03/13
6.99

Wait
UNTIL
Dark

THE NIGHT STALKERS

M.L. BUCHMAN

sourcebooks
casablanca

Copyright © 2013 by M. L. Buchman
Cover and internal design © 2013 by Sourcebooks, Inc.
Cover illustration by Paul Stinson/Artworks

Published by Sourcebooks Casablanca, an imprint of Sourcebooks, Inc.
P.O. Box 4410, Naperville, Illinois 60567-4410
(630) 961-3900
FAX: (630) 961-2168
www.sourcebooks.com

Printed and bound in the United States of America
VP 10 9 8 7 6 5 4 3 2 1

To my book group.
An honor to belong among such writers.

Rosslyn Chapel, Scotland
Wine is strong.
Kings are stronger.
Stronger than these are women.
The strongest of all is truth.

Weight *n*.
The aerodynamic force that must be
overcome for a helicopter to fly.

Weight *v*.
To burden down.

Chapter 1

SERGEANT CONNIE DAVIS FELT THE METALLIC STUTTER before she heard it. It broke the rhythm of the music that usually floated in the background of her thoughts when flying.

She began counting seconds... four, five.

Again.

A third time to be sure.

"Major?" she called on the Black Hawk helicopter's intercom.

"What!" Major Emily Beale's voice made it damn clear that whatever Connie wanted had better be more important than the firefight going on all around them.

The copilot and the other crew chief, Staff Sergeant John Wallace, kept their silence. It surprised Connie that she'd heard it before Big John. He was the most amazing mechanic she'd ever met.

"We have," Connie estimated quickly, "about five minutes until lift failure. We're losing a main blade." And without that, ten thousand pounds of U.S. Army helicopter and her four crew members were going to fall out of the sky far too fast.

"You sure?"

Connie leaned out the left-side gunner's window to unleash another spate of fire from her minigun on the bunkered-in machine gun nest that was giving them such trouble tonight. A hailstorm of spent brass spewed out the window as she pounded sixty-eight rounds a second of tracer-laden hell down on the aggressors. More raw power than the cannons in Tchaikovsky's *1812 Overture*.

For the three long seconds that the nest was in her range, the tracer-green fire whipped and coiled across the sky like a nightmare snake. In three seconds she hurled two kilos of lead. Four and a half pounds didn't sound like much until you pumped it along as three thousand separate pieces moving at three times the speed of sound. She raked her flying buzz saw back and forth twice over the enemies' position in the time they were in view.

"She's right. Maybe ten minutes if you ride it soft," Big John chimed in. He might not have caught the problem, but as soon as she pointed it out he'd found the vibration rippling through the frame of the Black Hawk helicopter, had counted the seconds, and he knew.

It was her first time in full combat with him. But already he was a man she'd learned to really admire during training flights. A man she had real trouble not noticing. She kept finding herself watching him when he wasn't aware. Big John Wallace fully deserved his nickname and was also perhaps the most handsome man she'd flown with in a half-dozen years aloft.

That she was a step ahead of him would have been satisfying in any less hazardous situation. One look out the window was enough to wipe any thought of a smile entirely out of her mind.

Even at night, the Hindu Kush mountains of northeast Afghanistan looked ugly. And tonight's mission had taken their flight in deep, way past five minutes to safety, or even ten. Base lay forty-five minutes away, with four good blades, and the area around that ranked almost as unfriendly as the people shooting at them now.

They might be the Night Stalkers of U.S. Special Forces, the fliers who ruled the night. But if they went down here, they wouldn't be ruling the night for very long despite being the toughest gunship ever launched into the night sky.

"*Viper*, this is *Vengeance*." The Major, the first woman ever in the Night Stalkers, had long since proved her ability as a pilot and commander when fast decisions were needed.

Helicopters never flew alone into combat, and tonight's mission had paired them with *Viper*.

"We're losing a blade and running for home. Won't make it." Then she took one last turn, wide rather than her normal hard slam, giving Big John a final chance at clearing out the problem they'd been sent to solve. The copilot fired four rockets, and whatever they opened up, John drove home.

The shock wave hit them hard enough that Connie half feared they'd lose the blade now. …Four, five, shudder, still right on cue. Okay for the moment. She puffed out a breath she hadn't known she was holding as the Major turned south by southeast.

They were through the smaller of two mountain passes while everyone on the ground remained distracted by the massive explosion that continued to roll skyward behind them. No one on the ground remembered to fire at the speeding helicopter until too late.

"Roger, *Vengeance*." The radio crackled in her helmet. "Heavy One is moving, thirty minutes."

Major Beale ran down the throttle to ease the load

on the blade. They stayed low to avoid any stress from attempting a climb. That meant flying low through the next, very well-defended pass, assuming they didn't fold up and crash before then. Even with a good rotor, they'd already be up in high-hot limits. The combination of heat and altitude really knocked efficiency out of helicopters, the air was just too thin. With a bad rotor, they didn't dare climb out of harm's way.

The troops defending the pass less than a minute ahead were very unfriendly.

Connie thumped the ammo can with her boot—barely a quarter full. She opened her gun and tossed the ammo belt loose, snaking it back into the can. She snapped down the lid and pulled out a fresh belt from a new can.

Out of the corner of her eye she saw Big John, who sat back to back four feet away on the other side of the chopper's bay, making the same choice. Once again, they were in some sort of perfect synchronicity.

…three, four. Not good. She leaned out the window to spot the pass ahead. They were down in the gut of it. Open to fire from all elevations of both sides.

"Can I—"

"No." She and John cut off the Major in unison, almost making Connie laugh. No climbing, not on this rotor blade.

Connie switched on the night-vision goggles feature of her helmet. She'd turned off the NVGs to avoid being blinded by the rocket flare at the firefight. Now she needed any advantage she could find to see in the dark.

A wash of the world gone green projected across the inside of her visor. Leaning out the gunnery window to look ahead, she watched for the bright shimmer of gunfire or the sharp glow of running stick figures as fighters scrambled for position. They were there. A dozen or more. And several were higher than they were. She couldn't attack them, couldn't shoot upward, unless she wanted to take out what remained of their own rotor blades. Helicopters were designed to shoot down at things, not up.

"Major?"

"Stop asking and just speak!" Emily Beale was less steady than usual. Hard to blame her.

Connie swallowed hard and pictured it again in her head. She saw no better answer. It was either bet on the poor aim of the many gunners ahead of them or bet that the Major's reputation as the best Black Hawk pilot in all of the U.S. Army's Special Operations Aviation Regiment had been earned, rather than merely granted for being the first woman in SOAR.

"A roll is a neutral-gee maneuver." A slow barrel roll—flying straight ahead while rolling the copter over sideways, upside down, and back to right side up—actually placed very little stress on the airframe or rotor blades, if done correctly.

"Oh shit. She's right," John confirmed in that wonderful deep voice of his, making it almost sound rational even as the Major groaned.

Was it an act like this by some crazy or equally desperate pilot that had killed Connie's father? Why had she mentioned it?

"John, you'll be first. Then Connie."

Was this about to place her in the same unknown grave as her dad? Connie Davis. Just a name on the Night Stalker monument at SOAR headquarters. A short note in a secret file: Lost. Pilot, copilot, two crew chiefs. No survivors.

The Major aimed for the right-hand wall of the pass, almost head on. Moments before they would have hit the cliff face, the Major slewed the chopper back to the left. But not in a hard turn. In a long, slow roll.

The ground so close they nearly thumped their wheels on the rock passing at a hundred and fifty knots. At 175 miles per hour, death was only the slightest error away.

That was the moment Connie knew for a fact that Major Emily Beale had earned her reputation as the very best. Beginning the roll so close to the cliff wall reduced their availability as a target to those on either side of the pass. And it took advantage of the ground effect decreasing the stress on the blades. The Major had accepted the idea, planned the maneuver, and executed it all on fifteen seconds notice.

As the right side of the helicopter lifted, John's gun had a clear field of fire on the cliff face flashing by. He used the precious moments to rake the walls far and wide while Connie looked straight down at the ground racing by, going weightless in her seat.

They were so close that she watched the tips of the rotor blades swinging past sharp rock with bare inches to spare. She pushed back into her seat, her instincts taking control and trying to shove her body even another inch from impending disaster. The static electricity of the rotors striking dust in the air glittered in her NVGs, a green arc of brilliant sparks. So close to the rock, the sparks appeared to be inside it.

But with air-show perfection, the Major continued the roll, edging clear of the wall so that she didn't strike a blade. Now upside down, Connie had a disoriented moment to spot any fire John had missed. She only tagged one on the wall racing by so closely before she faced straight up.

In the moment of rolling silence, as she stared at the heavens, she recalled hearing John's gun fire just a few short bursts while they were inverted. That meant any remaining dirty work on the left-hand wall of the pass was going to be her issue as they rolled back to level.

Anticipating the moment, she leaned forward and drove down the triggers the moment she saw rock instead of sky. An arc of tracer-green fire poured from the six spinning muzzles. She swept her M134 back and forth as the chopper rolled, taking her aim at the cliff face flashing by in the night. Enemy rounds spattered against the airframe with sharp thwacks barely detectable over the roar of her minigun.

The threat detector flashed target information on the inside of her visor, and with instinct born of a thousand hours of practice, she swept the gun over position after position, cutting them apart faster than they could duck and cover.

And then the *Vengeance* was through the pass. The targets were falling astern at eighty meters per second.

Beyond the pass, the front range of the Hindu Kush mountains broke like a thousand-meter-high wave, collapsing in deep rolls and turbulent clusters. The flat horizon of desert formed in the distance.

…two, three. A distance they weren't going to make.

"Now, Major," John announced. There was no questioning the man, not when he used that voice. Six foot four and mountain strong with a deep voice to match. It was a wonder he could cram into the Hawk's crew chief seat, but he did.

Connie had never felt short, but the top of her head would fit under his chin, comfortably. Odd thought.

And he was right. Now, or they were going to fall from the sky.

"This is *Vengeance*. Going down. Repeat. Going down. Beacon hot."

It was a risk. Lately, the bad guys were getting their hands on night-vision gear. A lot of it was first-generation crap, but even that wouldn't have any trouble finding the brilliant, infrared beacon now flashing atop their chopper.

…One, two. The ground was coming up awfully fast. Connie glanced forward. Best not to interrupt the pilot at the moment, but she wondered at the woman's sanity. Major Emily Beale was a SOAR legend, but they were about to become just another footnote in the bloody history of the Night Stalkers. At her current rate of descent, they were going to dig such a deep hole in the desert that the sand might cover right over their impact crater.

Connie braced for the crash. This one was gonna hurt. And hurt bad. Assuming she was alive afterward to feel it.

Fifty feet up, she felt the shudder as the Major yanked the collective full up and cranked the throttle wide open. A calculated gamble.

The Black Hawk's twin turbines groaned in protest, then over five thousand horsepower roared to life. Connie heard them go right past redline, nearly six thousand. The blades howled as they clawed the air like mad beasts. She and John chanting a mantra to the blade in unison, "Hang on. Hang on. Hang on."

Twenty feet. Ten. Slowing, five.

Then the blade let go. Twenty feet of laminated polycarbonate arced off into the night. Three blades remained, horribly unbalanced, but before they could turn twice more, the Hawk slammed into the sand. Not even hard enough to ram the shocks against the stops.

The Major dumped power, and the turbines collapsed from scream to cry toward moan. But not fast enough.

Another blade broke but didn't fly free. It slammed against the tail of the chopper, then the cockpit, then the tail again even as the rotor slowed. For ten seconds of held breath, they all waited while it dragged and beat the helicopter as it spun its way to a halt. The final scraping groan of wounded metal told Connie that half the bearings in the rotor head would need replacement and probably the swash plate as well.

"Everyone okay?"

"We're fine." Big John rolled free of his harness. "Now!" he called and snapped a monkey line to the steel loop by the cargo bay door.

Connie had to blink a few times. Was she fine? They weren't dead. They hadn't been killed by the failure of one of these hell-spawn machines. What next? Right, clear the blades.

Her body reacted before her brain fully kicked in. The wonders of all those endless drills.

In moments, she'd grabbed a saw and snapped in her own three-meter line just outside the cargo bay door to ensure she didn't get left behind no matter what happened. Jumping to the sand and closing the door exposed the built-in toeholds that let her climb up the outside of the Black Hawk helicopter until she met John squatting on the top.

Major Beale and Chief Warrant Officer Clay Anderson stood outside their pilots' doors, FN SCAR rifles unslung from across their chests, watching the night. The IR beacon provided Connie with plenty of light to work by with her NVG visor.

With John on one side and Connie on the other, they set to work, first sawing off the broken stubs of the two shattered blades. The hand saws ripped through the honeycomb of the graphite-epoxy spar, though they slowed down at the titanium erosion-resistant edge. Thankfully, the saws had been designed to make it through in emergency situations.

Viper came roaring in, flashed by close overhead. The sharp sizzle of six rockets and the heavy chug of the M230 30 mm cannon pounded down over the backside of the next rolling hill. The explosion and bloom of smoke and fire roaring beyond the ridge announced the end of someone who'd thought to find easy pickings from a downed American chopper.

Together, she and John grunted the main rotor a quarter turn to get one of the remaining intact blades over the tail. Connie could feel the grind of the ruined bearings fighting every inch. Definitely a new swash plate, maybe the lifters as well.

John rapped his knuckles briefly on the rotor head. Same thought, they'd be replacing both. From almost the first moment they hadn't needed words to communicate.

But the *Vengeance* couldn't get a tow with the other blade pointing forward. Too much danger of it being caught by the headwind and kicked up into the lifting chopper.

The low thud of Heavy One, the massive Chinook helicopter inbound to carry them home, told her they didn't have enough time to unlatch the cut stub and fold it back in line with the tail and then do the same to the forward blade to move it into place for shipping. They needed twenty minutes and they had five. Maybe.

John started swearing about the waste, as they both set to work with their saws.

Viper circled wide to secure a safe perimeter around their craft, both drawing fire and answering it in a very definitive fashion. It felt good knowing that Major Beale's husband, Major Henderson, and John's best friend, Sergeant Tim Maloney, were close by watching over them. But the remaining fighters who'd been guarding the pass were on the move and time was running out.

The third blade dropped free and fell aside, even as the four-point lifting harness dropped from the hovering Chinook.

In moments, they had their damaged helicopter latched in and secure. They were airborne and headed back to base before Connie was even fully back in the cabin. She tossed a pair of thermite grenades out the door onto the stack of partial blades as they lifted clear. With a blaze of white fire and shooting sparks, the grenades cooked, then melted most of the blades and fused a patch of sand a dozen feet across into brittle glass.

The machine hadn't killed her this time.

That didn't mean it wouldn't next time.

Chapter 2

BIG JOHN WALLACE PULLED OFF HIS HELMET AND scrubbed his fingers through his sweaty hair, reveling in the sensation. Out of the corner of his eye he watched Sergeant Connie Davis as they and their broken Black Hawk were lowered into their position at the air base. The moment they cleared possible enemy sight lines, she began stripping the equipment.

Not her helmet, not the hot flight suit, not her harness. Always first things first by the book with Sergeant Connie Davis. Her minigun's ammunition belt slotted back into its case, her last round hand-cleared from the minigun's chamber, caught in the air, and stowed in the loose-round bag.

Every move in U.S. Army official order. Every bit of maintenance done as if she were a walking, talking training manual. An attempt to alter any of her actions was met with page and paragraph quoted from memory. He'd stopped checking her on that, mostly. He hadn't tripped her up yet, but he still had hopes.

He'd flown with her on a couple of training missions, but Kee Smith was his usual gunner. Except now she was Kee Stevenson and off having her honeymoon. Go, Archie.

Before Kee, John had thought no one would ever replace Crazy Tim, but even Tim bowed to Kee's marksmanship. And Kee ranked damned cute. Not his type, but real easy on the eyes, assuming you didn't tick her off and get a punch in one.

Sergeant Connie Davis, on the other hand, while awesomely nice to look at… he had no idea what to think of her. The woman never laughed, never smiled. Built at the U.S. Army factory and shipped to the front with all parts in certified working order.

Not his type at all. Sure she looked like the sitcom dream girl next door, the quiet, smart one. The Kate Jackson of the original *Charlie's Angels*. Taller than the feisty elf that was Kee, but neither the long nor leggy of Major Beale. He was typically drawn to the latter, but there were two issues there. One, Major Beale had married Major Henderson, and two, she was also perhaps the scariest woman alive. A good person as a commanding officer, but lethal at any distance. It was a wonder Major Henderson had survived his courtship. Actually, considering what they'd been through, he almost hadn't.

Kee barely came up to Big John's armpit, while the Major rose well past his shoulder. Connie stood tall enough to rest her head right on his shoulder. Her long hair would fall in its soft waves across…

Connie stared at him square on from three feet away across the Black Hawk's cargo bay.

"Sir?" Her helmet was off and her cascade of brunette hair flowed around her face almost exactly as he'd just imagined it, looking as if she hadn't spent the last six hours flying hot and sweaty under heavy gunfire. Her mirrored Ray-Bans were in place against the sharp light of the desert dawn.

"Sergeant, not 'sir.'" He responded automatically. He wasn't a commissioned officer. He knew he sounded rude, inconsiderate. Though her eyes were covered, he knew they were a soft hazel and set wide across the bridge of her nose. He also knew that they were the only part of her that indicated someone was home.

Meeting Connie Davis, you wanted to dismiss her as some cute Connie Homemaker. The girl next door brought to life right out of the television screen.

But he'd run into the wrong end of her very keen mechanic's mind more than once. Now she sat there, expressionless and unreadable, waiting for what he needed of her.

Those eyes. Even through sunglasses they pinned his brain somewhere he couldn't readily access. He cleared his throat to make it work. "Nice catch on the stutter." He turned back to clear his own weapon.

He barely heard her quiet reply of, "Thank you, Sergeant," before she exited the chopper.

He cleared the chamber round and stowed the belt. Time to get moving. Connie would probably complete the damage inspection by the time he'd made sure his weapon was cleared and locked. She'd probably have it analyzed and half repaired by the time he even had a chance to look it over.

He was either going to kill the woman with his bare hands or... He had no idea what lay on the other side of the equation.

And he didn't want to know.

Chapter 3

CONNIE LOOKED AT THE CREWS OF *VIPER* AND *VENGEANCE* across the mess tent, then down at the tray in her hands. Burger, fries, salad, and a large bottle of some fruity electrolyte drink. Even an apple crisp in the corner. The Army fed you well when it could, even at a forward air base like Bati. All of it appearing so normal and homey in an Army-base sort of way.

When she looked up, nothing normal at all.

Bati was a town in northwest Pakistan where, as far as anyone other than the locals and a few government officials knew, this SOAR air base did not exist. A dozen helicopters secretly located in a country that appeared so unfriendly to America. The squatting rights never mentioned, all part of some arms deal.

No choppers here, folks. And no Rangers or Delta Force operators being launched nightly into the battles raging across the Hindu Kush mountains of northeast Afghanistan. No, sir. No, ma'am. No base that showed up on any part of any world map except ones inside the Pentagon.

The choppers hunkered down in an abandoned soccer stadium of sprawling concrete and flaking whitewash. The same whitewash swirled about in bright flurries along with the brownout dust clouds kicked up by the rotor's downwash every time anyone fired up a chopper.

The chow tent was equally foreign, even as she moved

through it heading for where she knew she'd land. Where she always landed.

The place felt cramped with the day staff fresh from their racks, eating breakfast, and the night fliers eating dinner before watching a movie or writing a letter home, then crashing out through the daytime. They jostled, crowded, rubbed shoulders. Most had their turf staked down and staked down hard.

She headed away from the Rangers. All noise and bravado down at the far end, half of them moving out into the dawn light to eat on the soccer stadium tiers, plates in one fist and a tale of glory in the other. D-boys, the most dangerous fighters on the planet, were silent ghosts as always, appearing for food and then fading away as if they'd never been there. The only people they spoke to between missions were the Rangers who were stupid enough to bait them—a sport no Ranger could resist despite decades of failure.

The Chinook heavy-lifters, the masters of the giant twin-rotor helicopters, always took the corner at the front of the tent by the entrance flap. Shoulder to shoulder, each team snagged an extra chair to fit their five-man crews at a four-top. Closed circle.

The pilots of the half dozen two-seater Little Birds had a long table where they sat in neat pairs across from each other, pilot and copilot, though who sat on which side varied. Perhaps the pattern was unconscious. Connie considered their alternation as she moved past but could find no particular sequencing of either a mathematical or a psychological nature. Four of the Black Hawk crews, the transport versions of the birds, intermixed at random tables.

Then there were *Viper* and *Vengeance*. Supposedly her crew. The six members from the two DAP Hawks always ranged around a double table. DAPs were always a crew apart. Like police or nurses in the civilian world.

The two Majors commanding the Direct Action Penetrators typically sat off by themselves at one of the back tables. On the rare occasions when they ate with their crew, another table was dragged in. But typically two copilots and four crew chiefs ate, shared, and joked together. Captain Stevenson had been out for three months on med leave, and Chief Warrant Clay Anderson had taken his seat both in the air and at the table. And though she'd taken Dusty James's place on *Viper* when he'd taken a round, she'd never felt welcome in his seat at the table.

She'd not taken it while Dusty was gone. That was proper, it was his seat and now he'd come back to fill it. Had the bullet that found him that night flown six inches differently, she would be the returning comrade now welcomed. Well, perhaps welcomed.

There'd been no spot at all for a week, and she'd been assigned to a ground maintenance squad. They hadn't put her in another bird because Kee Smith had upcoming marriage leave. Now Kee, the only person on the base she'd ever really spoken with, was gone. In two weeks she'd be back and Connie would be reassigned again.

Should Connie take the seat that would only be hers for fourteen days? Would she know what to say if someone spoke to her? Everything she said always came out wrong.

Even her moment with Staff Sergeant John Wallace this morning. Something she'd said had been wrong. She could see his face change, but though she studied it carefully, she couldn't read it. Had he even meant the compliment, or had he been angry that she'd noticed the failing rotor blade before he had? She didn't know anyone well enough to ask.

He hulked at the table, perfectly at ease, with that big, welcoming laugh of his flowing across his friends as he told the story of their roll, holding his arms out and tipping them sideways, making everyone duck.

Even when he retracted his arms, his broad shoulder intruded deep into the space where Kee always sat. Kee was small enough that it didn't matter. And fierce enough that she didn't care.

But there was no room for Connie Davis.

She turned for her usual table and sat with her back to the crew so that she wouldn't have to watch yet another place she didn't belong.

Chapter 4

"TWO DAYS, MAYBE THREE."

"You have until dark, about thirteen hours, to make her air-worthy."

Big John slapped a hand as big as both of Connie's on the table. "Dammit, Major. You gotta be kidding me."

Major Emily Beale had signaled Connie to come over and sit at the table as the meal broke up. Now it was just the three of them, with the dirty dishes still rattling on John's tray.

"There is no damn way, Major!" Big John's voice filled the chow tent, but the few people remaining didn't even bother to turn and watch. John's booming voice was more of a constant than a surprise.

Connie considered the logistics of repairing the Black Hawk.

The Chinook was supposed to deliver a new set of blades in about six hours. Even now she could hear the bird starting up for the three-hour run each way to go fetch a fresh set from the aircraft carrier. They'd need to replace several panels on the tail boom that had been beaten up by the dragging of the second broken blade. And the star-cracked plexi window on the copilot's side. The rotor head was the real issue. Until they tore it open to see what had been wrenched...

"Problem here?" Major Mark "The Viper" Henderson slid in next to Major Beale and kissed her solidly.

It always made Connie blink. Their perfect ease about themselves and each other. They walked hand in hand from briefing to the flight line in thoughtless harmony, both absolute masters of their craft, two of the most accomplished and decorated helicopter pilots in the U.S. Army. They clearly wasted no time doubting themselves or each other. From a place of such confidence, they flew where merely earthbound mortals stumbled along under gravity's force.

"Major, you gotta talk some sense into your wife, sir." John held his hands out like a supplicant. "We just flew a full mission and you know my bird took it hard, but she's a good one and saw us through. Now Major Beale wants the *Vengeance* mission-ready in thirteen hours. It just ain't gonna happen. No how, no way. Please talk some sense to her."

"Mission-ready? Did I say mission-ready?" Major Beale spoke, all bright innocence.

John floundered at a loss for words, as if his pilot had just lied to him.

Connie rolled the words back.

"You said 'air-worthy,' ma'am."

John jerked around to face her and blinked hard. Once. Twice.

Emily Beale merely nodded an acknowledgment with a gentle swoosh of her straight blond hair. As if she'd expected Connie to catch that.

Connie had always thought herself unobserved. Time to upgrade her assessment, again, so as not to underestimate the Major's capabilities.

"Air. Worthy."

Connie could hear Big John roll it around on his tongue.

There was a huge difference. Making her flyable was quite different from ready to fly into combat.

Connie dropped the battered panels and cracked plexi from her mental list. She dropped the necessary checks of the backup systems. She dropped the two radios and the FLIR that had taken direct hits and needed replacement, alignment, and recertification. She juggled times and equipment layers. She put the FLIR back in but left off the fine recalibration. It meant working straight through the day, their night, but—

"It's possible."

"No!" John's hand hammered down again on the table that groaned beneath the blow. But Connie could see his mind working even as his body protested. Could see the calculations in his unfocused gaze.

"Wa-ell," Major Henderson drawled in a horrid, fake Texas accent. "We could always give y'all another tow if ya can't fix the *Vengeance* in time. You wouldn't mind arriving at Kabul air base dangling from a Chinook's underbelly like a limp piece of meat, would ya now? I know my wife, y'all's commanding officer, couldn't care no more than a snap of her fingers."

John finished his calculations as the Major finished his sentence. John nodded slowly, rearranging the details in his head. Connie could read it in the narrowing of his eyes, the firm set of his jaw.

"Thirteen hours. We can do that." He glanced her way.

The light emphasis on "we" was one of the nicest compliments Connie had received since arriving at Bati. Not that she doubted her own skills. But she knew her mechanical ability bothered Sergeant Wallace and this was the first time he'd acknowledged it directly as an asset rather than an irritant.

"Excellent." Major Henderson rose easily to his feet and took his wife's hand to help her up.

As they walked away, he drawled once more, "It's just a-knowin' how to motivate them thar troops."

John looked from Connie to the departing couple. "Did he say something about Kabul?"

Chapter 5

THEY MADE IT WITH TWENTY-EIGHT MINUTES TO SPARE.

John flexed his hand again, wincing at the pull across his barked knuckles and the long scrape that ran from wrist to elbow.

Twenty-eight minutes. Enough for a shower and a shave. Time to stuff his gear in his duffel and grab something better than the energy bar he'd stuffed down midday. He strolled toward the chopper in the evening light with his kit on his back, a stack of salami sandwiches in his hand, and a cold Coke in one of his thigh pockets.

Beale and Clay had pitched in where they could, but for the most part an officer's usefulness on a repair was measured by their increasing distance from the job. Front-seaters knew how to fly but were trouble beyond that. Major Beale had West Pointed in, never even working as a back-ender other than in training.

Every now and then a noncom made the jump to front seat like Clay, but no chief in his right mind would ever let them touch anything mission-critical again. Sure they thought they still knew, but they were wrong. Without constant study, no mere officer could keep up with all of the technology required to keep a Black Hawk humming.

Even if Clay Anderson had stayed qualified, a DAP Hawk was a whole different bird beyond that. Newbies thought the mods designed by SOAR couldn't be that drastic. But the Direct Action Penetrators were custom-built for SOAR and SOAR alone. Built from the ground up on a Black Hawk frame, but that and their name was about all that remained the same with the most common helicopter on the planet. There were whole layers of gear and electronics that no other helicopter had ever carried.

John stood now at the entrance to the hangar and admired their handiwork as he bit off another chunk of his first sandwich.

Fewer than twenty DAPs were spread across five battalions, among the rarest and definitely the most lethal weapons ever launched into the night sky. Also one of the most complex. Seventeen separate software systems, eight in the weapon systems alone, networked across four different media. And that was only if you didn't count the beamed-in ground reference, the satellite imaging systems, or the new drone feeds they'd recently installed.

The Major had made sure they were towed into the one Rubb shelter at the base. Covered in desert camo, the towering temporary hangar kept out most of the sand and all of the sun, making the desert midday heat merely intolerable rather than potentially lethal. The hangar also offered a ceiling-mounted crane that had been essential to the repairs.

John patted the side of his bird. She'd done good getting them home, and it still pained him that they'd been unable to complete the cosmetic repairs along with the critical ones.

The Hawk squatted, looking lethal even sitting still. In the air his baby looked downright terrifying. The squat and wide profile of the main fuselage was augmented by the weapons pylons reaching outward to either side from the midsection's roof. Two mounting hard points each, they presently held a nineteen-round rocket pod, a 30 mm Vulcan cannon good for punching fist-sized holes in anything less armored than a main battle tank, and two four-racks of tank-killing Hellfire missiles just in case you did run into one.

And she was good to go. Still needed calibration and testing, of course, but all of the chopper's working pieces were back where they belonged and operational.

No matter how Connie dug under his skin, he had to admit he couldn't have pulled it off with a lesser mechanic. Even Crazy Tim, who'd chipped in from time to time, hadn't come close. John felt bad for even thinking the thought. He and Tim had flown together since Basic. A decade in the air, mostly in the same bird. He knew Tim was a rock-solid gunner in any situation and a better-than-average mechanic. But Sergeant Davis operated on a whole different level.

Each tool he'd needed, Connie had slapped into his hand even as he reached for it. Even when she was deeply involved in rebuilding the flare launch system, the right part waited where he could reach it when he needed it most.

Where he'd have applied brute strength, she applied leverage, though she wasn't shy about asking for his help when his power was needed. Not that she spoke more than ten words in the dozen hours they'd sweated over the job. She'd simply preset, align, and then assume his strength would be applied at the required moment. She made it easy.

And those fine hands of hers. At first they pissed him off as they reached into places where he'd have had to pull panels and equipment to gain access. He didn't really appreciate them until he'd grunted down the FLIR camera head. Not just the forward-looking infrared radar had been blown to smithereens, but most of the network bus behind it. In a dance of those fine fingers, she'd repaired in an hour what would have taken him six.

The rotor had been the worst. They'd finally dismounted the whole thing and laid it out on a couple of tables hijacked from the chow tent. Standing on either side, they'd torn it down to the bearings and put her back together again.

All in silence. They both knew what to do. Four hours to tear down and paste the rotor head back together— less than half the time projected in any manual. Two hours faster than his and Tim's best. She was incredible.

He'd tried filling the silence with questions, but most barely elicited a single-word answer.

Her homes had been a list of military bases.

Her training had been her father and a list of jobs starting with Sikorsky, the Black Hawk's manufacturer, and moving through several of the primary electronics vendors before she joined the Army.

Connie's family... That one bothered him the most. Those questions had been answered with silence.

—◆—

Connie took a sandwich from Big John's open hand. He didn't startle the way he normally did around her.

She hadn't had time to grab any food or a shower. Halfway through packing her gear she remembered something she'd seen. Not directly, but from the corner of her eye. It hadn't taken her long to place the image, and it sent her scrambling back to the chopper, her kit bag banging against her back.

She'd uncovered the port-side turbine engine and there it was. As neatly snipped as if done with the finest shears, a quarter-inch of pressure-feedback-loop fuel line simply wasn't there. No bend or flex to draw attention to the damage.

A round must have passed within inches of her face during the firefight. She'd never heard the one that almost got her. Instead, it had come in the gunner's windows, missed her and the minigun, and punched through the cabin roof, drilling the neat 7.62 mm hole her mind had noticed, even if she hadn't. It had continued upward with enough energy to remove that tiny section of the main fuel system.

They'd been running on the auxiliary feed, part of a standard back-and-forth use of systems to make sure everything kept working. Last night no one had noticed, but tonight they would have the moment they tried to lift off, running again on the primary fuel system. They'd be facing an engine fire in the first few minutes of flight.

She bit into the sandwich, heavy on the tomatoes and mustard. Just the way she would have made it for herself.

"Thanks."

"You're welcome." John's voice was a low rumble.

They headed to the chopper together, moving with that same harmony they'd been working in for the last thirteen hours. She'd never met a man so easy to be with since her father. Perhaps not even him.

Chapter 6

THEY FLEW THE TWO HOURS TO KABUL HIGH ENOUGH that John and Connie didn't need to man the guns. They could leave the flying to Beale and Clay for this trip.

First thing in the air, they ran systems tests and some calibrations that could only be done in flight. But when it took John three tries to punch the right keys to run the wideband satellite-ground tactical system loopback test, he knew it was time to bag it.

"Major," he called on the intercom, "we're hammered."

"Crash out," was all the response he wanted or needed. He released his harness, snapped in the monkey line out of habit, even though the cargo doors were slid shut, and stretched out on the hard deck.

"Connie, let it go, girl."

"In a minute."

He watched her in the instrument glow, hunched forward, focused. Even in helmet, flight suit, and full SARVSO survival vest, there was no mistaking her for a man. She wasn't like the Major, too willowy to be a man, or Kee, too generously proportioned to be masked by a mere flight suit. Connie's standout feature despite full gear: she simply moved in a way that no man would, or could. A neatness. A lack of wasted motion. A… He wasn't sure.

He puzzled at it as sleep overwhelmed him and took him under.

—w—

Connie stretched, and every joint popped or cracked. She couldn't recall the last time she'd been this tired. Not since the month-long hell of Green Platoon training. Or perhaps during her SERE course. She'd survived, evaded, and resisted for the two full weeks of the field test. She'd never been captured, so she hadn't needed the fourth letter of the acronym, escape. She also hadn't slept more than thirty minutes at a time in fourteen days.

She leaned back in and squinted, but her eyes were too tired to determine if the readout was a "4" or a "9." She gave it up.

"Let it go," as John had said.

Glancing forward revealed Major Beale in rear quarter profile. Clay was invisible in his armor-wrapped copilot seat just six inches forward from Connie's right shoulder. She could just lean on the back of his seat and she'd be asleep in seconds.

The Major rarely spoke as they flew. Emily Beale ran a quiet ship, which was fine with Connie. The air waves were silent as well. They were just ferrying to Kabul. Too high to be susceptible to enemy ground fire. If there had been a briefing about their mission, she'd missed it while working on the chopper.

As if sensing her attention, the Major turned to face her through the gap between the seats. With a sharp nod, then a soft shrug, she communicated her thanks for fast repairs and her lack of knowledge regarding the reason for the move. No briefing missed. All communicated without risking waking John by using the intercom.

She turned to look at John.

He'd stretched out, his feet propped on their duffels strapped to the rear cargo net. His head reached most of the way to his seat. You could fit a stretcher and a doctor in the space he took. Maybe two.

But there was room beside him. Not as much as you'd expect in the cargo bay of a Black Hawk. If it weren't for all of the mods and extra ammo for a DAP Hawk, you could fit a dozen troops, or half a dozen with some serious in-country gear. But even with the DAP's unique load, there was room for her. She could see that he had moved to the side before passing out. Leaving more space.

For her.

She felt uneasy sitting there, looking down at the open space left by the kindness of a man still in helmet and full gear, unrecognizable if not for his physical scale.

But she didn't sleep well beside others. Too much of her life alone. Mother gone early, Dad on assignment. Her fading grandmother had made sure she was fed, but the rest of her life had been up to her. To her alone.

Even in the Army it was easy to be alone. To just be quiet. Stay out of the jokes, the pranks, the incessant rivalry to be the best at something. You could be accepted for your proven skills, the only test that really mattered once you were past the lowest units, and not have to interact or often speak.

Women were almost always afforded more space to sleep in the Army. Often cots when guys had hard ground. Or at least they were put with other women. And her time hadn't been frontline hardship. Except for frequent weeklong exercises and war games, most of her career had been in helicopters. Choppers almost always returned to a base at night.

If your bird was parked in the wild, you didn't sleep. You hunkered down wide-eyed and watched for bad news crawling through the high weeds.

Her body begged her to lie down beside him.

Finally too tired to think, she did stretch out beside the sleeping Staff Sergeant.

Hard against the opposite cargo-bay door.

Chapter 7

A HAND REACHED FOR HER. IT WAS A HAND CONNIE knew like no other.

It reached for her, begging for help. Only the hand showed, reaching through a tear in the skin of a shattered helicopter.

The heat of fire brushed her cheeks. And she breathed in the stench of kerosene igniting as Jet A fuel poured from a sheared gas tank onto the fire.

Her hands were too heavy. Too slow. Too weak.

Even as her fingers reached out, the hand slid out of reach. The helicopter's carcass falling away, tumbling earthbound while she remained trapped in the sky.

Trapped where…

Someone shook her shoulder. Shook it again.

By reflex, she grabbed the hand's ring finger and flipped it back hard, eliciting a sharp yelp. Her attacker withdrew rapidly, tumbling away to get clear of the pain as her instincts continued to drive the finger up and back.

Tumbling like a helicopter falling through a perfectly blue sky.

A big finger, a big hand.

She didn't know this hand.

It wasn't her father's.

Then she was awake and instantly knew the hand. Had been impressed by its combination of strength and finesse throughout the long repairs, its ability to make the finest adjustments or bend a panel by hand to custom fit an airframe that had been through too much battle to easily fit factory-fresh parts.

Connie let go immediately and tried to stammer out an apology as Big John began to massage his hand tentatively, as if he weren't sure it were safe to touch.

"We're landing in five."

Major Beale's voice sounded over the intercom.

Five minutes. Kabul air base.

Connie leaned forward and offered to inspect John's hand.

He withdrew it quickly and banged his elbow on the cargo door frame.

He hissed out a sharp breath.

"Everything okay back there?"

"Fine, Major." His answer rough and abrupt. "Banged my goddamn funny bone. Zinging like hell."

Again Connie could only sit and watch. Retreating meant she didn't care. Assistance from her clearly wasn't wanted or welcome. Helpless once again, she could do nothing but sit and watch as they touched down.

"They're waiting to load us now," Major Beale announced before John could stop clutching his elbow and cursing.

"Who?" He looked at his hand and flexed the fingers. That was going to sting far longer than his elbow. Connie didn't look like a fighter. He had to remember that you didn't get to SOAR without being the very best. Minimum five years in the Army and two years of SOAR training before being declared mission qualified, if you survived the entrance exams. A weeklong interview that he remembered with abject horror. It almost made the month of Green Platoon testing seem survivable.

"Try looking out your window."

He hitched himself up to his knees and looked out the shooter's window. He could feel Connie move behind him to peek over his shoulder. An absolute awareness that made him think thoughts he definitely shouldn't about a woman serving beside him.

He didn't see anything but a curving wall of gray.

Connie slid open the cargo door as the rotor wash eased and the engines wound down. Kabul, with its own unique odor of spiced lamb, too much mint, and fresh sewage.

Then his brain got the perspective.

Not a gray wall, but rather the side of a C-17 Globemaster III. Not a C-5, but still three stories tall of aircraft the length of half a football field.

What it also told him was that he had to wake up fast. Before the hour was out, he was going to wish he'd found some way to wake Connie without touching her. He flexed his hand again before unsnapping his monkey line, stowing it neatly, and stepping out of the Hawk.

He was assaulted by the typical mayhem of a military airfield.

The C-17 loomed above them, a towering mass in the night, each of her four jet engines about the size of the Hawk's cabin area.

Viper, Major Henderson's bird, had landed on the other side of the jet's tail. Even as John watched, the lower part of the tail unhinged and a massive ramp swung down to the ground. Two DAP Hawks on a jet transport meant something nasty was going on, that was for sure. And if they were ready to load... It was time to hustle and ignore the armament and fueling crews already swarming toward their birds.

John reached back into the cabin for a wrench. One slapped into his hand. Connie had already assessed the situation and was on the move with a wrench of her own.

He hated morning people. Even after a decade in the Army, he preferred to take a quiet half hour, maybe an hour. Get some coffee, and a plate of eggs and bacon, English muffin with strawberry jam, and a short stack if he was lucky, before he ever really considered being awake. Didn't happen all that much, but that was his preference. Now, he'd slept three of the last thirty hours and had to prepare his bird for transport.

He climbed up the toeholds leading to the top of the Black Hawk just as he had twenty-four hours earlier. At least here at Bagram Air Base, there was less chance of someone shooting you from the top of the nearest dune. The first order of business was folding back the rotors. Thankfully without having to saw off the blades this time.

They rotated the fixed blade until it was aligned with the still-battered tail section. Next they broke free the second blade's pins and swung it alongside its companion. As they tackled the next blade Connie actually spoke.

"How's the hand?"

John flexed it and tried to ignore the twinge that ran up the length of his arm.

He offered a noncommittal grunt.

By the time the next blade swung into place she spoke again.

"I don't like being touched."

"I guessed." Actually, he'd been worried. When she slept, the chill facade she usually wore—no, not chill. Aloof? Remote? Anyway, it had slipped off her like a shield set aside.

He'd woken to find her asleep beside him. And he'd watched her face. No longer so carefully expressionless. No longer under the fierce control she always wielded. Her sleeping face reflected her sleeping thoughts. A gentleness that spoke of the woman more than the mind within. Then, after he'd studied her enough to know he'd not forget a single aspect of her face any time soon, not the high cheeks, not the ever so slightly flattened tip of her nose, not the surprising length of her lashes, unobservable under the impact of those sharp, assessing eyes when they were open.

Then an abrupt shift: worry, strain—horror! He'd shaken her then to break her free from whatever so shrouded her features in terror.

And nearly had his finger dislocated as a reward.

Who knew what would have happened to him if he'd followed his first instinct and gathered her sleeping form into his arms.

"I'm sorry. I was—"

John left her the space of silence as they broke the double-pivot free and swung the forward blade back in line with the tail. It was perhaps the first time she'd voluntarily started a conversation, rather than responding to a direct question.

"I'm sorry." She moved away to fold down the tail rotor.

John reinserted the pin bolts before climbing down.

Down onto a pallet.

A pallet of parachutes. Big ones.
Shit.
He hated parachutes.

Chapter 8

THE C-17 WITH TWO DAP HAWKS IN ITS BELLY FLEW straight through. No Aviano Air Base in Italy. No Ramstein in Germany. Fourteen hours, two flight crew changes, and several midair refuelings, straight to the States.

They slept as well as they could on the hard deck. Everyone woke cranky after fighting to ignore the pounding roar of the four jet engines ramming them from Southwest Asia over the Mediterranean and finally the Atlantic. Water bottles and plastic-packaged sandwiches were handed round, all made with white bread that turned to mush and stuck to the roof of your mouth in awkward lumps.

John now had a crick in his neck that he couldn't crack loose to go along with his sore hand. He and Connie put in a couple of listless hours on the Hawk. They finished what could be done inside the cavernous space hurtling along at five hundred miles per hour and thirty-eight thousand feet in the air. Mostly the cosmetics, tail plates, and copilot window.

After they called it off as a job well done, or as well as they could, they moved to the benches at the head of the cargo bay. Crazy Tim had shoved a couple of crates around until he had a makeshift poker table. John had been taking Tim's money since Basic Training and saw no reason to stop simply because he was exhausted.

Even Major Henderson was yawning, but exhaustion

wouldn't be a problem for him; he never lost at poker. John always figured it was the price of observing a master at play, to sit down to a game with the company's commander. And he always dragged some winnings off Tim and Dusty. Usually enough to break even, but rarely did he make enough for a night out. Sometimes not even a beer's worth. Henderson was just that good. Clay had learned the hard way to resist joining in. Major Beale didn't play.

Major Henderson at least played low stakes with his own crew. Other crews weren't so lucky and had suffered badly at the table when the Black Adders helicopter company came to play. The name had been a natural extension when the company was formed by then Captain Mark "Viper" Henderson. Now, many of them had the striking snake tattoo, along with the flying Pegasus with laser-vision eyes that was the unofficial emblem of the Night Stalkers.

Connie sat down across from John.

"You play much?" he asked as Tim shuffled the cards.

"Never." Her typical one-word reply.

He did his best to hide a smile. An easy mark and some quick money in his pocket would be just fine.

He told her the rules once and she had it. Or claimed she did. That simple, silent, single-time nod of hers with no wasted motion. Recorded, registered deep in her weird-ass brain that never needed to look in a service manual to fix even the most esoteric problems on the Hawk.

Well, he was about to prove her wrong. They'd run through a couple of hands open and a few more for no money until she had the feel of it. Now they were playing for money, low money, but that wasn't the point.

Tonight, today, whatever it was, John would tempt fate and his wallet by throwing caution out the window.

"See your buck," he called loud enough to be heard over the roar of the Globemaster's engines. "And one more." John was nursing along a respectable trip jacks. A high percentage winner in five-card draw. He knew he had Tim beat just by how he sat. The simplest poker game to play, but very hard to win. He eyed the Major.

Henderson laughed and matched but didn't raise.

Crazy Tim tossed in his cards with disgust on top of his two bucks already in the pot.

Dusty released a massive yawn. "I'm out and done." He tossed his cards down, accidentally face up, revealing a low full house. When John exclaimed, Dusty looked at them again. "Sorry." He flipped the cards face down and crawled off to sack out on a bench seat. Too tired to even realize that he'd thrown down an almost guaranteed winning hand.

Connie inspected each player carefully. Laid down the one dollar to stay in and raised back. Four bucks in.

He had to see this. What the hell, he raised her back as well. Teach the newbie a lesson.

The Major hesitated. Hesitated too long, making it clear he didn't have squat, cursed quietly, realizing he'd been tired enough to give himself away, then threw his cards on top of Tim's. First time John had ever seen him falter.

Just the two of them now.

She waited. Did she somehow know to watch for his reveal, some facial tic that might give him away? Some twitch of his pinkie that he didn't know about possibly indicating the quality of his hand? Maybe she paused merely to test his confidence. To task him.

Well, he was up to that. She was probably trying to remember if two pair beat three of a kind.

At length, she matched his bet. Seventeen bucks. A very sweet pot in such a low-stakes game.

He laid down his three boys and sat back to watch her.

Without a word, no hesitation to double-check, she fanned her three ladies on top of his jacks.

Not a glimmer. Not the least hint that she'd figured out the cards and taken her first hand at poker. No hesitation, no uncertainty.

John glanced over at the Major.

"Nope. I didn't see it either. Let's go again."

"See what?" Connie's first words since she'd sat down and said that she'd never played.

Neither of them answered.

They dealt around again. Connie only took one card on the draw, classic two-pair move.

He drew... garbage. The temptation to play it out almost drew him in, but didn't.

This time the Major went for the ride on Connie's trip tens with his aces and eights pairs.

Connie's stack of ones and fives was growing.

Major Henderson didn't look so sleepy anymore and John couldn't figured out how he was losing money so fast in such a small game.

By the fourth hand, he and Tim were folding on the deal, leaving the Major and Connie to go at it. They were so intent that when the C-17 drove into an air pocket, dropping them a quick twenty feet or so and all of the cards and money floated weightless for a moment, neither of them glanced away. Mark merely slapped his hand down on the pot to hold everything in place until the flight resettled. They watched each other far more than the cards.

Thirty bucks down, John folded for the night. Tim had long since lost interest and fallen asleep stretched out on the deck.

The Major had to be fifty in the hole by the time he threw up his hands in surrender.

"Game over. Okay, girl. Give."

Connie had started straightening her winnings. She looked at him a moment, tipped her head sideways as if to relieve a crick, and then offered him her stack, over a hundred dollars.

"No. No. No. That's yours." He scrubbed at his face. "You've really never played before? How did you do that? How did you beat us?"

She finished with the money, slipped it into a back pocket, and began reboxing the cards.

"It strikes me as a relatively simple game in some ways. Between what is in my hand and discards, and the pattern of discards of others, I can discount at least fifteen of the fifty-two cards. Taken only in combination, the odds simplify further. Then I observe the players and that alters the odds. After that I simply need to know if I can make you believe I have a better hand, whether or not I do."

The Major grunted barely loud enough to be heard.

"Then John…"

The Major slapped his shoulder. "You've got to watch how you hold your hand, buddy boy."

"Not his hand. His mouth."

"My mouth?" A key to poker was knowing your own tell. Your own giveaway about the quality of what you had versus what other might think you have. Hearing about your own tell was rare and priceless.

"No. His hand. He holds it higher when it's worth less."

He did?

"No," Connie shook her head. "Not always. But when his hand is really miserable, he has a tiny bit of a smile. You, Major, are far easier to read."

He blanched. The inscrutable Viper actually blanched before the fair Connie Davis. John could get to like this woman after all.

"Easier?"

John could see the Major's lips move, but his voice was a stunned gasp lost in the unending roar of the jet's engines.

She pointed over his shoulder to where Major Beale sat perched on a crate just behind him.

Mark spun around to look at his wife. Her grin was sheepish.

"I'm sorry. I didn't know I was giving away your cards. I don't have much of a poker face, do I?"

"It depends," Connie answered matter-of-factly, "on which side you're on."

Mark burst out laughing and pulled his wife into his lap. The ramrod straight Major Beale curled against him just like any other girl.

John loved watching them. They'd been magnetic together since the first time he saw them, even if it took them a while to figure it out. And there was no woman he'd ever respected more highly.

Connie snapped the rubber band around the box of cards.

Here was another woman he couldn't help but watch.

Chapter 9

"PRACTICE." CONNIE SUCKED HARD TO GET HER BREATH in the freezing air now roaring through the Globemaster's cargo bay.

"Practice makes perfect." She whispered it like a mantra. It was how her father had raised her and the Army had trained her. And she agreed. But right now she was cold and tired.

"Excellent conditions for an advanced training opportunity." She could practically hear her past instructors barking that out.

After a mission, thirteen hours repairing their DAP, and fourteen hours in flight, they were just twenty miles short of Fort Campbell, Kentucky, the home of the 160th SOAR. Whatever was so urgent as to drag them across half the world didn't supplant a training opportunity. Not in Fort Campbell's mind.

Even with her helmet on, she could barely hear herself think. They were down from thirty-five thousand feet to seven hundred. The crews sat on the side benches, their knees pulled in tight, facing the two Black Hawks awash in the red light that let their eyes adapt for the dark. The helicopters loomed huge inside the Globemaster's bay.

The sound redoubled as the jet's crew opened the tail door. One section folded up into the ceiling, revealing the black of a winter's night in the heart of the Blue Ridge Mountains. No moon, no clouds to reflect back any man-made light. The other section of the rear door folded down until it angled down slightly below horizontal. Where the rear of the cargo bay had been now gaped a great maw of darkness waiting to swallow them whole.

"Drop zone in ten," the pilot announced over the intercom.

"Parachutes suck!" John leaned in and yelled near the leading edge of Connie's helmet so that she could just hear him.

A crew member in a harness strolled to the rear of the aircraft and chucked a small package out into the wind stream. The wind caught it, and in moments a little four-foot drogue chute danced beyond the tail at the end of a long line.

"Five."

"They're frickin' awesome! I love free fall!" she shouted back.

The crewman moseyed back to mid-ship.

"Drop! Drop! Drop!" sounded over the intercom.

The C-17 loadmaster popped the release, and the main chute was pulled out by the drogue. One second, the parachute filled to a huge size just past the end of the ramp, larger than the cargo door it had just exited.

The next second, the *Vengeance* Black Hawk MH-60M DAP shot by Connie's knees with a foot to spare. By the time it reached the door, the ten-thousand-pound bird was moving at the speed of an express train. Actually, the parachute was slowing it down to earth-bound speeds while the C-17 continued to roar ahead.

Another long webbing leash tied to Henderson's Hawk shot out the cargo door. It in turn dragged free the second bird's big parachute, and in moments the second chute and *Viper* were gone, moving even faster. It left Connie breathless in the sudden vacuum of the abruptly empty cavernous interior of the plane.

"Go! Go! Go!"

Magically the crewman materialized in the center of the cargo hatch. Both Black Hawk crews were scrambling to their feet from opposite sides of the cargo bay.

"Free fall makes me barf!" John shouted at her as they threw off their safety belts and jumped to their feet. Or rather struggled upright. Large survival kits dangled from the fronts of their vests to hang awkwardly between their legs.

They waddled past the jumpmaster as fast as they could. He checked the security of their riplines on the overhead rail before letting them waddle off the plane.

At the tail edge of the ramp, she turned to face John.

Connie yelled out, "Wimp!" and allowed herself to tumble over backward into the night sky.

She started the timer on her watch as she completed the first somersault. A heat blast and the burned-fuel smell of jet exhaust surrounded her for half a moment before she fell into clear air.

Connie normally loved free fall. HALO jumps were her favorite training exercise. High altitude, low opening, you felt as if nothing could hold you back. With the right gear, you could plunge seven miles from jetliner altitudes over thirty-five thousand feet to under a thousand feet in less than two minutes. Two hundred miles per hour without a vehicle or any more protection than a helmet and a high-altitude suit.

But not tonight, so Big John would be okay. Tonight was a LALO jump: low altitude, low opening. The line jerked her drogue parachute free just after she left the aircraft. It yanked out her main chute, and the harness grabbed her hard, jerked her painfully to an abrupt halt. From a hundred-plus knots to twenty in two seconds flat.

She checked the sky about her.

Seven other chutes, John close beside her. Good, the whole team accounted for.

The C-17 disappeared from all visibility even as she watched, the closing rear hatch cutting out the red interior lights. Gone. The jet had flown without lights for such a training run. At the limit of vision, the nav lights blinked on and then they were gone.

Below, the two massive chutes lowering the Black Hawks toward the open field of the drop zone were etched against the white landscape. Snow. It was going to be cold down on the ground reassembling the Hawks for flight. She steered for them. The freezing night air was chapping what little of her face wasn't protected by the helmet.

At a hundred feet, she dropped the survival bag on a long lead line. Fifty feet. Thirty. The bag hit the ground like an anchor. She stalled the chute and landed soft. A quick pull on the forward shroud lines and the chute spilled air, collapsing to the ground.

She jerked the quick-release toggle and started gathering her chute as Big John dropped in fifty feet to her left. The others ranged beyond him in a tight grouping. John set to work on bundling his chute.

"No barfing. Not even a gag. I'm disappointed."

All he did was snarl in reply, "Sixty minutes."

She checked her wrist, fifty-six and counting from when they'd stepped off the tailgate. The exercise hadn't specified which time to start, so she'd count from the "Go!" not the ground.

She saw John's nod. The burden was now on them. On that they could agree.

First, they had to check the chopper. Then put her back together. After that, perform the preflight check so that the Major could fly them back to Fort Campbell. Undetected.

And, more importantly, they had to beat *Viper*.

Fifty-five minutes.

———∿∿∿———

"Goddamn it!" Sergeant Steve Johnson looked out Fort Campbell's heli-field control-tower window.

"Hey, Jeff. How many Hawks were on the concrete when we came on shift?"

"I don't know. A dozen, give or take."

"How many were DAP Hawks?"

"Two. Why?"

"Well, now there are three." He had the satisfaction of hearing Jeff's curse. Jeff moved beside him and looked down at the floodlit field.

"How in the hell did they do that? And when?"

Steve ran the security recordings back. "Four minutes ago." Low and slow. They'd actually come sliding from inside a hangar he knew to be empty. He rolled back on camera four. There they were, dropping two crew chiefs to the ground. The smaller one did something quick at the edge of the hangar doors. He'd better let maintenance know they'd need to fix the alarm on the hangar's back door.

The pilot flew straight through, low enough that he'd barely hesitated at the threshold to retrieve the ground team.

"Slick." He'd seen Navy SEALs who were clumsier.

He rolled the recorder further back. Camera fourteen at the back gate.

Again the two crew chiefs slid out of the night with the grace of combat operators and captured the guard booth and its three inhabitants. They'd actually opened the gate so that the Hawk could fly through with her body well below any radar and her rotors just clear of the wire.

Steve called the booth. He didn't even have to ask the question.

The guards answered with, "They told us we had a choice—be tied up, face down out in the snow, or keep our mouths shut until you called us. We chose the latter, sue us."

Steve hung up on them without responding.

He was used to SOAR's pilots trying to outsmart Fort Campbell's security, an old game. Strictly against the rules, but most rules didn't really apply to the highly secretive 160th Air Regiment. One rule did though, always. Never, ever be seen. All else came second. And the tower worked hard to make that first one a real challenge. Very few got by them.

"You know what I'm thinking?" Jeff picked up his night-vision binoculars.

"Helicopters always travel in pairs?" Steve concentrated on the low clutter at the bottom edge of the field's radar sweep.

"And that just had to be Emily Beale's team. Had to be. So goddamn smooth."

The two of them shared a smile. That pretty much identified the other bird.

It took two more minutes, but their vigilance paid off. Not that they could have missed it. The low-sweep, outer-perimeter radar gathered up the second helicopter with ease.

Steve snapped on the infrared searchlight and swept the second DAP Hawk as it hopped over the fence, clearing the razor wire by no more than two feet.

"Greetings, *Viper!*"

"Get that damn thing out of my eyes!" Major Mark Henderson snapped over the radio.

Steve doused the light. "Welcome to Fort Campbell. Haven't seen you in a while. When did you get stateside?" He tried to sound sassy, but he couldn't figure how the Major had gotten past the first three levels of threat detection that surrounded SOAR's home base.

And how the Viper's wife had gotten past all six.

Connie spilled out of the Hawk with the rest of the crew to crow a bit over *Viper* being caught. While waiting, from forty-eight minutes to fifty-four minutes into the exercise, they'd scrambled to shut down the bird and strip helmets and vests in the cramped space. John handed around warm hats. They'd all hustled to tie down the blades and cover the key components.

Now, with shouldered duffels, they tried to look unhurried, even bored as *Viper* landed.

The message was clear: "We've been here a long while. Where the hell have you been?" They were both under the one-hour limit mandated by the exercise, but it provided a fine chance to rub in the victory.

While they waited in a loose line for *Viper's* rotors to

spin down, Connie edged up to John. "What did you do to the outer fence?"

"My first gig at SOAR was testing flight against the perimeter security. I found the backdoor password. A quick downlink over our new wideband and I hacked the system. I told it to look anywhere except where we were. Then I instructed it to reset after thirty seconds. *Viper* walked right into it."

She nodded, filing the information away.

"LtCGrimm1981."

Connie looked at him. Sharing an insider secret like that. He did it without thought, consideration, or negotiated trade. He shared the password because he had it to share and trusted her.

LtCGrimm1981.

Easy to remember, probably one of the more logical passwords in SOAR. Lieutenant Colonel Michael C. Grimm, one of the founders of the Air Regiment and one of the first to be lost, pushing the envelope that night-vision technology hadn't yet learned how to fill. The Night Stalkers' passion to develop night-vision gear now in use by the military worldwide could be traced directly to the night Michael ate a power line flying an MH-6 Little Bird at full throttle in a narrow river valley while leading a flight of twenty-two choppers on a nighttime training exercise. His was just the fourth of the hundred names on the Memorial Wall outside Grimm Hall. Lt. C. Grimm. Died 1981.

When Connie was standing quietly shoulder to shoulder with John like now, he didn't seem so overwhelming. Big and powerful, but with a kindness inside that his exterior did little to reveal. Even when he was exhausted and cold and viewed in profile, you could see his irrepressible merriness. Nothing like her father who had been quiet, thoughtful, guarded. Never speaking without thinking. She'd done her best to emulate him.

But perhaps she was missing something.

John made her feel... Connie wasn't sure. She'd never been good at placing words on her emotions, when she even allowed herself to consider them. Pain she knew. The pain that wrapped around her heart every time she thought of her father's death in an unnamed helicopter in an unmentionable place.

Around John, that constant pain eased. The tight squeeze that often made it hard to breathe let go just a tiny bit, and the sensation was quite heady.

A part of her heard John teasing his buddy Crazy Tim. A part of her heard the deep friendship that lay between them. But the words garbled and were washed away by the solid thud of her own heart.

Standing next to John, she felt that weightless moment she'd missed when jumping out of the back of the C-17 Globemaster III.

That incredible sense of flying.

Chapter 10

TWELVE HOURS.

Pure luxury. Twelve hours out cold with a hot meal and a hot shower on each end.

John had not one complaint. Well, not much of a complaint, though he could certainly think of one fine enhancement. And his opportunities were much better here. Not a lot of available women in Bati, Pakistan, especially ones not likely to knife him while he slept. There had only been four American women at the base—the Major, Kee the gunner, a day staffer, and Connie.

While Fort Campbell wasn't what you'd called a target-rich environment, in comparison it wasn't so bad at all.

He mounded up a short stack of pancakes, a couple eggs, bacon and sausage, English muffin, hash browns, and a coffee mug the size of his fist. A damn cute mess-hall orderly, with skin hued nearly the same color as the dark roast she poured, offered to refill his mug almost every time he set it back down.

They really knew how to live back here at the SOAR regimental headquarters. Instead of in a chow tent huddled at one end of a scorched and abandoned soccer stadium dotted with plywood tables, they were in Grimm Hall. He hadn't seen this many Americans at once in over six months. He'd seen bigger crowds in the Afghan and Pakistani markets, pressing, pushing, crowded mayhem, but that was different and dangerous as well. Here, with the SOAR training battalion and the first two fighting battalions, Fort Campbell felt like New York in comparison, all energy and purpose.

It didn't feel as if they were tucked away in the westernmost corner of Kentucky, just a couple of states over from his family. Maybe he could get some time to see them; it had been too long.

The orderly came around again to flirt a bit more. She was long, lean, and Army fit. A very nice combination. He wouldn't mind a little companionship. Wouldn't mind it a bit. Out of the corner of his eye he spotted Connie coming off the chow line. Without thinking, he raised a hand high to get her attention.

Even at the distance, he noted her eyes going a bit wide.

He waved for her to join him.

She started in his direction, looking as if she were grinding gears and couldn't quite engage her transmission.

"You could have said."

"Hunh?" By the time he looked in the orderly's direction, she was striding off without even the nice sashay of those splendid hips she'd offered the first few times around. What? Connie was just one of his crewmates. That didn't mean he didn't want to see the orderly. Connie was just…

He watched her as she approached. She was just… Something about her snagged his full attention. His world went quiet around her. Not as if he didn't want to speak, but as if he didn't need to.

"You sure?" She stood half a step from the other chair at the two-top table.

"I'm sure." And he was. Now that was interesting.

Cute, leggy, and willing orderly with skin the color of night. Cool and remote white-chick Sergeant Connie Davis who always ate alone. Always sat by herself. But there wasn't really a contest. Connie brought that incredible mind of hers. Also a gentleness that he'd bet would surprise her if he pointed it out. And the more he watched her, the more he liked her looks. No longer just pretty, they were becoming familiar.

He couldn't read that poker face that she always wore, not yet, but he caught hints through its mighty shield.

She cleared her tray, setting plate, napkin, cup of tea, silverware as if she were dining at home. Perhaps she was. He remembered that his question of home had been answered with a list of Army air bases. She treated her past as a closed book, but that didn't stop him from wanting to know more about her.

For one thing, she was nervous. He could tell by the way her eyes shifted to his even as she sat. Nervous around him?

"Something bothering you?" He dug up a mouthful of something from his plate but didn't taste it.

She fooled around with the toast on her plate, as if studying it for hidden secrets. A bite of hash browns and some more messing with her toast before answering. "They've been working on our helicopters since the moment we walked away from them."

Why did he feel that was a topic change, even if he couldn't quite pin it down?

"Not unusual. We're fresh in from a forward theater of operations. Frankly, I'm glad to have someone else muck out all that dust and grit. Every bit of it brings back dusty, gritty, and downright nasty memories. I mean, what am I gonna do if I don't find sand in my shorts and a dusting of brown dirt on my dinner? Have withdrawal? Go for it. That's what I have to say."

"They aren't cleaning. They're installing. New systems."

He dropped his fork. He didn't intend to. It simply slipped out of limp fingers and tumbled a piece of sausage into his coffee. A sheen of oil rose to the surface and shimmered across it.

"What new systems?"

"They didn't say."

"Didn't or wouldn't?"

Her shrug was eloquent.

He started to rise, then caught her expression. It shifted. For just a moment. Her eyes casting down to the left as if he'd sworn at her or something.

He dropped back into his seat. Sat and stared into his breakfast. What had been a banquet moments before now looked to be slowly congealing under layers of cooling syrup and long drools of dull-red hot sauce. He ate a piece or two of bacon, but his heart wasn't in it.

"What are they doing to my chopper?" he asked himself. Not looking up, not wanting to see the pain that had slid into those gentle eyes when he'd made to leave her alone at the table.

"Five external fittings." Her voice was unchanged. A glance showed her eyes were recovering.

"Huh?" He hadn't realized he'd spoken aloud and had momentarily forgotten about Connie. But now, so close, he could smell her. The freshness of soap and shampoo, with an underlying treat of spice. Not the home-cooked freshness you'd expect from a girl like her, but rather a bright, enticing drift just barely kissing the air.

"Two low forward, one low aft. Front and rear high."

"ADAS." He breathed it. It felt like a prayer on his lips. There'd been rumors, even a limited press release of initial testing. But field ready?

She nodded. Clearly her guess as well.

"This I gotta see. Are you done?"

Connie looked down at her untouched plate and his mostly full one.

Then she focused back on him and did the impossible. She smiled.

The warmth of it, the force of it, slammed him back in his seat. It lit her up with a radiance that nearly blinded. It made the rest of the room pale by comparison. It shifted her from merely beautiful to the most stunning creature he'd ever seen.

"Yes, I think we are." He caught her gentle emphasis on the "we," a testing sound, but couldn't make sense of it. Perhaps he'd imagined it. Or maybe he wasn't and she was a bloody nutcase. But that didn't fit.

She made a quick sandwich of her English muffin, scrambled eggs, and sausage patty before standing. He did the same and followed her to the tray drop window and headed for the airfield.

His last gasp of breath was still somewhere back at their table.

The rest of him was busy trying to figure out how to make her smile again.

Chapter 11

"WHAT DO YOU THINK?"

Connie jumped a bit to find Major Beale close beside her. The blasting heaters were loud enough to mask smaller noises in the hangar, and the Major moved so quietly.

"I've always liked it here."

And Connie did. They were in the Fort Campbell maintenance hangar that they'd flown through last night. Lower than an airplane hanger, it was made for helicopters. You could park a couple of the massive twin-rotor Chinooks in here, but a 737 not so much. The walls were lined with overhaul parts: pumps, rotors, racks of small parts, and anything else a mechanic could want. Every tool, lifter, and overhead crane imaginable stood available for the moment it might be needed. Through an open door she could see a full machine shop.

"I'd rather be flying. Makes me nervous to see that." Beale nodded toward the two choppers.

A half-dozen service techs, all in matching white coveralls with the vendor's red corporate logo, were attacking their birds. FLIR dismounted. Panels pulled topside and the floor plates stacked on a handy rolling cart. The Hawks' guts, especially the wiring control systems that ran through a Hawk's cowling and underbelly, were exposed for all to see. A section of cockpit control panel had been pulled out and set on a wooden pallet.

Another team was also replacing the rotor blades, though they'd only been reinstalled yesterday in Afghanistan. Actually, they were replacing the entire upper end of the rotor head to accommodate five blades instead of the standard four, and they'd already changed out the rear rotor as well. Being told five blades were "quieter" was an understatement. The Hawks were being rigged for stealth, at least in sound. Radar stealth would require replacing most of the chopper's skin with different components, but with this, they'd be much quieter. Something was definitely up.

Where the Major saw disarray, Connie saw the bones of the Hawk, and they were good bones. She liked being able to see all of the systems laid bare that she could normally only see in her head.

They stood in silence watching the process. There was a clear process flow of delayering the existing system and the first steps of layering in the new technology. She and John had reviewed the installation plans carefully and couldn't critique them. The vendor, as usual, knew exactly what it was doing down to the last meter of fiber optic.

Right now John and Tim were over at *Viper,* talking over something. Tim hauled off and punched John hard on the arm. Tim was shorter than John but powerfully built across the shoulders. Tim's blow would have rocked a lesser man but only made John laugh. He wrapped Tim in a headlock, knocking knuckles on Tim's skull as if trying to knock some sense into it.

"They're good together."

She nodded in response to the Major's observation. They were. Not just friends. Not just soldiers who had served side by side for a decade. They were part of the kind of integrated team that formed in the best chopper crews. Teams so tight that you trusted yourself and your crew like no other. So close that if someone took the bullet, all of the others hated that they weren't the ones who'd been hit instead.

For Connie's whole life, she'd been the outside observer. She'd never been able to pretend that she truly belonged. Always on the outside of the crew looking in. Someday. Maybe. Probably not. She knew herself too well. She'd met other introverts who could fake it, women who could pretend they fit in with the crowd until they only stood out to other introverts. But she'd never been one of those.

Connie wanted to move forward and see what the tech was doing on the forward mount, but she didn't want to break this moment she was sharing with the Major.

"How did you end up in SOAR?" The question was out before Connie knew where it came from.

Major Beale laughed aloud, that easy musical sound that would draw any male not already drawn to her blond beauty.

"The only way, the hard way."

Connie knew what she meant. Soldiers, enlisted like her and officers alike, tried time after time to qualify for Special Operational Forces, waiting a year at a time before their next opportunity to apply. Seventy-five percent of Army fliers, all with a half-dozen years or more prior military experience, couldn't make the cut.

The Special Forces trials began with the brutal month-long Green Platoon entry test. You couldn't tell ahead of time who would tough it out. The skinny geek with a compulsively bobbing Adam's apple bruted out twenty-mile hikes with fifty-pound packs and no sleep. Gung-ho G.I. Joes never made it out of the day-one mud pit.

They drove you past skills, past endurance. What saw you through was only one thing—motivation.

You had to want it, want it so bad that it was part of your inner core. So bad that your soul wouldn't be complete without it.

It was a bond she and the Major had in common, they'd both walked places few women had ever trod.

Connie recalled hallucinating on the firing range but still getting five rounds touching the black. Or waking up to discover she'd been walking with a full pack for hours, but couldn't remember ever starting out. But she'd wanted it. To prove herself to herself. To prove that her father had not died in vain, though she knew he had. So it was up to her to prove his sacrifice hadn't been wasted.

"I remember…" The Major was gazing over at the choppers. "I was standing just about where John and Tim are two and a half years ago. A beautiful summer night. A one-star general was facing off with me over a maneuver I'd just flown, well outside the original practice-mission profile, but I got it done. Thought he was going to bust my ass back to regular Army. If he was, he'd have to just do it. I wasn't giving in one lousy inch that I'd done anything wrong."

Connie tried to imagine herself being so sure of her own rightness that she'd face down a one-star, but she couldn't think of any scenario where that might occur.

"I had a Drill back at West Point who insisted he'd 'never trust some little girl to fly anything as expensive as a helicopter.' Put it in my damned Army file that way, saw it once." The Major shook her head.

"Eight years later, I stood right over there in front of the one-star considering whether it was worth the time I'd get in lockup if I popped him in the nose. I was so sure he'd say the same damn thing. Instead, he snarled at me, 'Captain Beale, I'll be damned if I'd ever trust such a hard-ass as you with anything less than an attack helicopter.' That's when he assigned me to the DAP. Best day of my life."

"What was the best day of your life?"

Connie turned to see Major Henderson had slipped up close behind his wife and was trying to pretend he was hurt by her last comment. With the slightest of motions Major Beale leaned back against his chest.

"The day I got my DAP."

"Not the day I proposed?" He didn't sound hurt, just teasing. Flirting with his wife. Slipping his hands around her waist.

"Close second, dear."

Connie wondered if she'd ever feel so comfortable around a man but couldn't imagine it.

That's when she spotted John waving in her direction, signaling her to come over and see something in the cockpit installation.

She hurried over with barely a parting nod to the Majors.

When Connie glanced back, Major Henderson appeared intent on his wife's hair, but Major Beale was watching her closely. Clearly seeing something Connie didn't.

She turned back to John and leaned in close to see how the ADAS cabling routed around the primary armor.

Chapter 12

At the beginning of day three at Fort Campbell, Connie pulled on the new helmet. It felt wrong, odd. She'd had her current helmet for four years. There had been various technology upgrades, but it had still been her helmet.

The ADAS helmet had been custom fit, just like her first, but felt wrong. She knew the feeling would wear off, but right now it was as distracting as a new pair of boots after wearing the old ones slipper soft. The fit was okay, but the weight was about a third less and in different places. It wanted to tip her head forward just a little. Have to watch out for that during high-gee maneuvers or when slamming through an air turbulence pocket.

Then the technician turned on the system and she forgot everything else.

Yes, she stood beside her Hawk, still parked in the middle of Hangar 14. But that's not what filled her vision.

Her point of view centered inside the Hawk, but the hull of the Hawk was invisible. Instead of leaning out gunner windows or cargo bay doors to see, she had a completely clear field of view. People walked around her in the soft grays of infrared outlines. The hangar walls were some distance in the background—eleven and a half meters to the south, her readout informed her. The resolution was astonishing. She could pick out the technicians she and John had been working with the last two days as easily as if they stood beside her and not on the other side of a ten-thousand-pound Hawk.

As she turned her head, the helmet registered the shift in orientation. The north wall of the hangar stood forty-eight meters from the center of the Hawk. The cameras perched around the craft fed their view across the inside of her visor. She could focus on the reality before her by looking through her visor or on the projected view by focusing on the inside surface of her visor. A quick blink and she managed to see both at once, the colored con-crete and steel-walled hangar world through the poly-carbonate of her visor and the gray-toned infrared view from the helicopter's new cameras projected across the visor's inside surface.

Standing on the hangar floor was a little disorienting. Clearly the helmet was set up to project the view angle as if she were in her normal seat and viewing much more remote objects while the helicopter was in flight. But knowing that, it wasn't difficult to compensate. A further turn and she could see herself, looking away from the craft. Boots, insulated camo pants, jacket, and globular helmet where her head should be.

It was strange seeing herself like that. She didn't think about such things. Mirrors merely reflected, but now she was viewing a real-time, thermal image of her-self. She raised an arm and watched herself do so in the same instant. On those rare occasions when ground crew were offering hand signals, she'd be able to see them clearly without half hanging out of bay doors.

Then she turned to the stern and she actually cried out.

Their "six" was clear. In any aircraft, a major problem was seeing what was sneaking up behind you. The back end of the helicopter was always in the way of viewing your six o'clock position. The pilot had to skew the chopper's body sideways again and again so the crew chiefs could keep an eye on what was behind, in addition to anything the radar revealed.

Now, because the cameras were mounted on the outside of the helicopter, she could see all around even if she were inside the chopper, everything except a thin wedge where the tail rotor sliced across the image. But there were times you wanted to check the condition of your own rotor, a trick completely impossible in a speeding chopper, right up until this moment.

The "Advanced Distributed Aperture System" (the vendor's techs insisted on calling it by its full name every time) consisted of nine distributed cameras in five mountings, all feeding a carefully interlaced view onto her visor.

She and John had been saying ADAS as a word, but the right word was "miracle." When she looked down, Connie's screen blanked. That made perfect sense. She was now asking the equipment to look straight down at the hangar floor and it showed her blank concrete, 2.2 meters below the Hawk's center. But in flight, she would see a landing zone or an underslung load.

John, also helmeted, stood a dozen feet to the side, apparently frozen in place as she was… except that his head wasn't moving.

She blinked to shift her field of focus.

His attention appeared riveted at a blank wall.

Then she did the triangulation in her head. If he were in his seat and looking through the ADAS, he'd be staring at…

Her! He'd been close by her side for three days, hovering inches away as they joined in the installation and training. So close that his rich, earthy essence had been a constant awareness even in the moments when he wasn't nearby. But he wasn't inspecting the equipment. He was watching—

Connie tore off her helmet and threw it aside. Only the quick grab of a tech kept it from bouncing and rolling across the concrete.

She slammed back into the harsh reality of Hangar 14.

The tech was trying to ask her what was wrong. All the noise of a dozen people working on two helicopters that had been buffered by her helmet now hammered against her, overshadowed by her own harsh breathing.

For three days she'd fit in. At least a little.

Emily Beale, once again standing back to observe the progress, slowly tipped her head a little to the side and watched her. Another inspector. Some question on the Major's features. A question without a good answer, as if she'd just bitten down on a lemon.

Connie didn't know. Didn't care.

John remained as he had been before, riveted. Staring at what she'd do next from his helmet world. Inspecting her like she was a goddamn bug on a platter. Like she was an oddity to be observed and would never fit in. The only one she'd ever fooled was herself.

She saw a door and headed for it. By the time she hit the push bar, she was at a run. The outdoor cold slapped her hard, but she was numb inside and couldn't feel it other than as icy knives in her chest. On the far side of the door she kicked into a sprint.

Connie ran across tarmac and taxiway. She ran over

the field and crossed the narrow two-lane road named Nightstalker Way. Ran until she slammed against the perimeter fence where it faced the trees and rolling terrain that surrounded this side of Fort Campbell.

Breathe.

She couldn't breathe.

And she had no idea why.

Chapter 13

JOHN FOUND CONNIE PLASTERED AGAINST THE PERIMeter fence like spaghetti thrown against a wall. Or a cartoon cutout. But this was no cartoon.

Her hands were clenched into the wire as if holding on for life. Maybe they were. Her face pressed against the wire. Her breath billowed in cloudy gasps into the cold morning air. Nothing beyond the fence except low hills and trees.

Night Stalkers were as steady on the ground as in the air. They prided themselves on their smooth and steady attitude. Same way they flew.

Let the Rangers brag to each other, pretend whatever battle they were about to para-jump into juiced them up. Maybe it did, or maybe that was just a fear reaction. Let the Delta operators crawl aboard a chopper dragging the bodies of friends back across the thin line of safety after a mission gone to hell.

SOAR provided the stabilizing touchstone to both.

John had seen this before. Reality slammed into you at the strangest of times. All that cool caught up with you, and the steel-hard casing every SOAR flier kept wrapped around their inner core blew out sideways when least expected. Never in combat. Too busy staying alive. Always when it was quiet. Then some little trigger set off the storm.

After the blowout, he'd helped buddies crawl out

of benders that left a trail of shattered relationships, wrecked cars, and empty whiskey bottles. Others imploded, becoming little more than walking corpses. He'd seen one walk into a spinning tail rotor because he simply didn't notice what was happening in the world outside his head. Only John's quick tackle had saved that one from turning the loss of an arm into the loss of a head. He rubbed a hand across his face, still able to feel the spray of hot blood there.

John fought against his instincts to rush forward and pull Connie into his arms, to comfort her, to keep her safe from whatever had set her off. He'd never pull an Army buddy into a hug, it wouldn't be right to make her an exception. Even though he desperately wanted to.

And he'd bet that with Sergeant Connie Davis, it wasn't the right choice.

Instead, he scuffed his boots through the tall, winter-dead grass to announce his presence, crunching on the thin crust of snow that remained between the stalks. Arriving at the fence, about a meter away from where Connie still stood motionless, he leaned his back against the chain link and then slid down until he sat on the ground. He dropped the coat he'd grabbed for her on the ground between them.

Damn! Kentucky was cold. He blew on his hands and wished he'd thought of gloves as well. A year in the desert lay just seventy-two hours behind him. And the winter weather, though crystal blue, hadn't warmed up enough to erase the couple inches of snow that had greeted their arrival. The only scent on the air was the sharp crackle and bite of cold.

For a while, he just sat and watched the air base. A

monstrous C-5 burned skyward from Campbell Army Airfield, probably loaded with a couple hundred troops or a half-dozen Army vehicles desperately needed somewhere else in the world. A Chinook wound up her rotors, then lifted out of the SOAR compound. The U.S. Army was going about its business.

He kept Connie in his peripheral vision.

Her breathing finally eased.

John saw her flinch as she pulled back from the fence and spotted him there. Looking up, he saw the bright red crisscross of the fence's wire pattern across her cheek, her skin pale from within, bright red with the cold on the outside.

He turned back to the airfield and waited. That was half the secret when the seal blew on a Night Stalker's shell—give them a little time.

Connie took a sharp step away from the fence, as if to leave him as quickly as possible. Then her knees buckled and she slammed back into the fence and slid to the ground close enough that he could smell her.

Warmth, not the feel but the flavor. And sweet, like dark chocolate or rich clover honey from the farm. Comfort. She seasoned the air about her with comfort. And salt. A leisurely glance at her profile revealed that her cheeks were dry, even if her eyes weren't. That was good. Tears were hard to deal with. A grown man breaks down and weeps, you thump him on the back and hand him a shot of tequila. A woman cries and what the hell is a guy supposed to do?

He considered handing the coat to her before she froze, but he didn't know what might set her jackrabbiting off again.

"I remember this time…" John decided the silence had gone on long enough. "We were sitting on our backsides during Green Platoon training. The Drills were on a rampage, busting down the newbies. And we were their eyes in the sky, except they'd rounded everyone up and were haranguing them for being sloppy enough to be caught. That the drill instructors had top-grade night-vision gear wasn't something you complained about being unfair. Not unless you wanted to run in place with full pack and gear and rifle held high for an extra couple hours."

He shifted against the cold wire of the fence before it could etch his back through his coat as it had Connie's cheek. The lines were fading now, but her color was still all wonky. She hadn't yet reached for the jacket partly wrapped around one of her ankles.

"So, we're sitting on our bird, killing time and waiting for the Drills to chase their captives through more sucky swamps. Crazy Tim came up with this whacked idea. I have no idea why I always listen to him. 'Hey John, you remember what it was like during our Green Platoon?' Man, did I ever." He shuddered. The SEALs' notorious Hell Week had nothing on Green Platoon followed by Ranger School. "Constant downpour for four weeks.

"These guys had it easy compared to Tim and me. The day wasn't all that much warmer than this, but it was dry. Not a drop of rain in three weeks. Well, we happened to have a water bag stowed in our gear, left over from a firefighting run the month before. We'd rigged the Drill's observer chair in front of it in the bird, so we hadn't bothered to dig it out. The water bag wasn't hurting anybody sitting in the back of the cargo bay."

He pointed up at the clear blue sky. "We dumped

eight hundred gallons of freezing lake water on the
heads of eighty grunts and eight drill sergeants. Man,
did the Drills chew our behinds. Like with so many of
Tim's plans, we hadn't thought about that part of it be-
forehand. Maybe Tim does and just doesn't tell me."
John shrugged. That actually sounded like Tim. Damn
the consequences if the joke was a good one.

"Later, one of the DIs told us how much they'd actually loved it. They'd stood up under much worse, but the
kids had no idea what had hammered them." He let his
laugh roll forth.

He didn't check on Connie. He just let her be a silent
partner. When their world blew apart, soldiers weren't
apt to find laughter, but at least they'd feel welcome or...

"I don't care."

John spun to face her as if she'd slapped him hard.
Why had he even tried to—

"I can't want to care."

Was she talking to herself? What the hell?

She turned to face him, agony across her features. "I
don't want to care, John. It hurts too much. Here." She
slammed a fist against the center of her chest and held it
there. As powerful as her smile had been, now the pain
etched upon her features battered him.

How had he ever thought her a heartless automaton?

"It kills me. Each time a little more. Right here." She
thumped the fist again for emphasis.

Hard enough to make him wince in empathetic pain.

"Everything I care about is dead. I can't bring it back.
I'd give anything if I could. I've given my life already.
If it would help, I'd give my death as well. Can you
understand that?"

He looked away. He did. How in hell had she fired a round right into his weak spot? Damn! He looked up at the sky and blinked hard. He knew what it meant to want what you couldn't have. Why the hell did she think he was in SOAR?

A glance showed that she'd turned to face the air base and the sky, her fist still in place over her heart, now clenched there by her other hand as she crouched on the dead grass and snow. Her shot in the dark hadn't been aimed at him. She'd aimed it at herself.

"I miss him so much." Her voice broke.

That explained it. She'd had a man and lost him. Another soldier? Or worse, the civilian spouse who couldn't survive being with a soldier. Some worthless dog he'd love to pound into a pulp if he ever met him.

That gave him a focus. Let him shove his own pain aside, back where it belonged, because whatever was going on here, it wasn't about him.

"My dad was the best man who ever flew." She hung her head and shuddered after wrenching the words out from the core of her soul.

He watched as she went fetal, arms wrapped tight around knees pulled in close. She didn't weep. But a shudder, then another, pulsed through her, so strong he thought she might break.

This time he didn't think or hesitate. Reaching out, he gathered her into his lap and wrapped his arms around her.

The shakes slammed through her.

Sometimes he found it hard to keep his hold on her. Some titanic battle was being fought. A battle for control. A battle against memories?

What the hell did he know? He just held her, held her tight until the shakes no longer started from deep, deep inside her, pounding their way through her body until he feared she'd shatter like a piece of fine crystal hurled against the wall.

Chapter 14

AT LENGTH CONNIE RELAXED ENOUGH TO COME TO her senses. For a moment, or maybe John imagined it, she just curled against him. Perhaps comforted. Perhaps simply exhausted.

She pushed back, pushing off his shoulder, and sat up.

The chill air slapped his chest, which had been Connie-warm a moment before. She moved aside and collapsed against the fence. Spotting the jacket, she dragged it on with rock-steady hands that had been shaking with the battle moments before. She sat back with her hands jammed down in the pockets.

Once again just two soldiers staring out at an Army base and freezing their damn asses off.

Then she rested a hand on his arm. A slender, warm hand that he could feel right through the heavy cloth.

"It was you, John." Her voice was hoarse with tension. "I saw you looking at me. Looking at me as if I could somehow be someone I'm not. I thought it was because you were somehow rejecting me even as a fellow SOAR. But when you came out here, I finally understood I was wrong." She squeezed his arm for a moment, then withdrew her hand before continuing.

"I like you, John. I've never respected a man so much since my father. But my heart died that day. I have nothing to give. You almost make me wish I did, but I don't. I'm sorry."

John considered saying he didn't care, but that was more about him not having had sex in too long. He half suspected that if he asked, right now, in this moment, she'd assent. She might be willing, but her heart wouldn't be there. And it wasn't what he wanted from her.

Didn't want sex from Sergeant Connie Davis? He tipped his head forward, then smacked it back against the fence with only minor pain and no more clarity. No, he definitely wanted sex with Sergeant Connie Davis. He hadn't before, but she'd shown him new parts of herself. The killer smile and the killing pain. But not just sex. He wanted...

She'd also just spoken more words to him than she had in the entire prior three months of serving in the same company.

He wanted... to know more about her. He knew it was a cop-out, but it was as close as he could go for now. Though he'd rather not freeze to death in the process.

———

Connie closed her eyes as she leaned against the fence. Hammered. Only word she could come up with. Hammered down hard. She hated the battle. Had fought it since the day her father hadn't come back. Ever. Thirteen years old and fighting the dark.

She'd never let anyone see it. And now John had... There was no way to ever live this one down. Now she'd always be on the outside. She liked this crew. Like flying with Emily Beale. Liked being on a bird so well maintained. You could feel the difference.

But she'd never belong.

She heard him get up to leave.

She heaved out a breath against the cold that sounded far too much like a self-pitying sigh. That would never do.

A deep, slow, calming breath and she opened her eyes.

Then blinked.

Twice.

But what she saw didn't change.

John stood not two steps from her, his hands tucked loosely in his jacket pockets. Even as she watched, he reached out to help her to her feet. A kind gesture. And with how her body was feeling after her internal war, he represented pretty much the only way she'd make it to her feet before she froze in place.

Carefully. Unsure. Not wanting to be cast off, she reached out.

He took her hand in his and pulled her to her feet as if she weighed nothing. The strength he demonstrated in such a simple gesture was a sharp contrast to how gently he held her hand. And then, as if moving on its own, his thumb slipped gently over her knuckles leaving a clear heat signature in its path.

His eyes. Dark, dark eyes, pulled her in.

Without thinking, without considering, she leaned in and kissed him lightly in thanks for sitting with her and holding her and, most of all, for not just walking away.

Even as she shifted back on her heels, the impact of the brush of their lips slammed into her.

"Interesting." She said out loud the only thought that came to mind. But her body had other thoughts.

Without intending to, she leaned back in. This time his hand clamped tightly on hers. When she tilted her head back, the kiss deepened with a long, slow luxury.

His lips were soft and tasted of winter and wood, his mouth gentle and downright luscious.

This time when she rocked back on her heels, she retrieved her hand as well. A bare breath of air separated them. John's eyes inspected her like... She didn't know. As if he'd stepped off a short helicopter flight to find himself on another planet.

All she could think about her own reaction was, "Really interesting."

How lame was that?

But that made up the totality of what she could think before turning back toward the hangar.

Well, her body had ideas even if her brain didn't. She could feel the smile making her cheeks hurt.

Chapter 15

CONNIE KNEW SHE'D BEEN AVOIDING JOHN. EVEN when they were standing only five feet apart, conferring closely with the technicians on the ADAS calibration requirement on the *Vengeance*, she still was avoiding him. Moving so that a vendor's tech or a tool cart always ended up between them.

Once, when the space got too tight, she made an excuse to go over to *Viper* and check how they were dealing with a similar issue.

She wasn't very good at being subtle, but she needed the distance and was doing her best. She could see that John wasn't stupid and knew what she was doing. And bless the man, he wasn't pushing her.

While staring at the readouts on the latest image overlap alignment test, Connie worked to unravel why she was avoiding John. First and foremost, Army Command Policy Regulation 600-20, especially Section 4-14 regarding fraternization. While the regulations didn't technically prohibit any relationship between two enlisted, he was a staff sergeant, a rank above her and therefore her superior, even if not an officer per Army regulations.

Which was a total dodge. She was avoiding John because when she kissed him, her mind had blanked. She normally had a dozen streams running simultaneously. Regs, flight conditions, audible and tactile feedback on a helicopter's condition, and a half-dozen others. She had

learned that keeping complex music in the background
of her mind helped her focus on other tasks.

Since "the kiss," her mind had gone very, very one
track. The feelings, especially tactile, of John's gentle
kiss and the desperate heat of her sudden desire for him
had clearly shocked them both.

Yes, distance was far and away the best policy. As
he crossed to *Viper* to check something with Tim, she
headed back toward *Vengeance*.

"Sergeant Davis. Big John." Major Beale called out
to them just as they passed each other midway between
the birds.

They snapped to attention in front of her, a little farther apart than standard rank and file. Connie felt stupid
for doing that. This wasn't goddamn grade school, but
she hadn't been able to stop herself.

"Follow me!" As the Major turned to lead them out
of the hangar, Connie glanced at John. Had they been
caught kissing at the fence? But that was three days
ago. He just shrugged, clearly with no idea of what else
they'd done wrong.

Once they were out in the cold sunlight, Major Beale
eased her stride until they walked on either side of her.

"You two in a mood to scare the shit out of some
newbies?"

"Sir?" Big John rumbled.

One step. Two. Three. And suddenly Connie got it.
She felt her feet grind to a halt.

The Major had stopped and was smiling at her,
clearly amused at what must be the look of horror on
her features.

It took only a couple of beats more before she saw

the same look she was feeling cross John's features. He looked ill.

In near unison, they both swore.

Chapter 16

CONNIE COULD ONLY RANK THE MAJOR'S SMILE AS wicked.

They were headed over to Grimm Hall so it could only be...

"You remember Assessment Week?"

"Shit, yes." Connie responded before she caught herself. "Sir."

"How do you feel about being on the other end of the stick?"

Connie reconsidered her initial reaction. First there was Packet Week where the complete Army records of every applicant to SOAR were checked and cross-checked until nothing remained hidden, not a bad report by a drill instructor, not a mission screwup, not a poor mark in fourth-grade multiplication tables. Packet Week trimmed half or more out of every applicant class to SOAR.

Then Assessment Week. Seven days of hell that often slashed the class by half again or more. She'd made it through, though to this day she still didn't know how.

Day one, brutally physical. Even the best-trained Army jocks were hammered by the end of the first day. Endless PT. Enough physical training calisthenics to bury an entire platoon. Then the dunk test. How did you behave when flipped upside down in a simulated helicopter into a freezing-cold swimming pool while physically exhausted and wearing full gear and blackout goggles? Five different scenarios. That wiped out a fair number of applicants, right on the first day. Rescue divers helped you out twice. You didn't get a third shot at it. Then still shivering from cold and muscle exhaustion, plan a full night mission.

Day two, psych tests. Mixed with more PT, of course. Six people drilling you for sixteen to eighteen hours. A long list of standardized questions that never ended. And the worst was, not a single word on how you were doing. Did you answer the question right? Did they ask that question because you didn't do enough pushups yesterday? Or because you did them wrong? Or because you screwed up a key soccer match in high school?

The SEALs in their Hell Week training were rewarded when they were the best or dumped into the ocean when they weren't. Even being sent back to lie in the freezing waves must be better than this. At least in the SEALs you knew you'd screwed up.

Not SOAR Assessment Week. Seven days of perfect deadpan. "Next," was all the feedback you ever received.

Day three, this must be day three. Interviews. Seriously sleep deprived, punch-drunk on brutal testing and no idea of how you were doing. Now, a never-ending rotation of SOAR officers asking you any damn thing. Pushing when your thoughts were too slow to form. Driving in at the least sign of weakness.

It was the day she knew her dream had failed, that they'd never accept her into SOAR. Not that year, not any year. She'd finished out the rest of the week just to prove she couldn't be so easily beaten and they could all go to hell. Only after she was out the gate did she tuck her proverbial tail and run.

She'd received her transfer orders to Fort Campbell two days after the end of Assessment Week. With no one to share her good news with, she'd simply shown up, and they'd taken her in. Two years later and the shock still sat inside her somewhere blinking its eyes in surprise.

Connie looked at John, who had stopped with her.

His features were still crossed with a look of revulsion. She couldn't blame him. That something as blandly named as "Assessment Week" could be so brutal wasn't right. But to be on the other end of that. It was an interesting idea. John didn't appear to think so.

"You've got to be kidding me." His voice held none of its usual depth or volume.

The Major just shook her head. The smile was easy on her fine features. "Sixteen in this class still. Packets knocked out twenty-three. PT, dunk, and psych took out another nine so far. They asked for help cutting the next layer of chaff."

"Why us?" Sixteen of forty-eight remaining. Two-thirds gone. Usually about ten percent made it through. They'd probably lose eight to ten more, though there'd been classes where no one made it through despite the rigorous prescreen.

"First, we've found that actual teams have a performance standard based on real-world experience that the psychs can't match. Second, in my case and yours, Sergeant Davis, women. Women at SOAR's level of engagement are a new factor. There are very few of us so far. They want to gauge the readiness of the men in this group to deal with the female factor. And there's a woman in this class. Maybe number five."

Connie started walking again, a bit mechanically. She had to think to make her legs move properly, but she managed to move almost normally beside the Major. John fell in on her other side.

"Five? You said number five, sir? Women. You, me, Sergeant Kee, and who?"

"Another one passed Assessment about half a year after you did, Ms. LaRue. Chief Warrant Officer 2. Pilot. She's still in training."

Who would be crazy enough to put themselves through that?

Chapter 17

"It can't be me." The Major was staring through the dark side of a mirrored observing-room window as if she'd seen a ghost. The Major stood to Connie's right and John to her left. This was the closest Connie had let him come to her in three days. Just a kiss. That's all it had been. Repeating her mantra of the last three days still wasn't making any dent in her desire to repeat the experience.

"What can't?" Connie looked into the room, seeking the Major's problem, but she saw nothing exceptional. Before them, on the far side of the one-way glass, sixteen glassy-eyed applicants stood in neat rows. They all wore Army sweats and coveralls. No insignia. No rank. Not during Assessment. All the same, enlisted and officer, gunner and master pilot.

"I know her." The Major didn't need to indicate who she meant. The only woman in the room was a head shorter than anyone else. A slip of girl with flaming red hair, ageless.

"How?"

The Major ran her long fingers deep into her straight blond hair, uncomfortable. Major Beale was never uncomfortable. "I—" She looked away, then turned her back on the room and faced Connie.

"I don't know you, Sergeant Davis."

"We've flown together for just two weeks and that—"

"Isn't what I'm talking about." The Major glanced over her shoulder as a captain began separating the applicants into groups of four, then she turned back to face Connie squarely.

"How far can I trust you, Davis? I don't know yet."

Connie could offer no answer. The only way she knew to create trust was to prove it was deserved. It couldn't be asked for. It couldn't be offered. It had to be proven and built. She was learning to trust Major Emily Beale the pilot, but she knew little or nothing of Emily Beale the woman. So what could the Major know of Connie Davis the woman?

And why? Did the Major want the woman to fail? Battle over an ex-lover? Or had they been grade-school playmates? What piece of the past did they share that the Major wasn't able to stand in front of her?

Connie kept her thoughts to herself. She wasn't going to queer the Assessment Week process either way.

The Major waited. Waited some more and then nodded.

"Right. Up to me. Okay. Here's a piece of information you shouldn't have. I can't be the one to face her because I'd be too soft. And because Trish would feel safe having me as one of her interviewers. Assessment Week isn't about safe. But—and do with this what you will—that soldier is what SOAR needs. Desperately."

She waited for Connie's acknowledgment. A brief nod was all she could offer. The Major loved SOAR as much as she loved her husband. She was a stand-up person. Absolute integrity. That was how the Major won the immense loyalty of people like John Wallace and Kee Stevenson. And Connie would bet that neither had been easy to convince.

They turned together and walked out of the observation room, down the short hall, and swung into the interview room. Connie, half a step behind, kept an eye on the woman. Of all of the recruits, she stood the straightest, no sign of the weariness that Connie knew would be wracking her very bones. The instant they entered the room, a genuine smile started to light up the woman's face.

Then Major Emily Beale walked by within a foot of her without any hint of notice. The woman looked as if she'd been punched.

No one said SOAR's Assessment Week was supposed to be easy.

Chapter 18

"TELL ME ABOUT THE LAST TIME YOU ALMOST GOT YOUR squad killed. What did you do wrong?" Connie watched as John drilled his question at the guy on the left of the line standing at parade rest. She and John sat behind a bare steel table facing them in a gray concrete room with no leavening decoration other than the U.S. flag.

Connie hadn't known that day three was unscripted. She remembered the round robin of SOAR fliers who had pounded her with questions, she just hadn't known they were making it up as they went along. It made sense. Yesterday had been the scripted psychological profile questions. Today was twenty hours of unscripted real-world tests.

The four applicants looked ragged. They'd probably been on their feet since midnight, and lunch was long gone with no break. Two were actually weaving with exhaustion and hunger. Three men—white, black, and Asian—and the one woman, Irish with red-orange hair and immensely blue eyes. A real mixed cadre.

"Answer, soldier!" John snapped out. His voice rang in the unpainted concrete room with its white T-hung ceiling and no windows. Four cameras lined up behind Connie, four cyclopean antagonists, one focused on each candidate. In the next room a psych board would be watching. The group assessment was to add the stress of performing in front of your potential future colleagues.

She and John kept the questions negative, aggressive, and potentially embarrassing.

Mr. White Guy's reply came out in a growl. And directed at John. Even when she asked the question, he always answered John as if she weren't there. Connie didn't wear any insignia. She could just be another psych tech for all the guy knew. Or a bird colonel. Either way, he was more and more aggressively not answering the questions she asked.

After three hours of it, she was ready to fail him without waiting for the end of the week. Not her call. And none were ever told during the week if they failed or not. They could quit or give up. But they never knew anything about their success or failure until they did or didn't get the order to leave their unit and come to SOAR. By keeping the person who'd already failed in the process, it kept the other candidates from getting any gauge on their own progress.

If she had her way, this one would be getting the lowest grade. "Failed, not approved." There would be no recourse after that. No way to reapply.

There was also "Failed with reason." Those folks were given a chance to work on an identified weak skill and reapply if they could face the process again. Then there was "Approved." Ten to twenty percent of each applicant pool made it to that golden ring. Once there, very few dropped out in the six months to two years of training that followed before they were declared mission-qualified.

She cut off Mr. Misogynist halfway into his justification about a mistake he'd made of under-hydrating. Connie'd seen that in the desert heights of Afghanistan.

A significant danger to the rest of the team. Dehydration clouded judgment and slowed reactions, endangering your squadmates. It also made your urine far more pungent and much more likely to give away your position during an extended hideout.

Connie drilled the same question at the other two guys, leaving him at a loss as to what to do with the rest of his story. The other two did better. At least they looked at both her and John when they answered. One principally answered her chest, despite the vest and jacket that hid most of her form, but maybe he'd been in-country too long and had forgotten what a woman looked like.

When your application passed Packets, you received an order to show up. If that meant getting your ass out of a Colombian jungle and flying through the night to get to Fort Campbell for Assessment Week, that's what you did.

Or maybe he was just a jerk.

John turned for the woman to answer, but Connie cut her off and aimed her next question at Mr. Chest-Starer. She didn't even give the woman the opportunity to answer most of the questions.

John had caught on quickly to what Connie was doing. Between them, they now let the woman answer about one question in five.

He sent Connie a look of sadness that she could just read through his poker face. He was too soft at heart, funny thing for such a top-notch soldier. The same generous heart that had held her out at the fence. She considered patting his thigh under the table but was afraid of being too forward, especially with a superior rank.

By the third time they cut the woman off, Connie could see the simmer forming. Over the following hour and a half, the woman's steam pressure rose to near explosion, but it hadn't come out yet. Best way to piss off an aggressive warrior? Ignore them as if they didn't matter. And in a female warrior, that was even more of a button. That's probably how she'd been treated more often than not throughout her Army career. And to have another woman treat her that way would be particularly galling.

Connie had only taken action against a superior officer once in her career. She had reported a critical deficiency and had her report dismissed because she was female. The Staff Sergeant had ignored her and signed the "Flight (Combat) Airworthiness Certification by Mechanic" release on a Cobra attack chopper.

Connie had reported it directly to the man's commanding officer. Upon investigation, the Staff Sergeant had been handed an immediate general discharge for intentionally endangering his squad with unsafe aircraft. After being caught threatening Connie's life, he'd been bumped to "dishonorable" and tossed in jail for six months. They hadn't treated him well on the inside, and he'd scampered for the hills when they let him out.

Connie wanted to know how this Trisha O'Malley, who Major Beale wanted, would handle being treated with so little respect.

"Permission to speak, ma'am?"

"Denied!" Connie snapped and she could see the woman's jaw clench hard. She fired off the next question. At least the woman had addressed her request to Connie. Smart enough to see who was baiting her.

"If we're downed behind enemy lines and have to lie low in a mudhole for a week, what am I really going to hate finding out about you?" Same pattern as the squad failure question, spread wider.

The guys came up with personal habits. Mr. Chest-Starer had tried to start a riff about the stink of his farts killing anyone who came too close. He almost got a laugh from Mr. Nasty-Misogynist-White Guy until they'd all glanced at Connie and her waiting silence. She let the silence drag out. The pair of them looked at the floor. Two failures in her book. Guy number three was honestly trying and might get a pass from her for this round. Have to compare notes with John.

At length she nodded for the woman to answer.

Her gaze locked on Connie's, her voice rock steady despite her knuckles being bloodless white where her fists clenched tightly at her sides.

"You're going to hate learning that I'm the one who will still be alive at the end of the week. And you'll really, really hate learning that I'm the one who will be the toughest bitch in the mudhole, ma'am." The thin smile she offered was as much challenge as triumph. But despite the anger, her control of her voice and physical actions, other than her hands, had been complete.

Connie learned two things in that moment.

She could absolutely trust Major Beale's judgment, no matter what happened.

And Trisha O'Malley would be a shoo-in.

Connie couldn't have answered the question better herself.

Chapter 19

JOHN FOUND CONNIE SITTING ON THE COLD GROUND with her back against the fence, out across Nightstalker Way. She looked okay. She was just sitting quietly. She appeared calm. The emotional cap was back on, screwed down tight, but he'd bet the internal war still raged somewhere deep inside. He put his own back to the fence and slid down beside her.

The afternoon sun was warm here despite the cold day. In minutes he could feel an ease roll over him. Being with Connie Davis was a quiet place for him. He didn't need to chat or joke or entertain. They could just sit together and watch the midday activity unfold across the base. The occasional chopper in and out. Some mechanics taking a short turn around the field to flight-test a newly serviced bird.

"I learned something today." Her voice wouldn't have carried more than a pace or two past him, but she wasn't whispering. It was a soft, inviting comment.

"What was that?" John shut his eyes and leaned his head back against the fence.

"I'm a stronger woman than I thought I was."

That snapped his eyes open. He studied her profile, She too had closed her eyes and leaned her head back to enjoy the sun. He suspected that she might well be the strongest woman he'd ever met. Major Beale was a hard-ass warrior despite her runway beauty. Kee Smith was as tough and stubborn as any man around her, except maybe her new husband. But Connie...

She was a woman first and a warrior second. Maybe third. Second was that amazing mind of hers. And all three of her aspects, he was learning, were incredible. She fought remarkably well, not with Kee's natural flair but as a highly accomplished soldier.

That brain. The one that thought up the roll in an Afghani mountain pass. He might have come up with that in a day. Or five. She'd done it in under ten seconds with exactly the same data he had.

The woman. That was the one that was blowing him away.

She looked amazing. Trim without being petite. Generous curves that bespoke wonders to explore. Now there was a thought that pushed against a man's imagination. Her long hair, falling feather-cut over her shoulders in waves so soft that a man would never be sure when he first shifted from not touching to touching.

Even with that, her face was what captivated him. The ultimate poker face of exquisite form. Unreadable until she smiled, and then she'd been struck alight. Her eyes sparkled, her quiet mouth developed into a kiss he hadn't erased from his mind despite three days of trying. And eyes he wouldn't mind staring into for a day or two or three, just to learn their shades and emotions.

John suspected that most people saw Connie Davis in the reverse order: warrior, technician, then woman. He had himself, now that he thought of it. Actually, pain-in-the-ass first, then all the others.

Now he had glimpsed beneath the hood of what drove her, seen her shattered in her fight with whatever

was going on inside her head, and seen her beat it back
down into submission. That was a strength he'd never
witnessed before. He wished he knew what she faced.
Could reach in and somehow fix it for her. Replace the
broken part.

He didn't usually do that. People had their issues. As
long as they didn't make those issues his, he was fine
with them. He'd roll along with the good times. Not that
he abandoned friends. He'd paste them back together,
let them sleep it off on his couch, but they could find
their own damn breakfast in the morning. That's all the
guys usually needed.

Your girlfriend broke up with you? Fine. John would
be there to thump you on the back, stand you back on
your feet, but it was up to you to deal with the mess
inside your head or get back together with the woman.
Some asshole insulted you? Who cares? That's their
little world of hurt. You didn't have to buy into it, and
you certainly didn't waste John's time trying to make
him buy into it.

But how could a woman as powerful as the one leaning on the fence beside him not know she was strong?

Apparently taking his silence as interest, Connie
continued.

"It was while sitting in on that Assessment Week
interview."

"No shit?" He'd hated Ass Week, as the few survivors usually referred to it. The failures didn't refer
to it at all. He'd hated it then and he'd hated it today.
Being on the other side of the table didn't help; it only
reminded him of how impossibly hard it had been. He
ached for every poor SOB who'd crawled through his

and Connie's sights. It was not a time he'd wanted to revisit in any manner, shape, or form. Seven days with no feedback. You always had feedback. School teachers, friends, family, your squad, your instructor, your flight… always.

For seven days, the only feedback was a dozen other guys all freaking out just like you. No idea if you were a success or a screwup. Even having Crazy Tim in the same test group hadn't helped, because they'd both felt so totally lost. They'd waited in fear for three weeks after testing before they received the approval to join SOAR, thankfully at the same time. He didn't know how he'd have taken it if one of them made it and the other didn't. The orders came long after he was convinced he'd failed and maybe should just quit the Army to save everyone the embarrassment of dealing with him. Only Tim's upbeat nature had kept his hopes afloat.

They treated you differently back in your old unit after a failed SOAR test. You no longer belonged where you were. You had wanted to leave your squad, tried to leave them behind, and then you failed. No one had to say it. You'd been tested and found wanting. They hadn't been tested, but they also hadn't failed. They still could have passed. Maybe.

Jumping to another unit wouldn't help either, they'd want to know why.

"Because I failed at SOAR."

He'd talked to some of the guys who had failed the different Special Forces tests, another place where a cut rate of fifty percent or more was normal. He learned that he was one of the few people who would talk to them.

"Damn, that was brutal for me. What could you

possibly like?" he asked Connie, still sitting quietly beside him.

"I found I liked being on the other side. Having made it. Not that I was better than them, though there were a couple where that was absolutely true, which didn't hurt my ego much."

He hadn't thought of it that way. They had made it. Crossed over to the other side.

"To know that as we sat with group after group, the smart ones, at least, wanted to be like me. They really wanted what I already had. And not just the validation of their skills. The good ones wanted to serve with the very best."

He nodded, even though she couldn't see with her eyes still closed to the bright sunlight.

"I understood that these people, and several of them were really exceptional, were fighting for even just the chance to achieve what I've already done."

John leaned his head back against the fence and thought about his own view of himself. He knew his own skills were topflight; they had to be to survive on Major Beale's crew. Yet, in a way, Connie was right. He hadn't really acknowledged that. He'd simply worked his way up and was afraid half the time of disappointing the Major or of letting down his team.

Maybe that was the reason he hadn't yet.

"God, John. You're so damned handsome when you smile like that. Does any woman resist you?"

"Not many," was his lazy answer before he caught himself.

He glanced over at Connie Davis, still sitting in the sun. Her gentle waves of hair glittering in the sunlight.

Her expression was open and easy. Her smile was there, not blinding, but bright enough to make him feel he hadn't just been stupid beyond belief. There was no invitation, but there was a zone of safety here.

That wasn't something a SOAR flier was particularly used to.

He liked the way it felt.

Chapter 20

JOHN STILL HADN'T PUSHED HER. THE MAN WAS DECENT down to his very core.

Connie cut across the parking lot between the temporary quarters to Grimm Hall for a meeting.

She would have to figure out how to thank him for that some day. And to thank him for coming to sit with her. The first time, when waves of the anger and sorrow and pain threatened to overwhelm her. The solo battle always wrung her dry. John had made it easier to face, or at least easier to ride through.

And the second time, just the easy companionship which was not something she was used to. And none of the pressure to get her in bed. She actually wouldn't mind that so much with John, but the pressure got old real fast. She was pretty enough and she was Army and she was female. That put her front and center in most Army guys' gun sights. And even when it was fun, it didn't stay that way for long. Guys either got serious and she was never going there. Or they stopped caring it was her and just wanted a body shaped like a woman, and she had too much self-esteem for that.

But John didn't bring the heat. He was just there, which was a gift.

Her only mistake had been trying to thank him with another kiss before they left the fence the second time. The impact hadn't lessened in the slightest. Her body had roared aloft as her brain had settled into soft and quiet. She'd let the kiss build a bit. Hell, it had blown her away like a blowtorch finding jet fuel. She'd never felt anything like it.

Felt it still.

John's kiss was a dangerous thing.

A lethal weapon.

A great power that could block her reason between one heartbeat and the next.

Despite doing her best to avoid him and his dangerous kiss since then—her own, personal version of Assessment Week that she wasn't much enjoying—her body still flashed cold and hot every time she thought about him, which was a true challenge while they worked together each day.

In the narrow hall outside the main briefing room at Grimm Hall, they asked for her ID. That focused Connie's attention back on the main track. This wasn't some minor checkpoint, they were actually running her ID through a scanner and studying the on-screen results. Time to push John to a sidetrack. She rarely thought about only one thing at a time, but the primary focus of her mind should not be on a man she wasn't planning to touch again. He was way too powerful. Way too dangerous.

Something unusual was up. They were already inside the SOAR perimeter inside Fort Campbell, but when they were done with her ID, they went to a finger scanner to confirm her identity.

After a solid week of training on the new ADAS equipment, the two DAP Hawk crews were ready for a serious test. However, the high security implied a mission, not a test. And that didn't make sense. They weren't ready for that yet.

Then they let her into the briefing room. In the center of a space that could seat twenty crews, she found a fight going on.

"No, Peter. Not no way. Not no how. This is not a safe flight."

A man in an elegant suit and with dark hair that fell in a soft wave to his collar faced the shouting Major Beale but stood at perfect ease. This was a feat of daring Connie had trouble imagining. Clearly civilian, he must not know any better.

Major Henderson stood beside his wife, his arms folded across his chest, but incongruously, with a small smile on his lips. Several of the DAP crew members ranged nearby, mostly looking uncomfortable.

John came through the door behind Connie. She could feel him before she could see him. Her awareness of him had been instantaneous ever since their long chat and second kiss by the fence. A kiss that had left her breathless and on the verge of begging for more.

She no longer needed an ADAS helmet to know when he entered a room, shifted positions in the helicopter, looked at her. She'd tried to erase that portion of her brain's operations, but that hadn't worked. And with each passing day she became less sure that she wanted to.

"Em," the suit addressed the Major with a dismissive tone that would have gotten a one-star general castrated. And yet he lived. That in itself was telling.

"You've always told me I didn't have any appreciation for what you do because I never served. It's a training mission. How dangerous could it be?"

"What's the name of the hall you're standing in?"

The suit glanced sideways at another suit, but the second guy was nearly as powerfully built as Big John if on a slightly shorter scale.

And, as the speaker turned, Connie saw one of the most famous profiles on the planet. She snapped to attention. She didn't think, she simply did. Felt John do the same beside her. The Commander-in-Chief, President Peter Matthews, stood there in elegant profile. She'd seen him on a tiny video monitor at a mission briefing half a year ago. But here? In person? She remembered that he and Major Beale had an ease together, but she'd never known how much of one.

"You're in Michael Grimm Hall," the big Secret Service agent answered him. Now that he shifted, Connie could see the gun bulge in the man's immaculate suit. He looked good in a suit. She did a mental shift. John would look amazing in a suit.

The President turned back to the Major, and her expression shifted even darker as she continued.

"Lieutenant Colonel Michael Grimm was a pioneer of SOAR and a pioneer of the Black Route. And it killed him and almost killed his copilot. People die on this flight."

Black Route. Rumor said that the two Majors had gotten engaged while flying a Black Route, which made no sense at all. It ranked as the most vicious test of any helicopter team on the planet. Developed by SOAR for SOAR. No one pushed the limits as they did. Nap of Earth, rarely over a hundred feet in elevation. A Black Route covered a thousand miles at night with three landings, each plus or minus thirty seconds.

"Sir…" Everyone turned to look at Connie before she

knew she'd spoken. "Nine helicopters have crashed on this route. Seven of those sustained at least one death and all sustained injuries. There have also been numerous mechanical failures from the strain requiring dangerous auto-rotation landings. Sir."

Beale nodded to her over the President's shoulder. Over his other shoulder, Major Henderson's smile grew. It implied a sense of humor he rarely showed, but Connie couldn't fit it into the situation.

"Out of how many thousands of flights? Is it more dangerous than getting on an airplane?" The President's question came fast, a quick thinker.

Connie ran some quick estimates in her head. "Less safe than an airplane. Far less safe than Air Force One, which has yet to report a single operational incident in seventy years of operation. But," she shrugged an apology to Major Beale, "statistically, if you discount the 1980s, the first ten years of skills and equipment development, Black Route is only a little less safe than a car. The numbers change drastically for combat, but Black Route training does bring out the best in a team and no one is firing at us during a training flight."

"There will be this time," the Major growled.

Connie couldn't think of what to say to that. Live fire during training?

The President turned back to face the Majors. "Only simulated rounds. We could order them only to fire at Mark. That would work for me. They could even use live ammo for that."

Major Henderson laughed. "Still pissed about losing at poker, are we?"

"I've been playing more lately, like a chance to win a

bit of my own back." There was some other level going on here that Connie couldn't follow, but it appeared to be ticking off Major Beale. Never a good choice.

"Only if my crew can play as well." Henderson winked at Connie over the President's shoulder.

They'd played twice since the flight. Even without Henderson's wife behind him, Connie had won neatly, pocketing fifty of his hard-played dollars each time. It didn't anger him, rather it intrigued him. She didn't like being thought of as a puzzle to be solved, but it was a way she'd found to fit in with the people around her and she'd not give that up any more easily than the Major gave up his money.

"It's a date." The President.

Wait a minute. She was supposed to play poker with the President?

Then the Commander-in-Chief faced Major Beale. "I'm coming, Em. Now can we get this mission under way?"

The Major clenched her jaw for several moments, turned to her husband who merely shrugged.

"The President's as stubborn as you are, honey. I wonder which one of you learned it from the other." He took one step farther from her. "He's nicer about it, though."

He hadn't moved far enough. Emily's four-finger jab caught him in the ribs before he could block. He winced as if it really hurt.

Damn, she was fast.

Chapter 21

JOHN CHECKED THE LAST OF THE WEAPONS. THEIR armament was all in place. For this exercise they'd dismounted one of the big machine guns. Now they had a rack of four Hellfire tank-killer missiles, a nineteen-rocket pod of Hydra 70s, the Vulcan 30 mm cannon, and a laser where they would normally hang a 20 mm chain gun for cockpit control. It would let them fire harmlessly at friendlies busy playing an unfriendly role.

His and Connie's miniguns were locked and not loaded, though spare ammo lay close at hand. Instead, a laser had been mounted in tandem with the six barrels for simulated warfare. For the twentieth time he checked the two observer seats now rigged in the center of the Black Hawk's cargo bay. Standard combat seats. He'd half expected them to put in airliner seats; this was the President after all. But they'd left in the ones used by the vendor's technicians during testing and calibration.

Connie finished the preflight check of the non-weapons systems and arrived outside the cargo door.

"Here." She handed him a stack of barf bags.

"Good one." He slid them into the elastic ceiling mesh where he or Connie could grab them easily for distribution.

She paused there. She had something more to say.

He waited. He'd learned that offering her a bit of silence was pretty much the only way to get her to speak when she was unsure of something.

"ADAS cameras. Stealth rotors. President riding along."

As she always did, she'd used the minimum number of words to set his thinking on a whole new track. He'd been excited by the new technology. And figured the President was just coming along for the ride.

Not Connie. She'd connected the pieces and just given him the heads-up that a major mission was in the works. One that needed a quieted helicopter, which meant going somewhere they weren't supposed to be or perhaps had never been before. The new cameras meant they were going somewhere deep where other feeds, like high-circling command platforms, wouldn't be available. And the President. That meant it was going to be damned serious.

A deep breath and a bit of a shrug, though John felt the pre-mission tension settle on his shoulders. It was what they'd signed up for when they went SOAR, but heavy missions always carried their own pressures.

He didn't question her conclusion for a second; he knew better than to do that. Always thinking, that girl.

Watching her, he'd learned. At the last poker game, he couldn't beat the Major, but he could read Connie. At least on occasion. He didn't yet know how, but his intuition usually warned him when she was way out in the wind on a hand.

He could read her a bit, except when she looked at him. What he'd at first thought was a blank stare, he now knew to be an intensely analytical process of assessment and review. But when faced with the wonder of those eyes, he couldn't tell what she was thinking at all.

Since their second kiss, she had returned to Sergeant Connie Davis mode. Calm, steady, the safety back in

place, all weapons secure. He liked to think there was
something more there, something more behind those
steadily assessing eyes. Did they see some shortcoming
in him? He and Connie hadn't found a moment alone.
But was it because they hadn't tried or because they were
crashing into their racks at night as exhausted from training as they had been from combat just a week before?

Before she could move away, he whispered her
name, "Connie?"

Those dark amber eyes turned upon him. And
Sergeant Connie Davis was nowhere to be seen despite
the flight suit and survival vest. Instead, the woman
who'd kissed him twice now stood just two feet away.

"Yes, John."

Then she turned and was gone.

It took him a moment to realize that she'd made it a
statement and thereby answered his question. The one
he hadn't known he was asking.

Yes, she was thinking of him. And with the way he
was discovering her mind worked, maybe she was thinking of him even more than he was thinking of her.

That was hard to imagine.

Chapter 22

THE TAKEOFF STILL SOUNDED ODD TO CONNIE'S EARS. The new rotors and blades had made the Black Hawk sound different. Over a hundred yards away, they'd be almost unidentifiable directionally. The noise signature had been changed drastically, and large caps over the rotor hubs would significantly decrease their radar signature.

"Half-stealth," the Sikorsky techs had called it. There hadn't been time for a major overhaul—replacement of all the skin panels, radar-deflecting enclosures for the weapons, wheels that folded into the fuselage, and so forth—but the Hawks were now significantly quieter. She liked the feel of that.

That they'd only taken the time to install "half-stealth" said that a real mission wasn't merely pending, but rather that it was pending soon. A hot one.

"Okay, *Vengeance*." Major Emily Beale's voice was clear over the intercom. "We still don't know what's coming, but we know it will be over hostile and unfamiliar terrain. It will probably be longer than a typical mission with multiple refuelings. This flight is intended as a shake-out of new equipment against friendly forces before we face the unfriendly. So let's show them what SOAR is made of."

A round of "Yes, sir!" echoed back. Connie looked past the back of Clay's copilot seat next to her shoulder and far enough around to see the Major in quarter profile.

Her thinly gloved hands rested lightly on the collective and cyclic controls. Her attention was straight forward, all of the woman hidden by her armor, vest, and helmet. She was the consummate commander and pilot.

Connie twisted far enough to glance at John seated back-to-back to her, his shoulders so broad that one brushed the back of Beale's seat. Already he was watching out the far side of the chopper, even though they were barely off the Fort Campbell tarmac.

Right. She faced her own window and stared out at the falling night. The place they always attacked was where you felt safest. She flicked on the ADAS feed to her visor and the night was replaced with a thousand shades of gray. A quick glance to the rear showed the Fort Campbell field falling astern. They were moving fast at barely fifty feet up. A narrow road slipped by below. Connie glanced down to see her spot by the fence—hers and John's.

Even as she considered that she'd like to try a third kiss with John, she spotted the figure. A bright thermal image, nearly white against the colder ground. Just outside the fence line, standing, shifting to follow their flight.

"Sniper low!" she called out.

Beale hammered the chopper to the side as a dazzle of red light from the ground, shown by the loose evening fog, missed her face by mere feet, a dazzling red dot on the ceiling of the cargo bay. Connie zapped the target with the laser alongside her minigun. The sniper held his rifle to the side in defeat. May have even waved before the trees blocked him and her section of fence from view.

Major Beale continued pushing the Hawk hard as

they flew west on the mission profile. Slipping the bird one way, then the other. Rise and turn. Working it. Training her body until the different reactions of the modified Hawk were once again second nature.

The next attack came a long time later, so long that complacency would have slipped in before Connie went through SOAR training. A hundred different lessons had beaten all the way down to her subconscious that there was no such thing as "safe" when you were in flight. Right after they passed by Jefferson City, Missouri, bright-green tracer rounds slashed across Connie's helmet display, intentionally wide misses but close enough for the targeting computer to trace back to their origin and provide her with a moving bull's-eye on her display. In a second the laser mounted on her gun was hot and she shot off a quick three-round burst to where her helmet identified the most likely source.

She glanced at the upper-right corner of her helmet's visor to read the information scroll. They were over the Skelton National Guard Training Site. Never heard of it. A report flashed in, briefly lighting the lower-right corner of her vision.

"Kill confirmed." That meant she'd landed at least one shot within ten meters of the target vehicle that had fired the tracer. With a minigun at full fire, she'd have sheeted the area with flying lead.

She heard a sound, someone clapping.

She turned to it, and all she saw was Major Henderson's Black Hawk flying tight on their tail and thirty degrees to the side in close formation. Shifting her focus from the ADAS display to the reality beyond her visor, she saw the President's hands returning to his lap.

Another shot, an out-of-focus blur across her visor, and she was too late to target it.

Thankfully, the Major rolled them down into a gully between two low hills, moving them out of range. The training system didn't mark them as hit.

Connie turned away, determined not to be distracted again. Civilians were a real problem.

The flight continued with little change.

At Nickell Barracks Training Center in Salina, Kansas, they swooped a dozen feet over a very startled guard shack, pulled up, and slid to an abrupt halt. The two Black Hawks each touched one wheel down on the sloped rooftop of Nickell Hall. Fourteen seconds ahead of schedule, they waited until zero time and left twelve seconds later, long enough for a whole squad to pile aboard each bird.

That close, the rotors were loud enough to draw people outdoors to see what was happening. But the choppers had been too quiet for anyone to think of them as being right on their roof. As the Black Hawks disappeared into the darkness, she could see in the ADAS that the soldiers below were looking in every direction except the right one.

She'd stood on the ground at Fort Campbell as the DAPs had been flown overhead with their new blades, and even though she knew the sound was unusual, she had trouble crediting the poor reactions of trained soldiers.

Three times they rose up for midair refuel. This was a real stretch of a flight. Usual Black Route protocols were a thousand miles, two refuels, and five to six hours of flight time. Tonight, they were profiled to arrive at the Nevada Test and Training Range after sixteen hundred miles of flight and eight hours in the air. In full fighting trim.

As they rose above the Utah-Nevada border for the fourth and last refuel, Connie glanced forward. On the lower edge of her vision, she saw the refueling probe extended forward, reaching out to just past the forward edge of the rotor blades. This was something she'd never seen clearly from the backseat of a helicopter.

A KC-135 Stratotanker trailed a pair of long umbilicals from the tip of either wing with target baskets at the end. Even as she watched, Major Beale drove forward and dead-centered her target with the 454 pounds of force needed to latch into the fueling system. A glance to the right past John, through the hull and past the weapon's pylons, revealed Major Henderson doing the same; two Hawks, each trailing just behind either wingtip of the Stratotanker. With the valves interlocked, fuel would be roaring down into their tanks.

She turned to check on their passengers. Secret Service Agent Adams's jaw was locked, perhaps a little too tightly. It was unclear whether he was fighting air sickness or still upset at the President's "needless exposure to undue hazard" he had voiced before the flight.

The President appeared to be in fine health, though his demeanor was much more serious.

"Sergeant Davis, is this what every day is like?"

"Well, Mr. President, first, I'd point out that it is night."

A bark of laughter from Major Beale sounded over the intercom.

Connie hadn't meant to be funny but could see how it could be taken that way, now that she thought about it.

"And second, there's a difference here. We know this

mission. We also know that those targeting us have been instructed not to hit us. Short of a mechanical failure, there are few unknowns and little hazard."

"Can you describe the difference to a layman?"

She puzzled over that.

John answered for her.

"Imagine, Mr. President, that you are going down the Grand Staircase of the White House. You've done it a thousand times, but think back to the first time. I expect it felt foreign or a little peculiar."

"Are you kidding? Lincoln trod those same stairs. Wilson, Truman... Scared the hell out of me."

"Good, better. Now, imagine that you're taking that first-time walk down those stairs and you're surrounded by the best protection ever designed by man." John patted the inside of the Black Hawk's fuselage.

Connie could see the President nod to the agent seated beside him. This was probably the least protection the President had traveled with since the day he was nominated. A single agent, and he'd chosen this man. That was high praise indeed.

"And imagine that maybe, just maybe, someone is waiting to kill you on the first landing and you can't see them coming."

Another bark of laughter sounded over the intercom from Major Beale. "He doesn't need any imagination to picture that, does he, Frank?"

The Secret Service agent merely growled in response as the President laughed.

John paused, but no one was explaining the joke.

"Now, sir," John continued after a moment in that deep voice of his, "imagine those two feelings combined for hours at a time. That monotony of climbing and descending those steps a thousand times, knowing that despite your training and your protection detail, the next instant may hold death even if you're good enough, even if you're fast enough."

The President was silent for a long moment.

"Is that the way it is, Em?"

"He pretty much nailed it."

Connie would never have thought to couch it in such terms. Never thought to describe it in the President's world. Never would have thought about the other person's point of view.

John did. He always did. For the hundredth time she was taken back to that ridiculous story he'd told her at the fence. When she couldn't find herself, when the pain was winning, he had reached out and told her that sometimes the world didn't have to make sense, at least not from one point of view. Those eighty soaked grunts on the ground had their worldview shattered in that moment, safe and dry one moment, just hanging out and resting up while the drill instructors did what drill instructors do. One of the comforting touch-points of Army training, being yelled at by your DI.

Until the blue heavens had opened with a deluge. And the drill instructors, who had "stood up through much worse," laughed.

"But why?" the President asked. "I've asked Em, but I still don't get it. You, Davis, why do you do it?"

There was a silence on the intercom. She could feel the others turning to her. Of course, they would know this about each other. She wanted to say something flip like Crazy Tim would toss off or funny but heartwarming like Big John. Something wise and thoughtful like Major Beale, with that touch of inner passion and spine of pure steel.

She searched for any answer other than the only one to be found.

"The best man I ever knew, my father, was murd— killed by one of these machines. I need to conquer it to prove that a Davis can't be beaten by a machine."

She turned away to face the night outside of the aircraft. Blinked hard against burning eyes. The silence that followed was almost harder to bear than the speaking of it.

She focused on the changing feel of the Black Hawk's flight as it gulped down a ton of Jet A fuel. Focused on testing her memory of the wiring diagrams for the ADAS and how those systems juxtaposed the underlying networks. And how the data systems aligned with power and control wiring. And that with fuel and hydraulics.

By the time she could see the entire Hawk's overlapping systems in her mind's eye, the entire Hawk's nervous and circulatory systems, her physical eyes no longer stung. Her vision had cleared. Once again she could glance forward and see the Hawks disconnect from the tanker and the refueling probe withdraw and tuck back into its casing, retracting out of the ADAS view.

Once again her field of view was clear.

Chapter 23

MAJOR BEALE CONCENTRATED ON KEEPING HER ROTORS clear as she backed off from the Stratotanker. A blink revealed nothing but darkness beyond her windscreen so she blinked back to focusing on the clear image projected on her visor of the tanker reeling in the two dangling fuel lines.

The additional fuel made the Black Hawk maneuver differently because of the additional mass in the tanks. The Major's body adjusted automatically to the change, leaving her free to consider Sergeant Davis's last statement.

So, Connie was Ron Davis's girl. She hadn't connected that, despite seeing his name in the Army file. Davis's file hadn't mentioned that the man named in the "father" box had also been a highly decorated sergeant first class. A chief mechanic for the 101st Airborne's Combat Aviation Brigade, the Screaming Eagles.

Useless. Army files, never the right information.

Emily had only flown with Sergeant Ron Davis once, one of her first Army training missions when she was still a wet-behind-the-ears second lieutenant fresh out of West Point. It had been just weeks before his flight was lost. He hadn't mentioned having a daughter. Nor much of anything else.

She could see the core-deep quiet of the man in his child. But did she have the heart? The heart that had taken Emily aside after that long-ago flight and told her how to fly her best. A lesson she'd never forgotten.

"Get out of your head, Lieutenant." Ron Davis had stopped them to stand out in the driving, chill rain that had hammered Fort Rucker flight school that night, where no one else would think to pause. As good a place as any for privacy on the busy airfield. Or maybe he was so focused that he didn't notice the weather.

"I've sat as a back-ender on a thousand flights and you're a goddamn natural. But until you get out of your head, you're gonna be just another chopper pilot. Some flight jocks crank rock 'n' roll to chill out that part of their brain. Some pick fights when they're on the ground. Some meditate. Some never shut the fuck up. Some kill the chopper and their crew by holding on too tight. You, you're a goddamned pillar of strength. I've never met a woman so tough who was still a woman. Accept that. Fly from that strength."

He'd cracked a smile, as brilliant as it was brief.

"And do me a favor. Any bastard who doubts you, fly his ass straight into the ground." She'd flown by that simple motto for the decade since and it had served her well.

Emily glanced over her shoulder to see how her newest crew chief fared. One of John's big hands reached across and rested for a moment against the center of Davis's back. Between one moment and the next, she shifted from head hanging down, fingers clamped on the handles of her minigun, to upright, a deep breath visibly taken as if she was starved for air until that moment.

Emily wished she could turn far enough to see John's reaction.

But maybe she didn't have to. Davis nodded without turning. John's hand patted her lightly between the shoulders, then withdrew from Emily's field of view.

She turned back to descend from behind the tanker. Their flight profile had them entering the Nevada Test Range from the southeast, so she and Mark had agreed to go true nap of earth and circle to the northeast corner through Tikaboo Valley. See if the ground testers were ready for what *Vengeance* and *Viper* were ready to hand out to them in the dark of the predawn hours.

Her equilibrium restored by John's kind gesture, Connie quickly checked her equipment and her surroundings. No one seemed to have noticed her lapse, her momentary teetering on the brink, something that had never happened to her before during a flight. Nor would she let it happen again.

She glanced back once more and, through the ADAS display, spotted a blur straight behind them. It shifted as Major Beale adjusted the trim, changing their flight line ever so slightly. Not an illusion of the new system. A fighter coming up on their tail fast. Nothing on the threat detector. Stealth. They were throwing a stealth jet at them as they came off the tanker. Never let down your guard when you're going to be somewhere predictable. Another five seconds and it would all be over.

"On our six," was all the warning Connie needed to give.

Without even taking the heartbeat to check for herself, the Major slammed over into a high-gee turn with a trust that still startled Connie. If her crew chief said something, that was now good enough for the Major. Warmed by the unspoken praise, Connie armed the laser and raked it across the flight path of the approaching jet.

Her own sensors rattled and chittered, near miss. Head-to-head now. Connie slid the gun forward on its mount and leaned forward until her arms and head were outside the gunner's window. She kept her fire as Clay fired the main laser, which would shoot a broader light in keeping with the increased threat presented by his larger weapons.

Someone groaned over the intercom, but Connie ignored it. No live rounds in this exercise, so no one was suddenly shot and bleeding out.

The jet's control wavered as some critical system decided it had been damaged enough to go off-line, but the jet kept coming. Not down yet.

"Viper," Major Beale called to her husband. "They're playing dirty."

He keyed his mic three times, two short and one longer. Two eyes and a grin, his electronic version of a smiley face. The Morse code for the letter *U*, the upward smile.

Connie hung on as *Vengeance* jinked high, low, left, then right to make a tougher target. But they remained in a general line head-to-head with the jet, firing the whole way in.

Another groan.

Connie knew from experience that the Hawk's crew flew in silence, so that would be the President or agent Frank Adams.

A glance up through the ADAS showed *Viper* in a high loop and roll. A quick trade of speed for a couple thousand feet of altitude and then he was plummeting nose down from above.

The lead jet faltered and dove to return back to base as a casualty. A second jet, which had been hiding directly in his leader's wake, never knew what hit him as Major Henderson shot his metaphorical tail off from straight above. With helicopters that flew at barely a quarter the speed, they'd just nailed a pair of America's stealth fast-movers.

"Ready to play?" She could hear the Major's smile in his simple question over the radio.

In answer, Major Beale just rolled *Vengeance* half over so her rotor was pointed straight at the ground and they were hanging upside down from their seats, then she cranked all the lift her bird could muster. They accelerated straight down while in inverted flight. Time to get where there wasn't so much open space. Jets didn't do nearly as well close to the ground.

Connie reveled in the free fall and braced her gut muscles for the roll-out at the bottom of the descent.

Chapter 24

JOHN HEARD THE MOANER SHIFT TO GAGGING. WITHOUT taking his attention off the skies, he fished out a couple of the barf bags and held them out. They were snatched from his hand.

A loud retch blasted the intercom.

"Goddamn it!" Emily cursed. "Shut off your mic, Sneaker Boy!"

"Not me," was the response, though the President's voice wasn't all that steady. "Frank's having a tough time. There," a loud click on the intercom, "I got his mic switched off."

"Fine! Now shut up. We're busy."

At five hundred feet, the Major turned their dive into a long roll, leveling out and pulling damn near max gees.

John huffed out a breath to decrease the pressure and tighten his gut even further. Heard others doing the same.

It drove him down hard in his chair and made him glad they'd had a week to break in the new rotors and blades while practicing with the new gear. He'd hate to trust a maneuver like that to new blades. The fact that they were a different blade type, stealth designed, continued to worry him. The Major hadn't killed him yet despite doing much harder stunts over the last year, a good sign for their continued survival. But as her chief mechanic, it was his job to worry.

He looked out his side of the chopper, and a rock

wall was flashing by at barely two rotors out. Two widths of their main rotor away, an irregular, craggy, chewed-up cliff whipped by at nearly two hundred miles per hour. It was weird to see the whole wall of it through the ADAS, rather than just what he could spot around the sides of the minigun. He tried to gauge real versus apparent distance to find some camera distortion effects. But in the dark, the cliffs looked impossibly close when they were visible at all. The camera offered the only really usable view.

He glanced down between his feet. Fifty feet above a dry stream bed. She must be flying extra high to keep the President safe. They'd all have to compensate for that, the extra height making them more likely to be in the radar of some damn ground-pounder playing at unfriendly.

They broke out of the canyon, and he scanned the skies out his side of the craft and made sure to include the stern in his scan. Connie had looked astern and spotted the fast-mover; he should have spotted it as well. He wouldn't forget again.

He also tried looking straight up and straight down.

"AA, two o'clock, very low."

The Major rocked sideways with a twist and put John's window square on target. The registers ticked off a couple of laser hits inbound, but not enough yet to declare them injured. He lit the laser rigged to his minigun and raked it back and forth in a swirling, flattened figure-eight pattern guaranteed to lay down the most damage in the least time with an extra twist at the center that Kee had taught him. He had the satisfaction of seeing the antiaircraft truck flash a red "destroyed" light within moments.

They were all a little twitchy about AA since Major Henderson had been shot down a couple months back.

———␣␣␣———

Connie let a part of her mind drift as she always did in battle. Not much, but enough. If she didn't, she'd lose her focus. But her dad had taught her that sometimes a little distraction went a long way.

Part of her mind always kept a running tally of the high-stress maneuvers so that she could anticipate failures. Major Beale was laying it on for President Matthews, though he'd pulled an iron jaw so far, pretty good for a civilian. Once the Secret Service agent had bagged his dinner, he didn't look quite so green.

Or maybe Major Beale was just having fun. There were things you could do at two thousand meters in freezing air that you couldn't pull off at the same altitude in Afghanistan's high and hot. The air got too thin at a hundred degrees for a helicopter to do much of anything interesting.

So Connie knew that she'd be checking the collective linkages and the swash plate sooner rather than later. She also wanted to keep an eye on varying wear due to the five blades and their strangely articulated tips that made them so much quieter.

In another track of her mind she also kept a running assessment of her own responses to the ADAS. The first problem with the ADAS became rapidly clear, as it had in testing—it was too damn good. It made you stop watching other indicators. She had to consciously remember to look inside the cockpit as well, because watching the projected world on her visor was so spectacular.

Enhanced infrared, it showed as black and white inside her visor, but she could see just how close the Major flew to rocks and trees to stay out of the sight and target range of possible threats. The pilot and copilot would have selections of heavy weapons targeting and terrain flashing across their visors. Another feed would include status of mission profile, planned versus actual position, and feeds from ground and airborne surveillance systems.

She and John had their own array of threat detection, engine status, and all the information from HUMS. The chopper's health and usage management systems provided extensive information and alerts to be filtered and managed. She flipped down into the subscreens for a moment, but all indicators were showing green. She knew from experience that HUMS was a little slow to pick up on sudden damage, such as being shot. It hadn't reported the damaged rotor blade in the Hindu Kush until the blade actually broke free. But for general wear and tear, it was a nice backup to her mental tally.

They passed over a small ground squad wearing the infrared reflectors that showed them to be friendlies. It took training to not reflexively pull the trigger when spotting armed squads deep inside hostile territory. Even with all her years of flight, Connie still had started to depress the trigger, but had resisted the instinct to hammer it down.

The copilot, Clay, took out another troop that didn't wear the badges, with John doing a little cleanup to be certain, as the Major slalomed through the snow-capped mountains of Nellis Air Force Base's test and gunnery range.

Connie also usually ran one more channel in her mind. Music. With Mozart or Bach or Handel. Her dad had played the oboe. It was her alarm clock for a thousand mornings, that sharp squee-squaaa of him warming up an oboe reed, even at the far end of the house. She'd never thought to ask him why the oboe and now she'd never know. At twelve, she hadn't thought yet to ask him all the questions a grown woman needed to know about her father. By thirteen he was gone, taking all of his answers with him to an unknown grave.

She sought one of Vivaldi's soaring tunes from her memory and relaxed into its familiar embrace which allowed her thoughts to focus on—

A flash came up on her helmet visor, intelligence from Major Henderson, peeking over a ridge about five kilometers to the east. The little glyph was almost lost in the sea of information, but not quite. A row of four tanks waited just around the corner, bunkered in, ready to score on *Vengeance* as they cleared the next ridge.

"Major?" She voiced the question to make sure that Major Beale saw it.

"Yep!" Emily Beale was on it, and those tanks were gonna go home dry. It wouldn't be happening for them tonight.

"Honey?" Beale called over the radio. She was definitely enjoying herself.

"Yes, dear?" Henderson was having a good time, too.

"How about shooting one of your cute little tank killers at the ridge in front of us?"

"In five, four..." Henderson interrupted himself, "Gonna hydrate 'em, dear?... One. Stay low... And it's gone."

Eleven and a half long seconds. Connie counted them in her head. Eleven and a half seconds while the tanks would be desperately trying to locate the deceptively muted blades of the choppers echoing strangely off the canyon walls. Stealth rotors sounded almost as if they were flying away, not toward their line of flight.

Eleven and a half seconds. An eternity in battle, though all they were doing was hovering behind the safety of the ridge. A Hellfire missile crossing five kilometers and traveling at Mach 1.3 would impact the other side of the ridge precisely...

She heard the krump followed by a rising cloud of dust as nine kilos, twenty full pounds of high explosive, smithereened the rock of the cliff face with deadly accuracy. Hit a tank with one, and there was gonna be a hole that started on one side and didn't end until it came out the other, no matter what or who it ran over in between.

As the cloud of dust rose above the ridge, Major Beale slid them up and forward into its shadow. They'd played this game many times in Afghanistan. When a dust storm came, you couldn't see much through it, but you could certainly use it, assuming you could stay out of its hot-and-blind kill zone. But here the dust was mostly cold, and those tanks sitting in the dark of the frozen desert were blazing hot in comparison to the surrounding landscape. Easy to spot.

"Half salvo away. Definitely going to rain on their parade." In moments, nine 2.75-inch Hydra 70 rockets were spread out in a slashing array. Small but mighty, the multiheaded serpents of mythology pounded into the earth a hundred feet in front of the whole line of dug-in tanks. Tall billows of sand and rock shot up into the air right in front of them.

"Think they all know they're dead yet?" Mark's Texas drawl was back, worse than in a poker game. "Let's jus' go on down thar and find out."

As *Vengeance* rode through the settling cloud of shattered cliff, Connie could look forward through the helicopter as if it wasn't there.

Major Henderson slipped up behind the farthest tank, its occupants still too startled to respond. No rotation of the turret, no one managing the turret machine gun. He hovered just above the top-center loader's hatch and began easing his Hawk's nose up and down, smacking the tank repeatedly with one of his front wheels. Inside the tank, it must sound like the fist of God knocking at the door.

Chapter 25

"NOW WHAT ARE YOU REALLY DOING HERE, PETER?" Major Beale fired the question they were all thinking directly at the President. Connie was still shocked at how they spoke to each other.

"And why the sudden, rush upgrades to our birds?" That was unusual enough to worry Connie significantly. She'd checked every enhancement a dozen times, but the changeover was still too fast for her comfort. She glanced down the table and wondered what each of the members of the two crews thought. She'd like to ask them and find out, but it wasn't her place.

They sat around a large dining table in a secure conference room at the Tonopah Test Range Airport. Flags lined one wall: U.S., Army, Air Force, Navy, Marine, Coast Guard... A banner for each fighting force that defended this country.

And for a hundred miles south and a hundred and fifty to the east ran the Nevada Test and Training Range. Nuclear tests and secret aircraft. Area 51 UFOs and Red Flag aerial combat training. Where Skunk Works had tested the fastest and the nastiest jets ever launched into the sky. U-2 spy planes and the SR-71 Blackbird had roared aloft here. The F-117 stealth fighter had been born in this baking desert. She'd cut her Special Forces teeth flying war games up and down this stretch of desert.

The President sat at the head of the long walnut table with Beale and Henderson to either side. *Viper's* crew ranged down one side, Dusty, Captain Richardson, and Crazy Tim. Connie, John, and Clay sat down the other side. No Secret Service, not even Frank Adams. No assistants. The remains of a fine Mexican meal of tamales, enchiladas, and as rich a beef caldo stew as Connie had ever eaten were scattered about the table. The food had been spicy enough to make her sweat, and her mouth still burned despite the sweet dessert.

President Matthews toyed with the last of his tres leches cake for a moment.

"I wanted to see what you keep telling me about my lack of understan—"

"Cut the bull, Sneaker Boy. This is me you're talking to."

John leaned in to whisper in Connie's ear, "Friends back when they were growing up. Wonder if they fought so much back then."

"You have no idea." Major Beale apparently had very sharp hearing. "Every conversation with Peter is a mental jungle like you can never imagine. And now that some fools made him President, it's even more deeply ingrained than when he was just the older pain-in-the-ass boy next door."

"And you love it as much as I do, Squirt. Admit it."

She huffed out a breath, then smiled at him. "I hate to admit it, but I do. Now give!"

"There's an assignment," the President finally spoke as he fussed with his cake some more, "a mission. It may be happening and it may be happening soon. I need a team on immediate call, and I need you to be able to do things that your commanders insist you can do. I wanted to see for myself. At least as much as a civilian can understand."

"And what did you see, Mr. President?" John asked.

Connie was amazed at how smoothly John stepped into the conversation. Distracting both the Major and her Commander-in-Chief from the next round of sniping debate with a perfectly natural question.

The President ate the last of his cake and washed it down with a sip of coffee before pushing both away.

"How many words would you have spoken if I wasn't there?"

Beale shrugged.

"Seventeen in…" Connie considered for a moment, "eight hours, twenty-seven minutes. Sir."

He looked at her a bit strangely.

Beale was clearly trying to hide a smile. Henderson didn't even bother to hide his.

"I'll wager that Mark's bird wasn't all that much noisier."

"Oh no, Mr. President." Mark reached out for a second piece of cake. "We had a running game of 'I Spy' twenty questions all across the country. You know 'I Spy?' Question one, 'Will it kill us in the next ten seconds?' 'No.' Question two, 'Will it kill us in the next twenty seconds?' 'Only if you don't move your ass.' That sort of thing. Helps the time go by."

"And you married him?" The President asked his childhood friend. In Connie's estimation, his voice didn't quite tease the way he intended.

"Guilty." Major Beale also didn't sound quite light-hearted. Had they been more than friends? How had she ended up married to her commander rather than the boy next door?

The President recovered quickly.

"I need a team with discretion beyond the norm. And I'm confident from prior experience of your absolute reserve when required."

"Oh shit!" She and Mark shared a look. "You ready to saddle up again, cowboy?"

"Wa'll," his Texas accent was back. It was lame, but it appeared to melt his wife's bones every time. "When yer nation cawls 'pon its finest, who be I to ar-gyuh with that?"

John and Crazy Tim groaned.

Major Beale must have seen the look on Connie's face. "You ever hear of black-in-black operations?"

Connie was still considering Mark's fake accent, even worse than before. He sounded like John Wayne run through a *Beavis and Butthead* laugh track.

Then Major Beale's eyes, which had been light and easy until that moment, became dark focused lasers of blue as Connie shifted to answer the Major's question.

She almost answered in the positive, but everyone already knew about black operations. No one outside of the operations team and the chain of command could ever be told what happened.

Of course, if you were a member of SOAR and had flown some black operations, it became fairly easy to pin down the ownership of certain world events. The explosion that had shredded a Russian tank factory, she'd lay good money that it was a U.S. Army black op. Then there was the meltdown that, for reasons still unreported, occurred at the Pakistan nuclear fuel facility, just bad enough to require outside experts to see what was really going on there, but not bad enough to create real danger. That one had SOAR and Delta Force finger-prints all over it if you knew how to look.

White ops were released to the news after they were done. Bin Laden's death, Hussein's capture, Grenada, Noriega, all of the help after Hurricane Katrina, a dozen others.

But black-in-black?

Connie shook her head.

Crazy Tim held up one finger and looked sick. He tried to put a funny face on it but didn't manage to pull it off. John held up three, which startled his best friend no end. Richardson, Henderson's copilot, just nodded his head. Clay and Dusty's faces, she suspected, matched her own.

"See the people at this table?" Major Beale slowly aimed her finger at Connie's chest and then tracked it slowly around the table in full-on, scary-as-hell com-mander mode.

Connie turned to look at each face in turn, as did the others.

"These people. Now. Right now. Really look. Etch these faces into your brain and etch them deep. These are the only people you may ever discuss this mission with. Not your future commanding officer, not your therapist or priest, not the next President. Not in your retirement. Ten years from now, stone drunk so bad that you break your nose walking into the wrong end of a Marine, these people and these people only. Are we clear?"

The steel was back, the fine meal forgotten as the Major leaned in and studied each face carefully. Connie felt pinned by the inspection, as if her soul had suddenly been bared. There was no doubting that Major Beale meant exactly what she said.

"Good. Now, this is the moment where you can walk out of the room. Completely voluntary. No reflection on your record in any manner, shape, or form. And I can tell you, if you walk out that door, your life expectancy is going to be much, much higher. Anyone?"

No one moved a muscle. Connie couldn't imagine that a Night Stalker would ever refuse a mission. Any mission.

"Go easy, Em. I don't even know if it's going to happen."

"That's one of the differences between civilian and military mind-sets that you always ask about, Mr. President. You aim for the best and try to avoid the worst. We soldiers always fully prepare for the worst. We train for it constantly and plan how to beat it every day, every hour. We're seldom disappointed and it's why we're all still alive."

President Peter Matthews looked much more sober.

"And with black-in-black, that usually isn't enough."

Chapter 26

CONNIE STOOD WITH THE GROUP AS THEY SAW THE President off with no one the wiser. He slipped out of Tonopah on a Gulfstream jet that would slide him back to Air Force One, parked overnight at Fort Campbell, as quietly as if he'd never left.

Connie and John spent nearly an hour packing their bird and freezing their fingers. Even the gloves couldn't insulate against the chill that had crept in as they sat in the warm conference room. Black-in-black. That implied missions that were never heard of. Missions, whether they succeeded or failed, that were never even known about.

Had that been what happened to her father, a failed operation rather than a failed machine? At first she'd blamed the manufacturers. That's why her first jobs were with Sikorsky and other vendors for the Black Hawk helicopters. When she hadn't discovered flaws there, she signed up with the military expecting to find slipshod work. Instead she'd worked with some of the finest mechanics she'd ever met—ones like John—who she was proud to work alongside.

For some reason, she'd never considered an operation gone bad. An operation so secret that no word of it could ever be released, not even to the surviving daughter.

When she and John finished preparing the DAP Hawks, the C-17 loadmasters took over and shifted

Viper and *Vengeance* onto the same aircraft that had delivered them to Fort Campbell. But Major Henderson herded the crews off before the vast rear cargo hatch closed like a giant mouth eating their Hawks.

"Not our flight."

The rear ramp closed, and instead of taking off, the plane was towed into a hangar and the doors shuttered her in.

Connie looked around the group. A secret mission without their helicopters. That didn't make any sense. Especially after all of the trouble to install and train on the ADAS and the upgrade to "half stealth."

They all stood there in their civvies, their heavy gear on the choppers, light backpacks and duffels stacked at their feet.

Another Gulfstream jet rolled up. They were all directed aboard and moments later were climbing up to twenty-thousand feet.

When they were up to cruise altitude, Henderson stood at the front of the cabin. Or tried to. The ceiling was too low. He stood almost as tall as John, and was nearly as broad of shoulder, but lacked the sheer physical power of a man of John's size.

Henderson crouched, then finally sat sideways on a chair arm that groaned in protest, and faced backward toward them. They sat in the seats arranged one per side down the length of the aircraft.

"Most of you have been in-country for near enough a year with too few breaks. The operational tempo is horrendous right now between Africa—north, central, and south, the Middle East and Southwest Asia, not even counting South America or the Pacific Rim. We didn't want to slam you from action to training and back into action. Though as you know, that's never stopped the Army before."

He got the laugh he was looking for. Connie found it easy to add her smile with Big John's deep and easy chuckle rolling it along, lightening the mood in the cabin even further.

"We don't know how long you have, could be up to a week, assuming it happens at all. All we know at the moment is that it isn't happening right away and that we'll have enough lead time to pull the team together."

They were all used to that. Three-quarters of planned black ops never happened, never received that final "go." Sometimes a month or more of planning went into a mission, only for the team to be informed they were no longer needed. Or they'd do the flight, only to find a dry hole where intelligence had bad information. It was just a normal part of their day.

"In about thirty minutes, we'll be dropping into Reno. Civvie side. Go play. I know it's winter, so go skiing or something. Do not, I repeat, not break a leg. Continental U.S. only. We want you to be ready to launch off the East or West Coast on six hours' notice. No Cancun, no Maui. Sorry about that. Keep your pagers on and your cell phones charged. Keep your gear packed but try to unwind a little. Questions?"

Major Henderson somehow sounded like a combination of Mr. Easygoing and a hard-ass drill instructor. Of course, there were no questions. He always ran his briefings that way, everything anticipated, questions answered before they were asked.

All except one.

Where the hell was she supposed to go?

Chapter 27

JOHN HAD WHOOPED WHEN HE HEARD THE NEWS. Home. Reno to Denver, connect to Tulsa, call up Paps and get a ride home. He could be home in four or five hours if everything lined up right.

"Home by dinner! Awesome!"

He punched the back of the seat in front of him hard enough to jerk Crazy Tim forward. Tim turned and they punched fist to fist hard enough that John's knuckles stung. He knew what his buddy would be up to, girl-hunting. They always swarmed around his broad shoulders and gentle eyes.

Tim let out a howl halfway between crow and wolf that set everyone laughing and talking at once. The plane was loud with both crews shouting over the roar of the engines. Someone raided the small galley and ran back tossing out cans of soda and bags of salted peanuts.

"Wait. Wait. What the hell's the date?" John shouted them down.

"December," someone called out. "I think."

"Fifteenth? Twentieth? I dunno." When every day was planned for you, dates weren't what you'd call important. The only time that really mattered was a major mission. Even then, you trained until you were ready, then they gave a "go" day. Dates didn't matter.

"December 19th." Connie's voice was a soft drift. As if she answered out of habit while her attention was elsewhere.

"Six days. Oh, come on, baby. Come to poppa. Six days. Let the mission prep take seven. Oh, please, momma. Please, please, please!"

Several of the guys looked at him as if he'd lost it.

"Christmas, man! Think about it."

That got them all going again. There was a chance of being home for Christmas. Crazy Tim started talking about his mom's Christmas garlic-roasted pork and green banana cakes. Sounded as if Henderson would try to get his folks out of their winter-bound Montana ranch to stay with Major Beale's folks in D.C. Clay was gonna hang in Reno and take a run at the tables. Dusty came from Oregon, said he missed the rain after a year in the desert, though he admitted that about a week of it would be plenty. Captain Richardson had a sweetheart in Maine, of all whacked-out places.

Connie...

Hadn't spoken a word.

John had sat across the aisle from her, as much by chance as plan. With the narrow fuselage, he could reach out and touch her shoulder easily when calling her name didn't get her attention.

"How about you, Davis? Where's you headin'?" He tried for Henderson's Texas accent but knew he messed it up.

She just shook her head.

The plane's attitude nosed down as the engines slowed, and the hum resonating the length of the cabin softened. Starting the descent already. The engine's diminished roar started to set up a waver, ever so slightly out of sync. John and Connie turned in unison to face the cockpit as the pilot caught it too and tuned them back up. Fast and assured. Military training. Sometimes on civilian flights the engines would be a quarter tone out of sync, which made John absolutely insane when the pilots failed to correct it. More than once he'd asked a flight attendant to deliver a note to the cockpit to fix it.

"So where—"

She shook her head again. Sharper. Without looking over at him.

He dropped back against his seat and stared out the window at the snow-shrouded Rocky Mountains as they flashed by below.

Where was she from?

He remembered her answer. A list of Army bases. Her dad, dead. That must have been hard. He couldn't imagine Paps dying, nor was it likely to happen anytime soon. John came from a long line of old men. Old Grumps still drove the combine at eighty-three during harvest, wasn't ready to let that task go to a mere youngster like his son who had only turned fifty-five last spring. Old men, all except his true father.

He shut his eyes for a long moment to bury the thought. Paps was his real father in every way that mattered. Every way except blood. John felt disloyal every time he thought of the man who'd died in a car wreck before John was even born.

When he managed to find level flight again and open his eyes, Connie still stared square at the back of Clay's seat. Not out at the amazing mountains towering below. What? Nowhere to go? Some crappy hotel somewhere, room service, and a stack of service manuals to study? No! It wasn't right. Especially not for Christmas.

John leaned over casually and patted her arm.

"Don't you worry none, little lady. Y'all are coming home with me. You'll be welcome and then some." This time the Texas sounded right. Like when Henderson was teasing his wife. It shifted and changed a bit.

She slowly turned. From that profile that made him wish he could draw until those gold-brown eyes focused on him. Really focused.

A gentle smile tugged up at one corner. Wry, perhaps a bit sad.

"I don't think that's the best idea."

"Y'all got a better one in that purty head o' yours somewhere?"

She shook her head without looking away. He couldn't have looked aside if the front half of the plane blew off.

The other corner of her mouth slid up, the first hint that her radiant smile lurked just below the surface.

Still no answer.

"We've got extra rooms at the farm. You'd be welcome. Ma's a helluva cook. And you'll be as safe as you want to be. Promise." He raised his hand in the old three-finger-raised Boy Scout salute.

That amazing smile cracked forth.

"What?"

She tipped her head ever so slightly to the side, studying him. Like one of her manuals. Except for that laser-bright smile that bloomed across her features. And the hair that draped to the side, inviting his hand to slip inside it to cradle her cheek. An invitation he resisted considering their present company.

"And if I don't want to be so safe…?"

The air whooshed out of him as if he'd just been punched in the solar plexus. Not a thing he could say to that one.

Chapter 28

THEY'D FLOWN TOGETHER FOR FOUR MORE HOURS, spent another three hanging out in airports, and were now rolling along in John's dad's truck as the sunset faded from the Oklahoma sky.

Connie couldn't puzzle out two facts.

First, why she'd said "yes" in the first place.

And second, had she actually flirted with Staff Sergeant John Wallace?

She'd done more than flirt.

She'd kissed him at Fort Campbell. Really kissed him. Twice.

He'd made her feel safe. Made her feel strong. Made her feel that she'd make it through another day.

And then she'd kissed him.

"That was interesting." About the stupidest thing she'd ever said to someone she'd kissed. But it was.

Never before had her knees gone liquid from a kiss, nor had her pulse pounded so loudly that she'd almost covered her ears so that John wouldn't hear the sound leaking out. There'd been an electric charge, like the wrong end of a nine-volt battery. Only it hadn't been the wrong end. Kissing John felt like leaning into the sweet heat rising off a fresh-baked apple pie.

Now she was going home with a superior. This could go wrong in so many ways, starting with making it intolerable to remain on the same crew, ending with a court martial, and who knew what in between. Well, neither of them were officers, so maybe not a court martial, but it sure wouldn't be pretty.

She could always bail out. It wasn't too late.

Except maybe it was.

They rolled through Muskogee and into the night. John played tour guide in between catching up on family news with his dad.

"The library's over there. Never went there much, truth be told."

He looked like he was five years old, twisting and turning in the front seat to face her in the back every ten seconds to tell her something. She'd insisted that he ride up front with his dad. Men his size didn't belong in backseats, not even of big, four-seater pickup trucks like this one.

"Look, Connie. That's the sub park. Too dark to see right now. Dad, are they having the festival there this year?"

Sub park. Versus main park? A festival in a subsidiary park. No. That wasn't right, but John didn't slow down enough to explain.

"Wouldn't be Christmas without it." John's father was slow spoken, with a voice as deep and comforting as his son's. "Your mom. She's making her butter pecan pies. Debbie's got her family churning out Christmas cookies by the boatload. Your Aunt Margaret is making her goddamn, sorry 'bout that, miss," he half turned to project his voice back to Connie, "Jello mold."

"I've heard worse, sir."

He nodded easily in acknowledgment. No need to speak his reply.

A quietness wrapped the air around John's dad.

Soft-spoken in comparison to his son. But other than that, and some hard weathering earned working a farm, he and his son were much alike. Big men. Powerful. Trim from using their bodies without being lean. Shoulders so broad that between him and his son, they filled the front of the pickup's stretch cab. She could only really see out the side window.

"Ataloa Lodge is right over there. Incredible museum if we have time and you want to go."

But what she found herself watching wasn't John's old elementary school or anything else out the side window, it was the two men. Their talk was an easy drift of stories about people she'd never heard of.

John shifted in his father's presence. In the air, he was pure business. On base, always larger than life, always with a personality big enough to fill his large frame, always the first with a story, a smile, a laugh.

Now, he was smaller. Not diminished, perhaps more himself. As if he now somehow fit his own skin. At ease with his dad. Temporarily forgetting about her in the backseat. No longer on any stage, unaware of any audience. Big John was gone and had turned into a John-sized man.

Connie had never filled her own skin. Her thoughts were the sole connections from her brain to the world. She sat somewhere inside her own skin and watched the world. She'd first been aware of this at Fort Rucker's day care. At five years old, she'd observed herself, as if a separate person, carefully drawing precise diagrams. Others grabbed crayons in fists and made flowers, houses, fighter planes dropping outsized bombs, or just scribbled multi-hued swirls.

She'd found some colored pencils and constructed a scale drawing of her father's Huey helicopter. Had drawn and erased, drawn again and erased again, until she captured the foreshortening of the twin-blade rotor that looked so oversized on the ground and so right during flight.

Five-year-old Connie had learned that day that she was different. That her peers for the rest of her school years, and later in her career, would be simply avoiding her. They didn't pick on her much, though she knew she was discussed behind her back. She'd been hurt for a while but then decided that not caring was a better use of her time. The few bullies who targeted her quickly experienced the fighting techniques her father had taught her.

She also learned that adults always looked at her work with an abrupt silence and little to say. Only her father would have shown her where her drawing didn't quite follow the fuselage panel seams and then have given her one of the multitude of hugs he said he always stored up while away on missions.

She knew her abilities, knew herself. And knew for a fact that she didn't fill her body. If you were to look inside her, you would see an incomplete person, someone missing a piece she'd never been able to find. It had driven her into the Army and finally Special Forces. It had stood her up through all the trials created to knock you down and out, driven her all the way to SOAR.

Yet John had made the same climb. And he was complete in himself. More than that, filling any room he entered. What had made him stand up to all the tests and trials? Being a tower of strength wasn't enough for Green Platoon. Being tough wasn't enough for the Ranger School. Being the best wasn't enough for SOAR.

Connie knew of the drive that had held her up through everything. And sitting here listening to John and his dad, maybe she could see the first piece of what drove John ahead. He loved the older man. Worshipped him. Would lay down his life for his father.

Once again she watched John, wondering why she was here. She couldn't imagine two people more different. He was big and loud and easy around anyone. Everyone liked John. And as far as she could tell, nobody liked her or ever had.

But they had one more thing in common besides a passion for helicopter mechanics. The man she would have died to protect was her father. The man she'd die to bring back from a place where he was unremembered except in his daughter's nightmares. Each of them would lay down their lives for the man whose blood they carried in their veins.

She loved to listen to John and his dad laugh. She smiled to herself in the quiet of the backseat, wrapped gently in their softening words.

But the true reason this man had turned soldier might be not having enough bravery when faced with Aunt Margaret's goddamn Jello mold.

Chapter 29

JOHN'S HOME, WHICH CONNIE'S IMAGINATION OVER the last few hours had built into a great, sprawling thing, wasn't. Not some modern McFarm, ridiculous in its scale. It was an average, everyday farmhouse. Generations had been born here, grown up here, and raised families here.

Stubbled cornfields ranged one way, and a series of large barns ranged in the other, disappearing into the evening dark. Some livestock pens, but mostly equipment bays with tall wooden doors that could admit a truck or a harvester.

The house was a modest two-story home painted a soft blue. The roof looked freshly replaced in the wash of headlights. A wide sunporch wrapped around the two sides she could see. An array of pickups was parked out front. How many people were here, anyway? They parked theirs and climbed down.

"Like ya wanted, John." His father led them through air just cold enough to show their breath white in the porch lights. "I didn't let anyone know you was coming back or the whole family would have rolled in."

"Tomorrow's soon enough, Paps."

As if suddenly remembering his manners, John turned to Connie.

Before he could speak, she shooed him ahead, an eager little boy glad to be home, ready to run up the porch steps.

He turned with one foot on the first step and checked in with her again. There was no one left alive to care about her feelings, so why did John?

Without feelings, the requirements of performance were much easier.

Was she the best mechanic? Could she be trusted in a firefight? Would she have your back no matter what was coming down? Sure. Those bars were easy measures. But how she felt... not so much. No one would use how she felt as a measure of anything.

But John kept breaking that rule. Kept caring.

Once more she waved him on.

This time he went, taking the five steps in two strides and crossing the deep sunporch in three more. If the door had been locked, he'd have blown it off its frame as he dove in.

Breathless from the strength of his emotions, she stalled on the third step.

John's father stopped beside her. Just stood and observed through the still-open door. A slash of light struck across the porch, almost reaching her feet. She shifted her boots uncomfortably. A line she wasn't sure how to cross.

"He thinks a lot of you, you know?"

She turned to study the man, but his eyes were hidden by the darkness. Her question must have stood clear on her face.

"He doesn't bring many Army buddies here." He scraped a boot across the edge of a step as if checking for mud despite the near-frozen ground. "Especially not a woman."

"Not all that many women where I come from."

This time it was her turn to try and read the silence, but she couldn't.

Again that slow smile. "You'll see what I mean. Give yourself some time."

He led her into the house before she could make sense of his comment.

Chapter 30

Paps Wallace led Connie into mayhem.

A half-dozen or more people swirled around John, all talking at once. A tall, slender woman was tucked under each arm in a tight hug. One graying, the other his own age. If the family resemblance weren't so strong, she'd feel jealous at how he held them and how they leaned their heads on his shoulders.

A man only a few inches shorter than John was thumping him on the chest in greeting. Two kids, three, four swirled about their feet. She kept trying to count them but they moved too fast, clearly caught up in the excitement.

An old man, gone lean and spare with age, sat where he clearly commanded the room, presiding from an old armchair that might match the years of the man it bore. Knitted pads of summer colors covered the arms. A small table by his elbow held a bottle of beer and a TV remote control. The screen flickered an old musical comedy and the sound had been muted.

Comfortable. Deep couches, a low table with a board game scattered across the surface. Worn throw rugs spoke of a long past and comfortable living. Photos on the walls, mostly of the farm and people. Myriad people. Connie had one small album with a few dozen photos of her mother and father, some with a very small Connie on her father's back. Another couple of Ron Davis and his helicopters. Here the photos were scattered everywhere. Some went all the way back to terribly formal black-and-white portraits from generations past.

A girl of maybe college age pounded down the stairs and threw herself at John's back. He barely budged as the dark beauty landed there and wrapped her arms around his throat. She planted kisses on the side of his neck and squealed out, "Johnny, Johnny, Johnny!"

He laughed and leaned his head sideways until they rested cheek to cheek.

Connie eased a step back. Then another. Headed for the door, but it was shut. Before the pressure could push her back against it, Paps placed a hand on her arm.

"Whoa there, girl."

His voice had been soft, but it plunged the room into sudden silence as they all turned to face her. A brother with John's shoulders, a mother with his eyes, two sisters with his handsome features transmuted to beauty, and an old man whose gaze missed nothing. Three young kids, there were three of them, gone suddenly quiet.

"This…" John partly extricated himself from the women who clung to him and the brother who'd come to rest with a hand on John's shoulder. The girl slid off his back to glare at Connie over his shoulder, her arms still about his neck and shoulders clearly saying, "Mine." A toddler, barely taller than John's knee, clung with arms and legs wrapped around one of John's legs.

"This is my crewmate, Connie. I asked her to come stay with us for leave."

They all turned in silence from facing her to John, then back. Then in a rush of welcome they stormed her until she bumped hard against the door.

"I'm Betsy, that big lummox's mother. And you, Paul," she aimed a finger at Paps's chest in accusation, "could have come up with something better than that lame-ass story about needing to run into town right before dinner. I knew something was up. I hoped." Then she smiled at Connie. "And that's why I made my fried chicken. The boy has a real weak spot for it. You can call me Bee, everyone else does. This here's Janice, my middle child. Two of these little hellions are hers and live just down the road a bit, the other one is just visiting, and that's Lawrence—"

"Larry. You fly? Like John does?" John's brother put in.

"—the younger brother." Bee rolled on as if he hadn't spoken. "The three of them in three years. If you ever think you've done something really and truly stupid, you just know for sure that someone on the planet has done something stupider." She tapped the center of her chest. "You've met my Paul. That's Grumps."

The old man nodded from his chair, looking very serious and patriarchal. But his eyes brightened as if he were laughing at some inner joke.

"And that one back there is Noreen. A late gift to my life and a constant challenge to my patience."

Clearly the great beauty of a handsome family, with not one bit of friendly in her gaze.

"Now you come into the kitchen before you catch your death. Johnny, you can double-up with Lawrence unless he has some new girl stashed under the bed. Put Connie in John's room. Paps, you bring in their bags."

Connie raised her black duffel with its I'm-just-a-civilian swoosh logo on the side in defense against the storm of words.

"Is that all you have? Mercy, child, how can you travel like that?"

Connie looked at John, helpless. He slung his arm around Larry's neck in a tight headlock and was scrubbing his knuckles across the man's scalp. Larry was almost as handsome as his big brother. The two Wallace boys must cut a serious swath among the ladies.

Chapter 31

CONNIE SLIPPED OUT AFTER DINNER WAS OVER. SHE'D not managed a single word edgewise since stepping into the house. John had answered questions for her when it was clear she wasn't going to speak. Couldn't speak.

She stepped off the back porch and was assaulted by a thousand smells she could only guess at. Some were obvious. The fried chicken dinner on her lips and the woodsmoke drifting from the chimney that led to the wood stove warming the large and crowded living room where the whole family gathered even now. The cold night air carried something different.

Afghanistan's night air had been tainted with mint and cooking lamb. The Muskogee night tasted almost as foreign. Hinted at memories she couldn't place, couldn't find.

Even the stars were foreign. A week ago the distant heavens had been bounded, held clear of the ground by the high silhouettes of the Hindu Kush to one side and the central Himalayans to another. At Bati camp, pre-dawn there, just returning from missions, the stars were held even higher by the ever-present rim of the concrete soccer stadium that had become their home. Here the stars flowed right to the horizon, a flatness that ranged forever away from her.

"Have you had sex yet?" The sharp, staccato words rapid-fired at her back.

Connie took a quick step for more distance before she turned to face her attacker. Noreen stood just three steps away. The light through the window built into the kitchen door silhouetted her against the house. No, silhouetted her against her home.

"No."

Noreen's arms were crossed in front of her.

"You trying to get him in the sack?"

"John deserves better than that." And he did. A man who cared so much about family.

Noreen grunted once. Her voice softened. "He keeps picking up these brain-damaged women. Sex and marriage seem to be the only topics they ever want to talk about. Most girls he brings home don't get that he's special. Like their heads don't work right or something, 2-D heads in a 3-D world. You one of those?"

Connie considered the question. She knew what she wanted. And it wasn't about family. She wasn't trying to find some man just like her father. She flew with SOAR because she'd earned it. It had taken her half a decade of study to reach SOAR, and even John was reluctantly admitting that she might be seriously good at what she did.

Was she here with John to be healed? Not likely. She was here with John because he'd asked. Because she'd imagined a quiet Christmas together with his mother and father. Because the last person she wanted to be alone with for Christmas was herself.

"No," she answered Noreen. "I fly with John. I know enough to truly appreciate his skills. Having nowhere else to go, I appreciate his kindness in inviting me."

"You planning to marry him?"

"Never!" The word blew out of her mouth across the night in a cloud of crystalline white.

"John not good enough?" The sharp was back in her adversary's voice.

"I don't believe in family. Not as a soldier, not when I could die crossing the next horizon."

They stared at each other in silence, three paces between them. One lost in the night, the other silhouetted by the home of her birth.

At length Noreen rubbed at her arms.

"You should come inside soon. John's already missing you, though he hasn't realized it yet."

Noreen turned back to the house. Before stepping through the door, she paused, as if there was something more to say. But then she continued through.

And Connie was left to stare at the old clapboard house, in wonder that John could be missing her.

No one missed Connie Davis.

Chapter 32

JOHN SLEPT LIKE THE DEAD. HE AND HIS BROTHER HAD shared the big, old double bed until they were ten and Grumps's sister had passed in her sleep. With her room opened up, John had the chance to sleep on his own.

He and Larry had traded stories long into the night. They'd talked about the farm. The success of the last season, the high cost of irrigation water versus driving in a couple more wells.

And they'd talked about flying, a little. The topic too foreign to any of them to sustain the conversation for long. His family didn't really get it. They liked that he flew as a mechanic for the U.S. Army. But they thought he'd do a tour and come home, as had he. Now that he'd been in the service a decade, the family wasn't so sure how to think about it.

Larry'd come to Campbell once on a visit and been smitten with quite a crush on then Captain Beale. He'd sworn to ten years of abstinence in mourning the day she'd gotten married. As John had expected, it had lasted about three days until Tamara Zulaski had thrown herself at him.

John had gone barhopping with Larry and Crazy Tim more than once during that weeklong visit. He and Tim drinking soda because they were always on call for flight duty, Larry getting mellow and happy, but no more. Larry and Tim had really hit it off, trading girl stories late into the night. John had brought Crazy Tim home a few times since. Each time, he and Larry had picked up right where they left off. They were his favorite two guys, but no girl could figure out how to pin either one down for more than a handful of months at a time.

When he'd noted as much to Paps, he'd laughed and tapped the center of John's chest and gone on about pots and kettles. John always had more than his fair share of luck with the ladies, but he didn't talk about them like war stories.

Paps was the one who came closest to understanding why John flew. He'd spent two years pounding the ground near the end of 'Nam. But his had been a different war. In a different era. One tour and he'd been done and come back to marry John's mother, have kids, and work the farm.

John lay a moment longer in the sunlight that streamed across the bed.

Thought of the one thing that no one had asked him. Not openly at the dinner table, not covertly before shooing him off to bed. The question that his brother had not asked him last night, except with a long silence before they finally slept.

Sergeant Connie Davis.

One helluva good question.

She'd stood on the edge of his awareness all evening. Observing. Smiling. A gentle touch that left him as aware of her as he was of his family. An easy mix, a happy blend.

He swung out of bed and planted his feet on the floor. Cold wood worn smooth by ten thousand mornings. John fished a fresh shirt out of his pack and headed for the bathroom. Coffee, eggs, and bacon scents wafted up the stairs. Maybe he'd get a shower later. He thought about all of his hard work in Nevada yesterday, then six hours travel, and he turned toward the bathroom hoping someone had left him some hot water.

———✦———

John thudded down the stairs a new man. Give him a mug of coffee big enough and strong enough to fuel a helicopter, and he'd be good to go.

No one in the sun-filled kitchen, but the oven was on warm. He hauled out the covered platter his mom had left in the oven. He briefly considered dishing some of it onto a plate. Instead, he grabbed a kitchen towel against the hot platter, picked up a fork, and dug in.

He leaned his butt against the warm oven and closed his eyes as he chewed. This is what it was about. At moments like this he couldn't remember why he ever left.

Then he opened his eyes and saw exactly why he had. It was to fly with people like the Majors and Crazy Tim. And Archie and Kee. It was to make these people safe in their homes with kitchens this warm and this safe in the freest country on the planet. The one who had borne him and the ones who'd taken him in as family.

Protecting them came at a price. And was worth every drop of sweat, every aching muscle, and maybe, just maybe worth the good people who had died beside him as they flew. He sent a silent prayer for safety to the folks still flying nightly sorties out of Bati air base. He glanced at the clock. Probably coming out of preflight briefing about now. Grab some food, then fly.

God but his mama could cook.

He shoveled down another mouthful of French toast with farm butter and real sorghum syrup and poured himself a steaming mug. Balancing it on one end of the platter, he wondered where everyone was hiding.

The kitchen clock answered part of that. Almost ten. Grumps, Paps, and Larry would be out working for hours already. Fixing a combine, turning the corn stubble under to rot until spring, weeding the south beet field. If they'd done beets this year. It bothered John briefly that he didn't know.

Noreen would be taking her first-semester, senior-year finals at Northeastern State. How did that happen? Twenty-two, an honors major in premed. Premed? She was supposed to be a model or married to the perfect man. Instead she was talking about emergency medicine. The first Wallace through college, and she was doing it with honors.

Mama must have gone to Janice's rather than the other way round so that the kids didn't wake him.

He started to laugh. Almost choked on a mouthful of homemade bacon, had to wash it down with more coffee. No, they weren't worried about his sleep. Mama and Janice would be out rousin' the troops. There'd be a hell of a party this weekend. Christmas just four days out.

There would be some serious shopping to do.

That stopped him. He'd grabbed some presents over the last month or so. Had a deal with Larry 'cause Janice couldn't keep a secret to save her sweet soul and Noreen was too much of a snoop. He'd mailed packages home to his brother as he found them in Afghanistan or Italy or wherever SOAR led him, and Larry would have them hidden away somewhere until Christmas Eve.

But he hadn't thought about Connie.

Wow! And what was he supposed to get her? Something to take apart and fix? He'd flown with her for three weeks now, been in the same unit for a dozen more, and he had no idea what to get her. "Pretty damn sad, Wallace. Pretty damn sad to not know that much about a person."

And where was she anyway? Probably off with Mom and Janice and the kids.

He chewed on another piece of bacon but stopped half through.

No. That didn't sound right.

She'd be more likely to be out doing the winter plowing with Paps. It had been good to see the two of them hit it off right away.

But she'd been quiet last night. Quiet even for Connie, which was saying something. He moseyed across the living room and down the hall, stabbing up some scrambled eggs.

But his old room was spotless. The bed made Army tight. Could bounce a quarter off the old quilt. He'd certainly never made it up like that. Her kit sat in front of his dresser, his old high school football trophies across the top. Her bag all perfectly neat, packed. She wouldn't even have to break stride to get her gear and be headed out the door. Exactly as Henderson had ordered.

He'd scattered his crap around, as much old habits coming to the surface as to piss off Larry, who'd always been too neat-freak anal anyway.

So, where was she?

He listened to the house. Nothing. No one here. Not a creak or groan in the old wood.

"Strange to sleep in your bed."

He spun fast enough that he lost the coffee mug. It spun through the air, leaving a trail of only a few drops. Thankfully, he'd drained it.

Connie moved forward from the door where she'd been leaning on the jamb and snagged the cup out of the air.

"You'd..." He swallowed against a dry throat. "You'd have made a good wide receiver."

"We never lost."

"We?"

"You don't think I've spent seven years in the Army and never played ball?"

He thought about the pickup games he'd played over the years. Army was rough, they played for keeps. Football played as a contest of who was tough and who was tougher.

"Really?"

She left him hanging for a long moment, then flashed that killer smile as she returned his mug to his platter. And stopped there, not two steps away. So close he could smell soap and shampoo. He breathed in again, and that unique scent of Connie came through. "Damn!" was all his brain managed.

"No. But I played first base in Fort Rucker varsity softball for most of high school. And no one beat us. Ever."

That was an image he could live with pretty happily in his brain. A uniform stretched tight on a beautiful woman. A woman athlete. One leg stretched back to touch the bag, leaning all the way out to snag the throw. Every curve of muscle etched clear in the moment.

He could feel the sweat on his brow.

"That's a sight I would have enjoyed."

Connie nodded. Not embarrassed. Not coy. Just matter of fact.

"So, are you going to eat all day?"

"I can think of something else I'd like to do more." Couldn't believe he'd said it.

For the longest moment, she simply watched him. Then she slid the plate from his nerveless fingers and slipped it onto the dresser top between his trophies.

Without hesitation, she took the step forward that placed her body against his, wrapped her arms around his neck, and pulled him down to her.

For the first time, his hands slipped around her waist. With women in his past, his hands had either encircled impossibly slender waists that had no strength to them or there'd been plenty there to hold on to. He liked women and was thankful that women liked him. They were a joy to hold no matter what size they came in.

But Connie's waist was the first that had ever fit his hands so perfectly. His fingertips rested against the soldier-strong muscles of her back right at the moment before they descended in that most feminine of curves. Connie had great hips. With his thumbs, he could feel the tight gut muscles from years of training, of a thousand miles run, of ten thousand crunches. In his hands, for the first time in his life, he held a woman of as near-perfect form as nature and the best physical training on the planet could produce.

Then she pulled his lips to hers and he was gone. Apple pie and cinnamon washed through his brain. Warm tropical and deep spice. Her mouth opened, welcomed, joined.

He'd thought Connie meek or timid. But that wasn't right. And his thoughts were in no condition to puzzle out the answer to that.

Rather, he simply fed upon those soft lips and the strong tongue. And pulled her in, never removing hands from hips. Pulled her in until their bodies pressed together in a way that allowed no secrets.

Her arms around his neck pulled her chest against his, twin swells of soft heat. And hip to hip… all he could do was groan into her mouth as she drank him in.

When at last she backed off, he refused to let go, and she didn't complain. She simply lay her head against his shoulder. Stood there and snuggled against him as if they'd stood like this every day for years. He rested his cheek atop her hair.

Soft. Her hair softer than it looked. Softer than he'd imagined.

"This is nice."

He could feel the gentle buzz of her voice where her chest still pressed against his. Nice? He'd had women say several things when he held them close, and "nice" didn't appear much on the list. But it was hard to be offended when she felt this way.

"Your sister wants to know if I'm trying to marry you."

His sister? Marriage? What?

"Uh, what did you say?" he asked before the statement fully registered.

She pushed back just enough to look into his face, but not to drive them apart.

"Of course I said I was."

That cleared his brain faster than a fresh mug of steaming coffee. He could feel the blood drain right out of his face, leaving a chill on his cheeks that slid down his spine. He'd brought home a crazy—

"Actually, I'm joking."

He tried not to reveal the relief that flooded into him, but when you held someone this close, there wasn't a pulse or a breath that wasn't clear as an onboard intercom between them.

"But it's nice that you care."

Again she slipped her head against his shoulder and sighed as she snuggled there a moment.

"Maybe we'll just use each other for sex?" He tried to make it light and funny. It came out a little choked from a throat gone dry.

She shrugged in his arms.

"Probably. Though it will piss her off pretty bad."

Like he was going to let little Noreen have any say in the matter of what he did with…

Sex with Connie Davis? Somehow he hadn't quite gone there. He knew her kiss blew his knees into butter, and her smile blew his brain into next week. He'd invited her home for Christmas, but he hadn't quite connected that they would…

Here? In his childhood room?

Now? Who knew when his parents were coming back?

But he could feel the heat returning to his body. To have this woman against him, skin to skin. To feel himself inside her. That most certainly got his body's attention.

"I told her I didn't believe in marriage. I can't tell if that calmed her down or upset her even more."

John felt the cold wash down his body again, an ice chill this time. Freezing every reaction that had begun pounding him moments before with its heat.

Connie sensed it, must have felt the change where they still pressed together. She looked once more up into his eyes. That assessing, measuring gaze of hers.

Then her expression grew serious.

He felt her moving away from him even though his hands still encircled her waist, rested on those incredible hips.

"I don't, John. Not for a soldier. Not when I could be dead the next moment. It's just not fair. What my father did…" She stopped, the pain a sharp slice across her speech. Then a whisper. "Just not fair."

Long before he could speak, she'd stepped from his arms, gathered his plate, and headed back toward the kitchen.

Chapter 33

"YOU OKAY, HON?"

"Fine, Mama." Though a day and another night home, John still hadn't puzzled out what he was feeling. Connie had shot his blood pressure to the moon twice in as many minutes, then he'd barely seen her for twenty-four hours.

He poked at his breakfast, but he hadn't slept well last night and his heart just wasn't in it. Again, by the time he dragged himself up, everyone was gone except his mom.

"You don't look so fine, Johnny."

Without even thinking about it, he snagged her around the waist and pulled her against him. She raised the hot fry pan she'd been serving him from so that she didn't burn him as he sat at the kitchen table. He breathed in the smells of home. A fresh-washed apron, flour, cooking oil, something sweet and something like forever, the smells that were always his mother. He'd been gone half a year and been home just a day and two nights. He'd never get enough of his mother's smell.

She kissed him atop the head, then shoved back, leaving a pair of fried fresh eggs on top of his toast, so rich and yellow they looked like they'd trapped the sun.

She returned to the stove. Setting the pan aside to cool on the back burner.

"I don't hear you eating my eggs. That's not like you, either."

John sliced his fork down until it clicked against the plate, releasing the yolk and snagging some toast along with it. He ate it, drank some juice, ate another bite, and looked up to see her sitting beside him at the table in the empty kitchen.

"It's that girl, isn't it?"

"Her name is Connie."

"I know her name. And you know that's not what I'm saying."

He nodded, he did know. Between him and Larry, his mama had welcomed a long line of girls into her kitchen. Sometimes it felt as if they followed him home like stray kittens. Michelle would just happen to ride the school bus five stops past her own house and just happen to realize it at his farm. Time after time. And she'd need a ride or an escort for the long walk back. Nancy showed up a lot on her bicycle. Later in her dad's pickup.

And Mama had fed each one, offered them comfort, sometimes advice. But none had stuck. Not Tanya. Not Bernice. And Mama had never said a word about Janine, the brunette who couldn't put together three words without "like" being at least one of them, or the redhead who'd lasted until she'd found out John had no intention of living anywhere beyond Muskogee or...

"So, what are you saying?" He cut off a bit of sausage, dunked it in the puddle of sorghum syrup he'd pooled in one corner of his plate.

"You're different about this one. About Connie."

He looked into her eyes. "As dark as the good earth," he'd heard Paps say a thousand times of his wife's eyes, "and twice as deep."

He set himself to protest. But you couldn't fake it

with Mama. He hadn't pulled it off when he was eight, eighteen, or now at twenty-eight. Keeping his mouth shut didn't even work, not when Mama was on the warpath. A quarter Cherokee that showed in her height, her long dark hair, and her spine made of adamantine steel.

"They none of them measured up to you, Mama. That was a problem. I'd bring a girl into this kitchen and she just looked ridiculous."

"There was Mary."

"Yeah, she was something. Way smarter than me, though. Had me figured out in five minutes flat. And she was after being a New York dancer, ballet was all she could talk about." And John could remember what all of those slim muscles had felt like wrapped around him. He could practically lift her in the palm of his hand, so light she'd felt more ethereal than real, and an inner fire of determination hotter than any rocket.

"She made it, too."

"Did she?"

"San Francisco Ballet, her sister told me just last week."

"Hot damn, go, Mary." He raised his orange juice in a toast to the west wall of the kitchen.

"But she wasn't Connie, was she?"

"You don't give up, Mama, do you?"

"Never! That's how I got your father to marry me."

He reached out and gathered her into his lap. How could he ever be lucky enough to find a woman like this one?

He'd barely spoken with Connie since yesterday morning. At meals she was quiet, never said a word. When he turned his back, she evaporated as if she'd never been there. She took up no space in the house. As he'd headed out to find her yesterday, Jeff had dropped by. Then Harold had showed up and dragged the two of them down to Miss Addie's Pub for a sausage-and-pepper sandwich, which had led to a beer at Dave's house and a trip out to watch the season's last pickup game before the holiday break of the Muskogee High School Roughers tossing the pigskin around.

Then more family had dropped in for dinner and hung out in the living room. Connie had been there and he'd been aware of her. Couldn't help it. No matter how she faded from everyone else's view. He could see her do it. Quiet, unassuming, patient, disappearing without ever leaving the room.

And watching, always watching with those amber eyes.

Until the moment he'd really looked away, and she was gone physically as well.

There were things he wanted to know. How it would feel to hold her again. Kiss her again.

And other things.

He squeezed his mama tighter to his side for a moment.

How could that woman not believe in marriage? It was one of those things where the words made sense, about not risking leaving behind a child, but somehow they were wrong anyway.

Chapter 34

CONNIE LEANED INTO THE SPANNER AND SHIFTED SO she could throw her weight against it. It wasn't going to budge. She needed—

Grumps stood close behind her and handed her a three-pound sledge.

Exactly! She struck the handle of the two-foot-long wrench once, twice, three times, ringing so loud it hurt her ears in the narrow bay. It might have once been a horse stall but now it held an ancient John Deere Unistyler tractor, one with the majority of its bolts rusted into place.

On the fourth strike, a shower of brown flakes flurried into the air and the bolt let loose all at once with a low, grinding groan and a high squeal of steel.

"Always the last one that's most stubborn." Grumps leaned on the half wall and watched her progress.

She used a triple block and tackle she'd rigged from the overhead rafter. The old iron wheel stood four feet tall, a foot wide, and probably weighed more than an entire Black Hawk crew, even one that included Big John. Leaning her weight slowly into the line, she shifted the wheel to lean it against the one she'd knocked free last night.

"Seems that way, sir."

Grumps nodded slow and easy. His hair was short and gray through and through. The morning sunlight washed over them both through the high windows in the barn, warm enough that she was working up a sweat. She stripped off her jacket and tossed it atop the half wall. The T-shirt and vest was plenty. And she'd never been one to mind a few goose bumps.

"Pop didn't believe in those newfangled rubber wheels that everyone was selling all of a sudden. Special ordered those old steel butt-grinders instead. Damn machine would just beat your behind to death by the end of a day."

She pulled out a large pipe wrench and slipped it around the driveshaft. Before she could lean in to test it, the weight of the wrench turned the shaft. Slow, but it turned and the axle, free of the two massive wheels, spun as well.

"Ain't that a lark?" Grumps nodded at her to keep going. He kicked an old metal and wood-slat milk crate upside down against a wall, sat down on it slowly, and then propped himself there.

She found a pan and set up to drain whatever fluids were hiding in the old crankcase. About what you'd expect, a heavy sludge oil so old and stiff it might have been formed right there, back with the dinosaurs. Then a slurry of water that had found its way in over the years, but the oil had stopped from finding any way out. Could certainly be worse.

"First time I ever drove her, she was brand new. Yep, 1938 was a damn fine year for tractors. Must say the next six or seven years sucked for everything else. I was too young for the war and Pop too old, what with me being a late child, but it was a damn fine year for tractors." He kicked his feet out on the old straw.

"I was ten when Pop told me it was time to learn to

get on in the world and five years was school learning enough for any man. I was never much good at school anyhow. And when he showed me this new tractor, his first new one ever, and told me it was mine to drive, well, I tell ya, I was still in short pants and barely as tall as that wheel there." He nodded at the pair stacked against the wall.

She tried to picture him. The little tractor didn't come much higher than her shoulder, but it had a stout, power-ful, can-do look about it. It must have looked huge to a young boy.

"I was a goner, I can tell you. It was all bright and shiny and beautiful and strong. Just like the first time I saw my Liza. Just a goner."

He left a long pause, and Connie glanced over her shoulder to see if he'd gone to sleep. He hadn't, nor did he look sad. He just stared up for a bit at the dust motes spinning in the sunlight shooting through a high window.

He blinked a couple times and looked at her.

"Last time anyone drove that tractor was my boy, Paul Andrew Percy Wallace, Paps to you young 'uns. I didn't let him on it till he'd made it through high school. Played football. Pretty good." Again that drifting silence.

Connie was okay with that. She'd never been com-fortable around people who needed to fill each silence with words. Grumps was comfortable to be silent with.

She dragged over an old wooden bench to start laying out the smaller pieces she'd already busted free. Stopped to blow on her fingers a bit. Not a hard cold, not like Nevada. But not exactly the Pakistan desert, either.

"Never was as good as John, though."

What wasn't? Who? Oh, Paps at football.

"What position did John play?" She took up the sledge again.

"Star quarterback. Senior year they got one game off the state championship for the first time in over twenty years. Haven't been so close since, either."

Connie looked up at the man not all that much smaller than his son or grandson, if you discounted the thinning of old age.

"With his size, I'd have thought he'd be a defensive tackle or something."

"Too smart. They had to find a use for those brains. And he was always good with his hands."

Connie nodded, she'd seen as much herself. Could still feel how he'd held her as if she were something precious rather than a woman to be manhandled. He'd shown her both strength and gentleness. Damn, she looked away. No worries about goose bumps now as her skin heated.

She tried to return her attention to the transfer case but with less luck. The way John's hands had wrapped around her waist, held her tight and close and... safe. Wow! That was a surprising thought. Before John she'd have defined "safe" as not being shot at. She'd have to think about that.

A couple quick raps with the sledge returned a tight ring. The transfer case and axle might be rusted on the outside, as the brown clouds shivering off the steel proved, but the metal was still thick and strong. She whacked it again, then propped the sledge's head against the steel and her ear against the butt of the handle. She couldn't hear any loose bits twanging or rattling inside and there hadn't been any metal shavings in the old oil sludge. Could still be trouble once she got inside, but it didn't seem likely.

"Like you. You're good with those fine hands of yours."

Connie moved the sloshing pan aside to where she wouldn't kick it into the inch or so of winter-dry straw that scattered over the stall's dirt floor.

"Been mechanicking a while." Grumps wasn't asking a question.

"Dad started me out young." The first toy she could really remember was a windup alarm clock designed to be taken apart by a kid. Maybe not a four-year-old, but all of the parts were big and well marked. She'd taken it apart and put it back together a thousand times, always impressed by the neatness of the winding mechanism, the prickly edges of the gears against her palm, the interlocking precision.

It had taken her a while to puzzle out how to fix its running slow, but she'd solved that in the end as well, reworking the timing counterweight with a small file. That was all before moving on to bigger projects. Assembling her first bicycle right down to bolting on the training wheels.

"I remember building my first go-cart. Scrap metal from my dad's collection of junk and a lawn mower engine I rebuilt from the block up. Thought I was seriously hot shit in that."

"How old were you?"

"Ten, I guess." She'd really been eight, but people looked at her strangely when she told them she'd been a skilled welder at eight. Hers had been the only go-cart at Fort Bragg to have a full cowling with all of the weld beads ground smooth.

"Did you win?" Of course, the old man would assume she'd raced it.

"Got whupped. Jimmy Jepps's dad bought him this fancy, duded-up, factory-built cart."

Grumps leaned forward, propping his elbows on his knees, and inspected her with narrowed eyes.

"What did ya do about it?"

"I disappeared into the garage for three months. Designed and built this primitive transmission that gave me a one-time upshift. Once I was up to speed, I'd throw this lever that jacked in a different gear, if I handled the throttle just right, and then I flew. I also painted her lipstick red. Blew the doors off Jimmy Jepps, then I put her away and never raced again."

Grumps smacked his knee loudly with his open palm. "Good girl! Showed that Jimmy a thing or two, I betcha."

Connie had. She'd proven she was smarter, more of an outsider, even stranger than Jimmy and all her peers imagined, which was pretty weird by third grade.

She focused hard on getting the axle out of the tractor's transfer case to bury the memories. The bad times along with the good times, like the cold evenings in the garage with her dad on those rare times when he made it home from tour. She'd always trained her mind to leave the past behind. Live in the present. Definitely not the past, and no real point in betting on an unknown future. There was only the now. That was all that mattered. She kept telling herself that so often that she almost believed it.

But it suddenly seemed important to know what had happened to that old clock. Now her life fit in a duffel bag and a small storage locker at Fort Campbell, one that was mostly empty.

"Been doing it a long while," she told the axle, grunting a bit as she slipped the inner shaft free and hefted it, hoping she could get it onto the bench for breakdown and cleaning before it slipped free from her oily grasp.

A large hand grabbed one end. John. She'd know that hand anywhere. Between them they levered it onto the makeshift table.

She glanced over at Grumps. He'd fallen asleep in the shaft of sunlight with his feet crossed in the hay and his head resting against the barn wall.

"This was his tractor."

She nodded.

"Almost bankrupted great-gran'da to buy it. Grumps drove it every day for thirty years to make it up to him. He made the success of this farm with this little machine."

They bent down together to inspect the driveshaft. She fetched the sledge and a massive pin punch to drive out the main joint, then glanced over at Grumps.

"Don't worry, he's pretty deaf. Larry said he sleeps through most anything these days."

She looked at John. Really looked at him as he watched the old man sleeping. Could see on his face how much he cared for—No. Scratch that. How much he truly loved the old man. Close enough to worship to leave no real difference.

She knew that feeling. Knew it and stayed as far from it as she could. There lived pain. Deep pain.

She aimed the punch and slammed the hammer down. Drove it until the pin flew loose and the driveshaft thudded to the ground.

Grumps stirred but didn't wake.

Chapter 35

ALL AFTERNOON THEY WORKED TOGETHER ON THE tractor. The silence of the farm a background to Grumps's gentle snores. John enjoyed the easy rhythm as he and Connie worked back to front, breaking the beast down to parts.

John dragged over an old milking stool and started cleaning the parts with a splash of diesel over an old bucket. No holds barred in the design of this machine. They'd planned for it to last by building it heavy and building it big. Not even twice the horsepower of a modern push-around lawn mower engine, yet she could deliver it year in and year out through the worst mud and hard-baked soil Muskogee could hand out. And a big enough bore that it took more than hard winter soil to slow the machine down. Not fast, but it won the race of sheer stubborn endurance.

Grumps had never let him fix up this tractor, though he'd started at it a time or two. The old man had always chased him off without ever explaining why. Yet here he'd fallen asleep perched on an old milk crate while watching Connie break it down.

John continued to clean the subassemblies as she dislodged them from the frame. Take 'em apart, clean 'em up, and reassemble 'em. It was soothing, easy work. A real pleasure.

Another pleasure of his current occupation was his

excellent view of the woman at physical labor. Her hair
pulled back through the hole of an old John Deere cap
Grumps must have dug up for her. If you saw her on the
street, you might not look twice except for the beautiful face and fine figure. Mr. Civilian, if he noticed her
shoulders at all, might think "gym queen." Whereas
John couldn't look away.

It was when she leaned in, when she flexed hard to
drive some resistant part into submission, that the difference showed. She didn't wear her muscles on her sleeve,
so to speak. But when those long womanly arms flexed,
the muscles stood out in clear and surprising definition.
Her strength lay beneath the surface, closer to the bone.

"Are all women like that?" he asked before he had a
moment to think about it.

"Like what?" She had the front steering assembly on
the run. At this rate they'd start building her back up in
another hour or so. Though the transmission would take
some serious time tomorrow.

Now that he'd asked, he wasn't sure of his question.
He hunted around the barn seeking the answer but not
finding it. The next stall down had the big combine,
more power in its power steering than in this whole
tractor. The other direction, in the next bay, an old GTO
hunkered on blocks. He and Paps worked on it together
when they were bored or Mama told them to get out
from underfoot.

"Keep their strength hidden?" That was about the
best he could find for it. He didn't wait for her answer.
He'd learned that conversations with Connie, especially while she was mechanicking, moved at a serious
mosey. Words clearly took second place to machinery.

He had the carburetor more than half torn down before she answered.

She stood up for a moment to stretch, cricked her neck off to one side.

"I don't." She squatted back down.

His hands were moving slower and slower with the more time he spent watching her. Squatting on the concrete inspecting the bearings on the front axle.

He couldn't imagine a woman who kept more pieces hidden. And each time he learned one piece, he wanted to learn two more.

"Hey, Connie?"

She didn't look up but instead reached in with a pair of needle-nose pliers and began extracting ball bearings from the thick grease in the steel race.

"Yes?"

"How about going out to dinner with me tonight?"

"Don't you want to be with your family?"

He did want to be with his family, but also, "I want to be with you."

"It's gonna piss off your sister."

John expected she was right.

"She's used to it."

And he just didn't give a damn.

Chapter 36

CONNIE LOOKED AT HERSELF IN THE MIRROR. AT LEAST as well as she could between the football trophies. She'd showered off the grease, even dug the worst of it out from beneath her nails.

Tan slacks, a gray cotton blouse, and a jeans jacket. She didn't have a parka with her, didn't own a dress except for her U.S. Army Class-As, and those were in a storage locker back at Fort Campbell where they'd been for over a year.

She looked ridiculous. Her friends, well, the flight crews that were still in Bati, were wearing armor and fighting for their lives in a country where both sides would prefer they were all dead. She shouldn't be here. She should—

She spotted Noreen's reflection in the mirror as the girl came to lean against the doorjamb to John's room. Arms crossed tightly over her chest.

"John's wearing a jacket. Only one place in town you can wear a jacket without getting laughed out. He's never taken a woman there."

Connie simply watched her in the mirror.

"You can't go dressed like that."

Connie inspected herself once more. "I look fine. Besides, it's the best I've got."

Noreen looked up at the ceiling, either counting to herself or cursing, it was hard to tell. She refocused on Connie.

"C'mon."

When Connie didn't move, Noreen took three quick steps into the room, snagged Connie's arm, and began to drag her out of the room toward the stairs.

Noreen's room was small, tucked partly under the eaves of the old house. The closets were low built-ins decorated as you'd expect with posters of bands. In contrast, a big quilt draped the bed nearly to the floor, lending the room a deep, homey feel. An old rug showed age, wear, and care. It was the insides of the closets that were a surprise.

They weren't packed with glitz or leather or any of the dozen other variations Connie had expected. They weren't packed solid with a disorganized array of items. Neatly arranged, there was space to see what hung in each spot, and the clothes were beautiful. Jewel tones that would offset Noreen's complexion. A neckline with an elegant, draped design to it. Pastels that would accentuate and warm her tones. A small rack of cozy sweaters and practical but feminine shoes.

Connie would expect someone of Noreen's beauty to have closets of slinky or... Well, there was more to the girl than first appeared.

In moments Noreen selected a forest-green top and handed it to Connie.

Connie stripped off her top, because it was clearly expected.

"Oh, give me a break."

Connie froze. "What?"

"You can't wear a sports bra."

"Why not?"

Noreen dropped onto the bed. "What hole have you lived your life in?"

"The U.S. Army and it isn't a hole."

"A deep and dark one, apparently." Noreen turned to a small dresser and dug around. Then she held out a pair of bras. "Blue or sunshine yellow?"

"What's wrong with—"

"I can't believe I'm doing this," Noreen muttered at the ceiling before focusing back on Connie. "First, it will make you look nicer, give my brother something he'll enjoy looking at from across the table. Second, I really am going to say this, crap! Second, if he gets that blouse off you, he should find something a little more interesting than a faded-out sports bra."

Connie looked down at herself.

"That's not going to—"

"Don't!" Noreen stopped her. "If it doesn't, fine. I'll sleep better. But you don't want to promise something that might make you feel guilty later and end up being even weirder around me than I'm already making you feel. Take the blue one. It's a good thing we're the same shape."

"You're kidding!"

"What, you want the yellow one? They're both fresh washed if that's what's worrying you."

Connie took the blue one. There was no possible way she was the same shape as this perfectly proportioned girl. Yet with just a few minor adjustments, it fit her neatly. The green pull-on blouse hugged her form and left Noreen nodding.

"Now a skirt. How are your legs?"

The first one she pulled out of the closet would barely cover Connie's underwear, a red leather miniskirt made with less material than her gun holster. She couldn't even answer.

"Just kidding. Wanted to see your face. I bought this the day after I broke up with Jeff to punish him."

Connie could feel herself smiling. "Did it work?"

"It was awesome! Six months and he's still begging to get me back."

"Does he stand a chance?"

"Not even a little bit. Total slimeball. I was young and foolish when I fell for him."

"Young and foolish six months ago?"

She grimaced, "Don't remind me."

"This is you." She held out a mid-length skirt with broad strokes of forest colors. They washed across the skirt and reminded Connie of that first refreshing break after a hot summer.

Connie stripped off her slacks and Noreen whistled.

"Damn! You got serious legs, girl. You sure you don't want the mini?"

Connie laughed. "Not even a little." She pulled on the skirt and swirled right and left. It made her feel light, even… she couldn't find the word.

"You clean up nice, girl. You are all woman. Wouldn't think it with what you usually wear."

Feminine, that was the word. She felt oddly feminine. This was a long way from jeans and a work shirt.

"You're fixing Grumps's tractor."

"Yes."

Noreen's tone had shifted. Enough for Connie to stop admiring the skirt and look up at her.

"Why?" Noreen's voice was carefully neutral.

Because Connie could. Because it got her out of the house when the people pressure built too high and squeezed in on her. Because…

"It wanted fixing. He's a man surrounded by home and family. It seemed like something I could give to him."

Noreen studied her for a long moment, started to speak, then changed the topic before she voiced it.

"Shoes. You need shoes."

"No heels," Connie had tried her grandmother's once, that was enough.

"You sure? Your legs in heels. They'd be awesome. And John being so damned tall…"

"As my commanding officer recently told, er, someone: not no way, not no how." Would it have been a breach of black-in-black operations to say that Emily Beale had been shouting it at the President of the United States? Probably.

Connie opened a cupboard in search of shoes and stopped dead.

"Hey! Don't!" Noreen rushed over and slapped the door shut.

Connie very gently pushed her aside and reopened the cupboard.

"Class-A uniform in Army green. ROTC." She turned the left sleeve outward to see the patches sewn there. "Noreen, that's a Ranger Challenge tab."

"Yeah. So?"

"With a Superior Cadet award on the left breast along with Dean's List and Shooter and a Cadet Captain epaulet."

Connie turned to face her.

The girl was looking at her feet.

Connie reached out and lifted her chin.

Noreen was blushing furiously.

"You don't blush about this. Not ever."

Her eyes were wide and watery.

Connie could only imagine the heckling and teasing such a beautiful young woman had taken wearing this to class and around a college campus in this day and age. She thought back to her own first uniform. How hard she'd had to fight to get it. How many back-breaking hours she'd spent working harder. Working smarter. In pain beyond speech. Heckled by every bonehead that had ever worn civvies. Harassed by any man-jerk who thought he could get away with it.

"Noreen!" She snapped it out, and the girl jerked upright.

"Don't you ever dare be embarrassed about that uniform. If you do, I'll come back and kick your ass worse than the Ranger trainers."

Noreen cracked a weak smile. "They were pretty damn tough."

"And they'll hand that out tenfold in the regular Army. But you earned it. If you ever doubt it, that's a Ranger Challenge tab right there on your sleeve." Connie didn't have to close her eyes to picture her own badges. Even as a technical specialist, you didn't get through five years in active duty and into SOAR without earning at least a few medals the hard way.

Her proudest possession, the SOAR patch, was almost never worn by any flier. In public, you wanted to blend in. On a mission, you didn't want to be downed and captured while wearing one. Enemy forces were not big fans of the U.S. Special Forces. Rangers wore their insignia everywhere. SOAR, Delta, SEALs, not so much.

"What do your parents say?"

"They're so proud that it's killing them not telling Johnny."

"He doesn't know?"

She shook her head in misery. "Graduation is tomorrow. I'm a semester ahead, so they're going to have a special ceremony tomorrow at the banquet. Please keep it a surprise? Please?" The young woman slid back into the girl begging a favor.

Connie pulled her into her arms and held her tight. She kissed Noreen on the cheek and whispered into her ear.

"He's going to be so proud of you, he'll just die."

Chapter 37

JOHN WATCHED NOREEN HUG CONNIE BEFORE HIS sister closed the front door behind them. He took Connie's hand and led her down the front steps, almost falling down them himself because he was too busy puzzling over what he'd just seen.

"What did you do to her?"

"Nothing." Connie climbed up into the truck easily, despite the skirt that flashed a fascinating bit of leg he'd never noticed in camp shorts.

"You did something. Whacked her on the head? Alien abduction? What? Just this morning she lectured me on how she didn't trust you. Now she's hugging you like I don't know what." John climbed in and cranked the engine over. He turned the heat up right away. She was gonna freeze without pants despite wearing his sister's long coat.

"Your sister's a very smart girl." They pulled out of the driveway onto the road. Two miles later he turned left on the highway.

"You're not going to tell me squat."

Her silence was eloquent. He glanced over and she was staring straight ahead. Staring and smiling like the cat that ate the blasted canary.

Shit, he wasn't going to get another word out of her on the topic.

Well, he'd wait her out. She'd have to give in at some point.

"I bet we could get the tractor running tomorrow."

Or not.

"Grumps would like that," was all he could answer.

Damn her.

—⁓—

He'd thought about taking another swing back to the topic of his sister as they arrived at Dave's, but was distracted by the aroma. Straight out of high school, he'd gone Army and Dave had gone cook.

"Best steaks in all of Oklahoma."

"Do they serve whole sides? I'm starved."

"Just smell that." He pulled open the door. A warm wave of broiled steak and garlicked mashed potatoes, of winter squash and herb dressings washed over them. They stood just inside the softly lit entry and inhaled the smell of heaven.

"Oh, that's so good!"

"Wait till you taste it. Let me take your coat."

He took her coat and made half of the turn toward the coat check. Then he cranked back, turning his whole body like a tracked tank, to face the spectacle that was Connie Davis. Her clothes clung to her in sumptuous delight. They accented curves he'd never seen, even in the minimal camp clothes of desert heat. The lines of form were accented in shadows of a green so dark that her eyes shimmered with the warmth of window lights guiding you home.

The neckline didn't plunge, but it felt as if it did. Where he was used to seeing her dog tags, a simple golden necklace with a teardrop stone the color of her eyes accented the fine definition of her collarbone and her long neck. Then the skirt made her light and airy. And legs. He wondered if his heart was going to pound this loudly all night. Connie Davis had amazing legs.

———

By the end of the soup course John's brain came back into gear. Or at least partly into gear. Enough that he paid more attention to her conversation than her eyes in the table's candlelight.

He was in so much trouble.

"Doesn't feel right, does it?"

John had to think if he'd missed the beginning of some topic change while drinking in the woman across from him and admiring the massive slab of Oklahoma beef spread before him. No. Connie's comment was out of the blue, except it wasn't. He knew what she meant.

"You're right. Funny how it hits you at strange times. It's about 6 a.m. there. Crews are probably just dragging into Bati after flying through who knows what shit in the 'Stanis." For a moment he inspected his plate and his appetite was gone. All those friends crawling hot and sweaty into the shower after a whole night of flying. Hopefully none of them on the way to medevac or the morgue.

"Suckers."

He jerked up to look at Connie in surprise. He could see by her expression that she was joking. Covering over the heavy thought with something light. She'd found some easy way around the pain that plagued every SOAR flier when on leave and their friends weren't. Knowing that not being there increased the risk for all of the others. Knowing there was some teammate that you might never see again because they'd been shot while you were gone.

"Yeah," he said, trying to think of why they were suckers. "Because, ah, there's no way they were smart enough to eat this good a meal last time they were stateside."

"Exactly." Connie punctuated the thought by waving a fork at him with a small scoop of mashed potatoes from heaven on it, though neither of them ate for a few moments as they sent good hopes winging back halfway around the globe.

Then they chewed in silence for a while.

"I didn't start out aiming for the Army." For Connie, this was actively gregarious, starting a conversation topic on her own.

"So…" He sliced into his porterhouse, which he almost could've done with the side of his fork. Dave was so frickin' good. "Where'd you start?"

"Where did you?"

She'd been doing that to him all night. By now she knew about his boyhood passion. He'd built go-carts, racing bikes, later rebuilt motorcycles. He'd paid for his own cars by fixing other students' cars for half the garage rates and still pocketing a tidy sum. Then the Army gave him the chance to work on helicopters and he was a lifer.

But Connie's past remained elusive. This time he waved a forkful of steak at her.

"Nope. I asked you a question, girl. Now you're going to answer it." He almost added, "or quit talkin'," but with Connie that just might get him nothing but silence for the rest of the night.

She shrugged acquiescence. "I grew up at a dozen

different airfields from Podunk, USA, to Ramstein, Germany. My dad got me cleared into the hangars, what with being a single parent and all. He taught me helicopters. I knew an awful lot before I was tall enough to get myself in the cargo door of a Huey UH-1."

She spent some time trimming a bite from her slab of prime rib and getting a little fresh ground horseradish on it.

"I started high school working part-time for a Boeing maintenance squad as a gofer. Dad didn't live long enough to see me airframe-certified at sixteen. Sikorsky hired me straight out of school, which was good because Dad's Army pension didn't go very far." She shrugged and started chewing.

He decided to try her tactic and let the silence grow until it filled the room around them. Until they sat in their own private world in the midst of the dark-paneled and candlelit dining room. Until—

A hand smacked him on the back so hard he almost fell into his dinner.

He didn't need to turn to know who.

"Dave! You son of a—" He caught himself before more than half of the dining room was facing him.

Dave's powerful hand clamped on John's shoulder, but he addressed Connie.

"Only guy I know who orders my fine porterhouse done Chicago-rare and then orders a root beer with it. Knew who it was the second I saw the ticket."

John tried to speak, but Dave ran right over him, "Yeah, yeah, yeah. You never know when you're gonna have to fly. Heard it a thousand times."

He reached out and shook Connie's hand.

"She's a keeper, John. Don't be stupid enough to throw this one back in the pond. A real stunner with a serious grip. And doing yeoman service to my prime rib. Damn fine beef, isn't it, ma'am? What are you doing hanging with this big lummox? Your car break down? You can stay with me while he gets out of his one and only suit and fixes it for you.

"Aren't you gonna introduce me to your lady? Nah, you get all tongue-tied every time a good one is slow-witted enough to get caught in the honey trap of those gooey, big browns of yours. I'm John—He's Dave. No, wait. Reverse that. Unless you're John and he's Dave. But then who does that make me?"

<hr />

"That would make you a U.S. Army sergeant," Connie offered. It was easy to return the chef's smile. Though she had to wonder why she introduced herself as a soldier rather than by her own name as a person.

"I'd introduce you," John clambered to his feet and wrapped Dave in a bear hug, "if you'd shut your damn face long enough to let a buddy get a word in edgewise." Dave stood only an inch and a half shorter. They crushed each other around the ribs in a way that would break a lesser man in two and then slapped each other's backs loud enough to startle the diners seated nearby.

A lot of history there. Connie felt the pinch. She didn't have history with anyone.

John wrapped Dave in a headlock and turned him to face her. "Connie, this useless piece of trash is Dave. Dave, Connie. He was my center for two years of football, we made a hell of a pair."

Dave poked John in the ribs and pulled his head free. "Center. A fancy way of saying that he kept running his hands over my butt to warm 'em up and then fumbling the football anyway which yours truly had to save."

He shoved John back into his chair.

"Stop messing with the chef. I've got steaks cooking. And no, you can't feel up my butt for old time's sake. Nice to meet you, Connie. Hang tough one more day, then I'll take you off his hands tomorrow night."

"You gonna grill?" John brightened up even more.

"Wouldn't be The Night Before The Night Before Sub Fest if I didn't have my smoker fired up." And with a running stream of words and greetings at half the tables in the place, he moved back toward his kitchen.

"The Night Before The Night Before?"

John dove back into his porterhouse. "The night before Christmas Eve. We always have a big feed out at the Sub."

Connie dug into her winter squash. This time she heard the capital *S*. She'd missed that in the truck.

"Sub Park. It's not a small section of another park."

John looked at her crossed-eyed for a moment and then laughed.

Connie loved that laugh. John's voice was always filled with it. Telling a story in the chow tent or in a full-on firefight. About the only time it disappeared was when he was focusing on some mechanical puzzle. And then it was only because his whole body went quiet as his brain and his hands took over.

"It's—No, if you—Hmm, no, that'd spoil it. Tell you what. I'll show you on the way back, we go right by it. Big moon tonight, should be a stunner."

She considered pushing, which was surprising in itself. She usually only pushed when a technician was busy assuming she was a girl first, rather than a mechanic first and second and third. But John made her want to know things, about him, about his life, even about his family. She wished she had someone to talk to about the way he spoke of his sister.

"So, what were we talking about before Dave showed up?"

"Sikorsky hired me straight out of school, which was good because Dad's Army pension didn't go very far."

"Right. After that you…" He forked up some mashed potatoes and chewed for a moment. "That was word for word, wasn't it? How do you do that?"

Connie had thought it would be obvious. Maybe it was only obvious inside her head.

"Photographic memory. Or near enough as doesn't matter. If I see it or hear it, I don't forget it. Sometimes I need a refresher, but not often." Most people looked at her strangely once they became aware of it. Like she was an automaton freak. She steeled herself inside to take the blow of John's shift. She knew she'd be able to see the shift away in his eyes first. Damn, she was enjoying herself. Liked talking to the man. Liked being on the inside of the warmth that poured out of him.

He sipped his root beer and stared over her left shoulder for a long moment.

She should have kept her damn mouth shut. It was the first time, maybe in years, that she'd felt relaxed enough to just talk. She didn't want John to shut her out. Wouldn't like how that felt at all. She did her best to raise her personal shield, which she hadn't noticed sliding down since the moment he'd invited her to his home. Since she'd kissed him out by the fence.

"Wow! That's why you never use the manual to fix the chopper. You worked at Sikorsky, so you know every subsystem. Because you can see it."

She nodded. Still waiting. Still waiting for the rejection.

"And the ADAS, you've already memorized the plans."

Connie blew out a breath. In for a penny... "Not the plans so much, but I can see the whole system and how it fits with all of the others."

Again that unfocused gaze aimed off into space somewhere behind her. So intent, she almost turned to look even though she knew the only thing behind her was a lush, burgundy curtain draped over the generous double-paned window she'd spotted when they drove up. It was easy for her to juxtapose the exterior and interior to line up where the windows were in the length of the drape-covered wall.

John was processing. Juggling pieces into place. Reliving their past conversations in light of this new data. Trying to figure out how to pigeonhole her in some place comfortable for his fragile male psyche. She'd seen it a thousand times or more over the years.

Then his focus snapped onto her face.

Her stomach gave an ungainly churn. Here it comes. The dismissive, "you freak" attitude.

"Does that mean you can't forget either?" Instead his eyes were filled with compassion.

"Not much." It took all the strength from half a decade of Army training to keep her gut tight and her voice steady.

"The bad parts with the good, huh?"

She couldn't answer. No one had showed understanding. Ever. There hadn't been all that many good parts. Some came to mind. Her father, her instructors, her first flight. And just about every moment she'd spent with John, especially since they'd started flying together just twenty-three days ago. Those memories stood out with near-crystalline perfection.

He reached out and took her hand. That great warmth wrapped around her chilled fingers. His thumb rubbed over the back of her knuckles.

"Such a gift isn't allowed without its downside, I guess."

A gift. She'd thought it was someone's idea of the best way to torture Connie Davis. Never let her forget anything.

Especially not the pain.

Chapter 38

JOHN EYED CONNIE AS HE DROVE THEM BACK. THERE she sat as calm as could be. For a moment, he'd thought that he'd lost her. He'd seen the blast-shield defense clamp down as she spoke of her abilities. There was a lot of hurt, but once again, he didn't know why. He took her hand, glad his dad drove an automatic these days. He'd wanted to wrap her into his arms and hold her safe, but the connection of holding her hand appeared to work as well.

Several times during the meal, one or the other had reached out and they held hands as they told tales.

They'd both steered toward safer topics. And had a great time. She flown nearly every rotorcraft airframe and, once he got her started, was comfortable talking about the differences and changes. In addition to working at Sikorsky, she'd consulted with Bell and worked for a year on the Boeing Chinooks.

He'd flown with Major Beale for almost a year and Major Henderson before that. They'd flown into and back out of some really serious shit. The kind only another chief mechanic could appreciate. They'd talked long and late over fresh deep-dish apple pie, homemade vanilla ice cream, and decaf.

But it was still there. He could feel it now, lurking just below the surface. The battle of iron will that always strove within Connie Davis. He suspected that he'd be nothing more than a pile of Jello if he had to live with something inside like that.

That immense strength that lay hidden along her very bones. Beneath that, an anchoring that hooked right down to the very core.

He swung left off the highway and into the Sub Park.

It wasn't often that no one at all was here, but it was past ten on a chill winter's night. Not a single car in the whole lot. In summer, the place would be packed with kids and picnics and tourists. He pulled up and stopped, shutting off the engine and just letting their eyes adapt to the bright moonlight. Enjoyed the feel of her hand in his for a moment more before letting go.

"C'mon." He slid out of the seat. Headed for her door, but she was down before he could get there.

They headed into the park.

He took her hand to steer her to the east of the park building. When he offered to release it, she didn't let go. He'd walked here holding the hands of many a girl over the years. There'd always be something to say, he'd be telling a story, trying to be entertaining. She'd be talking about some local news. They'd been comfortable walks and talks. The shared excitement of meeting up with a bunch of friends.

With Connie, it felt as if they'd done this a thousand times. Always walked hand in hand. He could picture them decades from now, still coming here. Still holding hands. It felt so right.

"That's a torpedo."

It wasn't like Connie to state the obvious. That meant the surprise of this park was working.

"Ton and a half. Delivered five hundred and

seventy-five pounds of Torpex at thirty-three miles per hour up to three miles out. That means you could have to wait up to six minutes to see if you'd aimed right, hoping no one blew you up in the meantime." Most of the DAP Hawk's traveled at supersonic speeds and would cover the same distance in under fifteen seconds.

She looked up at him, her face etched in the moonlight.

"Tour guide. Summer job." His own words sounded drifty. Her beauty in the moonlight simply—

He leaned in and tasted her mouth. This time she literally tasted of apple pie and vanilla. She also tasted of the promise of summer.

She leaned into the kiss until his mind was gone. He'd never been kissed like this. She dug her fingers into his neck muscles, holding their lips tight together.

When at last she pulled back, he stumbled forward.

He dragged in a breath and fought for rudder control to maintain his upright position. His head was spinning with the power of a simple kiss. What would it be like—

"Easy there, flyboy." Connie's voice was gentle with humor. "Unless you're planning on dragging me back to the truck, you'd better show me what you brought me here to see first."

The truck wouldn't exactly be his first choice. That's what kids did. For two grown-ups to manage sex in a truck wasn't going to be so likely. Not that the idea didn't have its attraction.

He leaned in for a light, easy kiss, ready to make a small joke about the potential joys of CQC, a little close-quarters combat in the backseat, but even that momentary brush of lips heated his skin until it flushed hot.

Giving up on attempts at speech, he held her hand

tightly in his and headed forward. He watched her closely, knowing the big surprise would be when they rounded the cherry trees.

Past the WWII three-inch gun and out onto the brow of the hill.

He couldn't have asked for a better setting. The full moon had risen an hour earlier, their breath the only clouds in the night. Moonlight washed the USS *Batfish* in soft golden light. Three hundred and eleven feet of World War II submarine stretched out before them.

"Holy shit!" Connie whispered on a breathless gasp. "What's that thing doing here?"

"That 'thing' is the number one Japanese sub killer of the Second World War. She knocked out three of them in just seventy-two hours. Can you imagine that? Three! That's a major portion of the number of confirmed sub-to-sub kills in the entire war."

"But John," she waved her free hand helplessly before her, "that's a submarine. We're in Oklahoma. And it's not down in the river, it's up here in the middle of a park. How?" The river was a trail of moon glitter in the distance.

He could tell Connie all the details of shifting the *Batfish* here in 1969. Towing mishaps, the Army Corps of Engineers lowering the river by three feet to get her under a bridge. Digging a huge channel into the middle of the park, then closing it off and pumping it full of water to raise fifteen hundred tons of submarine thirty-six feet, and finally dumping all the dirt back in to drive the water out.

But with Connie, the mechanical wizard that she was, that was a path to a thousand questions, and it would take away from the wonder of the soft moonlight and the aged weapon of war.

He leaned close and whispered in her ear, "Magic."

The smell of her overwhelmed him, and he nuzzled her for a moment in that warm cascade of hair over that exquisite neckline.

"Want to go aboard?"

"Well, yeah! But it looks closed up."

He pulled out Pap's truck keys and rattled them. "One of the advantages of a parent who heads up the restoration team."

Chapter 39

CONNIE STEPPED ABOARD THE *BATFISH* AS IF IT MIGHT break beneath her. But the decking was solid. And new.

"They just finished redecking her, over two hundred feet worth. I helped lay this section here when I was home on leave back in the summer. Isn't she a beaut? Tomorrow night is sort of her coming-out party."

Connie could only acknowledge with a nod. She hadn't been able to put together a coherent thought since he'd not lambasted her at the dinner table over her unusual memory.

When he took her hand on the drive back, she'd begun estimating his ability to control the truck if she suddenly jumped him.

Their kiss at the head of the park had actually made her toes curl in her shoes. Her brain was wrapped in a wild and heady mix of John's strength and his warmth. And his desire.

Men had wanted her before. But there'd never been one who couldn't stop himself around her. John needed to be in constant contact, holding her hand, nuzzling her neck. And what shocked her even more, she was equally eager to be in contact with him.

Beside her, John was babbling on about seven war patrols and Navy Crosses and Presidential Unit Citations.

And all she could really hear was her own labored breathing and her heart pounding so hard in her chest it actually hurt.

At the side of the conning tower, he inserted a key and stepped in through the door. Rather than being cold and dark, the interior was well-lit in the soft red of heat lamps and the air was warm.

"She's well enough insulated against the cold sea that we can keep her warm and dry with just a single heat lamp in each compartment. It took a while to figure out that we had to do something to beat the condensation. She gets over a thousand visitors a week in the summer. That's a lot of people breathing."

He led her down a ladder into the control room.

He kept up his tour guide thing through the bow by describing the Forward Battery and Forward Torpedo Room.

As they retraced their steps aft, John stopped and turned to her.

Connie readied herself for another mind-numbing kiss. For a total loss of willpower except the desire to immerse herself in his arms.

"I just remembered my question."

"What?" What was he talking about?

"The way I figure it, Connie, it simply isn't right that you know something about my own sister that I don't. Noreen is the stubbornest person ever born, and you win her over in a day. If not aliens, then it had to be blackmail. What do you have on her?"

Connie shook her head trying to make sense of how Noreen had suddenly entered the conversation. Nonlinear progression. She knew it was one of her weaknesses, but she'd always had trouble following sudden jumps of topic.

"Why won't you tell me? I know it isn't some wicked

use of that amazing memory you've got. That doesn't
make sense. It has to be you. You knocked over Paps.
Grumps is letting you fix his tractor, which I still can't
believe. Mama Bee is taking your side over mine, and
I didn't even know there were sides. And now Noreen.
My whole family is falling in love with you."

They were? She'd thought that she blended in well
enough. Pretended that she fit in, looked as if she belonged even if she didn't.

"How do you make friends so easily?"

Connie coughed. It was all she could manage. A
laugh, a scream, and a horridly tight choking sensation
collided in her throat and spilled out in a strangled noise.

"What? What is it?"

She turned until she faced back toward the bow of
the boat.

"Connie? You okay?"

She shook her head. In disbelief. At the sheer unreal-
ity of it. The ultimate loner being accused of making his
whole family fall for her. It didn't make sense.

His hands came to rest gently on her shoulders. In
moments his thumbs were digging into her tight muscles.

"What did I say? I'd apologize, but I don't know
what for."

She shook her head again, trying to clear it. "I'm
fine. Fine."

Blinking hard brought the world back into focus.

"I'm fine." She turned to face him, pulling out from
beneath his grasp of her shoulders. The concern showed
clear on his face. Another emotion she wasn't used to
having aimed in her direction.

"No, seriously." She was probably just caught in

the blowback of the family's joy of having John home for Christmas.

He studied her in doubt, his brow furrowed, his right eye narrowed suspiciously a little more than the left.

"Really, John. Your family is just being nice because they're so glad you're home. Being nice to the stranger you dragged in from the dark. They're a great family. Really."

He still remained undecided.

"Show me the rest of the boat." She patted his cheek, then kissed him lightly on the lips. "You're sweet to think I have some special power."

John huffed out a breath and then smiled, a bright, mischievous grin.

"Didn't think of that. Maybe you used magic on her. Just like the guys who got a submarine to Muskogee, Oklahoma."

"My secret is out." She winked and he winked back. The tension that had shot into her shoulders and neck eased back out. His family was just being nice to her. She could be comfortable with that.

Chapter 40

THE ENGINE ROOM REALLY SLOWED THEM DOWN. Connie's questions were more detailed than any tour John had ever led through the belly of the sub. And more insightful. She picked out operational necessities built into the design that clearly indicated failure of prior designs. She saw the evolution of the fuel injectors and air flow, the control systems and the maintenance accesses. She didn't just have an amazing memory. Even as they studied the ship she reminded him that she was also a damn fine mechanic.

He led her into the Maneuvering Room, the one guaranteed to strike any mechanic to the core.

"Oh, my, God." She stood with one foot still in the engine room and the other straddled through the watertight hatchway.

One of the smallest rooms in a vessel built of small spaces. Inches weren't wasted on a sub and this room represented the pinnacle of that design mandate. The overhead pipes barely cleared the top of his head.

"This room is fully suspended. It's sprung separately from the rest of the submarine to block vibrations from depth charges. It's the most heavily protected room on the whole sub."

"Of course it is." Her voice just a church whisper.

Here was the heartbeat of the sub. The four main engines and the "dinky" fed power into this room, as did the racks of electric batteries while running submerged. Here every decision was made about allocation of power to engines, to battery recharge, to living spaces. Let those in the Control Room think they ran the ship; every mechanic would know that here lay the boat's true heart.

"You can still feel it," her voice barely audible.

And he could. Forty years perched on an Oklahoma hillside hadn't changed the truth. The old ship had power.

Connie moved about the room, inspecting gauges, noticing everything. She jumped up and landed hard on her heels against the steel grates. The lightest shiver through the floor plates showed the tightness and size of the springs. Depth charges must have wreaked unholy hell on the occupants for such stiff springs to make any difference.

She halted in front of the main control desk. In a room of iron and gray-painted steel, the stainless steel levers shone like a beacon. Connie slid the levers, smiling as he had his first time at the smooth flow of their movement, unchanged in over seventy years.

"You know, Connie. You've been making me feel a bit incompetent."

Again that owlishly slow blink. "I have? How? You're the best chopper mechanic I've ever worked with. I learn something new every time I watch you working."

That took him aback. He hadn't imagined the Mechanical Wizard—Mech Wiz for short, as she was starting to be called behind her back at camp, or more often Mechanoid—learned anything from anybody, least of all him.

"I'm always impressed at the integrity of what you do. Not a single bolt is left uninspected, not a single shortcut is taken."

His laugh was automatic. "Would you skip a step with someone like Major Beale at the controls?"

"Not a chance." Her smile was a testament to the abuse the Major could unload on a machine. "If it can be overstressed, she's the woman to do it."

John nodded. "You also share her strength. A quiet power. It's mesmerizing."

Her smile bloomed slowly. Growing until it stunned him, until he lost the power of speech.

"I like being called powerful. I like the way it makes me feel." She reached out and grasped his jacket's lapel. She pulled him in, like a sucker at a poker table who just wanted to give all his money to this woman.

Their lips didn't meet with bruising urgency as they had before. It was power, but in perfect control. Slow and delicate testing. Her lips, as often as not drawn in a tight line of concentration, were the softest texture he'd ever experienced. As delicate as water, as strong as steel.

He slipped his hands inside the coat she'd already opened against the warmth of the sub. He held that perfect waist. This time he didn't fight the urge to slide one hand down the delightful curve of the back of the skirt. The thin fabric barely more than a suggestion between his hand and those tight, tight muscles.

She moaned against his teeth as he used that hand to pull her in. Close against him. He lifted her, supported her with two hands, raised her until she sat on the control desk.

Perched there, she faced him eye-to-eye. Ever so slowly, he traced the line of her neck, tasted the hollow at the base of her throat.

Her hands laced into his hair and held his attention there.

He wasn't about to complain.

And she didn't complain either as his hands explored her torso. The curve of her rib cage fit his broad palm as neatly as her breast cupped against the inside of his palm.

With the slightest downward pressure, she guided him to her breast. Through the fine blouse and sheer bra, he could almost taste her arousal, could certainly feel it.

He wanted this woman. Wanted her so badly he couldn't breathe.

He wanted to be inside her. He wanted to feel her come apart. Feel all of that perfect control slip away. Then he had a thought and cursed.

"I'm sorry."

"For what?" She pulled him back up and kissed him full and deep and slow.

"I didn't think to bring any protection."

Connie giggled in his ear before nipping it sharply. He'd thought her shy and found her uninhibited. Not shy, just quiet. Another one of her fascinating dichotomies.

"Someone else took care of that."

He pulled back enough to look at her. "You thought we might…" But she was shaking her head.

She reached into the coat pocket and pulled out a string of four silvered packets.

"Your little sister thought we would."

His little… Noreen. He was going to have to kill her, or at least lock her up in her bedroom until she was thirty, at a minimum, or get down and kiss her feet.

Connie twisted the strand back and forth. "She appears to have a pretty high opinion of your stamina." Her grin was wicked.

"Wa'll," John drawled in his best Texas. "This here

little boat does have eight compartments, not jus' four of 'em."

She reached into the coat's other pocket and pulled out four more.

All John could do was groan.

"I was right, by the way." Again that radiant smile that lit her up like a rocket flare.

"About what?"

"You look absolutely amazing in a suit." She leaned in and nipped his chin. "Now let's see how you look out of it."

―――~~~―――

John didn't let Connie off her perch on the control desk and it didn't bother her in the least. She liked being at a height with him, eye to eye. Liked the way he looked at her as if he'd ravish her in an instant. Chest to chest. The way he held her nearly stopped her heart as his kiss had accelerated it.

He held her tight in a long hug that was almost enough to satisfy all on its own. Not hurried. Not on the road to somewhere else. He simply held her as if that's where she belonged. And by that very action, she did.

And the way he undressed her so slowly, like a fragile and wondrous new system. A single released button of her blouse led to his hands, his lips, his tongue setting off on a whole new mission that made her body sigh with pleasure and hum louder than a chopper's turbine. A very well-tuned one.

He watched her fingers as she unbuttoned his shirt, such a long row. She waited until they were all undone before pulling the shirt open. Open to a world of wonder she'd only imagined. His chest was a landscape a woman could spend hours exploring, even on an initial recon mission. Shape, definition, power. She leaned forward and nipped his pecs with her teeth and he hissed.

When she took his nipple in her mouth and laved it with her tongue, she elicited a moan from him that she could feel rippling up his chest.

Each time she expected John to be like any man, running for home plate, he turned aside. Her bra remained long after her blouse. First he had to play with her hair and lean in for another one of those mind-searing kisses. Had to test skin to skin, his hands and arms so smooth across her back.

When at last he'd undressed her, he stepped back rather than forward. In the compartment that was only a half step, but it was away.

For half a moment old fears rose in her belly and quivered there, until she saw his eyes. Darker than should be possible, they inspected her slowly from her toes until his attention at long last reached her eyes. A look of the most desperate need she'd ever witnessed.

"Damn!" The softest whisper caressed her nerves. "I didn't know it was possible for a woman to look so amazing."

"That's just lust talking." Not that she was complaining.

But John merely shook his head at her words.

Some words formed there, some momentary concern crossed his brow. A concern she didn't like seeing.

She reached out and cupped her hand behind his neck, the contact shock as huge as their first kiss by the fence, and then pulled him back across the gulf of that half step between them.

It started as a kiss, her hand on his neck sliding over to his shoulder. And their lips. Their contact built in slow waves. His hand cupping her face before trailing down over her breast to her waist. The slow drawing in as they met breast to chest, belly to belly, and finally, his hands lifting her buttocks, pulling her to him. She slid her legs about his waist.

His entry, impossibly, almost painfully slow, staggered her with its shock of power. She felt his footing shift and she grabbed an overhead pipe to help steady them. Closed her eyes as she focused on the sensation of him filling her. Nothing like it. Ever.

When they were finally pressed hip to hip, she didn't want to stop.

She leaned back to drive them closer together, knowing his strong arms would never let her fall. She wrapped her other hand around the overhead pipes and leaned back, driving them together with the change of angle.

John kept one hand in the small of her back and explored her front with the other.

When she began to shift her hips up and down he actually cried out.

It was the last sound she heard other than the roar of her own blood carrying her away, far beyond free fall.

John could feel Connie's body vibrate as she rose and then drove back against him at a higher and higher frequency. The exquisite agony rose in him as he waited for her, watched her. She become no more than a blur in his vision until she exploded.

He could feel the pulses fire through her. Launching

from where their bodies connected, fire rocketing up her back and through her chest until it found voice in a low desperate moan.

It was the moan that got him. That tipped him off the deep end. A moan of such pure and perfect pleasure. It didn't get loud, it barely filled the small chamber, but it echoed from so deep inside that her whole soul lay open before him.

Even as he shuddered from his own release pounding through every nerve ending, he gathered her tight back against him.

She held on to him. More tightly than any opposing tackle who had ever sacked the quarterback. She held on to him and he to her as the waves flared through them both.

Connie tucked her head against his shoulder and nuzzled in against the base of his neck.

And, amazingly, he felt the slow trickle of hot tears slip down his chest.

Chapter 41

THEY DIDN'T FINISH EVEN THE FIRST STRIP OF CONDOMS, but it wasn't for lack of trying. It was from sheer exhaustion. Making love to Connie Davis wasn't something any man with even a lick of common sense would ever hurry.

All the concentration on details she brought to her life as a mechanic, she indulged on John's body. He'd never bedded such a woman. Not being a complete idiot, he knew he'd never find another like her again.

He wasn't just thinking about the sex, though his body ached from its need for hers and was sore from the sating of that need. John had also witnessed a woman of such deep-rooted passion that she made all others pale by comparison.

And play. He couldn't get over that. Connie's soul possessed a deep humor, another layer he'd never seen. She'd made him feel as if he was sixteen when he'd chased her buck-naked into the aft torpedo room, her bright laugh and quick-dodging steps leading him the whole way. And there she'd made several comparisons between a torpedo's size and his own before unlatching one of the crew bunks chained to the wall and pushing him down on it.

She'd inspected, explored, teased until he ached for her past tolerance. Connie had practically crowed with triumph as she'd straddled over his hips and took him from above.

Even as they finally dressed he could still taste her rich earthiness, the saltiness of her sweat, and the sweetness of her kiss as she'd sprawled back for him on the amidships crew's mess table and he'd feasted on her body right past sated and into madness.

His legs barely had the strength to climb back into the conning tower.

Connie awaited him there in the three feet between the attack and observation periscopes. She had one hand on the controls for either scope.

"There's only one rule. No matter what you do to me, if I remove my hands, you stop and we trade places." Her grin was wicked.

He knew she was as exhausted as he. That, or she was an insatiable demoness who had already sucked out his soul. So he slipped up to her and kissed her the best he knew how. He kissed her and thought of the splendid use they'd made of each other's bodies. He kissed her and thought of how strong and powerful she made him feel, not on the outside, but on the inside. He thought about how happy he was every moment he was with her.

When he felt her arms wrap around his neck, he enjoyed the sensations for a moment longer and then pulled back just enough to see those lovely eyes.

"I guess I have to stop now." He tipped his head to indicate her hands, which were wrapped around him rather than the periscope controls.

She nodded in chagrin as she rested her forehead against his lips and he kissed her there.

"Your turn."

"God, woman. Rain check. Rain check."

She laughed and nodded her head before turning for the exit hatch.

———

The house was dark when they returned. John turned off the engine and lights.

Connie didn't want to get out of the cozy warmth. Didn't want to leave this little world of two people. Surprisingly, she understood that world. Had found an ease and comfort with John that she'd experienced with no other.

In that house, she could feel Noreen sleeping with a knowing smile on her face. She could feel Grumps dozing as if he still sat in the sun. And Bee and Paps and Larry. All watching her. Wondering how she'd be with their boy.

She'd surprised herself that she could be at ease with John. More than at ease. Silly. Giggling. Playful. It was a whole side of herself she'd thought dead and buried in some foreign land along with any remnant of her childhood. In John's arms she found a joy she'd never experienced anywhere else.

She knew how to be with a helicopter crew, and tonight she'd learned part of how to be with John. But not with a family. That was a world far too foreign to imagine.

He climbed out and came around to open the door. As if aware of her reluctance, he took her hand and raised it to his lips. The kiss he planted on her knuckles gave her legs the strength to move.

When he made to follow her through the dark house and into his bedroom, she stopped him with a hand on his chest.

"John, your family," she kept her voice low.

He gazed up thoughtfully at the ceiling and shrugged that he didn't care.

Did she? It was his family. That wasn't her issue. Unnerved in a way she hadn't been all evening, she pictured them together in John's bed. More intimate than anything they'd done in the submarine. Too intimate.

But she also knew that in his arms there was a feeling of safety. That maybe with him, the nightmares wouldn't shock her upright in the middle of the night. Images of tumbling helicopters and groping hands already burning in fire.

"I want to wake up beside you." Even in a whisper, his deep voice was loud enough for the world to hear.

She put her fingers over his lips and could feel his smile.

She cocked her head and listened to the silence of the night.

That was something she'd like as well.

Chapter 42

CONNIE WATCHED JOHN ROLL INTO THE BARN WELL after sunup. He wore old coveralls, a thick knit hat of orange and yellow wool with earflaps and a ridiculous pom-pom, and a sheepish grin that looked pretty damn cute on him. He also brought three large mugs and a thermos of coffee that Connie was absolutely ready for.

He first served Grumps where he'd again perched on his milk crate to officiate. With no more words than a "Thank you" from her, they turned to the tractor.

John inspected her rebuild of the front end and offered a sharp nod for a job well done. They started reassembling the engine in easy harmony.

Grumps picked up the story he'd been telling her before John arrived. A tale of Old Man George losing his two boys at a bridge across the Rhine and how it had taken the heart out of the old man and his farm.

"That's how we got the property to the west. We'd been planning to replace this old tractor in '53, but Jeff died in Korea and none of his kids wanted the place. That brought us the south beet field. In 1960, Greg's girls married college boys and none of them wanted the farm, so we picked up another couple hundred acres from him. Da' and me, we started taking shifts, worked this old machine sometimes twenty hours in a day during the planting and the harvest."

He nodded at the work they were doing. "Each

purchase brought us some new machinery, most of it too worn to do half of what was required. I rode this little beast here right up to '66. I almost drove her two more years to get her to her thirtieth anniversary, but we desperately needed a huskier machine. That's the year I bought the JD 4020 down the end of the row there. A hundred horsepower instead of nine." He waved his mug toward the far end of the barn.

"And I finally got my butt off them damn steel wheels Da' had bought for me."

She and John laughed together.

They worked in silence, reassembling the engine while the old man catnapped.

"Must be a hell of a mission coming up." Connie startled slightly, not having noticed Grumps wake back up.

She and John exchanged a careful look over the nearly finished block and head assembly.

"What makes you say that, Grumps?"

"One thing, you're both hurrying a job like there might not be time to finish. Oh, not criticizing the work, this old bitch, pardon my language but it's true, been wanting a fixing for many a year and you two are doing her proud. But you're in a hurry. And I seen your girlfriend there check her pager twice this morning."

Connie carefully didn't meet John's gaze this time when he glanced over. She'd leave it for him to handle.

"Well, could be."

"Would be," Connie thought to herself. The range of new gear. They didn't make upgrades like that in such a hurry unless there was a damned good reason. This mission was going to happen and it was going to be hot when it did.

"Then again, might not." John's voice was smooth and steady. "You know how unpredictable these things are. I didn't want to tell Paps or Mom, they'd just start to worrying."

"Mum's the word, boy. Mum's the word." After a brief pause, Grumps started a tale about a tornado that had come through and torn out exactly one row of corn down the entire length of the northwest field.

Larry drifted in and was soon put to work with a wire wheel knocking off the outer rust. Eventually Bee and Noreen brought out a huge platter of sandwiches and were soon outfitted with paintbrushes and a couple gallons of glossy green paint. About the time Grumps slid into a nap, Paps showed up with a fresh painted sign. John Deere green and yellow on a sheet of steel, but he turned it to the wall before anyone could read it.

——•——

When Connie fired her up, John started what turned into a huge round of applause. He couldn't believe what she'd done. Somehow, she'd entered a family already so close and brought them even more together. It had been a long time since they'd all worked together. Between the farm and the house and schooling and him in the Army, they'd been scattered a thousand different directions. But Connie had brought them all together to do something wonderful.

She made a few quick adjustments to the carburetor, and the old tractor settled into a soft purr.

She tried to get Grumps to take the helm for the test drive, but he refused even as he stood with a hand tucked around her arm.

"No, girl. My butt is done and gone with that machine. The old wench, pardon me, requires a younger behind than my bony old one. Just don't ride it too long or your bottom won't be nearly so pretty." He winked at John. "Thought I was too old to notice, didn't you?"

John just gathered the old man in. This farm, this family had been the dream of one man and an old tractor. Grumps thumped him on the back, still pretty hard for such an old man, before turning to watch Connie climb aboard.

She adjusted the idle, drove out the clutch, found first gear, and eased it back in. The old machine barely coughed as it dug in and drove forward for the first time in more years than John had been alive.

Again the applause rose, Grumps starting it this time.

Noreen leaned in. "Hey, Knothead."

"Yes, Meddler?"

She merely grinned impishly in response.

"You do get that we're applauding the woman this time and not the tractor."

He nodded.

"And you know that she still doesn't get that?"

He knew.

Chapter 43

IT SEEMED LIKE HALF OF MUSKOGEE HAD TURNED OUT for The Night Before The Night Before banquet. The display lights were on now and washed the length of the *Batfish*, though her conning tower disappeared upward into the darkness. The field was a patchwork of glowing fires in the picnic fire pits they'd installed three summers ago. People gathered about the warmth and flowed from one fire pit to the next, clasping steaming mugs of cider to aid the chilly passage between.

Connie would have felt battered by the mayhem of it, but the Wallaces kept her close and she felt the protection of the family. Felt the welcome. If only every person there hadn't known John quite so well. Within moments of each one greeting John, she could feel the looks turning her direction.

Some, like Dave, smoking a whole side of beef, grinning and giving her knowing winks. Others telling her what a good boy John was and how happy they were for him, though they never quite said why. And the young women, even the ones with a husband and a brood of children, eyed her as if to assess what she possessed, what she had that they hadn't.

Everyone was making assumptions and she liked it less with each passing moment. This had to be stopped. But every time she got near John, there was another friend, ex-girlfriend, old friend of the family, relation, or who the hell knew what.

When she finally tracked him to the parking lot, she was hitting her limit.

Before she could speak, he pulled her tight against him. Before she could protest, he pointed.

"Here they come."

Paps's truck pulled into the parking lot. As he pulled even with them, she could see the old John Deere gleaming as if newborn on the trailer.

Connie was rapidly drawn into unlocking and unloading the machine. When they tried to get her to drive it, she refused. This wasn't hers to do. She didn't want to be seen. Didn't want to give all of those people yet another reason to look at her.

"Grumps," she offered in desperation. "It's his. He should drive it. Or his son. Or his grandson. That's even better, John. The history of it all. You should drive it." Please. Anyone other than her.

He shrugged amiably when his father and grandfather waved him aboard.

It started clean with a thud and a roar. Everyone gathered close as he backed it off the trailer, shifted, and drove into the park.

She did her best to hang back, but Grumps took her hand and tucked it under his arm. Trapped, she headed to the park, though they lagged behind the others.

"The old beast never did move much faster than a walk, but I don't move even that fast anymore myself without a little help."

So they moseyed in behind John and the others as they circled the building, cut wide around the dormant cherry trees, and pulled into the head of the main meadow.

"Johnny's quite gone on you, young girl. I've never seen anything like it."

Connie kept her gaze ahead as the old man chuckled softly. Next time she and John were alone, that was another thing she'd be straightening out.

"Well, you'll see soon."

"See? See what?"

He just shook his head and left her to wonder as they arrived beside the tractor.

———∿∿∿———

Paps shouted for the crowd to quiet down.

They didn't respond much until John thought to kick the old engine a bit. It roared for a moment, as if digging in deep for one last time, drowning any conversation across the whole field. He let it drop to an idle and then choked it down into silence.

Paps stood at the front of the tractor, beside the plaque he'd bolted on but covered with a cloth.

"Welcome all to The Night Before The Night Before," his shout carried as John came down to stand beside him.

A round of cheers echoed across the meadow.

"Now, I know it's braggin' a bit, but it's a braggin' sort of night for the Wallaces."

Hoots and laughter came from the meadow.

"I remember my dad and granda' first talking about the USS *Drum* and then the *Batfish*. I remember him and many of your da's and granda's gathering around and doing the same. And here she sits, still proud despite more than thirty years beached."

John spotted Grumps holding Connie's arm and waved them forward.

Connie escorted him up beside John but faded back into the darkness before John could snag her hand.

"I need to thank each and every one of you who has labored these last few years on replacing her deck." He paused and John could feel the crowd hesitate. "But there's a side of beef cookin', so screw that."

Laughter and applause erupted. It was a good night.

"This old tractor is parked here for a reason. My dad was too young for World War II but not too young to work. He rode this tractor from four years before the *Batfish* was commissioned. Never too weary to help, he drove this tractor on many of your farms to help when help was needed. And like good Oklahomans, you did the same." He waited for the next surge of applause to fade like the former mayor that he was. "Old Grumps drove her straight through until four years before the USS *Batfish* came to stay on our good Muskogee soil."

This time the applause overrode him for several long minutes. During that time, he uncovered the steel plaque, then read it aloud when the crowd quieted.

"'This 1938 John Deere Unistyler L served twenty-six years on the nation's finest farmland keeping our people fed, while the USS *Batfish* kept our seas free for the same number of years. Donated this date to the museum.' I warned ya'll it was a bragging night!" He shouted down the next round of applause. "I'm almost done, then we can eat."

John felt a tug on his sleeve as Paps pulled him forward.

"First, I want a moment of silence for our nation's heroes. For those standing beside us," he patted John's shoulders, "for those not lucky enough to be home for Christmas, and for those fallen."

Caps were doffed, heads bowed. John could feel the silence. Could feel why he served. To guard these good people and this good family. He bowed his own head and thought of the people he'd lost and the ones he was still privileged to fly beside. He thought of his buddies still over in the 'Stans, at Bati field especially.

The silence hung in the night air until all he could hear was his own breathing.

Paps's gentle throat-clearing carried easily over the silent crowd.

"And now, my last announcement. I have another reason to celebrate. Sergeant?" He called out the last loud and clear.

John looked up abruptly, but Paps was facing back into the dark.

And there stood Connie in her uniform. Not her dress greens, but her ACU. The mottled tan, gray, and green of an Army combat uniform.

"By request, I'm pleased to present U.S. Army Sergeant Connie Davis of the 160th SOAR."

The crowd remained silent. John tried to make sense of it. She'd been wearing Noreen's big coat, but now she wore full uniform, billed hat, and her Beretta sidearm that she must have had on underneath. Somehow in the last twenty-four hours he'd forgotten the soldier that was such a part of the woman.

She dropped to parade rest and faced the crowd. Her earlier meekness had evaporated. The soft woman who'd slept spooned against him and woken him in the best way possible was gone. A SOAR Sergeant now stood and faced the crowd, and beware any who messed with her.

John could see that those fierce shields she kept around herself were firmly slammed into place.

"There are exceptional young people in the world…" Connie's voice, normally so soft, carried easily on the silent night air. "And they are often the ones you'd least expect. These young men and women face a challenge that most would shirk. They do what others not only can't imagine but wouldn't do even if they could. These people are to be looked up to and encouraged for they place one thing higher than themselves. It is their country."

John applauded uncertainly along with the crowd. Didn't she know this wasn't a time to lecture a crowd of Okies on patriotism? She was going to make a fool of herself if she continued with a recruiting speech. He went to step forward, but Grumps put a restraining hand on his arm.

"She knows what she's doing. Now stand tall, son."

His voice wasn't all that steady as he spoke. He'd never served. What was going on?

Connie turned smartly to the dark behind them and shouted out, "Cadet Captain Wallace."

Wallace? Who the—

Noreen stepped forward. But it wasn't Noreen. She strode forward in precisely gauged steps. Her dress greens immaculate from her green beret, her jacket decorated with several awards, her blue pants with the gold side-stripe, and shining black shoes. Her long hair back in a neat ponytail. White dress gloves accenting her hands in the bright park lights.

Connie motioned his parents forward as John's world turned under his feet.

Paps and Mama removed the three pips from Noreen's shoulders. They replaced them with the single gold bar of an officer before stepping back.

"Cadet Captain Wallace…" Connie spoke loudly enough for the crowd to hear. "Please allow me to be the first to salute the U.S. Army's newest officer, Second Lieutenant Noreen Wallace." And Connie shot his sister a perfect and sharp salute with her right hand.

First, Noreen offered a silver dollar to Connie, left hand to left hand, and then returned the salute. Connie took the coin and tucked it into her breast pocket, Noreen snapped down her salute sharp as could be.

Then they hugged.

The crowd erupted. Roars, cheers, hoots, and hollers.

John shook his head even as his sister came up to him. She saluted him.

Reflexively he saluted back.

Then he roared into her face, "What the hell, Nori?"

Chapter 44

CONNIE FLIPPED THE COIN OVER AND BACK.

She'd found a quiet place over by the park's track-mounted, five-inch gun, a large, nasty piece of work.

A silver dollar. The payment due from an officer for their first salute from an enlisted soldier. A tradition reaching back no one knew how far—1800s, 1700s? A payment for receipt of respect due the new rank and position.

Connie twisted it in the moonlight. Fifty years old.

Noreen had whispered as they'd hugged, "It's a half-century coin, so that we can look at it together when we're a half-century older."

Connie twisted it again in the moonlight.

She knew it was stupid. Knew she was digging her own pit but couldn't stop it. Couldn't stop the downward spiral.

Half a century.

Her father had been there for her just twelve short years. Her mother for three that Connie didn't even remember in her nightmares. Death awaited her and all she flew with. She knew that. Her goal was to give as much as she could while she could.

Sergeant Ron Davis had taught her that.

And her thirteenth birthday taught her that death waited in the dark for all of them.

She could almost welcome it. But someone had thrown her a lifeline; she now held a fifty-year old coin.

And there was more happening inside her that she didn't want and didn't understand.

As if called by her thoughts, a shadow came striding toward her through the night, outlined by the lights brilliant at the other end of the park. No mistaking the scale of John Wallace or the easy stride, even in silhouette.

He came to her as if shining with a light of his own.

He didn't speak. He didn't pause either. No thought of hesitation.

John simply walked up to her and folded her into his arms. She buried her face in his chest and breathed him in. Breathed in the quiet and safety.

"I can't believe Nori. I can't believe she did that and never told me."

Connie didn't need to ask his reaction, she could hear it in his voice. A sense of wonder and pride.

"She's going CSAR, that's why the premed. Can you imagine some poor, shot-up son of a bitch when my sister jumps out of a combat search and rescue chopper with a med kit strapped across her back? He's gonna think he's died and gone to heaven."

John kissed her on top of the head.

"I'm so proud that you stood for her. I'll never forget that. Never."

Connie could only nod against his chest.

It wasn't a moment she'd be forgetting soon either.

She held the coin hard in her palm.

Noreen had given her a fifty-year dream.

She'd never even had a five-year one.

Chapter 45

THEY WALKED BACK TOWARD THE BANQUET HAND IN hand. No hurry. But John's family waited for him there and Connie couldn't hold him back.

It was easier in her uniform. She knew who she was in her camo. She'd face the crowd, both the welcoming and the jealous. She'd be strong for John's and Noreen's sake.

They came upon the old tractor. Grumps was sitting on her left side. There was an almost natural seat there where you could sit on a frame member and lean back against the driveshaft housing.

He looked comfortable there, sleeping quietly. A bottle of beer held loosely in one hand rested on his thigh. How many times over the decades had he rested in just that spot?

John slipped the bottle free before it could spill.

"Come on, old man. You'll freeze if you stay here."

He reached out and then jerked back as if he'd been bit.

Connie stepped forward and touched Grumps's skin. Cold.

She checked for a pulse beneath the thick woolen scarf Bee had wrapped around his neck.

Nothing.

Her ear, just a half inch from his slack mouth, felt no brush of warmth, heard no breath.

She turned to John.

"John, you need to get the truck."

He didn't move.

"John!" she snapped out, and he jerked back to life like a puppet with half its strings cut. "John, you need to go very quietly and get the truck."

He nodded. Turned for the parking lot. Turned back. Turned away again.

Too much too fast. Connie stepped up to him and rested a palm against the center of his chest until his jumping gaze finally steadied on hers.

"Give me the keys, John. You sit here with him. I'll be right back."

He fished out the keys, then dropped them in her palm.

"Okay, John. You just sit with him, all right?" It was what was needed. She could remember the Army psychologists who always showed up whenever you lost a teammate. They spoke softly, they did their best to make it okay. And no one hated them more than the survivors of the team. Outsiders who didn't belong there. No one outside knew the guilt of being the one still alive when your crewmate ate a round. Just part of how the dynamic worked.

"Okay, John?"

He nodded his head. Then shook it.

"I can carry him. I can't—" He looked toward the bright lights of the park. "I can't let it ruin their night. Paps and Mama work so hard for this all year. And Nori, it's her night."

Connie patted his arm. "Just wait a moment. Then we'll take him together, okay?"

He squatted down and took the old man's cold hand in his two warm ones as if waiting for him to wake.

Connie trotted toward the edge of the picnic and spotted Larry. Exactly who she was after.

It took a moment to extract him from the woman chatting him up.

The woman said something like, "Isn't one enough for you?" before leaving in a huff. Connie had learned long ago to focus on what was important and ignore the chaff.

She towed John's brother to a quiet spot near the twin propellers of the *Batfish*, despite his protests, and told him the news.

It hit him as hard as it hit John, but he recovered faster.

"John and I. We're going to take him home. Just tell anyone who asks that's what we've done. Can you do that?"

"Yes... Yes. Good plan. Good." Then his eyes focused on her. "You're the best, Connie, for thinking about the family like this. John's a very lucky man."

Connie puzzled at the statement all the way back to the tractor.

None of them understood.

Not Larry, not Noreen, and not even John.

There might be the now, but there was no future. There was no point in planning for it either. People just died.

And they did it at the worst times.

Chapter 46

JOHN STUMBLED THROUGH THE DAY AS HE'D STUMBLED through the night. Visitors, well-wishers, helpers, family, and more family. Those handling it better gave him comfort. Those handling it worse, he comforted. No plan of action. No direction to turn anywhere on the farm that didn't remind him of Grumps. When a little girl sat in Grumps's armchair, he'd wanted to heave her to the floor. When Mama set out lunch, she used the bread-and-butter pickles she put up special for Grumps each year and John had to leave the room.

The house pressed in on him. The people squeezed at his heart until he couldn't stand another moment. Another instant.

He flailed about until he found the kitchen door and bolted through. He came to a halt a half-dozen steps past the porch, blinded by the low evening sun. Without turning, he could feel all that pressure and all that noise of the people in the house. Brimming over with stories and tales and, even worse, normal everyday goings-on, as if nothing momentous had erased all other concerns from the face of the earth. It built until he thought the overpressure might bust him at the seams. It drove him a step and another farther away.

Quiet. Just a moment of peace. He needed to go find Connie and just sit somewhere. Maybe go out to the sub and sit on the deck as the sun set into the west.

He hadn't seen her in a while, but he knew her. She'd be in the barn, fixing something. It's what she did. She better not have touched the GTO, that was his and Paps's project. Though at the moment, he wouldn't even grudge her that after the way she'd taken care of them all through the long, sleepless night.

Leaning forward, like a chopper tipping nose down to get some forward motion, he managed to place one foot in front of the other.

A large pickup rolled up in front of him and came to a halt.

More people.

He didn't need more people.

John cut wide of the hood, didn't look at the driver as they got down.

"She's not there, Johnny."

His legs kept going as Nori's words sunk in layer by layer.

"Where…" He trailed off when he looked up and saw her face.

"She's gone."

"Gone." There was a word with no meaning. Connie wasn't gone. Grumps was gone. Connie was just out in the barn. He turned again toward his goal, but Nori moved in front of him.

He tried to sidestep, but she moved again.

He tried to shove her aside, but she didn't move as easy as you'd expect from a girl. Solid she was. Farmgirl solid. Soldier solid. Right down to her boots.

Nori placed a hand on his chest.

"She left a message."

A message? Why would Connie leave a message?

"She said it was time for you to be with your family." Noreen swallowed hard. "And that was no place for her."

His next breath threatened to choke the life out of him.

"Where?" The word grated out of his throat so hard that it hurt to speak.

"The airport. I took her to the airport."

John started for the truck. He'd just have to go get her back.

"Johnny! She's gone!"

He turned, hand raised to wipe the words away. To smash the speaker aside, the bearer of such news.

Noreen stood square. Didn't flinch. Just faced him.

"Yes, I took her. When I said no, she just slung on her duffel and started walking down the driveway. She did this mental thing. Her face changed. It was her, but it wasn't."

John knew it well. "Her blast shield. Not even you could get through that, Nori."

He lowered his hand, one that he'd never raised against family. Never raised in anger.

"No way through that shield." As opposed to the pain that shot through him so hard he had to rub the heel of his hand against the center of his chest. "I guess not even for me."

Noreen stepped forward, only now did he see the tears streaming down her face, then she wrapped her arms around him.

He couldn't even raise his own to hold her close.

"I'm sorry, Johnny. I know how you feel. I love her, too."

Chapter 47

CONNIE HAD BEEN ONE OF TEN PEOPLE ON THE FLIGHT to Chicago. Snow had trapped her there and she'd slept on the terminal floor Christmas Eve. Then the equally empty flight to Nashville and one of three, including the driver, on the bus back up to Kentucky. She'd arrived tired after twenty hours in transit to cover the six hundred miles from Muskogee to Fort Campbell.

It had an upside though. No Christmas dinner Army-style. No Christmas morning with a bunch of duty personnel who wanted to be anywhere else and were morose about it. She knew them well, having been there almost every one of the last six years. And often as a charity case before that.

She slept through the rest of Christmas and woke just fine with the next dawn. Nothing from John. Nothing from the Majors. The unknown mission must be pending soon. They'd been told up to a week. And today was day six. No word yet.

Just her and a plate of scrambled eggs and hash browns in an empty mess. Two guys sat in the far corner nursing their coffee in shared silence. A couple of singletons sat as far away from each other as possible around the hall. This worked for her. Later she'd go work out, get a quick 10K run under her belt, maybe see if there was a training flight she could ride along on.

"Hey, Connie. You the only one here? Tell me you didn't spend Christmas here."

She looked up to see Kee Smith, now Stevenson, set a tray down across from her. Kee looked her usual, bright self. Bigger smile perhaps. No perhaps about it. The diminutive Sergeant glowed like the newlywed she was. Her shoulder-length dark hair swirling about her face as she moved with far too much self-satisfied energy.

"No, I didn't." She'd spent it on the floor of Chicago O'Hare.

Kee glanced up from securing a piece of bacon.

Connie didn't want to talk about it. Had managed for thirty-six hours not to think about it. And now... she still didn't want to.

"What are you doing here? Where's Captain Stevenson?" Then she made a guess. "Did you wear him out, Mrs. Stevenson?"

"Mrs. Stevenson! Ain't that a complete laugh? Still makes me all warm and gushy inside each time I hear it. Me! Gushy! It's so weird. Yea, I wore him out good. Army cots force a certain creativity even a sailboat doesn't require." Then Kee narrowed those already narrow almond-shaped eyes of hers. "And why does that feel like an illegal subject change from the master of following the rules?"

Connie shrugged and turned her attention back to her breakfast.

"Let me guess. Since you never were much of a talker."

Other than with John over the last week, Connie had spoken more with Kee than anyone else in a long time. Maybe in years. She'd been fascinated by the differences in their backgrounds. Kee, a street kid, who fought everything around her so hard. A woman who didn't think twice about walking up to a superior officer and telling him, "You're a complete idiot, sir." A master sniper and a woman comfortable with her own curvaceous form and the one-two punch it brought her of men's attention. Didn't faze Kee a bit to be the center of attention.

"Okay, I heard you were doing some training that Archie and I are supposed to start in about an hour. So, I'm guessing, since you're here, that your training is over and you're hanging out waiting for your next assignment."

Connie did her best to simply act normal as she ate.

"Now..." Kee was clearly enjoying herself, aiming a forkful of pancake across the table. "By that iron control of yours, I can see that there are about eighteen more layers to what's happening here. So, are you going to make me keep guessing, or are you gonna tell your tentmate?"

Connie swallowed some coffee against a dry throat.

"Big Bad John?"

Connie froze. And knew in the moment, she'd given a complete tell. The weakness of her hand of cards was now there for Kee to see.

Kee's smile only proved the point.

Then the heat roared into Connie's face. What could she do but nod? Now that her hand was exposed, she found she did want to talk to someone about it.

"He invited me home for break."

"For Christmas break," Kee clarified, as if it made a difference.

"For training break. I didn't really have anywhere to go but back here."

"And…"

Connie tried to think of where to go next. Too much had happened.

"So give."

Still the heat in her cheeks, but also the warmth of it spreading through her as Connie remembered how they'd been together. She kept imagining they'd pick back up where they'd left off, but every time she tried to picture that, pieces kept falling off. Fragments and sections of the image tumbling away as she'd always dreamed of her father's helicopter tumbling from the skies.

Kee's smile grew wicked. "Is he as well-endowed as you'd expect?"

"A bit voyeuristic for a newlywed." Girl talk, she could never get the hang of it.

"Newlyweds have one-track minds. Besides, a girl can dream."

"Well, then, uh, yes." When they'd had sex, he had filled her until she'd felt one with his body. As if they'd clambered right inside each other's skins. "Magnificently!" So much of him that even sitting here in Fort Campbell, her body heated with a greed to once again plunge down upon him. It was also a safe place for this conversation to go.

"Good! I'm way glad for you. He's one of the best men I know."

"The best I've ever met." And it was true. His skills, his compassion for her, his love and pride for his family. "He's an amazing man."

Kee sobered. "Are you being careful?"

Did she mean condoms or courts-martial? "Yes, to both."

Her companion shook her head and poked at her food for a bit. "I'm not talking about that."

Connie inspected her own dish, but the little food that remained didn't look appetizing anymore.

"I'm talking about why you're here and he isn't."

"His grandfather died. Sweet old man." As if that covered even a hundredth of what Grumps was and what he had been. "I was one person too many. So I got out of the way."

"You bitch!" It burst out of Kee like a hard slap. Her dark eyes suddenly gone black, her hands clenched into fists on either side of her tray.

"Ah, what?"

"You left him there? With a dead grandfather? He's told me how much he loved the old man, couldn't stop telling stories about him, and you walked away?"

"I didn't walk." She kept her voice calm and even. The closer people in the mess hall were looking their way.

"His sister drove me." She would have walked and that didn't sit too comfortably. She'd so needed to not be there. Couldn't stand all of the well-wishers. All of those people who had come up to a thirteen-year-old Connie grieving for her father and patting her on the head mouthing platitudes about how it would all be okay. Only it never was again.

"His sister should have punched you in your god-damn nose!"

The shout stopped all conversation in the room as everyone turned to face their table.

Kee pounded to her feet, knocking her chair over backward. She grabbed her tray as fast as you'd grab a fresh magazine in a bad firefight.

"No! Wait!" Connie called out as Kee moved off.

"Wait for what?"

Connie could feel the tearing inside. Could feel something wrenching apart. But what? She'd watched how much he and his family had needed each other. He'd moved from one weeping person to another, always leaving them better, stronger for having stopped.

She'd had to leave.

At first the barn. But that hadn't been far enough. The old horse stall no longer held a tractor. Still propped in the sun, the old milk crate Grumps had sat on looked broken down, ready to splinter and collapse.

She'd had to leave.

It hurt too much to stay.

Everyone she let herself care about died.

All she could do was fight to stay alive as long as she could. But she couldn't do it with Grumps so present, so alive in her thoughts.

Kee Smith was glaring at her. And Connie didn't know why. Didn't understand. All she'd done was leave. The family was fine. They'd had each other.

All she'd done was take care of herself.

John's family had welcomed her to their table. She hated eating alone. Always had, now that she thought about it. Now that she'd experienced how it could be to share oatmeal with Grumps while the rest of the house still slept, to sit over lunch and listen as Larry and John got into it about some pickup baseball game that had happened a decade ago, to sit across from John in the nicest restaurant she'd ever been to and feel as if she belonged.

"Please?" was all she could get past the tightness in her throat before giving up and staring down at the table.

She clasped her hands and crushed them between her knees, trying to find some center. Some place where it was all as it had been before.

She closed her eyes and held on. Just held on as hard as she could. Used her tricks, learned as a scared teen suddenly afraid of the dark. First, a little layer, an old windup clock, long gone. Then a go-cart and her first ham radio. A computer. Layers of her life.

Living with her father, she'd flown before she could drive. A Huey's rear rotor assembly, the insides of an M124 minigun, a Black Hawk's FLIR camera in a hundred parts waiting for an eleven-year-old to reassemble them under her father's watchful eye.

When at last she could open her eyes, she could see that a tray had been placed across from hers. Kee's hands rested to either side. They were no longer fists.

Threat sensors. Protective flare packages. Fuel and hydraulic controls.

"You're a mess, girl." Kee's voice was gentle.

Connie pulled one of her hands out from where she'd held it clamped between her knees. She tried to pick up her fork, but she'd driven all of the blood and feeling out of her hand and couldn't make her fingers grasp, turn, hold. Couldn't pretend everything was okay by taking a normal bite.

"He really got to you."

"I guess." Even the soft words hurt.

"It wasn't a question."

Connie rubbed at her eyes, trying to wake up. To shed all of the memories.

"Yes. I suppose he did. Time I got over it." She sat up straight, able to take hold of the fork this time. She did her best to smile at Captain Stevenson as he came up beside his wife.

Kee accepted his easy kiss. Then she leaned forward so that only Connie could hear.

"You ever say that again and you're going to really piss me off."

Chapter 48

THE CALL CAME AND JOHN PACKED QUICKLY TO LEAVE.

He could now. He'd had the days to mourn, though the grief was still a constant companion. The younger kids had made Christmas morning what it was supposed to be, and the grown-ups had managed to enter into at least some of the spirit of it.

Good old Paps had moved himself into Grumps's chair so that it wasn't an empty space in the room. "Good enough for him is good enough for me." Nori had gotten all sniffly and sat in his lap for a long while despite being a girl grown.

And fate and the Army had allowed him to be there one more day for the burial out in the old family plot and the wake that followed.

Mama stopped him as he headed for the front door. He hugged her hard but she didn't let him go.

"Paps is waiting, Mama."

"Let him wait a minute."

"Army's waiting." Once the call came, every fiber in his body shifted into action mode.

"They can wait a damn minute, too."

You didn't argue when Mama dug in her heels.

"I was so angry when your father died."

John felt the gut punch land. His bag slipped from nerveless fingers to plop on the kitchen floor. His next breath ached as his lungs dragged for air.

"Even angrier at him for dying before you were born than that drunk driver who killed them both."

He tried to turn away, but she rested a hand lightly on his cheek to stop him.

"Paul had been crazy about me from the first moment we met. Might've married him anyway if we'd met first. Grumps and Liza raised good boys. You know why we all call him Paps."

John knew, even as his mother repeated the rarely spoken truth.

"So you wouldn't have to choose which to call your father."

John closed his eyes. He couldn't face her.

"Why are you telling me this? Why now?"

Mama pulled him close and held him. Held him until he remembered the smell of home. Held him until he felt less frantic inside.

She leaned back and looked up into his eyes.

"Sometimes it does a body good to be reminded. Think about that the next time you find yourself really stuck. Think about the two good men you had as fathers."

He kissed her cheek, "And the one good woman."

"Damn straight!" She pushed at his shoulder. "Now get outta my kitchen, boy. You're holding up the whole operation."

He retrieved the bag and made it to the door and turned back to look at her. To look at the strength of a good woman.

"I love you, Mama."

She didn't turn from where she faced the empty stove. "Love you too, honey. Now scoot."

Chapter 49

JOHN CAUGHT A FLIGHT JUST ACROSS THE RIVER AT THE Oklahoma National Guard's Camp Gruber Maneuver Training Center, and three hours later he was pulling into Fort Campbell. His sadness had been replaced. Replaced with a seething anger that had grown over the last three days until it was a hard ball inside his gut that he didn't know what to do with. It sat there and burned. His mama had packed him a great lunch for the road and he'd thrown it out right after they dropped him off. He couldn't even eat the damned candy bar they'd offered him on the flight.

When he made it through security on the base, the only thing he could think was it was damn good he hadn't seen Davis or he'd be in the brig right now just for the thoughts of what he'd like to do to her.

He could understand, kind of, why she'd want to be gone. She didn't do well with people and there'd been a lot of people. But she'd left. She hadn't stayed to honor Grumps's memory. She hadn't stayed for him. He'd imagined more. He'd trusted there could be…

Thankfully, she also wasn't the first person he ran into on entering the lobby of Grimm Hall.

"Sergeant Kee Stevenson III, you are just all smiles and glows." He wrapped her up in a bear hug, lifting her feet well clear of the ground. She hugged him back and planted a big kiss on his nose.

"Hey, put down my wife."

"No! Mine!" He told Archie as he hugged Kee again. "Damn! Wish you were the one coming with us."

"Can't. We gotta get trained up on your fancy new toy. We hear that you proved it out at the Nevada Test Range and now we've gotta get up to speed."

He set her back down on the carpeting and extended a hand to Archie. "You caught a good one here, Captain. How's the kid?"

"You wouldn't recognize her. Jeans, turtleneck, and iPod. Not sneakers, though, boots. I think it's just in case she ever has to make a long walk again, which she won't. The music she likes is really strange."

"Indie rock?"

"Broadway show tunes. The kid is singing along all the time."

"Sweet!" He could just imagine it, the Uzbekistani orphan they'd adopted singing about climbing every mountain and dancing in the rain, a commodity she'd rarely seen in her life until a just a few months ago.

"We're outta here." Archie shook his hand again. "We'll catch up with you in a week or so, wherever you are. Where are you headed?"

"Can't be soon enough. And no briefing yet on where we're going. But they called us back in, so it's probably time to get back on it." John didn't ask Archie about the wreckage the bullet had made of his shoulder. Didn't need to. The man's grip was strong and sure, and his shoulders were as broad and muscled as they ever were on his slender frame. He knew the man would never fly pilot again, but they were training him up as an air mission commander at which he'd be awesome.

"Marriage looks good on the two of you." And the bite was back in his gut, so hard he almost gasped at the sudden pain. Damn Connie Davis.

"Really. It does."

Kee put her hand on John's chest and patted him there. He looked down into those dark eyes of hers.

"John. I know it hurts."

He flinched. He couldn't stop himself.

"Yes, I spoke to her and she's pretty screwed up about this. Walk softly there."

"Walk softly? Walk softly! Do you know what she—" He bit it off before it became a scream.

Kee was nodding. She knew.

"I'm not the one who needs to walk goddamned softly."

She kept her hand on his chest as he struggled to breathe normally.

"I'm not the one." And there was the problem. He really feared that he wasn't. But imagining Connie Davis with anyone else was almost as awful as imagining being with her and then having her walk out on him again.

"John, I've got a message from her."

"Screw that! I've had enough goddamn messages from her."

Kee sighed and looked back at Archie, who just shrugged.

"Are you on her side? Both of you?" John's anger burned.

Kee shook her head. "No, the only side we're on is our crew's."

"Well, as soon as you're back, she's off the crew anyway. Problem solved."

In a second, Kee had her fingers dug into his throat

and was pulling him forward, dragging him down to her foot-shorter level using as leverage his desperate need to keep his windpipe intact.

"The goddamn message is from me then," Kee snarled when they were nose to nose. "You know where to find her. Actually, it is from her because I don't know what the hell it means and I don't care. But I can see you damn well do."

Then she smiled like an angel, kissed his nose again, and let him go.

He swallowed and knew it would hurt to speak. He swallowed again. It would hurt for quite a while.

"And if you don't have this straightened out by the time we're back with the unit, I'm gonna kick your ass." She snagged Archie's arm and headed out the door. Called back over her shoulder as sweetly as pie, "And you know I can do it."

Yea, he did.

Chapter 50

THE WOMAN, SO TALENTED AT DISAPPEARING, WAS suddenly everywhere. In the mess eating with the Majors. Out working with the Raytheon crew, helping run orientation for the class that included Archie and Kee. When John finally gave up and went for a run that afternoon, he spotted the small figure sitting against the fence on the far side of Nightstalker Way. He could feel her track him as he looped out and around the airfield.

When the C-17 showed up with their choppers, they all loaded aboard.

Major Beale stopped him at the foot of the ramp until everyone had moved past them. They started cranking up the engines, and still he and the Major remained.

"John?" He didn't like the sound of her voice. He knew this voice. It was her I'm-about-to-issue-a-command-and-if-you-don't-do-it-I'm-going-to-tear-you-into-teeny-tiny-pieces-of-once-was-John voice.

"Yes, Major."

"Fix it!"

"Yes, Major." He wished there were some question of what they were talking about.

But there wasn't.

Chapter 51

JOHN TRIED. HE DUG DEEP AND TRIED.

On the flight he signaled Connie over, and they went through their Hawk inch by inch.

Even if he could bring himself to speak to her, his throat was too sore from Kee's iron-strong fingers to shout over the roar of the C-17's engines. So they did it in silence.

Even before they'd moved off the tail section and started on the twin GE turboshaft engines, they were working smoothly. John wasn't ready to congratulate himself, but after thirty hours of complete avoidance, it was an improvement.

Connie was at a complete loss. John was making her work but wouldn't speak to her. She'd tried to be in places where they'd been comfortable together. To somehow make it okay. She'd eaten with the crew, and he'd never come to a single meal. She'd worked with the crew on the ADAS, and he hadn't joined them.

She'd finally decided to give him the space, to sit out at the fence. She'd started thinking this was their place. It was where they went to work things out. But they didn't. He'd left the hangar, heading out on a run. She knew it was him despite the distance. Then saw the stumble when he spotted her. And watched helplessly as he altered his course abruptly away from where she sat, nearly running head-on into a parked Chinook.

So she did what she did best. She kept her mouth shut, her mind on the mechanics, and her heart shut up in a steel casing. Five hours to review everything they could while in flight. Every system checked out. Every bolt was well seated. Every ammo case loaded.

The silence had sapped her energy. She was dragging by the time they finished. Usually the quiet was her friend. A place where she found peace and purpose. A place where music came to her and filled the spaces.

There was no music today, no harmony in their work. Only struggle and duty. When they finished, she lay down on the cargo bay deck and slept on the hard steel.

She slept and dreamed of falling from the sky.

Chapter 52

"YOU ARE HERE AS A PART OF MY GUARD DETAIL, EM."

Connie looked at the three Secret Service agents who stood at strategic locations in the hotel suite. Places where they appeared unobtrusive but would be the first to any door or window. Long before President Peter Matthews.

They fit in well here, and the SOAR crews certainly didn't. The plush furnishings evoked the founding of Stockholm's Grand Hotel in the late 1800s. She considered touring the suite but felt too self-conscious under the Secret Service's vigilant eye. She sat at the far end of the living room at the broad dining table. Most of the others were clustered down at the far end in the circle of sofas beyond the grand piano.

Connie had never imagined a hotel suite like this one, never mind been in one. Everything was so perfect that she didn't want to move for fear she'd mess it up.

Major Beale's latest protest filled the room from where she was busy chewing out their Commander-in-Chief.

"Peter, you don't go to an international peace conference in an allied country and drag along a pair of stealth-adapted DAP Hawks for guard work. Why are we really here? In the Grand Hotel Stockholm, for crying out loud!"

"For now, a joint training mission with the Swedish Special Forces, a way to say thank-you to the Special Operations Group for their help in Afghanistan. Beyond

that I'm not sure yet. I think we'll know more tomorrow
or maybe the next day—"

"So we just hang out while you do whatever it is you
do here, Sneaker Boy?"

"Look, Squirt…"

Connie tuned it out. She could picture them as children, enjoying the argument for the sake of debate, of
mental jousting. Connie couldn't imagine anything more
exhausting. Give her a game plan. A place and direction to go. That worked for her. When she even thought
about people like this, who had minds that worked like
this, it made her tired. When she was around them, she
found herself pulled in. Sucked in by the power and
magnetism they projected on those around them.

But it served so little purpose. No matter what either
said, it wouldn't change the course of events.

She was so sick of words. And they never were the
right ones.

John wouldn't speak to her. And now Major Beale
was shutting her out. To be fair, the Major was shutting
John out as well. But that didn't make her feel any better
about the arrangement. Clay, the copilot, did his usual—
loud music on his MP3 and a ragged novel folded back
on itself so that the binding was broken past reading the
title within minutes of his picking it up.

She rarely spoke with *Viper's* crew. Except Tim. Tim
was funny, easygoing in a way Connie had always en-
vied. He radiated a charm that swept up all those around
him. He and John together were hilarious, always something fun going on. They were two very action-oriented
guys, as different as possible from the President's and
Major Beale's modus operandi.

Now that she knew Tim, she understood something
she'd missed way back when she'd first arrived at Bati.
He'd made a pass at her. Thinking back, that's what
it must have been. She just hadn't seen it go by. He'd
made her smile, at least inside, several times, but she
hadn't really connected it to anything beyond him being
nice. But the moment she and John had started being
close, Tim had eased back so gracefully that she didn't
even know he'd been being forward. Smooth operator.

Smooth or not, now that she wasn't talking to John,
Tim wasn't talking to her, either. Of course, there they
sat on the far side of the suite not speaking to the Major
or each other. Tim kept looking over at his friend, but
John wore a black cloud over his head like a monk's
hood and was unapproachable.

So she sat in the corner of the suite and stared out the
window. It looked across the harbor at Old Stockholm.
In the dusk, a small tourist boat slid into the harbor,
mostly empty, not many people braving the winter night
on the water.

The snow lay on Stockholm like a thick blanket, and
the palace shone in Old Stockholm across the water.

The Major was right. You don't go to a friendly
country and bring your personal army with you. A bad
tactical move. And this had been touted as a goodwill
visit crossing Scandinavia and culminating in Russia
and the Ukraine, which to her way of thinking, made it
worse. Masking it as a training opportunity with SOG
worked okay, but that was counter-balanced by where
they were sitting. The President of the United States
didn't typically invite two Special Forces helicopter
crews over for a beer and a chat.

Tomorrow's conference didn't help much. Leaders from throughout the region were invited to the hotel for three days to discuss the peace process, and the President had come to participate and listen. A friendly ear with a personal fighting force of his very own showing their teeth to the Swedish Special Forces.

She sat up suddenly. Something wasn't right. The hand the President was playing didn't make sense. Unless he knew something. Something he wasn't willing to share with the very people he needed. What would make sense?

A threat. There was a threat to—

John sat down across the table from her. A quick glance showed that no one else in the room was paying them any attention. Except for Major Beale from the far end of the room, but she never missed anything. She did turn away a little abruptly when Connie spotted her. Great. Just great.

John wasn't merely making Connie miserable, he was also screwing up her career with one of the finest commanders she'd ever met.

"What the hell is wrong with you?" She kept her voice low.

John sputtered before croaking out in a hoarse voice, "Me? I'm not the one who screwed up."

"I don't need you telling me what Kee Stevenson has already rammed down my throat."

"Your throat?" He massaged his windpipe. "What did she do to yours?"

So Kee was on a rampage against both of them. She'd rammed Connie's own words back down her throat until she'd nearly choked on them and apparently done something similar to John.

Well, to hell with her, too. Connie'd been fine. It was
John who'd gone all weird over a little sex. Too bad really, it had been great sex. There'd never been a chance
that it would work out to anything more. Not for Connie.
And when Grumps died, well... she'd... She'd just been
in the way, that's all. In the way so she left. Simple.
Keep it simple and focus only on what she knew. She
still flew.

"So we're good now? We just fly together."

The color drained out of John's face, and his fists
clenched.

Before she could puzzle out his reaction, a deck of
cards landed between them.

"Enough planning. Time for a little poker." Major
Henderson slapped John on the shoulder, and he
flinched as if he'd been shot by a much bigger weapon
than Mark's palm. Crazy Tim took a chair on her left,
and to Connie's right, the President took a seat.

Tim gave her a worried look, clearly taking his
friend's temperature accurately. With a brief shake of
his head, Tim communicated that he didn't know how
to fix this one from the outside. It was sweet of him to
even think about it, but everything was fine.

Maybe if she kept telling herself that, it would
come true.

Major Beale crowded down between her husband and
the Commander-in-Chief. When Mark protested, she
held up her hands in self-defense.

"I won't look at anyone's cards. I'll just run drinks
and such."

Dusty, Henderson's gunner, squeezed along the wall
to sit beside Tim.

The card players had Major Beale back on her feet, running for sodas and sandwiches and a pizza and something called Swedish butter strips that Tim insisted on, until the table was well covered and she finally went on strike and sat back in her chair.

The President started shuffling the pack. Connie tried not to feel weird every time she looked to her right and saw him just two feet away. A pair of Secret Service agents flanked him on either side and a step behind. The big one, Adams, stood directly behind her chair, looking much more daunting than he had when riding in the back of the helicopter.

"Is your stomach feeling better, Mr. Adams?" She couldn't leave it alone. Never miss a chance to look down on another service or make them think you did.

"Better than your wallet will by the end of the evening, ma'am. Thanks for asking." He said it with a perfectly straight face, but Major Beale laughed for him.

"You wanna try your luck, Frank? You can have my seat."

"Not a chance, Army. Not with your husband sitting at the table. I've seen him play."

Mark Henderson winked at her. Not at his wife, at her.

Chapter 53

THEY'D AGREED TO START LOW, SO JOHN TOSSED A couple of dollar chips against Tim's pair and the President's possibly low three of a kind.

Mark matched the play, unreadable as always to John. The President folded.

John watched Connie carefully.

She looked at John from across the table. Looked at him like a stranger. Looked at him as if there wasn't something between them. But there was. He knew it. Something that ran deep. So far down neither of them could see it, but there it lay nonetheless.

And she'd blown off what they'd shared. "We just fly together." What the hell was she tripping on?

Well, screw her. Tonight she was gonna pay for it. She was going down.

She matched his two and raised one more.

Tim folded.

John knew she was bluffing. Knew it for a fact. He saw the play, would have raised her—he was still a dollar shy of the table limit—but decided to force her to show.

Mark studied the two of them, then set his cards face down on the table. Tapped them a couple times, then tossed in his dollar chip.

"I'm gonna pay to see what's in your hand there, Sergeant Davis."

She turned over a broken straight. The Major's pair of kings went nowhere against John's three nines.

He pulled in the chips, leaving one behind to the ante, and grunted out, "Deal."

This time it was the President who stuck and forced John to show his hand. Connie's two pair edged his by a single rank.

John had kept his hand steady and didn't have a god-damn thing to smile about, so there'd been no tell, no giveaway. She hadn't read him, it was just the luck of the draw.

—◦◦◦—

Major Emily Beale had been watching her husband play poker for the better part of a year, and not much threw him. He joked, he fooled around, he enjoyed himself whenever he was watching people. It had taken her a long time to learn that he actually enjoyed himself doing just that pretty much all the time. Especially when others couldn't see it. When he was in full-on Viper mode was when he was really laughing it up inside. It certainly would have helped if she'd known that little fact during their crazy courtship.

She knew now that he'd thought her shooting a laptop in a camp tent was one of the downright funniest pieces of justice ever handed down in any military court, of-ficial or otherwise. He had a wit and humor that she'd learned to love and that had the added benefit of guar-anteeing her life was never dull.

He'd gone quiet before the first twenty dollars had shifted back and forth around the table. And she knew his quiet mode was when he was being really intrigued

about some aspect of human nature. She wanted to drag
him aside and ask what the hell was tickling that hidden
funny bone of his, but she couldn't break up the game.

So she watched.

After about half an hour, Crazy Tim threw up his
hands and pushed back to watch, too. At least a hundred
bucks down.

Fifteen minutes later, Dusty, who'd been hanging on
by just the tiniest thread, got swept off the table despite
holding a low straight.

Peter ended up being quickly sidelined though stick-
ing in, more due to tenacity than common sense. He had
to buy in for more chips twice.

The more she watched, the more she understood that
this was a game between three people: Mark, Big John,
and Connie Davis.

What she didn't understand was why Mark was playing the way he did. Usually he was loud in poker, not
quiet. And he'd bet strong or soft or fold based on some
strategy of power she'd never understood. Now he was
betting consistently and those bets were consistently
low, never raising. His stack of chips was constantly
shrinking, which was also unusual.

He'd once tried to explain to her how the game worked.

"There are four levels to poker." They'd been lying
together alongside his favorite trout stream, just enjoying the day and each other rather than bothering the fish.

"First, as a beginner, you're worried about your own
cards. Second, later, you're worried about what you
think others have. The third level is," he ticked them off
on her fingers, "when you're worried what others think
you have. Fourth, and this is where it starts to get really

fun, you've learned that the cards no longer matter. At that level it's all a mental game of making the other guy think you've got what you want him to think. You almost don't have to look at your cards."

She'd asked if there was another level.

Another two rounds at the table and she finally spotted what had caught Mark's attention a dozen or more hands before. Maybe all the way back at the first hand.

This game wasn't between the six who'd started or the four still in the game. It was really between two people. And they were playing at a whole other level. They were playing Mark's fifth level. He was just staying in to keep it interesting, bleeding his chips as slowly as possible.

The two players were building up sizable stacks of chips at everyone else's expense, but that didn't matter, either.

They weren't playing poker.

This was warfare.

—⁓—

John slapped down two black chips, made sure he put a sharp snap into them as he slammed them down on the table. Because of the low-priced game they were playing, the black chips were ten dollars.

"Hey, ten-buck limit, dude. Can't you count?" Crazy Tim.

Screw him.

John watched Connie. No tell. Her eyes didn't travel to Mark or the President. Skipping the order around the table, she reached down into her own pile and pulled out four blacks and threw them on the pile in the center.

Mark whistled.

The President tossed in his cards with a weak laugh.

John slapped on two more blacks to match her bet. Let her stew on that.

"Wa'll…"

Henderson and his goddamn, weak-ass, fake Texas accent.

"I've jes' gotta see this 'un." He dribbled from on high, four black chips, wiping himself out.

Connie tossed down her cards. Three aces.

John tossed four hearts down on the pile of chips one at a time, holding the fifth, twisting it back and forth in front of Connie's face for just a moment, before slamming it down and revealing he really had a flush that pounded the shit out of her lousy aces.

Major Henderson started laughing. Started soft, but it grew. Others at the table joined him uncertainly.

John just wanted to smack him. Might be worth the time in the brig to shut the man up. He kept his eyes on Connie. She didn't look aside either.

Out of the corner of his eye, John could see the Major flash his hand at his wife and the President before laying the cards out on the table in a neat fan.

"Threes and twos, the nicest little full house of the night. Come to Daddy." He swept the chips over to himself in a big pile.

Before the cards and chips were even clear, Connie smacked down five blacks as an ante.

John was reaching for his own chips when the Major caught his wrist.

He pulled against it but didn't get very far. He might be a few inches taller than the Major and several inches wider, but the man was seriously powerful. Henderson kept John's hand pinned to the table when he tried to free it again.

"Enough, you two." The joking Mark Henderson was gone, so was the quiet poker player. This was the commanding officer.

"You're both done here. Now take it outside."

Connie was up and gone before Henderson even released John. Pushed past the President and the Secret Service agents as if they were mere slalom gates to be shoved aside in her race for the door. She snagged her jacket as she shot out of the room.

John was no more than ten steps behind her.

Chapter 54

"JUST STAY THE HELL AWAY FROM ME!" CONNIE COULD feel him close behind her as she shot out of the Grand Hotel lobby and into the street-lit night. Snow. Over to her right, a bridge. Strömbron. Get out and away. It was all she could think to do.

The freezing weather slapped at her as she crossed onto the bridge toward the palace and Old Stockholm. She could feel the heat of her cheeks in sharp contrast to the night chill.

Damn the man. "Damn you, John Wallace!" she shouted loud enough for him to hear as she crossed onto the bridge. She didn't need to turn to know that he continued to stalk her. Matching her pace. Boiling as deeply inside as she was.

Anger pounded at her. Drove at her. Drove her.

Across the bridge, she continued past the palace. She took a left, past the palace guards in their sharp blue and black.

She hated this. The anger so deep, so vast she became lost in it. She hated losing control. This wasn't who she was. It wasn't who she wanted to be. If only it would stop. A massive wall blocked her progress just past the lights of the palace.

Left or right or… She couldn't decide. She continued until the wall stopped her and she laid her cheek against the cold stone.

The anger boiled up inside until she couldn't hold it in. She retched against the wall. And retched again. She'd eaten nothing. Couldn't remember when she last had, her stomach knotted past tolerance. Fort Campbell maybe? All that came up was a thin bile.

And she couldn't stop. It was like she was heaving her soul out against the wall. The pain scorched through her. A line of agony starting at her gut and driving up her chest and out her throat.

She fell to her knees and heard a soft, "God damn it!" from close beside her the moment before John's strong hands wrapped around to support her. One across the small of her back and the other supporting her aching gut muscles as they once again tried to heave the anger out of her. The poison that had been killing her for years and she'd never been able to stop.

"Breathe, damn it."

She heaved again, her chest aching in need of air.

"Okay, Connie. Honey, just focus on my hands. Focus on my voice. It'll be okay. It'll work out. Don't ask me how, I don't have a frickin' clue, but it will. Now, just focus on my voice and breathe before you pass out."

She tried. She really did. And got half a breath before the next spasm drove it back out of her.

Chapter 55

WHEN AT LAST CONNIE STOPPED, JOHN PULLED HER IN. She was shaking now with the exhaustion and the cold.

He didn't even think about it, just swept her up in his arms and looked for a place to go. Behind was the palace, but the hotel was too far. She needed to get warm now.

He turned left and headed for the end of the building's stone wall. It opened into a narrow street to the left. Shops and cafés lined the far side, but they were closed and shuttered at this hour. To the right, a broad square opened before them. The front of the building she'd been sick upon soared above them. An older couple came out a door at the top of a half flight of steps leading to the massive doors. He headed over and the couple held the door for him, letting a warm light spill down the stairs.

He nodded in thanks as he carried Connie through. She lay against his chest and shook as the shivers wracked through her almost as hard as the sickness. She'd wrung herself out but good.

Through the doors, he stumbled to a halt and for just a moment forgot about the woman in his arms. He'd crossed into another world, one of gold and wonder. She'd been sick against the wall of a church. A cathedral.

Pillars of red brick soared fifty feet or more to the distant ceiling. He wandered forward across a diamond-laid aisle of marble between rows of worn wooden pews.

A pulpit fit for a pope soared above the congregation. Fanciful carvings evoked an era of knights and kings more than God and angels.

He reached the center of the nave and staggered to a halt.

"Holy crap."

Despite the shivers that still shook her, Connie stirred and looked to see what had stopped him and caught his attention. He'd never imagined she could feel fragile, but she did.

"What in the world?"

A statue of a great gray horse, twice life-size and dressed in golden armor, stood upon a massive pedestal. Astride his back, an equally ornately clad knight wielded a golden sword. Beneath his feet, a lance driven deep in its chest, a fearsome dragon struggled for the last time. He lay on a deathbed of human skulls, broken bones, and harsh rock.

"Well, ain't that something."

"St. George and the Dragon."

Of course Connie would know who it was.

"The knight and the horse represent the Kingdom of Sweden, the dragon her vanquished foes, mostly the Danes."

She turned her attention back to him. "You can put me down now, John."

He considered for a moment, but that was all. "Nope. Can't say as I will. Things make sense when you're right where you are. And they haven't been making sense when there's any distance between us. Besides, I have some questions." He headed over to sit in a pew across the wide central nave that would let them face the statue.

The cathedral was empty at this hour, anyone with common sense having long since gone to bed.

She tried to push out of his arms but was still weak enough to make her easy to hold. He could see her considering some more drastic actions but then, thankfully, dismissing them. She might be a woman who was wrung out, but she was U.S. Army Special Forces. His throat was still sore from the last female soldier who'd been pissed at him.

Finally, she lay her head back on his shoulder. "So ask." Her voice was filled with infinite exhaustion.

He considered the hundred questions, the thousand, but one burned brightest among them.

"Why did you leave?"

"It was time for your family to be—"

"Connie," he cut her off and fought to keep the heat he felt out of his voice, "you are sitting in a cathedral that's probably older than our country, probably a couple times older, and that seems a pretty lousy place to be telling a lie."

"I'm not. I really thin—"

"Okay. Different question." He stared up at the statue for a long moment. Was it possible she didn't know why she'd left? Sitting here in this old church, with her curled so wonderfully in his arms, maybe it was time to slay a few dragons. He didn't know them all, but he could make a few guesses.

"I know you care about people. I know you do. You cared for Grumps, didn't you?"

"I…" She buried her face in his shoulder a moment. "I fixed his tractor."

"You. Fixed. His. Tractor." That was an answer?

Either he was wrong about the woman or he was losing his mind.

"Yes."

"And that means… what? That you like fixing tractors?"

"No. Well, I do, though that was my first one, but that wasn't the point."

"And the point was?" It was like pulling teeth to get past her shields.

She struggled up from his lap until she sat upright across his knees, half turned to face him.

"John, you have this family. And… and they love you." She waved her arms as if encompassing the world and almost pitched herself from his lap. "I've never seen anything like it. Tighter than a flight crew. As close as my dad and me. Maybe even more." The last a surprised whisper, then a throat clearing.

"Your parents are so proud of you, and Larry worships you, and Noreen wants to be just like you. You're the ultimate big brother symbol brought to real life."

"They're just my family." Mostly.

Before he could follow where that ugly-ass thought led, she jabbed his shoulder hard enough to hurt right in the nerve cluster. If not for layers of shirt, vest, and parka, he'd be on the floor whimpering right now.

"No! Don't! Don't you dare belittle them for even a second. You have no idea. I—"

This time when she went to stand, he let her go. Doubted he could hold her back if he tried. She strode over to the statue and back. Sharp, purposeful strides of a soldier, though her arms still wrapped tightly about herself. She still fought the bone-deep chill.

Twice, three times she made the journey over and

back, stamping across the old stone floor and back. Odd-shaped stones with engravings… crypts. She was walking over the graves of kings long dead and buried.

She stopped in front of him and faced him square on.

"How many times did Paps help with your homework? Can you count how many meals your ma has made for you? How often did you stop what you wanted to be doing to babysit your little sister? How many thousand lessons did you learn from Grumps about how to be a man?"

"How should I know? A lot. It's what you do."

"It's what you do." She let her repetition stretch into silence. "It's what you do, John. You probably won't understand this. No reason you should. I'll be glad for you if you can't." She cricked her neck to one side, and he could hear joints popping in the midnight silence of the cathedral.

"My mom died when I was three. I don't remember her at all." She spoke fast and hard, as if giving a lecture. As if maybe if she said the words fast enough, dead enough, she wouldn't feel them, even though he could see how much each one cost her.

"Maybe that's when remembering things became so important to me. My dad, him they shot down when I was thirteen. Somewhere unknown, unrecorded. That's my family. Done. Gone. A feeble grandmother who lived off an Army pension, feeding me if she remembered. No one. From seventh grade on, whether I succeeded or failed was up to me and me alone. The only thing that poor old woman did for me was hang on until I was sixteen so that I didn't have to enter the foster care system. Shopping, homework, paying the electric bill, fixing the water heater. That was all me."

He wanted to reach for her. For fear she would crack like old stone and crumble before him, never to be put back together. But her eyes stopped him. They weren't looking at him. They were focused somewhere over his head, much farther away than the cathedral walls.

"And then I met Grumps. You know, he came to me my first morning there at your house. At your home. I was standing in the kitchen trying to figure out if it was okay to make breakfast before anyone was up. He never said a word. We made oatmeal together, leaned back against the counter side by side as we ate it from mismatched bowls. Not all Army issue, but old bowls, with chips and history and care. He headed outside at first light and I just followed along. I don't know why. Guess I was supposed to."

She blinked and squinted against the dawn light she was seeing in her too perfect memory.

"We watched the sunrise over those endless fields that surround your place. They go on forever, John. You've lived among them. Stable. Always there. You can't appreciate the wonder of that. All that work and heart and the soul of all that dark, rich soil. And the generations of effort that it took to make and maintain those fields.

"After sunrise, he led me into the barn to this beat-up old rust-bucket of a worn-down tractor. When he patted her on the radiator, I knew. He loved that machine. He loved it like the land. And he was sharing it with me…"

Now her face did begin to crumble. Her jaw shook, she started blinking and couldn't stop. She leaned forward so that her hair spilled over her face as she covered it with her hands.

"He shared it with me. Because he knew. Though we'd never spoken a word to each other. He knew what I didn't have. Could see the hole in me where I'm supposed to have a heart. I'm a goddamn walking, talking Tin Man, John. So, Grumps gave me a reason to be there. To be with him. He believed that I was a whole person. You have no idea what that feels like."

As her knees went loose, he gathered her back into his arms.

"Oh god, John. I miss that old man so much. How can you love someone that much who you've only known for three days? How?"

He held her as she wept against his shoulder. Not the wracking, silent, dry-eyed battles that she fought with her inner demons. She wept softly from simple grief.

How can you love someone that much who you barely knew?

He held her tighter.

It wasn't so hard. Not so hard at all.

Chapter 56

CONNIE FELT WRUNG OUT, DRAINED TO THE VERY CORE, as she lay in John's arms with her head resting on his shoulder. She considered adding embarrassed to the list but finally rejected it. In an odd way, she felt good, light even. Free of the burden she hadn't known she carried, didn't know what it had been. She simply felt free from beneath its pressing weight.

She slid from his lap until they sat side by side with her leaning safe inside the protective curve of his strong right arm. They held hands across, his left to her right, and gazed at St. George and his golden sword raised high before the final deathblow to the serpent below.

They sat quietly for a long time in the pew. Just at peace. Stopped. She'd leaned her head on his shoulder and he'd rested his cheek on her hair.

When the night could get no quieter, Connie finally found the space inside to speak. Though she kept her voice to little more than a whisper, it seemed to fill the cathedral. Not with long, creepy echoes, but as if it enjoyed traveling about the space.

"I'm sorry, John. I shouldn't have left, but I didn't think I had a choice. I couldn't get far enough from the memories. Everywhere I went, there was someone talking about Grumps. When I went out to stand by the fields, I'd remember the three mornings we had stood there together in silence and watched the sun come up over those beautiful fields. In the barn…" She let her voice trail off because she couldn't find the heart to speak of it.

It seemed wrong to compare the ornate and golden wonder of Stockholm Cathedral with an old barn, but standing in the latter was as close as she'd ever come to a religious experience. In the empty tractor bay, with the sun still shining down from the barn's high windows, she could hear Grumps's easy laugh. The old pine walls whispering with his stories. The air even more quiet than when he napped in the sunlight.

"You have an amazing family. Grumps. Your mother and father—"

"He's not my father."

Connie could feel the tension shoot into John even as he bit off the last word too late.

His cheek came off her head. She had to grab quickly to keep his arm wrapped around her. Trap it there to keep him in place.

"Whoa, John. No, you don't. You don't get to give me this monster lesson in not running away and then do the same yourself. Especially not after a statement like that. What do you mean Paps isn't your father? You're so much like him."

The silence lasted a long time. The rigid tension that she could feel in his arm no longer held her close but rather stayed frozen where she'd pinned it across her shoulder. She could see his jaw clenched against the words.

Finally, all at once, like an old keeper nut finally letting go of its rusty bolt, the tension drained out of him.

"A drunk killed my father. Ran him over outside a restaurant in Tulsa."

"How old were you?" She could see him swallow hard. She blinked hard. They'd both lost fathers. Her heart bled for him.

"I wasn't any age. I wasn't born yet."

"But how…" She could see it hurt him just as much as it had her, maybe more. He'd never even known his own father. At least she'd had that before she lost him.

"My mama loved my father, she told me that often. And like you, she loved my family. Grumps and Liza took her in, as if there were any question, though she's still surprised to this day. And Paps, apparently he was mad for her since the first time he saw her on John's arm. I'm named for my father. Paps convinced her to marry him even before I was born. She says it took a goodly while, but she'd learned to love the man who she'd thought only showed her kindness. A proposal and kindness she'd accepted in a 'fit of common sense,' as she called it."

Connie twisted a little in the pew until she could rest her hand on that beautiful broad chest of his. Until she could feel his heart beating through the heavy flannel shirt that showed through his open jacket. Until her own heartbeat echoed his.

"Mama belongs there. Bore Paps three more children. She's family. I've always felt outside of that. Not my family."

Connie jerked her hand back, felt as if she'd been burned. This man, so loved by his family, so in love with his family… And he thought he didn't belong! She'd never had family. Not since the day her father burned and fell out of the sky.

How could he foreswear such a gift? How could he be so thoroughly and completely wrong?

Her fist clenched, curled tighter than any knight grasping the pommel of his golden sword.

And she pounded that fist against John's chest hard enough that the air whooshed out of him.

His curse would have echoed around the church if he'd had enough air to create more than a whisper.

She half rose to drive another blow.

John caught her fist just inches from his chest. She managed to drive home anyway and he grunted.

Before she could attack him again, he finally leveraged his much greater strength to pin her hands together.

She considered head-butting him to see if that would drive some sense into him.

"What the hell, Davis?"

Connie rose and jerked her hands free. She took a half-dozen steps away. Stared down at the gravestones that carpeted the floor. That were the floor. A thousand years of family spread below her feet until the names were erased, worn away, and forgotten with age.

She strode back to stand in front of him. When she raised her hands he flinched. She paused for a moment, hands open until they both relaxed a bit, then she rested her palms on his shoulders. Sat across his knees.

Not knowing what else to do, she kissed him lightly and looked deep into those wonderful, dark, pained eyes.

"Paps is so goddamn proud of you. You're his favorite. Can't you see that? I don't know why. I mean you're so goddamn stupid. But he worships you. Your whole family does."

John tried to shake it off, but she rested her hand on his cheek to hold his focus on her.

"You didn't see it. When you drove the tractor into

the Night Before the Night Before, your mama had to wipe Paps's eyes so others couldn't see he was crying. He's that proud of you. Larry wishes he could fly like his big brother but he loves the farm too much. Your little sister is a U.S. Army officer because of you, for crying out loud." She dug the silver dollar out of her shirt pocket and held it right in front of him. So close his eyes crossed as he tried to focus on it.

"Here's proof." She looked at the coin herself. Still couldn't make sense of how it made her feel and she rammed it back into her pocket, careful to button the flap over it.

"I've never seen someone who belongs so deeply. I don't know how you could ever leave. I doubt if I could if I had that."

John studied her a long time. Looked at her until she removed her hands from his shoulders, though she resisted the urge to wipe at her face to check it for bearing grease or some other smudge that made him study her so.

"They're the reason I left," John whispered. "I fly to keep them safe."

Connie could only blink as she sat across his knees and saw the truth in his eyes. His heart was bigger than the world. The amount of love it held was something she could only pretend to understand.

At long last, he raised his hands, cupped her cheeks, and pulled her forward. He kissed her on the forehead, a kiss befitting the magnificent cathedral.

Ever so gently he shifted her until once again she sat inside the curve of his arm. Until once again her head rested on his shoulder and his cheek on her hair. Without a word, they sat together and watched until the predawn light colored the stained-glass window and dappled the great, golden warrior with its light.

Caught in that moment before he slayed the dragon.

Chapter 57

BEALE RAN *VENGEANCE* RIGHT UP THE THROAT OF A fjord. It narrowed on both sides, sheer cliffs.

Connie watched astern in the dual vision her helmet afforded. In the infrared view displayed by ADAS across the inside of her visor, she could see *Viper* in tight formation, just two rotors back and off to the side.

Beyond the visor, the outside world was all darkness. Inside the Hawk, she could see the four Swedish Special Operation Group operators dressed in white and dead-branch camouflage. Even their weapons were painted white, except for the blue stocks that indicated they were loaded with nonlethal training rounds.

The SOGs were watching through the visors of their borrowed ADAS helmets. They were being fed the view only as the tactical displays were too highly classified to share, even with friendly special forces. They pointed and gestured as if they were looking out a window. Their Swedish remained soft spoken to not interfere with flight operations, but she could hear the wonder in their voices. Connie already had trouble remembering any other way to see the tactical world outside the chopper.

She was glad to be aloft. She could feel the edge coming back. A week on the ground had dulled reactions. They needed this training run far more than the Swedish SOGs. The unofficial word was that the real mission was finally coming and it was coming hot.

Time to get ready.

Connie glanced forward as Major Beale drove into the head of the fjord. It closed abruptly from a quarter mile wide to a space too narrow for even a Little Bird, never mind a Black Hawk. The passengers in the back became quite excited, shifting toward the rear of the chopper as the head wall rushed at them, filling their visors with the minute details of what they appeared to be about to crash into. The four SOGs were finally pressed back against the cargo net to which they were clipped.

They stopped talking entirely as Major Beale pulled up the nose and converted speed into climb, cresting the headwall by less than a dozen feet. Her rotor stirred a cloud of snow as did *Viper*'s, who'd shifted left to fly beside her. That brought many sounds of relief in Swedish.

"Drop in twenty," the Major announced.

The commandos scrambled to change out the ADAS helmets for their own more familiar gear.

"Ten."

Connie popped her harness and snapped in a monkey line. She slid open the cargo door on her side and kicked out a fast rope as John did the same on his.

The Major yanked the chopper to a halt.

"Go!"

The guys didn't hesitate; this was more familiar territory than riding in a helicopter flown to the very edge by SOAR. They jumped out the doors and wrapped arms and legs around the inch-and-three-quarters, heavy-woven rope. In seconds they'd slid the twenty meters to the ground. Not bad, they were down clean in less than ten seconds from the "Go."

"Clear," she and John called in unison.

The Major slid back the way they'd come as Connie hand-over-handed the rope back aboard. In combat they'd just slap the release and be shed of the things. In standard training exercises, they'd send a cleanup team later to gather the ropes. But this time they'd decided not to litter a foreign country or risk losing them in the falling snow, and hauled them back aboard the chopper.

John slapped her on the shoulder, job well done.

She did the same to him.

By the time the ropes were coiled and stowed, and the cargo doors closed, the chopper hovered once again below the ridgeline of the fjord. The sound of the stealth rotors bounced oddly off the steep canyon walls. Not the heavy thop, thop, thop of a four-blade Black Hawk. Faster, softer, smoother. It made more for a feeling of floating than flying.

A little woozy from lack of sleep, Connie slid back into her seat and snapped in. She knew how to compensate for it. Had been trained in the required extra attention to detail, to drink juice in little sips to keep the blood sugar up. If they did any weapons work, she'd need to lead her target just a little more to compensate for slower reactions on the trigger. But she didn't begrudge the loss of sleep.

They'd spent the day planning and briefing for tonight's mission. Giving the two SOG squads daytime training rides to familiarize them with what a SOAR Black Hawk was likely to do. Though it still hadn't prepared them for Major Emily Beale in combat mode.

And last night. She'd always cherish last night.

She and John had sat quietly a long time. Just at peace. Stopped.

With the dawn, she told John about her father. How they'd fit together. Belonged together. She could see now that her father had not been a man filled with joy like Grumps. But he was filled with dedication. To his country and to his daughter. And that too had been a fine gift.

The priest had found them there, still leaning against each other, more asleep than awake. And the cathedral, a dark shroud of mystery in the night, now glittered with the morning light streaming through the stained glass. In the daylight, the dragon was less fearsome and the horse and knight were bolder and even stronger.

They'd arrived back at the airfield with barely time to eat and shower before the first briefing, but it had been worth every minute of it.

———

The Majors landed the helicopters in a small cove near the head of the fjord for thirty minutes. Connie had flown with commanders who would use the opportunity for a break, start a snowball fight or something. But that wasn't standard practice aboard *Vengeance* or *Viper*. Even on a training flight, Beale kept the rotors ticking over, ready to respond instantly to any emergency call. Thirty seconds faster off the ground could mean someone's life in combat.

Normally they simply sat and waited, a skill any Special Forces operative had long since mastered.

Connie was just settling into a systems check when Major Beale spoke over the intercom. "Sergeant Davis. Let's take a walk together. Clay, you've got the ship."

Connie glanced forward, but the Major had already

peeled her helmet and was out her door. A glance at John simply revealed a shrug. Connie peeled her helmet and popped the cargo bay door. John tossed her his ridiculous red-and-orange woolen hat as she exited into the slap-cold of a Swedish winter night. She pulled it on and almost face-planted in the snow as it slid down over her eyes.

She shoved it back on her head and followed Major Beale into the night. They walked half along the hard, tide-packed sand beach of the little cove, the clouds blotting out any hint of light. Only the faintest hint of white from the small breaking waves kept Connie on track.

"I asked you a question two weeks ago."

Connie didn't have to ask for clarification. Could the Major trust her? No one had ever asked her such a question before. She'd always been able to prove herself. But Major Beale operated at some higher standard than any of Connie's prior commanders.

"I remember, ma'am."

"I'm still having trouble answering that question."

Connie tried not to feel the slap. Even though she knew she wasn't good at it, Connie tried to see it from the Major's point of view, just as John had explained military risk using the President's point of view.

They had flown together for just over a month. And during that time the Major had seen Connie run from the hangar panicked that John might like her. Next Connie had offered a horrid rift in the Major's crew when she and John had fought so. But they were past that now. That should be obvious.

"As I said before, ma'am, trus—"

"I know. I know. Must be earned."

The silence stretched for another hundred meters down the beach.

"Last night's poker game was one of the nastiest, most spiteful things I've ever seen. The two of you battering at each other's defenses until it was too painful to watch. I almost cried out in relief when Mark ended it."

They'd fixed that.

"I half expected one or both of you to come back bloody. I sent Tim after you, but you were too fast and he couldn't find you."

Connie was thankful for that little bit at least. Barfing herself senseless against a church wall was not a side of herself she'd like many people to see.

"That you somehow resolved that without bloodshed makes me feel much better."

Again the silence continued until they neared the end of the strand.

"I considered aborting the mission for personnel reasons until I could get a crew replacement. I actually had them spooling up a jet to get Kee here, but she's not ready. Now I have to decide if you are."

The footsteps in the darkness stopped beside her. Connie stopped and turned, able to see the Major as the faintest of outlines against the waiting Black Hawks.

The silence stretched until Connie caught herself shifting foot to foot to stay warm.

"I flew once with your father."

Connie gasped. It was all she could do.

"What was he like?" Connie had never had anyone to tell her. She'd imagined him a thousand ways in combat versus at home, but never found anyone to ask.

"Quiet, like you. Brilliant, like you. Dedicated, like you."

Connie liked that. Liked honoring her father by being like the best parts of him.

"I keep thinking of a piece of advice he gave me just weeks before his death."

Connie held her breath so that she wouldn't miss a word, unable to believe that she would get words from somewhere other than her memories.

"You're a natural mechanic, Connie. I've never seen the like, nor has Mark, nor has John."

She nodded for the Major to continue. Connie knew the gesture was invisible in the darkness, but she couldn't have managed to speak if her life depended on it.

"He was also a man of great heart. A man I'd have been proud to have on my crew. He cared about those he flew with. Perhaps more than he cared for his own life. I don't know what happened to him. I also still don't know if among all that you've inherited from your father, you also inherited his heart. That's what I need to know."

The major didn't wait for an answer. She turned and began walking back to the choppers.

Connie finally whispered into the empty darkness, "I need to know, too."

Chapter 58

CONNIE RETURNED TO THE HELICOPTER JUST MINUTES ahead of the prearranged "go" time. John took the woolen cap and squeezed her hand through the thick wool. It steadied her heart rate. Calmed her nerves.

At the predesignated second, Major Beale yanked the collective and shoved the cyclic forward. In moments they were up and out of the fjord and racing along at ten meters above the ground, well below tree level.

The heavy overcast and light snow were ideal. They'd be nearly invisible and the rotor noise was muted by the descending flakes. A blizzard would be even better. Be nice to see how the stealth mods behaved in a high-wind, zero-visibility attack scenario. Already the ADAS was proving a more than fair replacement for the FLIR.

Connie watched as they flew along the wide track of a groomed cross-country ski trail that rolled and dipped along the gentle snow-shrouded hills, finally opening out over a small road. From there, a farmer's field led to a swath cleared by recent logging. The route was longer than their original path in, but it kept the Hawks well below radar level and didn't recross territory where they might have been spotted earlier or even tracked. If the SOG commandos hadn't finished their job capturing the Swedish air hangar that was tonight's training target, they'd need all the stealth they could find.

Viper followed close behind, they were right in the groove.

"Ten miles," Clay called out.

Connie caught herself checking her gun and kicking a boot against the loaded ammo can. No live ammo tonight—it would be a battle of training lasers—but habits were part of survival, so she didn't stop her full weapons systems check.

They slipped over a high bank and down into a riverbed, following it north and west. This would get them within a mile of the target.

Connie saw a weather update from the copilot flash up in the visor. The only thing that really mattered was cold. It was a dozen degrees below freezing and they were barely a thousand feet above sea level. No compensation for high altitude or hot, thin air tonight. The Hawk was running at full performance. Of course, now they had to watch for icing conditions.

"Two miles."

The target, one of the Swedish Air Force's Gripen jet hangars, had been warned, but not warned. They'd been rearmed with Simunitions weapons, fairly indistinguishable from the real thing except that they had solid-blue painted stocks and would only take specialized, nonlethal rounds. But no special security protocols, standard patrols only.

"Silence from the ground team," Clay reported.

"Power up," the Major called out.

It was weird to not hear the miniguns' electric motors spin up as a high whine on the edge of her hearing. Instead she heard distinct clicks as the lasers were switched to standby. Tight enough beams to register hits on body sensors, but diffuse enough to not blind if they impacted someone who didn't have his specialized goggles in place.

"Thirty seconds. Training weapons only."

Connie glanced down at the FN SCAR strapped across her chest, blue stock folded in. Good to go.

She counted halfway down in her head, then the Major broke cover and rolled over the last kilometer up the road at full throttle. They passed the red stoplight halfway there.

The Swedes were very smart. They didn't depend on large, centralized bases for their air defense. One big bomb in the center of an air base runway and everything would go to crap. England had learned that lesson the hard way in WWII. Sweden planted her jets in pairs in underground hangers all over the country. Their runways were straight stretches of road with a stoplight at either end. Set the light to red to stop car traffic, roll out the planes, and take off from deep in the safety of the surrounding trees; the jets were invisible except from straight above until they were already at fighting speed.

The fact that the light was red could mean the attack by the commandos was a success and they'd blocked the road in preparation for the Black Hawks' arrival. Or they were about to face down a pair of Swedish fast-movers head on.

With a roll of her thumb Connie zoomed her ADAS view out to the limits. Nothing ahead. Not even any sign of the hangar. There'd been the stoplight on the empty stretch of road, so this had to be the right road. Even as she felt the Major pulling back on the cyclic to slow them down, a reflector, bright in the infrared searchlight, arced through the air and landed in the middle of the road.

Beale flew one rotor past the beacon and thumped down onto the road with *Viper* one rotor back. Two seconds early.

Turning to the side, Connie could see the hangar, its broad doors set back into the hill beside the road. One of the bay doors stood open, and bright flashes of Simunitions fire glittered in the night.

John rose out of his seat and slammed open the cargo bay door, readying to assist anyone in the evac area. Connie swept the area with her laser-simulated minigun, careful to avoid the SOG commandos with the infrared reflective Swedish flags on their gear. Crazy Tim "killed" the jets with two quick bursts of red light.

Connie could hear that the rotors were flat but at full chop, ready for instant departure.

The commandos rolled in, four guys, with two prisoners and a stack of laptops and paper notebooks. This was over a DAP Hawk's weight limit in Afghanistan. But, she had to remind herself, they were now low and cold and they weren't carrying a full weapons load, which was the real limiting factor on crew-carrying for the DAP. She usually carried so much hammer force that excess crew was not an option.

They were aloft twenty-eight seconds after arrival and sliding off into the night. They swept less than five feet over a Volvo sedan parked at the red light. The driver, who'd gotten out to stand beside his car and see what he could see, plastered himself on the road as they roared by close overhead. No running lights and moving at one hundred and fifty knots and now, with the stealth upgrades to her rotors, too quiet for anyone to properly judge the distance. The motorist never knew what blew by him. Connie could learn to seriously like this. Rolling right, the Major was back in the riverbed and on her way out.

They dropped the commandos and their "captives" on a Swedish Navy Visby-class corvette anchored off Stockholm. The ship had a single helipad, so the *Vengeance* and *Viper* took turns disgorging the SOGs and their captives. It would give a chance for the SOGs and the Swedish Navy to razz their captured Air Force brethren. A replacement crew would already be in place back in the hangar.

The Swedes made a big deal over them before they left. Not in how neatly the operation had gone, nor how interesting their helicopters were. Connie had expected both of those.

No. A customs inspector came out and insisted on seeing their military IDs and their passports while Major Henderson waited overhead. This struck her as especially odd. Sweden was a member of the European Union, which meant U.S. forces didn't need their passports to cross into any country for a fair way around. The inspector pulled out a stamp and whacked each of their passports with an exit stamp.

"You have now taken exit of our country."

No one knew what to make of it. This wasn't covered in the exercise briefing. They'd just been thrown out of the country.

Within ten seconds of both DAPs being aloft, they were redirected over an encrypted circuit.

They didn't return to Stockholm's Arlanda Airport but instead continued out over the Baltic Sea and landed on the USS *Germantown*, a Whidbey Island-class dock-landing ship. The deck crew rolled the *Vengeance* aside while they were still shutting her down to make room for Mark. In moments both *Vengeance* and *Viper* were tied down to the deck and secure.

Connie and John worked in easy harmony double-checking the tie-down work of the Germantown's crew. Maybe they really had resolved whatever in the hell was going on between them. Connie certainly hoped so.

A CSAR Hawk was also on the deck, though there was no crew about.

"That's an 'M.'" Connie pointed it out to John.

The rotor blades on the combat search and rescue bird were wider than a standard blade. Not just CSAR, it had SOAR's MH60-M upgrade. Having that bird sitting on the deck next to the DAPs was not the most encouraging sign she'd ever seen.

A blast of wind brushed her aside, until she had to grab a handhold on the Hawk to stay upright. An AgustaWestland AW169 with French civilian markings settled out of the night onto the deck. Not quite room to land with the three Black Hawks aboard, so it hovered with an open cargo door over the edge of the deck.

A man in U.S. Naval Commander insignia came up. "Here is the rest of your crew." He nodded toward the helicopter.

Four guys, each with enough gear to bury a mule, jumped down and landed lightly despite their loads. She recognized the leader, having flown with Colonel Gibson many times in Afghanistan.

"Hey, Michael, thought you were still in the sand," Major Henderson greeted him jovially.

The Delta Force operator inspected the overcast sky and the flakes of snow drifting out of the cold sky.

"I might wish I still was."

CSAR and Delta Force. The night just got a whole lot more interesting. And the mission suddenly too real. Here they were in Europe, but their passports were clearly marked as having left. Now, with D-boys along, it meant they would be flying down the knife's edge.

The Naval Commander shouted to be heard over the sound of the departing AW169. "We've taken the liberty of moving your gear aboard from your hotel. Let me show you to your cabins to change into civvies. Your boat leaves in five minutes."

Five minutes didn't leave Connie time to ask, "What boat?"

She patted the nose of *Vengeance* for luck, then they all hurried below to change.

Chapter 59

"NOW THIS IS TRAVELING IN STYLE." ON THE LOWEST deck of the landing ship, Connie climbed into the backseat of a Saab 9-5 and John slid in beside her. Certainly one of the more surreal things she'd done lately, climbing into a luxury automobile when the nearest land lay at least twenty miles away through a dark and snowy night.

Two of the D-boys took the front seat. Colonel Gibson and the other D-boy loaded up with the two Majors in the car beside them. The rest of the crew loaded into a third one. With the typical imagination of the Swedes, the three cars were black, silver, and gray.

A loud thump and whine shook all of the cars, louder than the idling ship's engines. The back end of the ship unhinged. A massive landing ramp fifty feet wide and just as long lowered, exposing the night sky and the rolling waves of the Baltic Sea. The three cars were parked on an LCAC, a seriously large landing craft. These were not the little twelve-foot-wide landing craft of the Normandy beaches that chugged along at ten miles per hour and could dump forty troops or a jeep in the low surf.

The Navy's modern idea of a landing craft was fifty feet wide and ninety feet long, flew on a cushion of air, and could deliver an Abrams MBT. Last Connie had checked, a main battle tank weighed almost seventy tons. All three cars together weighed less than five, a load so small as to be laughable.

She was in a car on a landing craft, parked inside the cargo hold of a U.S. warship. Sometimes the Army was just too cool for words.

With a roar that hurt her ears despite the car's insulation, the fans of the landing craft screamed to life. All around them, the large rubber skirt of the landing craft inflated. In a moment, they lifted a few inches off the deck and were sliding out of the back of the ship, down the ramp, and into the ocean.

"It makes perfect sense." She had to shout a little for John to stand a chance of hearing her. "If you want to sneak into a friendly country you've just left, climb aboard a ninety-foot-long military landing craft. What? We're going to just drive to the nearest road and drop off three cars full of Special Forces troops?"

He nodded in response, she could just make out his grin that went with it. In the darkness of the backseat, despite the D-boys sitting in the front, she risked brushing her fingers along his arm, as if steadying herself. She wasn't afraid or worried. She simply liked the feeling of touching him.

They roared ahead, the craft weaving a little as it weathered the chop on the Baltic Sea.

"How fast?" John shouted, but she could only shrug.

One of the D-boys, neither of whom had yet to speak their names, called back. "This lightly loaded, she can cruise at seventy knots. If there's trouble..." he shrugged.

At over eighty miles per hour they were moving almost half the speed of a Black Hawk. Except this ship weighed eighty tons empty, compared with the Black Hawk's eleven tons fully loaded.

When they slowed, it was a major relief.

In moments, the deck angle changed as if they were climbing some hill out in the ocean. With the air cushion inflated, there was no way for the occupants of the center cargo bay to see anything. That was up to the hovercraft's crew perched up in their little forward turret two stories above the deck.

Another minute and the fans wound down to a mere roar. Connie could feel the thump as they settled to the ground. A loud hiss sounded as the forward air bag deflated and the front ramps lowered. A one-lane dirt road started not ten feet in front of the ramp.

Their car slid into line third and they were off.

She glanced over her shoulder to see the gates raise and the massive bulbous nose of the craft reinflate. Even before the cars crested the first rise of the road, the hovercraft slid back into the dark night.

———

Connie woke twenty minutes later by the car's dashboard clock. The other two cars were nowhere to be seen. They were on a busy highway pulling into early-morning Stockholm traffic.

They turned off and into Old Stockholm, right back where they started. This was crazy. John smiled at her again. She'd napped with her head against the door. She wished it had been on his shoulder but was glad her instincts had won that battle. Sleeping on John's shoulder would not be a good choice in front of the Delta operators.

Together they looked to their left just before the palace. The streets were too small, too winding, but right

down there St. George still stood upon the broken body
of his dragon. It was good to know. She squeezed John's
arm for a moment, and he flexed the muscles beneath her
fingers in return as they drove over the bridge she'd run
across and away from him just thirty-six hours before.

At the hotel's curb, none of the other Saabs near
them in line seemed to be the ones belonging to the
other two crews. A valet met their car and handed the
driver a marker.

The four of them clustered just before the carpeted
entrance to the hotel.

"Where…" Connie stopped when she saw the driver
hold up the marker. It had two tags. A large bronze disk
with a three-digit number stamped on it to reclaim the
car. And a paper tag that read, "Mezzanine Conference
Room 14."

The nameless D-boy tore off a tiny bit of the "4" and
dropped it in the garbage bin by the door. Just inside,
the rest of the "4" and part of the "M" went into a
standing ashtray.

Connie stopped watching him after that.

It took them some effort to locate Mezzanine
Conference Room 14. It didn't appear on any of the
discreet conference room maps placed conveniently
about. It was a small, innocuous door at the end of
a long hallway that appeared to have only restrooms
and a water fountain. Three layers of security greeted
them. The first, dressed as a hotel busboy, was cleared
by showing her military ID. The second by a finger-
print scanner. The last, a visual by Frank Adams, the
Secret Service agent in charge of the Presidential
Protection Detail.

She thought about how she'd behaved the last time she'd been in front of him at the poker table and did her best not to look away in embarrassment.

He nodded to her politely. "Ma'am." Then he smiled slightly. "We're also well-trained in what not to see. You have no worries."

Connie blew out her breath and smiled in return. "Uh, thanks." Not brilliant, but she didn't have anything much better anyway.

"Though you may want to rethink..." He glanced down at her hand.

It was clasped in John's. She shook it loose. It was clearly a surprise to both of them.

She didn't know what to say.

"We thought," John rumbled out easily, "that we'd be less conspicuous if we appeared to be a couple."

"Good thinking, sir, ma'am." Then Agent Adams winked at her.

"Connie." The least she could offer in thanks was her first name.

"Yes, ma'am." She could hear the silent laugh as they crossed into the room. On duty, she'd be "ma'am" or Sergeant Davis. And probably off duty as well.

The inside of the room was something different than she'd expect in the only five-star hotel in the country. It had the luxury. Dark paneled and deeply carpeted in a luxuriously rich blue, and the ceiling was ornately carved in plaster painted in splendid blues and golds. A large oak table dominated the room. But that's where "expected" came to an abrupt end.

The entire middle of the table was a glass screen that was lit from within. On it glowed a detailed map she didn't recognize. Along one wall ran a bank of monitors and computers that would be far more fitting in a combat command center, each station fronted with a high-back, carved chair from the "expected" category for a banquet rather than for the technicians who must sit there. The seats were empty at the moment. Some serious comm and isolation gear. She and John walked over to scan a tall rack of electronics.

Unless this room was very isolated, perhaps with steel plate in the walls and ceiling, there were going to be a lot of very angry people in the hotel. No cell phone or other wireless device was likely to be working anywhere close by.

"Serious shielding," Tim whispered over her and John's shoulders.

"Hey, buddy." John grabbed Tim's arm around the bicep and shook him in a friendly way. A friendly way that would cause a lesser man to flap about as if hurricane tossed.

Tim merely punched John in the arm.

The last of the D-boys drifted in, barely stirring the air as he moved. Behind him the doors whooshed closed, and Connie could feel the air pressure change as they seated home.

Tight door seals. Shielding. Three layers of security. The Grand Hotel offered its guests a great deal more than massage and pickled herring with room service.

Sixteen people in the dark-paneled room.

Two Black Hawk crews. Four Delta Force operators. President Matthews and his Chief of Staff, Daniel something. And two people she didn't know.

"If everyone could have a seat..." The President

waved them all to their chairs around the table as Daniel blanked the table screen.

"Well, Em. As you suggested, plan for the worst. This is bad and the timeline is suddenly very short."

None of them spoke. Clearly the President was waiting for some response, but they all got it. They had trained for years for moments like this. They were here, ready to go, move on.

He cleared his throat.

Looked off to either side, but the two nameless people in the room were keeping their silence as well.

"Before I continue, I need to reemphasize the priority of secrecy on this mission."

"Then perhaps, Mr. President..." Emily didn't quite cut him off, but it was a close thing. "Perhaps some introductions are in order."

The President nodded.

"Daniel Drake Darlington is my Chief of Staff." He looked like a blond, blue-eyed poster boy for a surfing club stuffed into an impeccable three-piece suit. But Connie could see his eyes roving the room and inspecting them one at a time. When his study reached her, she had the impression that the complete detail of her Army file flickered through his memory. Perhaps verbatim. Might be interesting to compare notes as she made her own assessment of him.

The Commander-in-Chief. Self-confident, assured, or trying to appear so. His glance traveled a little too often down to Emily's end of the table. The President looked worried and found some comfort in seeing his childhood friend in the room.

"I'll let Daniel make the rest of the introductions,

as he did the last three months of footwork with our other guests. Except to say this. Gentlemen…" He addressed the two outsiders. "This is the very finest the U.S. Special Forces has to offer. I would trust them with my life. Actually, I have a couple of times."

Connie looked down the table at the two Majors. For once Emily Beale's face was completely unreadable, but her husband acknowledged the compliment with an easy smile. She knew Major Beale had saved the President's life, had done it on national TV. But that Major Henderson had been involved hadn't made the news. And neither had ever said a word. A prior black-in-black operation?

The President sat back and Daniel leaned forward.

"To my left, your mission specialist, Dr. Thomas Williams."

The small, round-faced man waved cheerfully across the table.

A civilian. She didn't need to see anyone else's look to know what must already show on her own face. The risks of the unstated mission had just doubled, at a minimum. Towing along a civilian on a military operation simply didn't work.

"My name," the last unidentified man's accent was deeply Russian, though his English was clear and fast with British overtones, "is Aleksander Rodchenko Fyodorov Stepanov."

Connie didn't need any further introduction to the man. Short dark hair, suit impeccable, he was a fit man in his fifties. He was also one of the power elite in the Ukraine. Not currently in power, but a major player.

"I am the one in need of your help. My task is twofold,

though yours, because your President is a pigheaded politician who underestimates his enemies, is only one."

The President nodded politely in answer to the slur, but it was a good thing they weren't playing poker at the moment. The tension in the hand the President was dealing clenched his jaw too tightly for the polite smile he wore.

"Before he continues," Daniel leaned forward, "I must emphasize that Mr. Stepanov was never in this room. You've never met him. He's never been seen with the President of the United States except in the company of many others during the daytime conferences occurring here at the hotel. Right now it is near midnight and Mr. Stepanov is asleep in his suite on the third floor. Are we clear?"

Mr. Surfer-Boy Daniel was suddenly almost as fierce as Major Beale when she was in a mission briefing. Connie merely nodded her head as others did the same around the table.

Mr. Stepanov pointed his finger at Dr. Williams beside him and then swung it slowly around the table indicating each of them. His assessing gaze followed his finger until he had completed his circuit.

"I need you, each of you." He sat back in his chair for a moment.

"Only together can we stop the next holocaust."

Chapter 60

"WELL," THE UKRAINIAN STATED SOFTLY, "DID THAT get their attention, Daniel? I cannot tell."

John was doing his best to remain stone-faced. Holocaust, not genocide. The man's English was good enough that he would not mix up the two. He was talking about a nuclear threat.

"No pressure? Huh?" John whispered to Connie, but it sounded into the silent room louder than he'd intended.

"Ha!" the Ukrainian barked out. And laughed aloud. "No. No pressure at all, big man. I like him. What's your name?"

"Sergeant John Wallace, sir."

Stepanov nodded and shifted his attention to Connie but kept his finger aimed at John.

"And this one, he is a good fighter? He is good man?"

"The best." Her answer was so fast that it sounded spontaneous to John's ears. "The best." He liked how that sounded.

"Are you, how they say, sweet on him?" He switched his finger and attention. "Are you sweet on her?" Then he nodded to himself before John could think of a reply to form in front of his commanding officers and the Commander-in-Chief.

"Good. You two understand. You remind me of my grandmother and my grandfather whose names I bear as proudly as my heritage. They were an architect and an artist. They always worked for the highest ideal, for the purest form. I remember that with each choice I make." He pointed again back and forth between them, indicating a connection that John felt but had thought remained hidden.

Tim looked at John wide-eyed. They'd known each other since Basic, and he could read Tim's face as easily as in a poker game. Something along the lines of, "No f'ing way. My best buddy can't fall for the fatal disease of being in love." Or close enough.

John considered for a moment and decided that it was true. So he sent Tim the slightest affirmative.

Tim collapsed back in his chair as if he'd been shot and his palms briefly raised outward. Clearly stating, "Not me. Not ever."

"Connection is important," Mr. Stepanov continued. "Me, I have a love, too. She is my country. But she is not an easy mistress. When that bitch Mother Russia came apart, my poor Ukraine, she did not recover well. Since 1991, we have tried to put ourselves back together. Some parts we do well, some parts," he shrugged his big shoulders eloquently, "we do not so well."

John studied the man. They held each other's gaze for a long moment and then shared a slow nod. This was a man John wouldn't want to get in a wrestling match with. One fighter knew another.

Daniel leaned back in. "Aleksander is the leader of the opposition party. The thing we will not help him do is to take over the Ukrainian government, though he is likely to win the next election even as things now stand."

The Ukrainian shook his head slowly. "Only if you do not count the corruption of Gregor and his good buddies and the influence of the army on voting day and—"

"And," President Matthews cut him off, "we do think it would be greatly to our advantage to have Alek sitting in the president's chair. But we can't interfere in another country's politics."

John very carefully didn't look down the table. He and Crazy Tim and then Captain Henderson had aided a nasty little coup in Western Africa not all that long ago. Different time, different administration. The dictator's unexpected fall had also aborted a genocide campaign before it really had a chance to get rolling.

"You said holocaust, sir." Leave it to Connie to never lose the thread of the conversation. "That is not a word that I expect you bandy about lightly. And we still don't know Dr. Williams's specialty."

"Oh," President Matthews shrugged negligently as if he'd forgotten to mention it by simplest forgetfulness, "he is our number one expert on Russian nuclear weaponry."

The temperature in the room must have just dropped ten degrees to explain the collective shiver that went around the table.

Chapter 61

"WELL, THAT MUST BE MY CUE." DR. WILLIAMS BEGAN quickly typing on a keyboard and the table lit back up, displaying a large area map.

Connie had thought he might be the hidden card in the deck. His innate cheerfulness might be real, but that didn't get you a seat at this table.

"A bit of history." The map illuminated with national borders outlined in bright yellow. He zoomed back and then nodded in satisfaction.

"It's 1990 and the USSR is about to disintegrate like a poorly designed shrapnel grenade." As he spoke, a counter in the corner of the table's screen started scrolling day, month, year. As it scrolled, the borders shifted, broke, shifted again.

"In 1991, the Ukraine gains her independence. However, a large portion of the Soviet Union's nuclear weapons now suddenly belong to a country that doesn't have a government or economy of her own. Or a military. On the day she declared her freedom, she became the third largest nuclear power on the planet after the U.S. and what would soon become known once again as Russia."

The map was being covered in blue dots the size of a dime, dozens, hundreds. Connie leaned her knee against John's beneath the table as the dots kept multiplying, each one capable of destroying a major city. He leaned back, hard. The dots finally stopped, nearly obliterating the Ukraine behind them. She gasped for a breath she'd forgotten to take.

"Nearly two thousand warheads for rockets and bombers."

Two thousand. Obliterate the two thousand largest cities in the United States and America would cease to exist.

"Everything bigger than Madison, Wisconsin"— Williams waved nonchalantly over the table as if shooing flies—"wiped off the map. Then the radiation and the nuclear winter that would follow close behind. And next retaliation with much larger American and then Russian arsenals. Not a first choice scenario."

The dots started to go away as the days continued to roll by. With each one, Connie came closer to being able to breathe again.

"A very smart leader." The Ukrainian took up the tale. "My good friend Leonid Kravchuk proposed for the Ukraine to become a nonnuclear nation and sent the warheads one by one to Russia for disassembly and destruction. Regrettably, he couldn't manage to hold political power until the job was finished."

Several of the dots turned to question marks.

"Kuchma, who replaced Leonid," Aleksander said in his deep voice, "he is not so much a smart man. But he is a very dangerous man."

"Right." Williams let the clock continue to roll, and the question marks began to blur and split. "These weapons were 'lost,' hidden away during the confusion of those times. Leonid used what little was left of his power to seek them out. As a reward, Kuchma, who had been his prime minister, tried to have him executed. Several times."

"But my friend Leonid is a very smart man. He is still alive." The Ukrainian held up two fingers.

"There are two weapons left. The woman who should have taken command of the country would have finished Leonid's work. She was instead caught and tried for a bit of embezzlement. What is embezzlement in the Ukraine? It is just another way of doing business. A little problem we could have fixed later."

"Yulia's opponent has done far worse, but he was not caught. That was not good for us. That was not good for my Ukraine. Yulia tracked the two missing weapons but was unable to locate them precisely, even with Leonid's help."

"And that"—Aleksander leaned forward—"is where I come in." And he rammed a finger straight down upon the broad map before him.

The many question marks slowly resolved into two. Then, as the timeline neared the present, they jumped about the country several times, sometimes apart, sometimes together. When the calendar stopped running, they became two sharp dots once again.

And they were together.

"Yesterday I received confirmation of this after many long months of work. Today I know where they are. By tomorrow?" His shrug was eloquent. "Who knows where they will go."

President Matthews leaned forward. "And that…" He let his gaze drift over all of them. "That is where you come in."

Chapter 62

"YOU HAVE FOURTEEN HOURS WHILE THIS SHIP STEAMS south. Tonight at dusk we go aloft. Let's get the choppers geared up and then get some sleep."

John, with Connie at his side, hit the *Vengeance* where the bird was tied down on the rear deck of the Germantown. Crazy Tim and his fellow chief attacked *Viper*. He and Connie stripped the training lasers, verified three times that none of the hand weapons on board had the blue-painted stock of training equipment. He knew of more than one time a crew had gone into real battle, and some poor idiot came up with a weapon that couldn't shoot past a hundred meters and wasn't lethal even if it could.

They remounted the 20 mm chain gun in place of the training laser on the weapon's pylon, struggling to make their fingers work in the winter cold augmented by the ship's twenty-plus knots of induced wind chill. A quick double-check showed the fuel tanks full to the brim. A not so fast series of calculations, with double-check, and they loaded up the limit of ammunition they could fly with.

"Did you calc for the new rotors?" John asked Connie, tucking a stray hair behind her ear so that he could see her profile more clearly as she pored over her pad. She sat cross-legged in the main bay of the chopper, the wind loud beyond the cargo doors, but a small center of focused calm where she sat.

She leaned her cheek into his knuckles for a moment, taking away his breath. He'd been so angry at her that it almost didn't make sense how much he wanted to keep touching her. Perhaps he'd been more angry at the loss of her. Piled on top of his anger at losing Grumps, that was a world of hurt he'd been trying to unload on her.

"We picked up 153 pounds for the extra blades, the extra fitting weight on the rotor head for the fifth blade, and the radar cross-section reduction hubs on the main and the tail rotors. I got that, but the ADAS has to be added in and the FLIR taken away, but not its cabling. The FLIR's cabling is still in place. The center of balance shifts a bit as well."

That described it. That was it precisely. She'd shifted his center of balance. More than a bit. He no longer stood up straight when he was standing alone. Beside her, then his world made sense. With her at his side, that's when it felt right side up.

"I think…" She checked her notes again, tilting her head ever so slightly to the side as she did when thinking intensely. "It's only about a half-inch forward, so it's not a real issue. Then I subtracted enough ammunition to compensate for the estimate Dr. Williams provided as the most likely warhead weight adding back in for likely fuel usage. We need to…"

As an experiment, he ran his hand down her hair and over her back. He could feel her shiver and her voice trailed off into silence.

He spoke into the silence as she turned to him.

"I think the chopper's all set."

At her vague nod, John slid the clipboard from her suddenly nerveless fingers. Connie had kept trying to concentrate, trying to double-check a calculation that they'd already made a half-dozen times in the Stockholm conference room.

But all she knew was how close John sat beside her. How he'd been there for her. Time after time. While she fought against her past out at their fence. When she'd finally heaved her pain up onto a Stockholm sidewalk. When she'd finally let herself weep for the death of an old man who'd been kind to her.

She leaned into him and breathed him in. Despite the heavy winter gear, he was John. Her head resting against his chest was the only place the world went quiet. The only place the demons stopped chasing her. The moment of contact was the moment her mind relaxed, let go. Stopped.

"Now we just have to wait until dark. C'mon, you. Let's get out of the wind."

They closed up the Hawk and headed through the heavy double-doors toward the ship's decks immediately in front of the hangar deck.

"Are you hungry?"

She couldn't speak, just shook her head. The only thing in her mind was John's smell. The earth-rich feel of him. Her need, her desperate need to be close to him. Around him. On him.

"I'm with Tim. You've got a single berth?"

She nodded and pointed down the left-hand ladder.

The door to her berth wasn't even shut before she attacked his clothing. Parka, vest, shirt laid open in layers until she could lay her cheek against his bare chest. Until she could place her ear there and hear his heart, feel it, pulsing against her.

Only as she lay against him did she become aware of his hands cradling her close. Of his lips brushing the top of her head.

She felt as if she were finally coming alive. His broad chest, a place of such safety, was a miracle. She leaned back enough to look up into his face. It was deeply shadowed by the weak morning light coming in the lone porthole.

She'd never wanted anyone the way she wanted him. Never.

And their night on the old submarine was much too far in the past. She ran her hands down across the smooth, powerful belly and down over his pants, rubbing her palm hard against him.

"Whoa!" The wind knocked out of him.

Connie stopped his mouth with a kiss.

He went for gentle.

She wanted rough. She shoved his clothes back off those awesome shoulders. Dragged them down far enough to trap his arms when she pushed him back against the closed door. Digging her fingers into those magnificent muscles, she elicited a deep moan from both of them.

Shedding her own clothes with yanks and pulls that seemed to take longer than humanly possible, she managed to get her bare chest against his. She tossed her dog tags over her shoulder, out of her way except for the thin chain. She rubbed back and forth against him using anything, everything. Her fingers, tongue, teeth, hair, her own chest.

He actually whimpered when she suckled him, his massive pec muscles twitching as she did so.

When he struggled to free his arms from the layers of coat, vest, and shirt, she shoved a palm against the center of his chest to keep him pinned against the door.

With her free hand, she stripped his pants down to his knees.

She slid down to rub him between her breasts.

All he did was groan. She loved having control over such a powerful man.

His breath slid into a low moan as she took him between her teeth and ever so gently teased him.

"God damn it, woman." He pushed off the door again.

This time she wasn't fast enough and he slipped an arm free.

In moments he had his hand on her shoulder and pushed her back to arm's length.

"Just hold on a moment." He hung his head and gasped for breath.

"Why?" She reached for him, but still he held her off. That heady mix of John's massive power and how gently he kept her shoulder in his grasp was killing her. She didn't fall for men, but John was breaking that rule. And she knew an answer to that.

She nipped the inside of his wrist and slammed back against him the moment his grip loosened. Body to body she ground against him. Letting the heat inside her find a simple channel. It was always best that way. Let her body generate the heat.

Connie could sit at a safe distance inside her own mind and simply enjoy.

She slid a hand down to cup John, who groaned and then, in a single move, grabbed her.

One hand behind her neck, he slid his other hand,

clothes still dangling from his forearm, between her legs and grabbed her buttocks. In a move that gave her a moment of perfect free fall, that half moment before the parachute opened, he raised her high, then dropped her onto the bed.

"Now just hold on. Just one little damn minute." John scrubbed at his face.

Connie took the moment to shimmy out of her pants.

He stood over her, looking down as he cleared his clothes off his arm.

When she reached for him, he blocked her hands.

Then he traced a finger along her temple, over her cheek, across her lips, down the curve of her neck.

"You are the most beautiful thing I've ever seen."

Connie looked away. She couldn't face those eyes. She could face his chest, his hips, his powerful legs. But not those eyes that looked right inside her.

"So are you." And she blushed. She never blushed about sex. But the heat roared over her face and down her body. And he was. John was beautiful. That he wanted her, even for now, was... nice. She knew the word was lame, but it was all she could dredge up.

He kicked off his pants and lay down beside her. Once more his hand brushed down her length trailing heat, so soft, so gentle, so strong that shivers ran the whole way to her toes.

"Now."

John had seen the change. And couldn't believe it. Noreen's words came back to him. "We're applauding the woman, and she doesn't get that."

Did Connie even know that she was as gone on him as he was on her? She'd blushed. For the first time, the woman he'd seen so uninhibited about sex that she constantly short-circuited his hormones was also present at this same moment as the quiet but brilliant woman she presented to the world at large. That integrated woman, the two halves so far apart but coming from the same place inside, simply hit his heart, right to the very core.

He knew she wasn't ready to be told that. And he didn't want to make it all so serious. He knew she still needed time.

So he repeated himself, "Now."

And then he jumped her.

He kissed, he tickled, he made her laugh, he made her writhe, and he made her crest over and over and over. Each shot upward a miracle, a moment when she was perfectly woman. Not Connie, not mechanic, not cerebral, not even primal. It was a moment when she transcended all of those and simply rode the pulse of their lovemaking in such amazing harmony and bounty.

When at last he entered her, she simply clung, her face buried against his shoulder, her legs wrapped tight about him, her hands gripping his shoulders like she'd never let him go.

"Look at me." He ground it out. "Please, Connie, look at me."

She threw her head back against the pillow, but it took her a long moment to force her eyes open and then to focus. And when she did, he lost himself in the woman and in those gold-brown eyes.

Chapter 63

CONNIE HAD NEVER BEEN TO THE PLACES JOHN HAD sent her.

"Nice." Who the hell had she been kidding? "Nice" belonged on the same scale as "interesting." Her mind just went to stupid when trying to describe how John made her feel.

John had rolled them over so that she lay atop him, a good trick on a narrow Navy bunk. As sleep overwhelmed her, she slid to the side, still inside the curve of his arm, one leg thrown over his hips. A closeness necessary due to the narrow bed, a closeness mandated by how it felt when their bodies were touching.

Once again her head rested against his shoulder. Through narrowing eyes she could follow the slow rise and fall of that miraculous chest of his. Her own personal place of safety.

Together in so many ways, they slid down toward the sleep they so desperately lacked.

His hands, which had dragged a blanket over them and then delightfully traced her from shoulder to buttock and back and again, slowed, and finally hooked over her waist.

Her head, ever so gently raised and lowered by his chest as his breathing slowed, left her feeling lightheaded, dreamy.

As she drifted off to sleep, a voice spoke from the

darkness of her drifting thoughts, a voice from the past perhaps, ever so softly.

"I love you, Connie."

She slept without dreams.

Chapter 64

CONNIE AWOKE WITH NO QUESTIONS ABOUT WHERE she was. John's gentle breathing was still regular with sleep. She knew how much time had passed, could tell by how she felt and her internal clock that it was late afternoon, despite the heavy gray out the porthole glass.

She had never been one to lie abed. Her father had called her his "personal alarm clock" because of how she simply sat upright fully awake.

This afternoon she didn't want to move an inch. John lay warm beside her. His arm still draped lazily around her, he'd held her even in his sleep.

She rolled until her nose rested against his skin and breathed him in, deep and warm. She could really, really get used to this. John had definitely spoiled her for any other man.

What was she thinking?

There was only one man she wanted. And he lay here beside her, holding her in his sleep.

And how long would that last?

She didn't have to consider that for very long. She knew John. Knew his heart and the way he gave it to his family was the same way he'd give it to her. He would be true and loyal and everlasting, right until the moment one of them died. Knowing him, probably long after even that if she were first to go.

Connie blinked against the harsh afternoon light.

There was no way to go there. Happily ever after didn't exist for the likes of them. Death was too imminent an acquaintance. She knew what she wanted, didn't she?

She breathed in the heady, rich, dark scent of a man grounded on the earth who merely chose to fly.

Her body answered, it certainly knew what it wanted. At least that she understood.

She slid a hand down and teased him awake, so slowly, so gently that he didn't truly wake, not even a flutter of eyes as she shifted over him.

A soft groan as she slipped him inside her.

Then, as she worked her hips back and forth, his hands drifted up to hold her hips.

She rested her hands on his chest and leaned down to kiss him until he truly awoke, her tongue on his, and every bit of him reaching deep inside her.

His cresting and release was as gentle as a dream that carried her along for the ride.

And when at last they were both sated, she lay down upon his chest, knowing his hands would wrap about her and keep her safe.

Chapter 65

"OKAY," MAJOR HENDERSON WAS SLAPPING HIS FISTS together on the flight deck.

John noticed he was doing the same and did his best to stop. Throughout the day, while he'd slept, the ship had driven south and right into a cold front. Now the sun was setting and the Baltic Sea was tossing a fit that rocked the ship actively enough that he had to brace his feet wide to keep his place. The merest hint of land graced the southern horizon. It wouldn't have been noticeable except it was the one thing not moving in the rolling sea.

All the while they'd been steaming south, he'd slept with the woman of his dreams curled about him.

The woman he loved.

Once he'd admitted it to himself, it was completely obvious what Paps and Grumps and Mama and Noreen had all been talking about. He'd been crazy for Connie for a long time, he just hadn't known it yet.

As he lay there before they'd slept and realized that there was only one woman for him, ever, it had been so simple to say "I love you" for the first time in his life. He'd never been one of those guys who offered the words to each woman he was with. In his book there were a few things you just never joked about: how a woman looked, that you loved her, and marriage.

He blew on his hands to keep his fingers warm.

Dangerous territory there. Once he told the sleeping woman that he loved her, the next piece had been obvious. When you loved someone like this, you married her. You shared your life and your dreams, your successes and your failures.

He considered saying so to Connie when she woke in his arms as if she'd always been there. And again after they'd had splendidly delicious wake-up sex. But some part of him hesitated. Perhaps it was the wiser part of John Wallace telling him to keep his mouth shut for the moment.

It had almost burst out of him when she'd come out of the tiny shower with water drops still dancing on her skin. She moved with that loose-hipped walk of a woman well satisfied, wearing nothing but her dog tags and her radiant smile.

"I do so love looking at you." He'd had to say the word in one way or another, and it came out almost as a wheeze. "You're magnificent."

"John!"

"Hunh? What?"

Tim elbowed him sharply to draw his attention back to the briefing.

John blew on his hands again and faced Major Henderson. "Sorry. Not awake yet."

Mark offered him the thinnest of smiles. He wasn't buying John's excuse for a second.

"Okay, in review from yesterday's briefing. Sunset in about twenty minutes. We need to be done in fourteen hours, though twelve would be better. Poland is allowing an overflight, but they'd rather we didn't show up officially, so we're staying below two hundred feet the whole way to Kraków. Refuel there, they've promised us a tanker truck in a farmer's field less than twenty klicks from the Ukrainian border. Four hours in-country max, come out with two nuclear weapons in sling loads."

He pointed to the crew readying the CSAR bird on the other end of the freezing deck.

"That's our only backup. They'll be flying in formation with us but holding at the border. They're on need-to-know basis and are not presently privy to mission details. Any questions?"

They all looked over to watch the third crew. Unquestionably SOAR. The way they moved, the gear they wore. Not stealth, no ADAS, but these were not folks to be underestimated. They flew into full battle with a gun and a stretcher and were notorious for getting their people back alive.

They didn't have the heavy weapons of a DAP, but they had door guns and an underslung chain gun and Vulcan cannon. The kind of medic you'd want coming for you.

"Their pilot," Tim yelled just loud enough for John to hear him over the wind. "Damn, but she's hot."

"Don't get your heart caught." It was an old line they used to bandy about.

"Not like you. No woman is gonna trap this boy." Tim elbowed him again and directed a nod across the deck. "But see this one."

One of the CSAR crew pulled off her woolen hat. A cascade of mahogany hair spilled down the woman's back. For clearly it was a woman. A long, slender one. Major Beale had said there was a fourth, another woman in SOAR. Without turning their way, the woman pulled her hair back into a rough ponytail and pulled on her helmet. She climbed aboard to copilot.

A glance showed Tim completely mesmerized. John elbowed him to bring his attention back to the briefing, adding enough extra oomph in payback that he almost sent Tim sprawling to the deck. Only the driving wind kept him upright as he staggered for a moment.

Connie raised a hand.

Mark nodded to her.

"And if the weapons aren't there, sir?"

Mark looked grim. "That's a thought we aren't going to follow right now."

The flight through Polish airspace was uneventful. They'd been given clearance for the primary training corridor of Poland's largest helicopter manufacturer. It ran from Gdansk on the Baltic to Kraków near the Ukraine border. Neither PZL-Swidnik nor the Polish Air Force were flying any missions tonight, so the corridor should be quiet, and it was. By nature of being a training route, it avoided city and towns, even houses when possible, making it ideal for their current mission.

Connie wished Colonel Michael Gibson and Chief Warrant 3 Dave Grant weren't sitting in the two seats against the cargo net. Not that they were paying her any attention. They were doing what Delta Force operators always did on boring flights—they slept. It didn't matter that the Major was following a high-speed, low-altitude slalom course between hills and down rivers. It didn't matter that they'd just had a full day's sack time. D-boys always slept while flying into action, probably because once they hit the ground, it might be days before they'd have another chance.

She wished she could talk to John. Not about anything much. About how well she'd slept, about how worn and loose her body felt, about what she'd like to do to him next time.

There was some girly part of her that wanted to go back to the moment before they'd fallen asleep and simply wallow. It might be the most contented she'd ever been. And the memory of her dad's whispering, "Love ya, short stuff." A phrase that had tucked her into bed every night he was home from assignment.

Except last night it had changed. Her memory was unsure, tentative, clouded by how her body had gloried under John's devout attention. But the phrase had shifted, she was sure of it.

"I love you, Connie." The voice a soft rumble against her ear. He hadn't repeated it this morning. He. John. It had been John's voice.

Connie almost choked herself on her harness as she spun to look at John.

His attention remained focused outside the chopper. She could tell by his head motion that he was performing slow sweeps of the area using his ADAS visor.

Colonel Gibson had opened one eye to watch her, his hand resting as lightly on his M4 sniper rifle in wakefulness as it had in sleep.

She forced herself to turn back and do her own scan. Nothing to see except the night and the countryside that could have been anywhere. Fields and farmhouses, livestock showing as clustered groups of heat outlines. The cows were the brightest thing visible, even more than the carefully shrouded heat signature of *Viper* running clean and true just three rotors ahead or the CSAR crew running three rotors behind.

John's words meant nothing. Men always said such things, whether it was to get sex or after sex. "Love" was a word that slid easily off their tongues. Yet it didn't seem like something John would say idly.

They were going to have a serious talk at the end of the mission.

Assuming they made it back alive.

Chapter 66

THE POLISH ARMY HAD PROVIDED A FUEL TRUCK WHERE and when promised, but it didn't have the fastest pump on the planet. John took off his helmet and scrubbed at his hair while they waited. The cold air felt good against his scalp. They had at least ten minutes with nothing to do but wait.

He didn't have to see Connie's face to know he was in trouble. She grabbed his arm and guided him out into the night over the sharp crackle of the corn-stubble field. Her fingers would be digging in painfully if not for the padding of his flight suit.

A few dozen paces into the dark, she jerked him to a halt and turned him to face her by leveraging the grip on his arm. The two choppers and the fuel truck were bathed in a soft red glow that did little to light the darkness of the overcast and moonless night. The building rain sparkled a bit, reflecting the red.

"You can't!" Her voice was a hiss.

"Can't what?" Though he could guess.

"Say what you said!"

He cupped her face in his hands and kissed her lightly on the lips. Too dark for anyone to see.

"What? That I love you. Yeah, you're going to have to get used to hearing that, aren't you? Will that be a problem?"

"A problem? A problem!" She sputtered for a moment

before waving her arm at the broad fields. "Look around you, John. What do you see?"

He took his time, turned his face to let the chill rain cool his cheeks and forehead. "Beautiful night."

She jabbed him in the ammo pouch on his vest. There was no give there, and most of the force was transmitted straight to his chest. It hurt. Of course, she'd know that.

"We're in a Polish field on the way to the Ukraine to retrieve nuclear weapons." She shouted it into his face.

"You could say it a little louder. I don't think the fuel truck driver or the CSAR team quite heard that." John knew he shouldn't be enjoying this moment quite so much, but he was. Seeing Connie at a complete loss was simply too rare an event.

"The chances of us getting out of this unscathed aren't high. And when you add that to the next one and the one after that... John, be reasonable. Love is the one thing a soldier can't afford."

"What about the Majors, or Kee and Archie?"

"They're idiots." She muttered it half under her breath.

He grabbed her shoulders. Grabbed her hard and shook her. "Don't you dare say such a thing. Damn it, Connie. Have you ever really looked at them? Those are some very happy people. Open your eyes and see what they share. Don't you want that?"

"But they could be dead tomorrow. Dead tonight." Her voice caught, stumbled.

He almost responded with another shake. Almost told her how stupid she was being, when he realized she wasn't. Not from her point of view. Her mother and father had died. Even old Grumps. He still couldn't get over how deeply the old man had touched Connie's heart. Then he'd gone and died on her. It must make for a pretty dark view of the world.

So, instead of shaking her, he pulled her into his arms and held her in the night. She went quiet. The tension didn't drain out of her, he could feel it through all the gear that separated and protected them, but she came to rest there. It made him feel so damn powerful, as if he could fix the world, that a woman who didn't believe in safety had decided that the one safe place for her on the whole damn planet was curled against his chest.

He whispered in her ear as she quieted.

"I love you, Connie Davis. Never said that to a woman who wasn't family before. I'm likely to keep saying it as I like how it feels when I do, so you'd better get used to it." He debated stopping there, knew he should, but what the hell.

"And just so you can start thinking about it, I feel that I should give you fair warning. One of these days I'm going to ask you to marry me. And when I do, your answer is going to be yes. Just in case you were wondering."

"Not a chance." She spoke into the curve of his shoulder. But her voice didn't have quite the conviction that he'd bet she meant it to have.

Chapter 67

EMILY BEALE LANDED THE *VENGEANCE* SOFTLY BESIDE *Viper* and dropped the four D-boys barely a mile from the compound. They slid in behind a tall but completely decrepit barn that should mask the noise of their landing from the target.

The new rotors let them get far closer than she would normally risk. Still she'd rather have landed farther out, but there was too much flying time and too little ground time in the mission profile so they had to keep moving fast. Five hours back and forth across Poland, half an hour refueling time each way. With three hours flying time over the Ukraine, that left them only three hours of darkness to complete the mission. They had only one night to pull this off.

She settled in to wait for the signal to come forward.

Aleksander Stepanov's information and satellite imagery pointed to a very small compound that followed the old rule: if you want to hide something, leave it in plain sight. A small airstrip outside the farming community of Krasyliv boasted a couple of crop dusters, two MiG fighter jets, and, incongruously, a pair of Douglas DC-3s, which Stepanov claimed had been converted for bomb delivery. Fly the DC-3s low and slow to deliver the weapons to target, with fighter jets for cover. Made a certain amount of sense.

The four Delta operators faded into the night with

dart guns that fired a ten-hour dose of knockout juice in their hands and silenced sniper rifles across their backs.

Viper and *Vengeance* sat for an hour in absolute silence.

Emily really wished the ADAS had sound as well as sight.

At the fueling stop, Emily had felt positively voy-euristic watching her two crew chiefs out on the field. They looked close. He'd held her so long that it made Emily feel all mushy inside and made her wish she and Mark were somewhere safe and quiet.

But there was still something going on. Whatever had passed between them at the very end had changed everything. John had strolled back toward the fueling truck with a bounce in his step that could only be called smug.

Connie had remained where she was. As if rooted to the ground. Frozen. It took her a long time, a minute or more, before she started shaking her head. Clearly, some-thing shocking was being denied. Then she stopped, did that sideways crick of the neck they both shared when clearing their thoughts, and stood straight. And Emily would bet a full night of Mark's winnings at poker that whatever had surprised the unflappable girl enough to root her to the ground was now being rationalized.

Finally, as if nothing had happened, Connie's image, outlined so neatly in the dark and projected by the ADAS on Emily's visor, had walked out of the dark back to the helicopter, but not along the same path as John.

Emily had spun the control to shift her view past the fueling to the stern of the chopper as Connie crossed well behind the tail.

Exactly in the six, directly behind, Connie stopped

and looked up. Not at the new tail rotor, but at the fixed rear camera.

Emily had expected the girl to bow her head and scuttle aside as if embarrassed at being watched.

Instead, Connie nodded her head in acknowledgment of being observed and circled to the cargo door to enter the aircraft.

Emily had tried to look otherwise occupied when Connie returned to her seat, but she knew she hadn't pulled it off. When she slid her visor up and looked over her shoulder, Connie was turned in her chair enough to look at Emily.

Busted.

Emily nodded in acknowledgment, exactly as Connie had moments before.

Emily fiddled with the control of the ADAS for lack of anything else to do while they waited behind the barn. Farmer's field, bored cows, the side of a barn so long abandoned that she'd half feared the wind blast from the rotors would knock it down.

She'd never gone into the field feeling so unsure about her crew. She knew that's what was eating at her. Their performance was without question, but at the moment, the reliability of that performance with them sitting back to back just two feet apart in the main bay was worrisome.

Clearly Connie and John had solved some issues, they were no longer fighting like angry pit snakes. But they were—

"Starting," was the message that broke the hypnotic silence.

All other questions fell aside.

Emily started a timer on one of the biggest LCD screens in the console.

By minute two on the mission clock, she and Clay had completed the warm-start preflight checklist. By minute three, she started the turbines, easing them up to speed slow and soft.

Dead on minute four, she eased up on the collective and raised one meter up and shifted twenty sideways to clear the barn.

By four minutes thirty, she was less than ten seconds from the airfield and still hadn't heard from the D-boys.

"Steel!" she called to her crew.

The motto of the DAP Hawks was "We Deal in Steel." They were the nastiest gunships in helicopter history. Her crew knew what the motto meant.

Clay tapped his main two screens over to weapons' targeting, leaving a hundred percent of the actual flying to Emily.

She could hear the high whine that told her Connie and John had the miniguns hot and spinning, their attention wholly on the tactical information being displayed on their visors.

Emily slewed hard at the end of the runway, watching to make sure she didn't bank too hard and bury a rotor in the dirt. Then she ran *Vengeance* right down the center line.

Viper would be coming from the far end, but twenty degrees out of her line of fire.

A line of tracer fire ripped out of the dark of the starboard side. John answered back with a barrage even as the rounds hammered into the side of the Hawk. Not loud enough for antiaircraft. Standard machine gun, so most hits wouldn't get through the Hawk's skin.

One round shattered the side window in Emily's door, big machine gun. Another round followed that one in and slapped her helmet hard enough to jerk her head to the side and make her ears ring. Still alive, so the remains of the window and the helmet must have done their job, though her neck would be sore for days from the sideways whiplash of the impact.

"Goddamn it! Someone shoot that bastard."

John finished shutting them down before she even finished speaking.

Five figures moved across her field of vision down near the hangars. She almost fired by reflex before she spotted IR reflectors on their shoulders. Thankfully, Clay spotted them as friendlies as well.

"Center is clear!" over the radio from the D-boys.

"Circling wider for other guards," Mark called out.

Emily brought her bird in as *Viper* circled up and down the remote airstrip a few more times, looking for heat signs marking any other gunners.

Michael hurried over with a slender woman between him and another D-boy. Her hands were zip-tied together at the wrists.

She was babbling in Russian, clearly upset about something. Not one of Emily's languages. Archie had always handled that one for her, but he wasn't here. Clay shook his head when she looked at him. Every SOAR learned a couple languages. A full crew could generally cover most situations.

"Damn it! Doesn't anyone here speak—"

"She wants to come with us."

Connie.

Chapter 68

THEY'D GATHERED ROUND. THE D-BOYS FACED OUTWARD in a defensive perimeter. Except for Michael. Major Beale had left the rotor just ticking around, ready to go in an instant. *Viper* roared by close overhead. A rapid spate of fire indicated another machine gun guard.

The nasty burr of a minigun firing lasted under two seconds. Apparently enough to kill another target.

Connie had trouble following the Ukrainian woman's accent. She did a running translation as well as she could for everyone listening.

The woman was shouting to be heard. Too loud. Too fast.

"If they find me, her, with no bombs, I, she will be dead. Please take me with you. No one here. No one here." Connie pulled enough out of the translation to listen to the woman's words rather than simply translating them.

"She's telling us she has no family, no friends. But she keeps talking about another. Someone else we must take with us."

"Who?"

The woman wouldn't stop talking, a barrage of words poured from her tight mouth and narrow face. Her short-cropped blond hair and motions spoke of military.

"Who must we take with us?" Connie shouted it right into her face to get the woman's attention.

She stumbled back a half step, all that the D-boy's grip on her arms allowed.

"You are here to take the bombs, yes?"

"Yes."

"You are American. You will destroy them, not use them?"

"Yes."

The woman's shoulders slumped as if the fight had suddenly gone out of her.

"Good. That is good."

Or perhaps it was relief.

"I can help you take these two. But there is one more you must get."

Not a who, a what. A bomb.

"Where?"

———— ∿ ————

"A hundred kilometers from here." Connie told the whole tale again to Major Henderson after he landed.

With the help of the still-bound Gerta, the Ukrainian soldier, and two of the D-boys, John and Crazy Tim were extracting the two bombs from the DC-3s. The other D-boys were disabling the fighter jets without destroying them, which would draw too much attention. They slipped lengths of steel pipe into the turbine engines. Any attempt to start them, and the engines would shred themselves. Even the fussiest preflight inspection was unlikely to find them. Connie had to admire the economy of their actions.

"How much do those bombs weigh?"

"About fifteen hundred pounds apiece."

"No real way to carry two on the same bird."

"Any weight we can shed from them?"

Connie pulled out the satellite phone she'd been given. She rammed down on the Emergency button. Speed dial, uplink through a satellite, specially shifted to give them eight hours of coverage rather than the more usual fifteen to twenty minutes, back down to the help she needed.

She explained the situation to Dr. Williams. He sat a thousand miles away, seated in the command area that replaced the upstairs First Class lounge on Air Force One.

"Yes, you can shed all of the weight you want." He sounded thoroughly cheerful even though he'd been sitting in close quarters parked in a remote corner of the Stockholm airport for a full day already.

"That is, if you don't mind being radioactive afterward. The Russians didn't build these models with finesse. These are older designs, brute force. Thick steel insulation. You could lose the guide fins, but you'd still have to take the bomb apart to save a hundred pounds. If you don't mind taking six hours to do it and have some good radiation gear on while you're doing it."

He was happily describing what steps would be required to do that when she hung up the phone.

She looked at the Majors. "That would be 'no.'"

Major Beale grabbed her husband's wrist and looked at his watch.

"Whatever we do, it needs to be in the next ten minutes."

The guys, with Gerta's direction, had one nuke in a rolling cradle and were already lowering the other out of the second DC-3.

"We could just take these two and get out of here."

Mark didn't look happy with the suggestion even as he voiced it.

"Tomorrow morning, the Ukrainians wake up and find two of their precious nuclear weapons are gone. We'll never see the third one again."

Connie walked away into the night. She'd talked to Aleksander. A man named for two grandparents who had been great artists and great lovers. They had inspired each other to great successes. They had been successful before the Russian Revolution and had become famous in the Communist regime as well.

Aleksander had said they must get both bombs or destroy the second one. Because if they didn't, they were likely to see it falling out of the sky all too soon.

"Kuchma, he is not a man you should trust to be rational." She could hear Aleksander's heavy voice.

How much death would there be then? These were not small devices like the World War II weapons that brought Japan to her knees. These were state-of-the-art weaponry from the height of the Cold War. The devastation of even a single device would be catastrophic.

Aleksander's insistence that they retrieve both of the weapons only emphasized that they must steal all three.

Two artists who had done something.

She strode back to the Majors, who had lapsed into silence.

"I have an idea. But you're going to hate it."

Chapter 69

JOHN HAD ROLLED OVER THE TWO BOMBS JUST IN TIME to hear Major Henderson shouting at Connie.

"That's goddamn insane. No way! Request denied!"

John jogged over the last few feet to stand beside Connie. He wanted to check that she was okay but saw she had her unflappable military-grade blast shield in place. Not even the Major was going to get through that.

Connie kept her silence.

Mark cursed and stalked away.

Major Beale, who'd been standing close beside her husband, had her arms crossed over her chest and was nodding slowly.

"Do it," Beale said in a soft voice.

John followed Connie over to the bombs, not wasting her time asking what the plans were.

She pulled out the card that the geek had given to her back at the hotel. She was actually using it rather than trusting her memory. Not that John blamed her. Apparently she'd have to do something drastically wrong to blow them up, but that was a pair of nuclear bombs she was disarming.

John hovered close, handing her tools and poised to grab her if something went wrong, as if he could protect her from the mushroom cloud that would consume them all in the first few milliseconds if she screwed up.

While they worked, John could see the Majors and

the rest of the crew shift a half ton of rockets and ammunition from *Viper* to *Vengeance*. That's what Henderson must have hated so much.

To whisk two bombs to safety, they'd have to lighten *Viper* by moving excess ammunition to *Vengeance*. They couldn't leave the excess weaponry here to be found. Nor could they blow the weapons up because they'd draw too much attention.

That meant that Beale and her crew would be going alone after the third bomb. Helicopters didn't fly alone. Not if they wanted to survive. But they would this time.

Connie reached down inside the panel she'd unscrewed with a pair of wire clippers. Three sharp clicks of the cutters chopping wires. Quickly, without hesitation, working with that perfect surety she brought to all things mechanical.

It was only as she pulled her hand free of the guts of the second bomb's control circuitry that John saw her face was bathed in sweat despite the cold night and near-freezing rain.

"Doing good, Connie. You're doing good."

She offered a weak smile.

"These are dead now. It's the next leg I'm worried about. Even refueling here, it will be a real stretch."

One of the D-boys drove up in a rusting old truck with fading Russian letters written across the side and the unmistakable picture of flames. They began fueling the *Vengeance*.

"What's worse is that we'll be burning extra fuel to carry *Viper's* weapons, but Mark can't carry the load and the bombs, and we can't leave them here."

John again considered just blowing them up, but that

would alert the Ukraine to their presence. He felt the chill penetrate right through his flight suit.

The Majors were having a final argument.

"I need Connie and John." Emily Beale was standing her ground. "You know your guys aren't as good if we get into trouble with the third bomb."

"Fine, then I'll fly them."

John held his breath while all Major Beale did was stare at her husband in silence. Mixing a crew in mid-mission was never the best bet, and Henderson, by the way he was cursing, knew it.

Colonel Gibson, the D-boy leader, trotted over. "Let's go!"

Henderson swore, hugged Beale for a moment, then headed for *Viper*.

Tim came over and grabbed John's hand in a powerful handshake. "See you soon, Mr. Big Bad."

"Deal, crazy man."

John had to blink against the emotion. It was the closest he and Tim had ever come to saying good-bye because of a mission. He appreciated the sentiment, Tim was the best friend a man could have, but he didn't like the feel. He faced northeast. They were flying into a potential world of serious hurt.

Then everything was moving fast. *Viper* was aloft. In moments they'd taken up the slack on the two bombs now rigged in a towing sling. They eased aloft, dangling from the chopper's underbelly by five meters of wire.

Henderson made the lift clean and turned back to the northwest and the Polish flight corridor.

They all clambered aboard the *Vengeance*. Beale and Clay up front. John and Connie in the middle. Colonel

Gibson, one of the other D-boys, and the Ukrainian woman in the back. John didn't like having her along, not one bit. But she was the only one who knew where the other weapon lay.

As he pulled on his helmet, he heard Major Henderson's voice soft over the encrypted radio.

"Emily Beale, you come back in one piece, goddamn it!" Soft, but harsh with feeling.

"Yes, dear."

"You don't have to sound so damn cheerful about it."

"Yes, dear," Beale replied, not one bit less chipper.

SOAR lived to go where no one else could and this was definitely one of those circumstances. But John tried not to think about it as they lifted to a half-dozen meters and turned northeast toward the heart of the country.

He definitely tried not to think of the buildup of security the nearer they'd fly to Kiev.

And absolutely not about Connie's stated fears that there'd never be enough time before death found them.

Chapter 70

COLONEL GIBSON AND CAPTAIN GRANT WERE SCOUTING the area. Now the two Delta operators were lying low in a natural gully in the middle of a field about two miles away from the helicopter and a quarter mile from the target. They'd pulled back far enough that they dared whisper over the radio. The Black Hawk had been parked behind a copse of trees for almost an hour, and time was running very short. They really needed to be headed back to Poland somewhere in the next ninety minutes, and that wasn't seeming very likely.

Connie listened to what the D-boys had to say and didn't like it one bit. She wished she hadn't thought of this scenario in the first place.

She flipped Gerta out of the circuit, just in case the woman understood more English than she appeared to.

"An unguarded house and garage. Colonel, what if she isn't telling the truth? And this isn't the place? What if all that's in there is an old Ukrainian couple?"

The major turned in her pilot's seat and faced Connie. "What do you think?"

Well, that would teach her. Ask a question and have it shot right back at you. Connie thought about it and turned briefly to study the woman crouched in the back of the helicopter, her hands tucked under her arms trying to keep warm.

Finally Connie knew. Unless Gerta was dealing from

a cold deck with more skill than Major Henderson, the cards were clean. She had no one to miss her; that was a sadness that Connie recognized in Gerta's eyes. Add to that her wish to defect, the slope of her shoulders at the idea that she wouldn't be believed, her adamant insistence that this was the place, and the timbre of her voice.

"She's telling the truth."

"Then where is it, parked next to a goddamn rusting Lada sedan?" Colonel Gibson did not sound happy. "They tried hiding the first two in the open. I'd bet they'd do the opposite with the third one if they were smart. Heavy security."

Connie considered. Closed her eyes and tried to picture it logically. How did you lock something down that you didn't want anyone to discover but not run the risk of a large number of people knowing about it. You didn't do it with more people. They wouldn't use a base's worth of forces. This was a closely guarded secret. Even Aleksander had not known about it.

When she and John had wanted privacy, and what they'd thought to be secrecy, all they'd had to do was close the submarine's hatch. No one went there at night, not without a key.

Could it be so simple?

She flipped Gerta back into the circuit and chatted with her a bit more.

"You press the buzzer on the front door. They check your face. Then they let you in. The face is the key that provides the security. If you look wrong, you get the grumpy housewife or the front end of an Uzi. If you have the right face, you get in. Very few to know, very few to track."

"Well, they aren't going to like my face." Colonel Gibson and his companion had left the chopper with their faces heavily blacked for night work.

There was a long silence.

"Sir?" Connie asked.

"Yeah, I know." Gibson sounded pretty unhappy. "We're headed back to get you."

Emily cut in, "Stay where you are. My people move quietly. They'll come to you. Sergeant Davis, you make it clear to your pal there that if she cooperates, she gets a free ride to the promised land. And if she screws with me, I'm gonna drop her in the Baltic Sea in a long line of pieces no bigger than my goddamn thumb. And she'll live through at least the first hundred. Are we clear?"

"Clear, sir." She translated the message as literally as she could.

Gerta nodded easily.

"My commander…" Connie stared Gerta straight in the eyes. "She's not kidding."

Gerta's nod was a little tighter this time, her eyes a little wider.

"Go! John, you've got her back. Let us know when you need the cavalry."

———

It took them a precious half hour to cover the distance to the D-boys following a stream along the stubbled cornfield, then crawling through the winter wheat. And fifteen more before they were in position around the house. Half their time was gone.

This couldn't be it. Small, gray, perhaps once painted white long ago. No guards. No dog. No visible cameras.

At Connie's nod, Gerta stood, straightened her jacket, and strode purposefully to the front door.

She punched the buzzer as the D-boys lay to either side of the stoop, one having circled half a mile around to get there. The two of them in full camo gear looked like nothing so much as a pile of windblown leaves lying along the foundation.

A harsh light flashed on, making Gerta blink hard, standing on the stoop. But she didn't raise a hand to shield her eyes, simply squeezed them shut for a long moment. Some other rule of the security. If you followed reflex and raised your arm, you'd probably broken the first of a dozen security steps.

The D-boys to either side were barely lit by the backwash of the bright light. Unmoving. Eyes nearly slitted closed.

From her perch at the corner of the house toward the garage, Connie could just hear the speaker demanding Gerta's identity. John stood close enough behind her that she could feel his rapid breathing against the back of her neck. They both held SCAR rifles with the stock folded in for CQC. She really hoped it wouldn't come to close-quarters combat. Gerta would be the first dead, and she'd probably be next.

A shudder ran up her spine. Odd. Connie considered her own feelings. For the first time, having death as an inevitable end didn't seem so okay.

Gerta responded by holding up her ID.

Connie thought about the future, and an easy image of John rose to her mind.

Another spate of Russian from the speaker took Connie a moment to translate. "Why are you here at two in the morning?"

That was the question they'd discussed how to answer but hadn't come up with a good response. Or any response at all, really.

Gerta was up to it. "Open the damned door before I kick your collective Ukrainian behinds and I'll tell you."

"So give me the goddamn pass code, already."

Connie could imagine John and herself years from— She brushed the thought away. Now was so not the time.

"Marilyn Monroe," Gerta offered in her thick Russian. "37-23-36."

Measurements. Crap. What was it with men and Marilyn Monroe? Half the passwords Connie had ever cracked were some variation on that.

Another grunt, and then the sharp buzz of a heavy magnetic lock on a steel door sounded from the worn wood. Another proof of the right place.

Gerta pushed it open and stepped in, and the D-boys slid in beside her so smoothly it was hard to see them. Not even the slight pop of silenced gunfire or the soft gurgle of a slit throat. The guards must be somewhere else in the building, opening the door by remote.

Connie started counting to five as instructed.

At three, John moved around her, gun at the ready.

Connie cursed for at least a half second before she followed him.

Gibson had chocked the door open, as per plan.

A flight of metal stairs ran down straight ahead. Gerta was just stepping off the bottom step, waving to someone Connie couldn't see. The two D-boys were low and close behind her.

Gibson, crouched in the dark at the base of the stairs,

shot his silent dart gun at a target Connie couldn't see from the head of the stairs.

Three seconds later, there was the soft thud of a falling body.

Instead of going down, Connie moved through a door to the left of the stairs and entered the main house, looking for the sleepy housewife cover-story, fully aware that she might be walking into the sights of a Kalashnikov rifle.

She rolled right and low as she crossed the threshold, John perched left and high to cover her.

But there weren't any housewives. Or rooms. It was an open hangar almost exactly the size of the Mi-24 Hind gunship parked in it. The back of the house clearly opened outward on heavy tracks.

Definitely the right place.

She and John circled it quickly, but the room, which took up all of the ground floor other than the entryway, was unoccupied. A quick check showed the Hind chopper was empty but ready for immediate flight.

She slipped a remote-controlled C4 mine from her thigh pouch and read the code.

"3, 2, 3." Was that Monroe again? She flashed her fingers to John.

He pulled a remote detonator out of a thigh pocket, dialed the radio frequency in, and slipped it back into the pocket.

Connie peeled the back off the mine and stuck it on the underside of a fuel tank.

The rest of the bay was empty. They circled back to the stairs and Connie followed John down into the silence.

At the base of the stairs they looked and listened. They could see Grant and Gerta. She crouched behind the D-boy, a large stainless tank shielding them from most possible attacks.

Michael Gibson was nowhere to be seen.

"Damn!"

She barely heard John's whispered oath. He slipped into the room and opened up her view.

Suddenly she was glad to be behind the broad shield of his back.

The bomb was the least of their worries. A vast underground laboratory stretched off into the distance.

Two brief cries and a soft thud sounded in the distance.

"Clear!" Michael called on the headset.

Connie pulled out her phone and shot five photos in an arc across the room and hit Send.

A minute later, as they were moving forward, her phone buzzed.

"What is it?" she answered.

"Heavy water, I think." Dr. Williams didn't sound so chipper. "They're gearing up to build more bombs."

———

John groaned. This was a whole other world of hurt.

The bomb itself was sitting on an elevator that would lift it right up into the hangar. Wheeled carriage already in place. He could deal with that.

But every time he turned his back, Connie wandered off to some other part of the lab and he had to scramble after her. They were halfway through the room when he spotted Gerta moving toward them, something in her hands.

He raised his gun, zeroed on her forehead, and clicked off the safety.

The woman froze.

He dipped the barrel toward her hands, then zeroed it back on her face.

Ever so slowly, not moving a muscle she didn't have to, she opened both hands. A set of keys.

Connie shifted into his range of view but didn't get in the range of fire.

Some of the heavy slog of Russian shifted back and forth between them.

She signaled for John to lower his gun. They'd be better off with her dead. He hated carrying around someone he didn't trust. But she'd gotten them through the door. He did as Connie said.

The Ukrainian handed the keys to Connie and led her back the way she'd come. The keys unlocked a small safe, more of a cabinet. He could have just kicked the damn thing in. Inside were laptops and some backup external drives and USBs.

Connie swept them all into a bag. Then she slung them over the woman's head and shoulder, pinning her arms awkwardly. Connie pulled out her Ka-Bar and used the tip of the knife to slice the zip-ties around the woman's wrists.

John didn't like it one bit.

The Ukrainian massaged her wrists and started talking again.

"Only the three guards," Connie translated. "Tomorrow is New Year's. Everyone else has gone home."

Gibson slid up beside him. "We can't leave this."

John could only nod in agreement.

Connie kept snapping pictures on a quick tour of the room and sending them to Dr. Williams via the satellite uplink.

Back on the phone. "Anything here going to be upset if we blow it up?"

Good question. John was all for blowing it up anyway. It wasn't their soil, and it wouldn't be their mess to clean up.

Connie nodded and turned off the phone, jamming it back in the pouch.

"Just the bomb."

"We'd need a lot of something that goes bang." Gibson had been looking around. "But there's nothing in this room."

John didn't even have to look at Connie to know they shared the same thought. He started to reach for his headset, but she was already speaking into her microphone.

"Major. Soft and quiet, come around the back, and park close."

She pointed up and John moved out.

By the time he climbed the stairs and found the door controls for the back of the building, the Major was settling the Black Hawk outside. The top of the door swung out and down, extending the hangar floor another twenty feet. Slick.

The *Vengeance* jinked. First time in over a year of flying with her that he'd seen Major Emily Beale flinch.

He looked over his shoulder, then did his best to hide his smile. The fully armed Hind helicopter sat immediately behind him. At under a hundred feet from nose to nose, that was enough to chill anyone.

He'd have to tell Connie. This was too good. The Major had nerves of something other than steel.

The smile was wiped from his lips and his thoughts

when he turned. Connie and the bomb were riding the lift up through the hangar floor. Creepiest damn sight he'd ever seen. Even watching the two they'd pulled out of the DC-3s was only odd. Now it was just a woman and the nastiest-looking bomb he'd ever seen.

"This one's bigger," Connie called out. "We're going to have to lose a lot of weight."

John scared up a couple of handcarts. It only took a few minutes to set up a man line, shifting Major Henderson's extra missiles onto the cart.

When Gerta arrived, she didn't even need to be asked. She moved right into the line and began moving weapons.

John made sure his gun was loose in his holster, saw Gibson shift the sling on his sniper rifle.

The woman must have noticed, but she did well at hiding her nerves as she moved to help with the next Hellfire. With the missiles weighing in at a hundred pounds apiece, he didn't need the help, but she was pitching in. That was good.

Connie had her card from Dr. Williams back out— how to disarm "the bomb" in five easy steps or some such. She pulled a cover in the nose of the bomb and was studying the inside.

They had the cargo bay cleared and were starting on their own weaponry. The Major was letting go of two Hellfires and half of the 2.75s. Ten of those totaled another hundred and thirty pounds.

He felt Connie freeze, even though his back was mostly turned to her. In seconds everyone stopped moving and turned to look at her without actually turning.

She remained frozen, one arm elbow deep in the bomb's guts.

John slid up to her and looked down at the blinking green light on the bomb.

"What?" He hadn't intended to whisper.

"I don't know." She was definitely whispering back. He didn't like that at all.

She pulled out the phone very slowly and tossed it to Colonel Gibson, who caught it midair.

"Speed dial 1. Blinking green light on the flight circuit board after I jostled the blue wire on the protective cap over the detonator."

John didn't move. He wanted to run, but no way he'd leave a teammate alone here. And no chance he was going anywhere without Connie.

"Model?" Gibson relayed the question back to her.

"How the fuck should I know?" Her hiss was beyond anger. "It's big, it's nasty, and it's lying here just dying to kill us."

John rested his hand on her shoulder. "Remember, we've been through worse. It's just a sling-load of freezing water falling from the sky."

She started nodding. Slowly at first. Then stronger.

"John, grab the nose cone."

—∾∾—

Connie trotted to the Hawk and fetched the electric screw gun and set to work. Screws. Better than rivets. But did they have to use so many? She couldn't get to the detonator circuitry without removing the flight controller board. But she didn't dare move the controller board again.

So, she'd pull the whole nose cone and come up the damn thing's backside.

She began undoing the screws as fast as she could, the green light still blinking its unknown threat at her. One flashlight, two, then three aimed at her hands. She glanced up to see. Everyone stood in a circle around her, as far from her as they dared but not watching anything else.

If she screwed up, the bomb would fire, sweeping outward in a titanic wave. She and John would have one or two final milliseconds together while the trigger fired. After that it would all be over in the next microsecond or so. They, the circle of watchers, the two choppers, the house, and the lab would be gone by then. Another second and the initial fireball would be expanding in a supersonic shock wave. The mushroom cloud might take two whole minutes before it reached the stratosphere. Explosions were fast things.

No pressure. Shit!

She couldn't get to the screws on the underside without craning the whole bomb off the cart. No time for that and she didn't dare move it.

"Okay, John." She set aside the screw gun and slipped her hands beside his. She was pretty impressed at how steady her voice sounded. "We're going to lever the nose cone off, break it downward. But the instant it lets go, don't let it drop. Whatever you do, don't let it drop."

She braced herself to help cushion it from a fall.

Gibson called out, "Williams says don't do that. Not until he knows the model. Does it have—"

"Tell him to shut the hell up."

She saw Gibson close the phone and shove it into a pocket.

John released his hold, the nose cone didn't give

much. He leaned on the nose cone in stages, pressing downward but keeping his fingers beneath to catch it.

Connie laced her fingers under the nose cone, focusing on the catch, letting John do the bending.

The cover shifted to reveal a narrow gap along the upper edge. John slipped his fingers into the crack for leverage. If he slipped, it would pop back into place and sever his first two knuckles all the way across.

Gibson moved forward, but she waved him back with a shake of her head. There wasn't room for a third, not and be sure of their footing.

John grunted as he leaned into it, heaving. He braced a foot on the undercarriage. She could practically hear his muscles groaning under the strain.

Then it gave, ever so slightly. The half-dozen screws on the underside of the housing couldn't take the immense pressure and torque and started working more like a hinge.

It let go all at once. Heavier than she expected. It took both of them to the ground, but they stopped it before it hit the hangar floor.

John stood, shifted, got his stance, and then cradled it half torn open.

At his tight nod, she knew he had the nose cone's weight, but she shouldn't be too long about it.

"John. The old bird. Not the Huey. Medevac, Korean War. You know, like in MASH."

"Angel of Mercy, the Bell H-13s."

"Right. This looks like those radios." She poked around for a moment. "But I can't figure out the green light. It's still flashing."

"They. Always copying. Our circuits. Describe." It

was a grunt. This time Gibson did move up and help John ease the load. But there was no way Gibson could hold it by himself. No way for John to move forward and look.

So she described it. Half homemade bread-board wiring, half circuit board. "There's technology here I haven't seen since my Dad's Huey. The green light isn't even an LED. It looks like a big, fat Christmas-tree light."

"I'd wire it like the Bell 212."

Connie cursed under her breath. "I never touched one of those."

"The detonation cap is hooked up how? Blue and red to the det cap, green to the frame?"

"Yes." She traced them but didn't touch.

"Bet the green is loose. Don't wiggle it. Push it into the clamp on either end."

"Still blinking. Oh damn, John, it's blinking faster. I don't like this." She wanted—so much. Somehow she could see so much of it, today, tomorrow, some time, a lot of time. But a blinding light washed across it. She'd wanted. A wash of glaring fire. But now it was too late.

All was gone but the light of an explosion.

The light of a burning helicopter tumbling out of the night sky.

"Connie."

Someone was calling her.

"Connie, goddamn it."

"Dad?" A whisper that didn't even reach her own ears.

"You aren't going down the way your father did. You can fix this."

She grabbed for a breath.

John.

Connie managed to blink the nightmare from her eyes.

Saw her hands were still steady on either end of the wire, even if she wasn't.

"You with me, girl?"

"I'm with you, John." And she was. He was right there. "I'm with you."

"Okay." He blew out a breath hard. "Okay."

"The rest of you get the goddamn extra rockets downstairs. Twenty-minute timer on four C4 packs. Go."

Connie could feel it get just a little bit easier. John was there. He'd help. Twenty minutes, that was good. They'd either be ten minutes away and moving fast or they'd be in the center of the first nuclear cloud on Eastern Bloc soil since 1990.

"Talk to me, Johnny."

Emily had almost stroked out when Connie froze with her hands deep inside the bomb.

"Talk to me, but make it fast." Connie's voice was shaky, but it was there.

That told Emily what she needed to know. If anyone could solve it, they would. If he hadn't healed her with a word, he'd certainly helped her. Held her with his voice. They were a team. The two of them were far more capable together than either separately.

Twenty minutes. That made John's plan completely clear and he was right. Either they'd be clear or blown to hell. Time to really get moving.

They'd set the excess explosives on the elevator and move them down to the lab, trigger them on a timer, and watch the whole place go up in the ADAS rearview.

Emily got the others moving the last of the excess

weapons onto the elevator. She considered stripping the weapons off the Hind.

When she leaned down to inspect it, she saw the C4 already planted there. Standard issue. "Nice work, team," she whispered but didn't call out because she didn't dare risk distracting them. Emily had four more in the pouch slung over her shoulder. On her next trip by, she snagged the control from John's thigh pocket.

So, there was a reason to smile tonight. Her crew was a step ahead. Right where you wanted them to be.

They were still talking it through, John and Michael holding the nose cone in place, Connie now up to her elbows inside it.

Emily ganged a pair of the C4 packs on the floor directly beneath the chopper. It should blow a big hole in the floor. Then the helicopter with all of its weaponry would fall through the hole, taking two, maybe three seconds to reach the lab level. The pack that Connie and John had placed would blow up the helicopter during its fall, so that it was really burning before it blew itself apart. Finally trigger the pile of weaponry in the lab to finish the job. Shouldn't even be enough left behind to identify any U.S. military goods. Between their weapons and the Hind's, it was going to be a very hot fire.

Once the missiles were piled up in the lab, she slapped her last two bricks of C4 right in the middle and ganged them together. Emily quickly keyed in the numbers and set the three timers for twenty minutes.

She pressed her stopwatch first, then started each of the three in turn. She'd take the extra second of advantage of her stopwatch being a beat ahead of the first explosion.

Clay was holding two flashlights for the bomb crew.

Emily grabbed Gerta and the spare D-boy by the shoulder, and between them they got the load sling rigged. She wanted to be ready to lift the bomb the second it was disarmed. They finished in time to hear John say:

"Now, take that section of orange wire you just cut out and short it between the high side of the big, fat capacitor on the right and ground. There's gonna be a hell of a spark."

Connie looked at John. But it wasn't a question.

It was an answer.

One that Emily rarely witnessed, even among the most tightly knit flight crews.

Perfect trust.

Emily half expected the girl to mouth a good-bye of some sort, but her trust in John was too big for that.

They nodded in unison, then Connie shoved the wire ends down into the bomb's innards. A spark of actinic white flashed so brightly that Emily had to shield her eyes and look away.

Wrong choice!

But it wasn't.

They were still standing there.

John was the first to laugh, pure relief echoing out into the night.

Chapter 71

CONNIE LAUGHED AS JOHN AND MICHAEL LET THE nose cone fall free.

They all whooped, loudly for a moment, then hushed. Then it built again. The normally reticent D-boys pounded each other on the back. Emily hugged her copilot.

Gerta gave voice to a deep Russian belly laugh.

Connie grabbed John even as he flexed his fingers to get the blood moving back into them. She dragged his face down and kissed him a good smack.

He scooped her into his arms and swung her in a circle until it felt like she was flying.

She heard the sharp, ripping sound right next to her ear. A bullet flying through where her head had been a moment before, then a loud, "Thwack!" against the helicopter behind.

John must have heard it too, because the next thing Connie knew, the air had been slammed from her body and she lay on the hangar floor beside the bomb, beneath John.

A cry! Under the bomb cart, she could see someone crashing to the ground. Not even raising his hands to catch himself. A brutal slap against the concrete.

John rose to one knee above her, his rifle lined over the top of the bomb, seeking a target.

Behind him, Colonel Gibson stood upright, sniper rifle up, night scope casting a green glow across his features.

Connie could hear each bullet come in. The sharp

snap of near misses, the sudden tap of rounds that hit something hard, metal or concrete.

Another cry. She couldn't see who.

She saw Gibson fire a quick double-tap. Then one more.

She had her pistol out and was rising to kneel beside John, but she heard nothing.

For a moment, she thought her hearing was gone. That had happened to her once in training. She'd never heard the instructor shout "Stand down!" signaling the end of the exercise because she'd been in full-on combat mode. Sound had become extraneous as she'd focused her mind on the practice of a hostage rescue raid. The instructor had not been pleased at the simulated round in his back.

But no one else was moving or firing.

Then she heard Major Beale's voice, "Crap! Mark is going to be really pissed at me."

Chapter 72

THE D-BOYS WERE GONE INTO THE NIGHT. NO QUESTION who had gotten the shooter. Colonel Gibson had drilled him twice in the heart, once in the forehead.

A car had arrived unnoticed at the other side of the house. Someone coming back uninvited. Maybe a shift change. Who knew.

It appeared he came alone, but the D-boys had gone to make sure.

Connie wrapped the blanket around Clay. She'd have patted his face good-bye, if he'd had one. Two rounds, maybe three, to the back of the head had blown out the other side. Gerta folded the blanket closed. Between them they managed to lift his body into the back of the chopper.

Then she returned to check on John and the Major. He'd cut a big flap out of the back of Emily Beale's pants and her underwear.

"Damn! I liked these pants."

"Shut up, Major!" Connie called out. "Quit whining."

Connie got back the bark of laughter she'd hoped for. It was hard, bitter, but it was a laugh. That's what Connie wanted. Needed, because she could see John's hands shaking. He was the best medic among them, but that someone had shot Major Beale was... wrong. The Major, always invulnerable, the proof that *Vengeance* would always triumph, had been shot. Blood was dripping down the backs of her legs and staining her pant legs with far too much red.

The bullet had entered from the side. Thankfully passing through clean. It bled out of the entry and exit wounds, but not hideously. Not arterial. The bullets had been hollow-point. It was the only thing that explained what had happened to Clay. If it had hit the Major's hip, the bullet would have mushroomed inside her and created a damage path that would leave nothing they could do for her. Instead, a purely meat shot had passed through both buttocks leaving four neat holes.

As it was, John smeared antiseptic, then a dab of glue to seal each hole. Best they could do in the field. He tapped some cotton patches to keep it clean.

Major Beale shifted slowly upright, testing her leg, her bandaged butt out in the wind.

"We need to get out of here," the Major called out.

Connie nodded. Even shot up, the Major kept her sense about her. The timers were running. She glanced at them, they didn't need to be stopped and reset. There was enough time to get gone. The two on the floor still showed twelve minutes.

So fast. In the last eight minutes, they'd disarmed a nuclear bomb, Clay had died, the Major had been shot and bandaged, and the shooter had been taken down.

Connie shied away from Clay's death. They'd all be miserable soon. They'd all been in the services long enough to know the crushing doubt of why the bullet chose the man next to you and the deep guilt that had often made her wish she'd been the one to take the round. Even knowing the cycle wasn't going to spare her. But the time wasn't now. After the mission would be time enough for grief and guilt.

Connie moved in. Pulling the Major's arm over her shoulders to support the weak side where the bullet had drilled deeper into the muscle, Connie helped her hobble toward the chopper.

"Can you fly?" The Major's voice was low, low enough to be private from those around them.

"I can get around an airfield. No more than that."

"Good. That's more than John. I need a copilot."

"Why?" The question slipped out even though it made some sense. Maybe she'd need help on the pedals with a shot-up butt.

"Because I've been a bit dizzy since I got shot in the head at the first airfield. Whacked it again pretty hard just now when I fell. Don't alarm the others, but I need someone beside me in case it's a concussion."

"You're alarming me!" Connie tried to keep it light, but that didn't work so well. She wasn't even close to qualified to handle a DAP Hawk on a low-level flight across foreign soil. None of them were, other than the Major. And they were probably two hours of hard flying from safety.

"You'll do fine, Connie. You may be the most capable woman I've ever met."

Connie helped the Major up into her seat after she spread a blanket for her to sit on as an extra cushion.

"After me, that is."

Chapter 73

THEY CLAMBERED ABOARD THE BLACK HAWK. GIBSON stayed down to guide the sling over the bomb and hook on the attachment points. He climbed back up the fast rope more quickly than the most agile squirrel. As if the very devil was on his tail. Or a nuclear bomb.

The Major called out, "Ten minutes." And laid down the hammer.

Connie sat in the left front seat. She could look back between the seats and see John's back, his hands tight on the handles of the minigun. Colonel Gibson would be sitting directly behind her in Connie's seat, also watching the side and rear.

Gerta sat in the cargo bay with the other D-boy. Behind the cargo net lay Clay's body, forgotten for now.

Connie returned her attention forward, letting her hands ride lightly on the controls. Getting the feel for it. Even the most mundane action the Major did had something different about it. A nuance, a finesse that made Connie feel less and less competent with each passing moment. Then, as she recognized some of the techniques and she could pretend her hands were making the motions, she grew more confident. Not enough to fly, but enough to help.

The count rolled down.

All hell was going to break loose in Ukrainian airspace in about sixty more seconds.

Fuel was going to be dicey. They'd burned their reserve getting here. If they got into a dogfight, they weren't going to make the Polish border. Who was she kidding? If they got in a dogfight with her at the weapons controls, they were going to be dead.

And if they kept moving at this speed, they weren't going to make it there either. Burning fuel too fast as they pushed ahead just below redline on the turbines.

But Connie didn't complain. Until the explosives destroyed the underground factory, farther away was the only place she wanted to be.

—⁓—

Connie glanced back inside the helicopter. The D-boy and Gerta were leaning their heads out into the brutal wind. John looked at the stern of the helicopter when she glanced back, clearly studying the ADAS view.

She spun her control to display straight back.

Connie saw the flash.

"Stage one, the floor beneath the chopper," the Major announced over the intercom.

Even as she finished speaking, the flash bloomed higher.

"Stage two, that should now be a flaming Hind Mi-24 falling through the hole."

Then a blaze of light roiled upward obliterating the darkness, momentarily overloading the ADAS cameras.

For a moment Connie feared there'd been another nuke that they'd missed and just triggered.

"And that, ladies and gentlemen," the Major sounded very pleased with herself, "is two hundred pounds of good American explosive and half that again of Russian helicopter. And that's not counting the fuel in the chopper or the missiles. Hope you enjoy the flight. Tonight's forecast is for smooth sailing and low turbulence. Because if we don't have that, we're going to run out of fuel and fall out of the sky with a nuclear weapon strapped to our belly."

They saw the occasional jet or helicopter flying high and fast toward the explosion. But not one of them noticed the DAP Hawk, blacked out and running silent in the other direction while carrying a nuclear weapon ten feet off the ground.

Chapter 74

CONNIE COULDN'T REMEMBER THE LAST HOUR OF THE flight. She knew that forevermore it would be a hazy time of high adrenaline and near panic. As they'd moved through the Ukraine wilderness, she slowly picked up more and more of the flying. Not good enough to do it on her own, but she was doing the heavy motions and Major Beale the finer tweaks.

It felt like some maddening video game. At best-fuel cruise speed of one hundred and fifty knots, trees, houses, whole hills popped up in endless, mind-numbing succession. An unending slalom, every object requiring instant attention because at less than a hundred feet up, they were constantly less than a second from becoming a hole in the ground. One thing for sure, Connie knew she hadn't been built to be a combat pilot. Ever.

She'd tried speaking to the Major, but that distracted them both. Their communication was completely silent, transmitted from control stick to control stick, from woman to woman.

Connie felt the trust grow with the flight. The Major was letting her do more and more, but was always there to correct before her missteps became too dangerous.

The last fifty miles, Connie had also been holding hard to keep the Major from overcompensating on her corrections. A strong hand to steady the increasingly erratic shifts Connie could feel through the controls, see through the ADAS display.

Together, they settled softly by the refueling truck.

She called over to the CSAR craft and the crew swarmed toward *Vengeance*.

Connie only had a moment with the Major before she was lifted out and onto a stretcher. They'd stripped off their helmets and looked at each other.

Emily's face was white as paper, her eyes blinking constantly for focus and sweat running freely off her brow.

"We there?"

"We're there, Major."

She snaked out a hand, pulled Connie over by the lifting ring on the front of her vest. She kissed Connie on top of the head.

"You done good, Connie. You got us home."

"No, you did, Major." Then they took her away. "No, you did, Emily." The name felt right even though there was no one to hear her. Emily Beale had gotten them home, shot up, and probably with a concussion, but she'd done it.

And Connie had sure helped. She'd "done good." Having a woman she respected and liked as much as Emily Beale say that was quite something. Connie would be holding that close for a long time.

"Hey, y'all."

Connie startled as the long, slender brunette from the CSAR team swung into the Major's seat. Her smile was huge and bright. Perfect teeth in a magazine-ad face. No wonder Tim had been so gob-smacked by her. She was stunning.

"You gonna fly us home?"

"I, uh…" Connie stumbled on the words, knocked back a bit by all the cheerful energy that suddenly filled the seat of the quiet and thoughtful woman who just might be becoming her friend. "I can't fly."

"Not what the Major says. She says you did great. Willing to fly copilot for me, too?" She stuck out a hand, not waiting for an answer. Her hands were fine but her grip was Army strong. "Lola LaRue. I know. Couldn't you just die? My daddy always joked that he'd hoped I'd grow up to be a stripper. Men are such jerks."

Connie knew one man who wasn't a jerk. Not by a long stretch.

"It's gonna take them a good twenty minutes to fuel us up if you wanna go stretch your legs. I haven't flown the DAP in a while, so I'm gonna check some things over if you want a break."

Connie released the harness and stepped down, her legs nearly folding under her.

Colonel Gibson stood close by her, doing something to the satellite phone they'd used.

"Nice job, Sergeant."

"Thank you, sir." Connie wondered how much more undeserved praise she'd get over this before she could stop it. "What are you doing there?"

"Making a copy." He slid an adapter into the phone and two green lights started blinking. When it stopped, he pulled off the adapter, unplugged a small USB drive, and handed her the phone.

"I'm sure Dr. Williams will want the full-res images on this."

She slipped the phone into a pocket. "Who gets the copy?"

"The President did mention that it would be awful if a copy of these images fell into the hands of someone, perhaps the Polish Army, along with instructions to leak the images. It just might help our Ukrainian friend find his way to power. The President felt we would owe him that if we retrieved the bombs."

Connie nodded. "The President is a good man."

Gibson nodded. "I heard you say your father went down in the service."

"Yes, sir. Sergeant Ron Davis, Screaming Eagles."

"Well, you did him proud today."

"Thank you, sir."

Gibson moved a few steps away, then stopped abruptly and turned back to face her.

"When did your father die?"

"His chopper burned just over ten years ago."

Colonel Gibson looked at her closely.

"Burned." He left the word in the air between them.

"That's what I was told. Crashed and burned, no remains."

The Colonel looked off into the night for a long moment. In profile, the soft light from the refueling operation revealed a soldier old beyond his years. One who had fought too many battles, seen too many friends die.

Then he glanced around before indicating she should follow him into the darkness away from the others.

She could see John coming over, but she sent him a hand signal to stay back. Colonel Gibson was clearly not interested in a crowd, no matter how much she just wanted to curl up in John's arms and let the shakes of nerves and adrenaline roll through her.

Gibson moved quietly and evenly. She idly wondered

if dance was part of a Delta operator's training. His motions were so smooth that the frozen grass barely moved.

Twenty paces from the chopper, they turned to watch the CSAR bird carrying Emily Beale lift off and head north into the night.

"Sergeant First Class Davis?"

She almost corrected him. She was sergeant, but not first class.

"Oh, yes. He was my father."

"Request permission to shake your hand, Sergeant. I didn't know. I should have seen it."

Connie held out her hand but barely returned a proper handshake in her confusion.

"It is an honor and a privilege to fly with your father's daughter."

Her expression must have revealed her bewilderment.

Again he gazed off into the night for a moment before reaching some decision and refocusing his attention on her.

"I was on his last flight. We went down hard. And dirty. Where doesn't matter, but it was very, very unfriendly."

He looked up and over her shoulder, watching a different place. A different time.

"My squadmate was dead, along with the copilot. The pilot was out with a nasty head wound, and with my broken leg I wasn't going anywhere too quickly. Your father hid us and walked out. Two days later, long after I assumed we were going to end up dead, a farmer's truck rattled up and he waved us aboard.

"Your father got us out. What we didn't know was that he was shot up worse than any of us. Dead from internal damage before we reached the border. He stayed alive long enough to save our lives, no matter what it cost him. Maybe he knew he was dead already and was simply too stubborn or dedicated to die until he got us out safe. He didn't burn, ma'am. He went down standing tall."

The Colonel refocused on her. He snapped a sharp salute. "An honor and a privilege, ma'am."

Connie numbly returned the salute.

He tossed the USB lightly in the palm of his hand. "I'd better go make sure this accidentally falls into the wrong hands." Then, he moved away into the night with his light, dancer's step.

Connie's knees finally let go and she sat down on the frozen grass with a soft crunch.

John moseyed up and sat down beside her. Just a breath of night air between their shoulders. Quiet. The way he was sometimes. When he was happiest.

When he was with her.

Where was she happiest? Flying in her father's footsteps? That had shifted tonight. Not when Colonel Gibson finally answered the long-lost question of how her father had died. That was good to know, good to finally put to rest, but seemed less important than she thought it would be when she had imagined discovering the truth a thousand times over the years.

No. The moment when it all had shifted had been standing in the hangar of a Ukrainian bomb factory. It had been in that moment. Facing death. With her fingers in the heart of a nuclear bomb. When the least mistake would bring the death she'd always expected. Make it all finally come true forever after.

But then she'd looked up and seen John's face.

She'd seen another woman.

Another Connie.

She'd seen the one loved by a man. The one that someday would bear his children. And while she watched their grandchildren lie in his strong arms, Connie and Noreen would look at the fifty-year coin, now a hundred years old. The coin Connie still had buttoned in her pocket.

She had seen herself with a future. With John.

Clay might be gone. But she was alive.

Connie pushed to her feet and dusted her hands together, brushing the bits of grass to the ground.

"Yes, by the way." And she strode off toward the chopper.

"Huh? Yes, what?" John stumbled to his feet and came after her.

"The answer is yes, I will marry you."

She got three more strides, two more than she expected, before he grabbed her arm and spun her back to face him.

"You will?"

"Of course I will. I love you, John."

His eyes rolled closed as he pulled her against his chest. That broad, marvelous chest.

She heard the pilot call that they were ready to go.

"And, John…"

"Yes?"

She got a step clear, partly turned away on her heel.

"I will bear your children."

The stunned look that flowed over his face told her that her work here was done. It put a real bounce in her step as she returned to help fly the chopper home.